GHOST MARK

Praise for Ghost Mark

McLean's writing is as ingenious as her protagonist, ranging from grunge to repartee to sophistication to laugh-out-loud snarks. Ghost Mark is Gripping. You won't put it down till it's done.
—Ottawa Review of Books

A captivating nail-biter that will leave readers thirsting for more!
—InD'tale Magazine

Will keep you on the edge of your seat . . . an intense, riveting, and fast-paced novel.
—Literary Titan

An exciting blend of action, mystery, suspense, and thrills with a supernatural kick that will leave you wanting more!
—Ann Charles, USA Today bestselling author of The Deadwood Mystery series

This mind-bending, supernatural thriller is a riveting romp through the dark streets of obsession and murder. A story that tugs at your heartstrings and lingers in the mind long after The End. Unputdownable!
—Sue Coletta, award-winning author of The Mayhem series

A sexy noir crime novel starring a bold intelligent superhero who seeks justice for past transgressions in a gritty Vancouver landscape.
—W. L. Hawkin, author of The Hollystone Mysteries

Praise for the Dark Dreams Novels

McLean's writing is clear, gentle, relentless, and original.
—Ottawa Review of Books

JP McLean's novel is a fresh and original mystery thriller with a side of budding romance. The twists and turns will keep the reader in suspense until the very end when all is shockingly revealed. This gripping tale should be on every bookshelf this year!
—InD'Tale Magazine

Blood Mark is an enthralling dark fantasy novel with captivating characters that will appeal to anyone looking for a crime thriller with a unique supernatural setup.
—Literary Titan

A deliciously addictive fever dream of a mystery with a surreal beauty akin to a David Lynch film. I loved it!
—Jennifer Anne Gordon, author of
Beautiful, Frightening, and Silent
winner of the Kindle Award for Best Horror 2020

Featuring a fearless, badass heroine and plot twists that will leave readers breathless, J.P. McLean's Blood Mark is a gritty, sexy, fast-paced thrill ride from start to finish.
—E.E. Holmes, award-winning and best-selling author of
The Gateway series

An explosive new series that combines mystery and magic into a can't-put-down thriller.
—Eileen Cook, award-winning author of
You Owe Me a Murder

Titles by JP McLean

Dark Dreams Series
Blood Mark

Ghost Mark

Scorch Mark

The Gift Legacy
Secret Sky

Hidden Enemy

Burning Lies

Lethal Waters

Deadly Deception

Wings of Prey

The Gift Legacy Companion
Lover Betrayed (Secret Sky Redux)

Novellas
Crimson Frost (A Supernatural Noel)

GHOST MARK

JP McLEAN

Jo-Anne P. McLean

WINDSTORM PRESS

Ghost Mark
Dark Dreams ~ Book 2
First Canadian Edition

Copyright © 2022 by JP McLean
All rights reserved.

ISBN
978-1-988125-63-3 (Paperback)
978-1-988125-64-0 (EPUB)
978-1-988125-70-1 (Audio)
978-1-988125-65-7 (PDF)

Edits by Donna Tunney, Amanda Bidnall, and Ted Williams
Book cover design by JD&J Book Cover Design
Author photograph by Crystal Clear Photography

This is a work of fiction. All of the names, characters, places, organizations, events, and incidents, other than those clearly in the public domain, are either products of the author's imagination or are used fictitiously. Any resemblance to actual persons, living or dead, is entirely coincidental and not intended by the author.

No part of this publication may be reproduced, recorded, stored in a retrieval or information browsing system, or transmitted, in any form, or by any means, without prior written permission from the publisher or, in the case of photocopying or other reprographic copying, a licence from Access Copyright, accesscopyright.ca, 1-800-893-5777, info@accesscopyright.ca.

Excerpt from *Scorch Mark* copyright © 2023 by JP McLean

Cataloguing in Publication information available
from Library and Archives Canada

For my first reader, John.

I have never yet heard of a murderer who was not afraid of a ghost.
—John Philpot Curran

1 | Jane

Guilt was a nagging constant in Jane Walker's life, a gargoyle digging its claws into her spine. She inhaled a heavy breath and steeled herself to return to work. Jane used to love her nursery job at Positively Plants in Vancouver's West End. But seeing Pieter in his wheelchair every day, and his mom, Anna, with her cane, ate away at her conscience. And then there was Buddy. She wanted to believe that he had survived her unforgiveable lapse of judgment—the lack of a death certificate was a glimmer of hope—but it had been months now, and she hadn't found him.

"You done?" Ethan said, reaching across the brushed-steel bar for Jane's plate.

Shaken from her thoughts, Jane looked up. "Yeah, thanks." She rested her fork beside the cold French fry she'd been scooting around her plate and nudged the dish in his direction, catching the slight lift at the edge of his smile that was just for her.

The mirror on the wall of bottles behind him reflected the sunlight that soaked through frosted windows, brightening the room. The effect was amplified by steel tables and blond-wood chairs, the product of a recent renovation. Music drizzled in the background, but tonight, when the line formed outside, Riptide's lights would dim and the music would thump.

Ethan set Jane's plate in the bussing bin beside the glass washer. A wayward New Year's streamer lay drunkenly underneath.

Jane checked the time. "Guess I'd better go."

Laughter erupted from a table of safety-vested construction workers across the room, who dwarfed their table. Fanny, their server, waved them off and bustled up to the bar.

"They giving you a hard time?" Ethan asked, as she loaded her tray with the pints of beer Ethan had just pulled. Ethan was notoriously protective of the staff, not that Fanny needed it; though petite, she was a career server and could fend off the worst of the liquid lunch crowd.

"They wouldn't dare," Fanny said, picking up her overloaded tray and starting back.

Ethan turned to Jane. "You coming over tonight?"

Her relationship with Ethan Bryce was still fresh, exciting. He was the first man who'd seen beyond her birthmarks, back when she had birthmarks. The first man who'd loved her without an ounce of pity. That he was also ripped and handsome was a delicious extra.

"After eight, okay?" Jane slid off the bar stool and pulled on her jacket. "Thanks for lunch."

"Anytime," Ethan said.

She grabbed her helmet and started for the door, but the sound of breaking glass startled her. She swung her head toward the commotion. Fanny was looking in her direction, but quickly darted her gaze away, with an apology to the construction worker, whose beer she'd just dropped.

Jane paused, wondering what had spooked her, and stepped forward again, not noticing that a wall of a man had veered into her path. She knocked into him hard enough to loosen her grip on the helmet, and gasped as it fell to the floor, bounced, and landed at the feet of the man's companion.

"Sorry," she said to the brick wall she'd bumped into. The man acknowledged her apology with a curt nod, no smile. No wonder Fanny had dropped a glass. He stood his ground, a boulder in a stream, flotsam flowing around him. He ran his hand over the dome of his clean-shaven head.

The other man stooped to pick up her helmet. Raindrops glistened on the shoulders of his canvas jacket.

"Thank you," she said.

He glanced up as he handed her the helmet. Jane sucked in a breath. His eyes were mismatched, one hazel, one brown. She scrutinized him, a more perfect version of the man she remembered. Jane could hardly catch her breath. She'd been searching for him for months. "Buddy?"

A spark of recognition flashed in his eyes before the man frowned. "Ah . . . no." He looked at his friend with a shrug that suggested Jane had been overserved.

No? He was beefier than the Buddy she knew, and taller, but Jane had only ever seen him in a wheelchair. And Buddy was just a nickname. Might be that in this altered reality, he didn't have that nickname. She reached for him, stammering while her tongue caught up to her memory. "Dylan?" That was his given name, Dylan O'Brien.

He stepped back, raising his arms like she had some kind of contagion. "I don't know you, lady." He then turned and continued toward the bar. The wall that was his companion dismissed her as well and moved alongside him.

But how many people had those eyes? It had to be him. She called after him. "Is your mom's name Mary?"

He rounded on her, annoyed now. "You got the wrong guy."

From behind the bar, Ethan caught Jane's attention and shook his head. A warning. She knew better than to ignore it. Though it killed her, she left Riptide without another word, wondering what it was Ethan knew about Buddy. And how long had he known him? She took some comfort in having seen him, in knowing he was alive, but she'd have to wait until tonight to learn the reason for Ethan's warning. The wait would be torturous. Her curiosity about this version of Buddy was an itch she was dying to scratch.

After work, Jane parked her Rebel 500 in the gravel patch underneath the second-floor bay window. She removed her helmet and headed inside the old Victorian mansion that had been renovated into disjointed apartments.

Until late last year, she and her best friend, Sadie Prescott, had shared the one-bedroom unit in the basement. But in the aftermath of Jane's kidnapping—instigated by Rick—Sadie's former john, Sadie had moved out and taken over the studio unit down the hall and adjacent to the poorly insulated utility room that housed the noisy furnace and boiler. It was a financial stretch for Jane to cover the rent without a roommate, but she'd paid off her Rebel, and that helped.

Both Sadie and Jane's apartment doors hung open, the only two units on that floor. Jane stood on the threshold of her own place and peered inside, past the worn velour sofa to the kitchen beyond. "Hey, Sade."

Sadie, who had her head in Jane's clunker of a fridge, straightened. "Good. You're home. Do you have fresh basil? I'm trying a new recipe." Sadie's blonde curls were tied in a knot on top of her head.

"Sorry. There might be a packet of dried, though. Try the cupboard."

Jane set her helmet on the floor and hung her biker jacket on a hook by the door. Though Sadie hadn't lived with her for months, she frequently made herself at home here. Jane didn't mind. They'd stitched up the gash Rick had caused in their lifelong friendship, and it had left only a small scar. She liked having Sadie around. They'd been inseparable since their group-home days. More than best friends. Fierce friends. The kind you'd protect with your life, and they had—with fists, and knives, and words as sharp as finely honed steel.

"I collected your mail," Sadie said. "It's on the trunk."

"What are you making?"

"Penne pesto."

It was exactly like Sadie not to have one of the main ingredients of a dish she was cooking. "There's a jar of pesto in the cupboard."

Sadie found it. "Great. That'll work."

Jane sat on the sofa and absently flipped through her mail. She stopped at the government envelope with the British Columbia Crown Counsel's logo on it. The prosecutor. "Shit."

"What is it?" Sadie came to sit with her.

Jane read the letter. "Looks like it's started. I have to arrange my first meeting with Crown counsel. Ms. Monica Fowler."

Jane had thought the trial was still months away. The man responsible for her kidnapping, Dr. Roderick Atkins, aka Mr. Rick Kristan, was safely locked up. She and Sadie had known him as Rick and still referred to him that way. Rick had learned Jane could manipulate the past, and he'd mistakenly thought he could starve her to the point she'd do his bidding and kill his brother.

"I am so not looking forward to reliving those events on the witness stand." But unless Rick pleaded guilty, Jane would have no other option. She handed the letter to Sadie. "So much for wishful thinking."

Sadie straightened her spine but wouldn't look at Jane.

Jane pulled the letter out of Sadie's grip before her friend could spiral. "Rick is responsible for what happened to me, not you." Sadie never used to hold on to regret. She was a free spirit, often touting their old mantra: never look back. But she had a firm grip on her guilt over what had happened to Jane. It saddened her to see the change in Sadie.

Jane steered the conversation in a happier direction. "Guess who I saw today?" She told Sadie about bumping into Buddy at Riptide.

"You sure it was him?"

"He was taller than I would have thought. About Ethan's height."

Jane's phone rang. "That'll be Ariane. You want to say hi?" Ariane

Rebaza was the professor helping Jane navigate the minefield of her visiting dreams.

"Nah. Another time," Sadie said. "Come over when you're done."

Jane understood Sadie's reluctance. She hadn't yet shaken off the shame of admitting to Ariane that she had been a prostitute, and that she had played a part, albeit unwittingly, in Rick's scheme to get his hands on Jane.

But Jane had forgiven her. They'd both made mistakes.

Jane answered Ariane's call and turned on the video. She recognized Ariane's kitchen in her family's home in Lima. Ariane was a slight woman in her thirties with olive skin and expressive dark eyes. Her long ebony hair was pulled back in her customary ponytail. To Ariane's left sat her grandmother, Yessica, an elegant if birdlike woman with a nest of white hair piled on her head. To her right was an elderly woman named Rosa Yupanqui. Rosa was sturdy and thick-necked with cropped steel-grey hair and hard eyes.

The elderly women were from what Ariane called "the old families." They held the knowledge of the old ways and passed it on to the next generation. The younger generation scoffed at their lore, but not Ariane. She was a renowned Inca scholar who'd dedicated her life to exploring and preserving their history.

And now Jane was caught up in it as well. After learning of her dreams, Ariane and the old families had identified her as *una testigo*, a Witness. As was Jane's late mother, a woman Jane had only seen in her dreams. The old families hadn't known about Jane or her mother. In Peru, Witnesses hadn't existed for more than a hundred years.

Rosa's face split into a wide smile. She spoke Spanish, which Ariane translated. "Rosa is asking if you've dreamed yet." Ariane's accent had gotten more pronounced since she'd left Vancouver to return to Lima.

"No. Nothing yet." Jane hadn't had what she called a visiting dream since her twenty-fifth birthday more than five months before. Rosa understood Jane's reply without translation, and her smile faded. Rosa had great hopes that in one of her dreams, Jane would be able to locate a family heirloom, a ritual offering bowl. The very bowl responsible for the blood marks that had now faded from Jane's body.

Rosa and Yessica exchanged words that sounded like grave disappointment.

"Tell her I'm sorry. If I ever figure out how to choose what I dream of, I'll try to find the bowl for her."

Ariane translated and, after further follow-up in Spanish, the two elderly women nodded.

"They've been praying for you," Ariane said, with a mischievous smirk. "But I'm not sure you'd appreciate it; their prayers are for your dreams to return."

Jane forced a smile. Her dreams weren't like other people's. Hers were dangerous. She dreamed of the past. And at times, unpredictably, she slipped into those dreams. When that happened, one misplaced step could change history. Buddy and Pieter were living reminders of that.

Jane had dreamed of the night Buddy was born—the same night Pieter was born. On impulse, Jane had helped Buddy's heavily pregnant mom navigate an icy patch of pavement at St. Paul's hospital. Jane had thought she'd prevented a life-altering fall. But all she'd done was delay the accident and change the victim. Now Pieter was in a wheelchair instead of Buddy.

"Gracias," Jane said. "Please tell them I'll call you if I dream again."

"Not if," Ariane said. "When."

2 | Sadie

Sadie returned to her own apartment. If Ariane's previous calls were anything to judge by, Jane would be at least an hour. She unscrewed the lid on the jar of pesto, dipped her finger into the oily mixture, and tasted it. "Mmm," she mumbled, thinking it needed a little more garlic. She set the jar on the counter and fished a dirty pot out of the sink. After she gave it a quick scrub, she filled it with water and set it on the hot plate for later.

She wasn't much of a cook, but since she'd had to cut back on eating out, she'd had to get used to the daily grind. And that's what it felt like. A grind. The tiny kitchen didn't help. Could you even call it a kitchen? It was six feet of counter with a combination hot plate and half fridge on one end, a handful of shallow cupboards, and an exhaust fan that moved the air around at best and was as loud as a jet engine. It was a good thing she didn't have much kitchenware.

She wandered back to the table she used for a desk and sighed. When she'd committed to the online bookkeeping course, she'd neglected to factor in the monotony of it. She also hadn't figured that she'd have to get her high school equivalency before the gatekeepers let her into the accounting program. But Jane and Sadie's former social worker, Nelson Leonard, had pulled some strings and secured her a seat in the accelerated GED program. It had taken eight intensive weeks of study, but when she passed the exams, she'd never been prouder.

The irony of being a legit student, after faking it for years as one of Cynthia Lee's teacher's pets, had lost its humour. Every month, when her rent was due, she thought about how easy it would be to pick up the phone and take one of Cynthia's gigs. Sadie mourned the shopping haunts that she hadn't visited in months. A thousand dollars for a few hours of work was more profitable and not nearly as mind-numbing as introductory taxation.

But she'd promised Jane she was done with the easy money. More importantly, she'd promised herself. So she sat down, refreshed her screen, and picked up where she'd left off.

An hour later, Jane tapped on her door. "You're a lifesaver," Sadie said, rubbing her face. She closed the laptop and pushed her books and papers aside.

Jane flopped into a beanbag chair Sadie had found at Goodwill. "How'd your date with Mike go?"

Sadie had collided with Mike inside the door of the classroom on the first day of GED classes. She'd been running late, and he'd been unimpressed. He was a brute of a guy, tall, inked, and built like a pro wrestler. Just her type. He ignored her, but her instincts told her he was paying attention. She dropped her phone number on his desk on the day of the final exam.

He called. They'd been tearing each other's clothes off for coming on three months now.

"He took me to the diner on Fourth, the one with the lineup on Sundays. Went back to his place. Gotta give him full points for stamina, but he could use more coaching on style."

Jane laughed. "He's dating the right chick for that advice." She picked at the seam of the chair. "Have you told him yet?"

Sadie rolled back from the desk and gazed out the stubby excuse for a window. Before Sadie had been sent into the system, she'd been raped by her dead mother's boyfriend. She wasn't even a teenager, and he had her working for his protection. People who had never experienced that life, who thought little girls wore tutus and pigtails, would never understand how normalized sex for money was on the streets.

"It didn't come up." Sadie had played out a dozen different ways to tell Mike about her past, but she couldn't bring herself to follow through. And she didn't want to think about it anymore. "How'd it go with Ariane?"

"She's translating a stash of diaries she says look promising."

"From a Witness?"

"Yeah. Guy named Pedro. He died in the mid-1800s. The old families have been helping with the search."

"They must be disappointed your dreams haven't come back."

"Ariane said they pray for me," Jane said, quirking an eyebrow.

"As in pray you'll dream again?"

"Yeah, but she said it with a laugh."

Sadie knew all about the dreams Jane had been having since she was a kid. Dreams of the past, of people she knew suffering at the hands of abusers. Sadie would have dismissed it as bullshit if Jane hadn't proved her truth, recounting episodes from Sadie's history she'd rather have forgotten.

"How was work today? Did mean mom take her happy pills?" Sadie hadn't thought Anna Bakker, Jane's boss at Positively Plants, could be any more of a bag, but after Jane's abduction, Anna had stepped it up. It was almost as if Anna blamed Jane for her own kidnapping. As if Jane going AWOL was a personal affront to her and the store.

"I wish there was something I could do for her."

"You're doing it. Showing up early every day, staying late. She's lucky to have you." What Sadie didn't voice was that Jane's continued attempts to ingratiate herself with the bag made Sadie want to scream. Jane didn't even need the damn job. She was sitting on an inheritance—a whack of cash from the Walkers, the couple who'd adopted her. Jane was only two years old when they'd died in a fire, but they'd had life insurance. Jane had learned of it last year, after her twenty-fifth birthday.

Unfortunately, Jane blamed herself for the fire that killed the Walkers, despite Sadie and Nelson's countless reassurances that she couldn't possibly, or reasonably, have been responsible. But Jane couldn't let go of the fact that her little two-year-old hand had been holding a spent match when they found her safe and sound on the burning home's front lawn.

The shopping spree they'd initially planned had been eroded by Jane's misplaced guilt. Jane was now determined not to spend the inheritance on herself, which drove Sadie batty. Jane didn't even remember the Walkers, but somehow, she'd gotten it into her stubborn head that they would want her to spend the money on needy kids. Sadie was still working out how to fit herself into that category.

Sadie got up with a stretch. "You hungry?"

"Starving."

Sadie plodded to the stove and turned on the burner under the water pot. "Can I ask a favour?" She and Jane had traded favours all their lives, but this one felt more important.

"Sure."

"I have to find a company where I can do an internship. I thought you might have an in with the accountants who manage the Walkers' money."

"It's worth a shot," Jane said. "I'll ask them."

"Terrific," Sadie said, relieved. She took a chair beside her. "So tell me about Buddy."

"He came into Riptide. I wouldn't have even noticed him if I hadn't dropped my helmet. Buddy picked it up, and I noticed his eyes. One hazel, one brown."

Jane's obsession with this Buddy character hadn't subsided since the day she'd learned what had happened to Pieter. She had been certain he'd eventually show up, and now he had. Sadie couldn't wait to meet the guy.

"Did he recognize you?"

"Said he didn't, but I think he was lying. Didn't know the name Buddy, though, or even Dylan. But Ethan knows something about him. He warned me off after Dylan insisted he didn't know me. I'll drag it out of Ethan later. I'm going to see him tonight."

Sadie held her tongue. Jane didn't want to hear Sadie's jaded opinions about Ethan. Following Jane's abduction, he'd been unbearably arrogant about Sadie's choice of side hustle.

"While we're on the name subject, have you made a decision about changing yours?" Jane's original name was Baby Jane Doe. Her adoptive parents had kept the name Joyce, given to her by a hospital nurse. But last year, Jane had learned her birth mother had wanted to name her Beth. Ever since, she'd been waffling about changing it legally.

"I've given it a lot of thought," Jane said. "Honestly, I think it might be asking too much of everyone."

"Why would you think that? It's the name your mom wanted for you. Besides, BMW is classic." Beth Morrow Walker. The name Jane had chosen honoured her mother, Rebecca Morrow, and her adoptive parents, the Walkers.

"I've been testing it out," Jane said. "Ordered takeout at the falafel place the other day. They must have called out for Beth four times before I realized it was me they were calling. I felt like a moron."

"Yeah, but a classic moron."

3 | Ethan

Ethan heard Jane's motorcycle enter the back alley and glanced out his kitchen window. The caged light above Riptide's back door had burned out. He made a mental note to replace the bulb on his next shift.

Jane had no idea how hot she looked straddling that bike. She parked her Rebel beside his Fat Boy, dismounted, and waved when she looked up to his window. Jane wasn't like other women he'd known. She was completely unoccupied with her looks. The birthmarks she'd had most of her life had warped her perception of herself. And even though the marks were gone now, she still avoided her reflection. She didn't even wear makeup. But she didn't need to. Her beauty was ingrained in her confident stride, the way she swung her silky hair like a sword, the ferocity of her loyalty.

He'd experienced the rejection of women who'd cringed when they saw the burn scars on his stomach, but not Jane. She hadn't flinched, hadn't even looked away. She was formidable and nonjudgmental to a fault. And that fault had a name: Sadie Prescott.

He raced out of the apartment and down the three flights of stairs. She smiled as he opened the door and greeted her with a kiss. Her lips were cold. "Let's get you warmed up," he said, taking her helmet.

Rather than summoning the doddering elevator, they jogged up the stairs. He imagined the tenants on the eighth floor were either very fit or very patient.

He pushed open the door to his apartment and set Jane's helmet on the end of the bed. Other people might have found his bachelor unit on the small side, but it was all he needed, a place to bunk. The money he saved in rent was going to a better cause: his new acreage in the Sunshine Valley. He was impatient to get back out there, to move his Airstream in, but the property was still covered in snow.

"Tell me about Buddy," Jane said. "Why'd you warn me off?"

"He goes by the name Joey Hampton. His partner, the big guy? His name's Garvin Burman. You don't know them, and you don't want to know them."

"Joey is Buddy, I'm sure of it. I looked up the mismatched eye colour thing. It's called heterochromia, and it's rare. That guy is Buddy. His real name's Dylan O'Brien."

He took her hands. "His real name is Joey Hampton. I know it kills you, what happened to Pieter and Buddy, but you've got to let it go."

She looked at their hands. "I just want to know what happened to him, that's all."

"You don't. Trust me."

"How do you know him?"

He dropped her hands. "Want a beer?"

"You're changing the subject." She pulled off her boots, careful as always to check that her boot knife—a knife she was remarkably deft at handling—remained in place.

He propped his hands on his hips. He knew she couldn't let the Joey topic go. "The Buddy you knew doesn't exist anymore," he said, and headed to the fridge. He pulled out two Coronas, popped the caps, and handed her one. "Joey Hampton is a piece of shit, and his partner is the disposable wipe he's stuck to. Feel better?"

She laughed. "Hardly. I need more. Don't be so stingy with the details." She hung her coat on the back of a kitchen chair and sat down.

"Joey and Garvin are the thugs I told you about. The ones who have Connor's nuts in a vice." Connor Boyd, and a partner Ethan had never met, were Riptide's owners.

"You said Connor denied it."

"Yeah, ages ago. I don't believe him. He's changed. Something's going on." He took the other seat at the table. "When he fired Jerry and made me day manager, he said it was temporary. Brought in the new night guy. Said he knew my skills were wasted on days and he'd hire another day manager. It's been five weeks. He's not even looking. Makes me think he wants me out of there after six." The day manager worked late morning until 6:00 p.m. In the history of Riptide, there'd been maybe five daytime brawls that needed his level of skill. The night shift is where he belonged. The regulars knew him, knew his reputation. And those who didn't and chose to be aggressive, learned it soon enough. No one got out of line on his watch.

"Did you challenge him on it?"

"Tried. He reminded me he owns the joint and he'll get to it when he goddamn pleases." Ethan took a slug of his beer.

"That doesn't sound like Connor. I thought you guys were friends."

"Yeah, me too. But he hasn't been himself. Not since those two showed up." Ethan considered Connor one of the finest men he knew and the most easygoing boss he'd ever had. "And a few weeks ago, he changed my QuickBooks access. Now all I can see is inventory. I have no idea what the balance sheet or the bank balance look like."

"Don't you help with the books?"

"Not anymore. Says he's doing it himself. Wants to get a better grip on the finances. Which would make sense if he knew how to use Quick-Books."

"He knew enough to change the passwords." Jane turned her bottle in its ring of condensation.

"You only have to sign in to do that. He doesn't know thing one about generating reports, doing the payroll. If he'd asked me to show him how to use it, I might have believed him."

"He's shutting you out."

"He's trying. I'm not that easy to get rid of. I don't know what they've got on Connor, but it's serious." And Ethan was patient. He'd find out.

"I wonder where he lives."

"Who? Joey?"

She looked up, and he could see the curiosity behind her gaze.

"Leave it be, Jane. He's not Buddy, and he's mixed up with some serious shit."

"Don't worry. I'm not going to stalk him."

"No?" Ethan knew how determined Jane could be. But she was deep in thought again, drawing spokes in the beer's condensation ring, and didn't catch his skeptical tone.

"You think Joey or Garvin could be Connor's partner in the business?"

"Not a chance. His partner was a university mate, his age. Fifties, despite what all the ladies think. Joey and Garvin are late twenties max."

Women flocked to Connor's easy smile, beach hair, and the dimples that erased ten years from his birth certificate. "What do you think they're up to?"

"I wish I knew."

Jane sat forward and propped her elbows on the table. "Tell me more about Joey. How long have you known him?"

Ethan sighed. Jane wouldn't be easily distracted from Joey. She'd been curious for too long. "First time I saw him in Riptide was around Halloween. He was with Garvin, as always. They looked like trouble, so I kept an eye on them. They came in a handful of times after that, had a beer, and left. A few weeks later, Connor started coming out to meet them, and they'd go into the office. I followed him once. Just to check on him, but he shooed me out of there as if I was butting into a secret club meeting, persona non grata."

"Is that when he fired Jerry? Put you on days?"

"Soon after, yup." Ethan stretched his leg to the side and nudged her foot. "We aren't going to spend our whole night talking about Riptide, are we? Tell me about Ariane. Did you learn anything new from her tonight?"

Ariane had a PhD, so she was legit. She was also the only one who could shed light on what Jane experienced. And since Jane's marks had vanished, Jane had grown increasingly uneasy. Her sleep was fitful, and she was always on edge, waiting to fall into one of her paralytic dreams. It had been months since she'd had one, and he'd never seen it first-hand. Truth be known, he wouldn't be upset if it stayed that way. He hoped those wild dreams of hers were a thing of the past.

Jane told him about the diaries Ariane was translating, and how she hoped they held clues to controlling her dreams. Ethan still found it difficult to wrap his head around how her dreams worked, but he didn't doubt her. Not after she'd told him about the night he'd been burned. Only someone who'd witnessed the accident would have known those details.

But at least she'd moved off the Joey topic. He was a threat. Garvin may have been more senior in whatever organization they belonged to, but Joey was smart, observant, and he moved like a fighter, light on his feet. Garvin moved like a bull: head down, barrelling into anything in his path.

When they'd drained their beers, Ethan collected the bottles and set them on the counter.

"I got a letter from the Crown counsel's office," Jane said. "It's started. They're prepping for trial."

They'd both been dreading this day. Lawyers were clever. One slip-up in Jane's testimony was all it would take to paint her as delusional. If that happened, Rick and Andy would walk away unscathed.

"The police collected a shit-ton of evidence against both of them."

"Let's hope it's enough."

He closed the blinds while Jane updated him on Sadie's progress with her new career. Ethan was glad Sadie was trying to turn her life around, but unlike Jane, he hadn't forgiven her for putting Jane's life in danger. And he found Sadie's naïveté disingenuous. Hookers weren't that stupid.

He sidled up to Jane and offered her his hand. "Care to join me?"

"Depends." Jane's mouth eased into a seductive smile. "Where are you going?"

He held her gaze as he pulled her into his arms and kissed her. "Thought we'd go for a walk," he said, guiding her backwards to the bed. With each step, another piece of clothing dropped to the floor. "And then maybe play a game of doctor." The few clothes that remained peeled off easily once Ethan and Jane were horizontal. He couldn't imagine ever tiring of caressing her, kissing her in places that made her shiver, watching ecstasy cross her face when he was deep inside her.

Afterwards, they spooned, content to linger in each other's arms. She didn't always stay the night, but he hoped she would tonight. She'd had a beer, which was always a positive sign. He fell asleep thinking about a second round of doctor they could play in the early morning hours before she left for work.

Ethan woke to a shrill ringtone that sent adrenalin shooting through his arteries. It was Riptide's security alarm. He apologized to Jane as he scrambled out of bed in search of his phone. A cyclone had strewn their clothes about. He tripped over his jeans, and his phone dislodged from a pocket, skittering across the floor. The alarm's message blinked the warning that the main entrance had been breached.

The piercing cry of an arriving siren had him rushing to the window to jerk up the blind. Lights flashed from the street beyond the alley. A fire truck blasted its horn and rolled past.

"I've gotta get down there." He bent to pick up his clothes. The sirens continued to blare, no doubt waking the whole building. "Sorry, Jane. You don't need to get up." She lay on the far side of the bed with her back to the window. He switched on the lamp, sorted out his jeans, and pulled them on. He yanked his T-shirt over his head. Jane still hadn't stirred.

"Jane?" He reached over and placed his hand on her shoulder. "I'll be back as—" He pulled his hand away and stared at her skin. The marks she thought had vanished—the blood marks that had mysteriously disappeared—weren't gone at all; they were blindingly white and glowing beneath her skin.

He crept around to her side of the bed and lifted the hair away from her face. The marks were back, luminous. He paused, staring in disbelief. He pulled the sheet off. All of her marks were back. And she was deeply asleep.

He covered her again and sat there, not knowing what to do, but knowing he couldn't leave her like that.

4 | Jane

Visiting Dream

Jane wakes in a darkened bedroom. Boisterous male voices leak in through thin walls. Jane gazes around the room. Shoved up against a wall is a single mattress dressed in rumpled bedding. A well-thumbed Spider-Man comic rests upon a soiled pillow. Children's clothing and stray toys are strewn around the stained carpet.

She's aware she's in a dream and knows she doesn't want to be here.

A glance at her torso reveals that it's translucent, semi-solid, a ghost. Fear hits her as she realizes she's naked. *Why?* Ethan's face flashes in her mind. *Ah, yes.*

She rubs her arms for warmth, and her attention drifts to her right forearm and the back of her left hand. The blood marks that had snaked around her body and disappeared months ago are back. White now. The shock of it registers, but her reaction is muted. A curiosity.

She notices the mark on the back of her hand. It's changed: round now, not square. She touches it. Her vision waffles, and a wave of nausea hits her. *That's new*, she thinks as men's voices boom out again. She needs to cover up, and she gazes at the rumpled bedsheet. But no. Mustn't touch anything. *Why?* A sense of disconnect frustrates her. It's as if a barrier stands between her and her memories. Important memories.

Where is she? Outside the window, colourful leaves on a tree branch quiver in the wind, casting shadows on the walls. It's autumn. No curtain on the open window. She peers outside. A streetlight glows beyond the tree, illuminating the night. She's on the second floor, third if there's a basement level. A *No Vacancy* sign swings crookedly from a white post beside a crumbling front walk. Cars line the street. One has plastic taped in place of a missing window. Another has a mismatched quarter panel.

The clank of beer bottles draws her attention back into the bedroom. Light spills across the carpet from the door, which hangs half-open. Strips of faded flowering wallpaper have been peeled from the walls. The smell of nicotine permeates the air.

Cautiously, she picks her way through the castoff toys and clothing, toward the door. She glances through the hinge-side crack and sees a sliver of kitchen cupboards, a counter cluttered with dirty dishes.

Banter comes from the kitchen, but the men who are speaking are out of sight. She moves to the door's opening and chances a peek. Three men. The one facing her, with sunken cheeks, has his elbows on the table and picks at his nails with a knife. Another she sees side-on. He wears an undershirt and balances on the back legs of his chair. The third has his back to her. His black T-shirt is stretched over what looks like rising dough, and his thighs spill over the edge of the chair.

"Huan, get me a beer," says the beefy man.

She hears the sound of a refrigerator door opening and then closing. A boy comes into view, places a can of beer close to the big guy, and then flits out of sight.

"You're doing the mule tonight, kid." Beefy man's voice.

"Can't. I'm going to Cameron's."

The beefy man leans back, and when he does, Jane sees a handgun on the table. He reaches into his front pocket. "That wasn't a request. You're going. Here."

The hollow-cheeked man glances in Jane's direction. She darts back behind the door.

Silence.

"You bring someone home again, kid?" Jane fears it's the hollow-cheeked guy talking, the one who was facing the door. He may have seen her.

"Take it!" Beefy guy.

"I'm gonna get jumped with that much cash." The boy's voice.

"Don't be stupid. No one's going to mess with you. Not if they want to keep breathing."

"Kid! I asked you a question. Who the fuck's in your room?"

Jane glances at her body, ghostlike and visible. Again, she scans the floor, desperate for something to cover herself with, but a sweat-inducing fear of touching anything stops her.

"No one," the boy says. "What if the cops show up?"

"You're twelve. What are they gonna do? Drive you home? Enough with the excuses."

"Mom'll kill me."

"Yeah? Look at her. She's passed out. Now get going, or I'm gonna be the one who kills you."

"Where's your bonehead friend, Cameron?" It's the same voice Jane fears belongs to the hollow-cheeked guy.

"How do I know? Probably upstairs in his apartment."

"Leave the kid alone." A new voice. Must be the guy in the undershirt.

"I saw something in his room."

"Can I take my b-ball?"

"I don't give a shit. Vamoose, kid. Your slot's 1:30. You miss that meet, and I'll use you for shootin' practice. Got it?"

A chair scraping. Footsteps.

"Probably a fucking rodent." Undershirt guy.

Jane backs away from the opening, past the hinge-side crack in the door.

"See that! Not a fucking rodent."

There's a thump that sounds like Undershirt's chair righting itself.

Jane scoots along the wall as the bedroom door slams open against the wall. The hollow-cheeked guy stands backlit in the doorway.

His gaze zeroes in on her like a homing beacon. Jane covers herself with her hands. "Who—" He takes a tentative step forward. Confusion clouds his features. "What the fuck?"

A shout nearby. "What is it?" Another set of feet thud toward the room.

Jane, desperate to escape, races for the open window. Her foot lands heavily on something sharp. She screams.

Jane woke with the cry still on her lips. She bolted upright and rubbed the arch of her foot, which was painful from having stepped on whatever the hell it was. Memories rushed back as she became aware of her surroundings.

Ethan stood by the window, phone in his hand.

"Hey," she said. A weak dawn light seeped into the room. The full weight of what had happened hit her.

"I'm sorry," she said, looking away. She hated that he'd seen her like that, out cold. Being pitied pissed her off. Feeling vulnerable made her angry.

Ethan took his time coming to the bed. Almost as if he was wary of her. He was fully dressed.

"How long have I been out?"

"Twenty minutes, give or take. Are you all right?"

"Yeah, fine." No need to dwell on it. Emergency lights flashed beyond the window. "What's going on out there?"

"Why are you rubbing your foot?"

She immediately dropped her foot to the floor. "Stepped on something. I'm okay."

He raised a questioning eyebrow, but she didn't elaborate.

"Where were you?" he asked.

"Some shithole apartment. A kid named Huan lived there with his mom, who was passed out, and three low-life drug dealers. I have no idea who they were or why I was there."

Ethan sat beside her and reached to brush the hair from her face. He pulled up an image on his phone and held it out for her to see. It was a photo of her face while she slept. The thick red blood mark that used to cross from mid-forehead to her left ear glowed white as if etched in glass and lit from within. She held out her right forearm, her left hand. There were no marks. "I saw the marks in my dream. But not glowing like that."

She touched the back of her left hand, remembering the newly round shape, the nausea, the rippled vision. But the effect was gone.

Ethan tucked his phone away. "Having seen you like that for myself, I know now what you mean about needing protection when it happens."

Here it comes, she thought, disappointed. "I have protection. Steel door, remember? Two deadbolt locks?"

"Not here."

She let out a sigh. "No, not here."

"I couldn't leave you like that. Vulnerable."

His words summed up Jane's fear. "I don't need to be babysat. It makes me feel weak." Jane shifted on the bed and met his gaze. "I hate to say it, but I can't sleep here anymore," she said, already regretting the loss of him lying beside her. "You can come to my place instead. You'll never have to feel stuck with me there. You can leave anytime."

"I don't feel stuck with you. I want you here. But I won't ever leave you like that. I'd kill anyone who did."

He was a good man, but he didn't understand how it felt to be a burden. She'd never let herself be that to him. "What's with the flashing lights?"

"How about I look into better security here? I don't think the landlords would even notice if I switched out the door, installed better locks."

"You'd do that?"

He leaned in and kissed her. "I'd do a lot more than that to keep you in my bed."

His words put a seductive smile on her lips until the flashing lights distracted her again. "You going to tell me what's going on out there? And why are you dressed?"

"Someone smashed through the front door at Riptide. Drove a shopping cart loaded with rocks into it. Set off the alarm." He took out his phone again and swiped at the screen. "The security camera caught this." He handed her the phone.

The figure pushing the cart was covered from head to foot. "Any idea who it is?"

"No. Best guess is a male, five-eight, one-sixty. He got away."

"But he wouldn't have if you hadn't been babysitting me."

"I couldn't have gotten down there fast enough anyway. He didn't go inside, just smashed the door and took off."

"Why break in if he wasn't going to steal anything?"

"Don't know. But I bet Connor does."

Jane arrived at work still haunted by her dream of Huan—and distracted from her time with Ethan that still had her tingling in all the right places.

The door to Positively Plants hadn't yet closed when Anna Bakker called out to her from behind the checkout. She had hooked her cane on the edge of the counter. "A customer in seasonal needs help."

The old Anna would have used a pleasant tone and said please. The new and decidedly unimproved Anna did not.

"I'm on it," Jane said, hurrying toward the Valentine's Day display.

Positively Plants was the last holdout gardening centre in the downtown core. The others had been squeezed out by high rents, but the Bakkers owned their corner-lot building. It had been cobbled together over the years, with a main building that fronted the street, an extensive greenhouse on the side, and a fenced open yard at the back.

This time last year, Anna would never have asked her to help a customer—the birthmarks on Jane's face put people off. But her marks were gone now, and she'd had to get accustomed to greeting the public. Still, her lifelong habit of hiding the left side of her face had proven difficult to break. Cutting her long dark hair to jaw length had helped, but she still felt more secure when it fell over her face like a veil.

After she helped the customer, she tidied what remained of the

Valentine's Day displays. She thought of Ethan as she rearranged the bedraggled bleeding hearts and the picked-over peonies. For the first time ever, she had a valentine.

Anna called out to her. "When you're done there, dig out the Paddy's Day decorations and bring them to the office. I'll see if there's anything I can reuse this year."

Jane's smile slipped. Decorating the store was something they used to do together. Those were busy days spent on ladders and filled with pranks and laughter. "Sure," Jane said, and turned on her heel.

When her shift ended, Jane trudged to the breakroom to change. From behind the flimsy partition that delineated Pieter's half of the room, Reyna's soft scolding pierced Jane's heart. Reyna was Pieter's care aide. The partition, Pieter's wheelchair, Reyna, Anna's cane: none of it would have been necessary if it weren't for Jane's unforgivable mistake, colossal screw-up, poor judgment. Call it what you will—she'd ruined lives.

Not that Anna or her family knew it was Jane's fault, but that didn't excuse what she'd done. They wouldn't understand even if she could explain it to them. In their reality, their lives had always been this way; both Pieter and Anna had suffered irrevocable damage when Anna was pinned under a car while in labour. All because Jane had chosen to interfere in the past. She'd chosen this for them. She hadn't known the implications of that choice at the time, but it didn't lessen her guilt.

Ethan knew what had happened. So did Sadie. But their reality had also been altered the moment Jane acted out in her dream and changed history. Neither of them remembered the Buddy Jane knew, the man in the wheelchair with mismatched eyes, a man she used to bump into regularly on the streets of Vancouver in the old reality, but whom she hadn't seen again until she'd bumped into him at Riptide. *Who are you now, Dylan O'Brien?*

5 | Sadie

Sadie stood and arched her back in a stretch. She'd been hard at it for hours and needed a break. But there was nowhere to go, save for a walk around the neighbourhood, and she was sick of that routine. Not being able to grab takeout or pick through racks for a new outfit took the fun out of it. And a trip to her favourite downtown shops was way too big a temptation.

Last year, after she'd bought the new car, tricked out her digs, and brought her new laptop home, she'd run the numbers enough times to know she had just enough money left to cover school and her expenses through to the end of her program. Every extra dollar she spent cut into her grocery money. Cynthia's payout sure didn't go far. Though it had seemed like a lot of money at the time, Sadie wished she'd negotiated for more on her way out the door of the Teacher's Pet business.

Perhaps another coffee, she thought, wandering into the kitchen. But all four mugs were in the sink, dirty. As were most of the plates and bowls and glasses. Her plan to keep up with the dishes wasn't going so well. She pulled a glass from among the few left in the cupboard and filled it from the tap.

Resting her butt against the sink, she looked over at the table where her computer and books waited like needy little trolls. It seemed more and more often she played the How Much Longer game. She had twenty-eight credits left to beat her way through to the end of the accounting certificate program. If she kept up her current pace, she'd finish early next year. But the new year felt a very long way off.

"Screw it." She stepped into her Ugg boots, shoved her arms into her coat, and left her impossibly small apartment. As she made her way up the front walkway, she called Mike. "I could use a break. You want to meet me for a coffee?"

They met at the diner on Fourth Avenue. It was late for lunch, but he ordered a burger anyway. It took a lot of calories to maintain that physique of his. She opted for a coffee.

"How's the job hunt going?" she asked. Mike worked at a gym, but he knew his body wouldn't hold out forever.

He sighed. "Employers look at this," he said, flexing a bulging biceps, "and they see a grunt. It's tough for them to see past it, see what I'm capable of."

Sadie stared into her coffee cup, his words bouncing around in her head. He'd just given her the perfect opening to fess up about her past. She took a tentative verbal step. "I know what you mean."

"Yeah?" he said, with a lighthearted laugh. "I doubt it. Anyone looks at you sees a gorgeous woman who'd be an asset to any business. And with your body?" He whistled. "They'd hire you just to work in the same room with you."

Sadie swallowed. She'd have to tell him eventually. Today was as good a day as any. She looked up. "Not everyone. I have things in my past that're like your build. Some people have a hard time seeing beyond it."

Mike arched an eyebrow. "What are you talking about?"

She took in a deep breath. "I used to work for a Teacher's Pet website."

He frowned. "I don't know what that is."

Sadie looked down to her lap, praying he'd understand. She gathered her courage and met his gaze. "There are men who like to pretend they're teachers. I'd play along. Be their student."

His frown froze. She waited for the pieces to fall into place. "Like . . . a hooker?"

She bit her lip. "It paid very well."

"You were a prostitute?"

She straightened at the change in his tone.

"Sorry, I just . . . Whoa. Did not expect that."

"Figured you should know."

"Yeah. Thanks." He looked away from her. Straightened his cutlery. Pulled the ketchup bottle out of the condiment rack. Put it back. "I, um, should go. Get back to work." He stood. "I'll uh, call you." He grabbed his coat off the back of his chair and walked out the door.

A moment later, the server arrived with his burger.

Sadie walked for hours to distance herself from Mike's reaction and put him out of her thoughts. It was dark outside when she got home. The rain had been relentless all afternoon. She'd done the right thing. Probably should have done it sooner. He'd either come around, or he wouldn't.

She dripped across the linoleum to drop her bags on the kitchen counter. On days like today, she longed for summer—for warm daylight hours with sunshine that extended until nine in the evening.

Then again, maybe not, she thought, glancing at the computer. Doing coursework cooped up inside when the sun was out felt all kinds of wrong. She groaned.

A knock at the door interrupted her drain-spiralling thoughts. She checked the peephole. Jane.

"Hey," she said, opening the door. "You want to come in?"

Jane stepped inside. "You been out?"

"Had to," Sadie said, shrugging out of her coat. "The books were ganging up on me. I bought wine. It's just screwcap, but you want a glass?" She headed back to the bags on the counter.

"Nah. I want a clear head when I call Ariane later."

Sadie resolved not to mention her discussion with Mike. Not today. It would only undo all the distancing she'd done. "Well, I'm having one." She might just drink the whole bottle. By some miracle, the wineglasses were clean. "Didn't you just talk to Ariane? What's up?" Sadie said, pouring her wine.

"I dreamed again. Fell asleep at Ethan's."

"Shit. You okay?" It would have been the first time Ethan had seen Jane in a dream state. Sadie knew Jane had been dreading it. But given how many nights she spent there, it was inevitable.

"Yeah."

"Who'd you dream about?"

Jane headed to her usual beanbag chair. "Some kid named Huan and the three moron drug dealers he lives with."

"You know them?" Sadie said, sitting on the bed.

"No. Nor their connection to me, but there'll be one. There always is. But there's more. My marks are back."

Sadie scoured Jane's face, her hands. "What do you mean? There's nothing there."

"In my dream. I saw them. Just like before, but they're white now. Like scars. Ethan took a photo while I was under." Jane pulled her phone from her pocket and swiped to the photo. "The damn things glow," she said, handing the phone to Sadie.

"Jesus, Narc. You're a fucking night light."

"A naked fucking night light."

Sadie searched her face for the joke, but she was serious. "You were naked? In your dream?"

"It got me thinking. Back when I was just a vapour in my dreams, clothes were never a factor. But ever since I've been visible, whatever I'm wearing when I fall asleep is what I end up wearing in the dreams."

"You're telling me you were prancing around buck naked in front of the kid and a bunch of drug dealers?"

"Yup. Makes me want to sleep in a coat of armour."

"That's wacked. What if they saw you?"

"They did. Or one of them did. I was in the kid's bedroom looking for a way out." She remembered the moment with a shiver. "He probably thinks he was hallucinating."

"Were you glowing like in the photo?"

"No. Translucent. Like a ghost, but more solid than I was when I helped Buddy's mom across the ice at St. Paul's."

"This is *so* not good. Your dreams were disturbing enough when you were a fly on the wall. Being visible complicates all the things." Sadie swirled her finger in the air.

"Tell me about it. I hope this isn't the new normal."

"How'd you get out of there?"

"I stepped on a LEGO or something. Hurt like hell, but it flung me right out of the dream."

"You woke yourself? That's rare." One of Jane's biggest frustrations had always been that she couldn't escape from the dreams. "Anything you can use?"

"You'd think. But when I'm in a dream, my memory is blank in spots. Like, I knew why I was naked, because Ethan, obviously, but I didn't know why I shouldn't touch anything, only that the thought of it terrified me."

"Maybe Ariane will have answers." Sadie took a sip of wine. "How'd Ethan handle it?"

"I didn't tell him about the being naked part; didn't know how he'd deal with that little gem. But he gets it now—why I have a steel door. Said he'd install one at his place, get more locks."

"I hear a *but* in there."

"You know how it is. I hate that he feels he has to protect me. I can protect myself."

Sadie stared at the floor, ignoring Jane's empty boast. When Jane felt weak, it brought out the worst in her. And she was just stubborn enough to give Ethan a hard time about it, too.

"You been shopping?" Jane asked, gesturing to the bags on the counter.

"Just groceries. And wine," she said, holding up the evidence in her glass. "God, I miss eating out. I could smell the souvlaki from the Greek joint out on the sidewalk. Nearly slipped in my drool."

"And you didn't cave in? I'm impressed."

"I walked all the way to Alma and back. Even went into the second-hand shop." Sadie shook her head. "Man, I hate living like this."

"It's a little more than a year. You can do it."

"I know, but I'm going to hate every minute of it." Sadie upended her glass. "Some days I miss my old life."

"You don't mean that."

"No. You're right." But she wasn't.

6 | Ethan

Jane hadn't been far from Ethan's thoughts all day. He'd walked her out to her bike at half past six and seen her off to work, but the memory of her in that paralytic dream kept popping into his head.

He knew the narcolepsy combined with cataplexy caused her sleep paralysis: that was a medical condition, something he understood. Something documented in medical books. But the dreams? Slipping back in time? Her glowing marks? That was straight-up supernatural. He put up a good front, but it unnerved him. He had no way to protect her from that, to protect himself.

And what if there were others like her? Playing with lives like chess pieces, pawns to be sacrificed... or not. One wrong step and—poof—a person simply ceased to exist. And no one would ever know. It was a lot to get his head around, and in the absence of her dreams of late, he'd been getting good at ignoring it. But now the dreams were back.

"Ethan? The bill?"

"What? Oh yeah. Leave it with me." He'd called the emergency glass repair place before he'd left his apartment. They'd already replaced the glass in the front door and vacuumed up the mess, and it wasn't even ten in the morning.

And Connor still hadn't returned Ethan's calls. He either had his phone turned off or was ignoring him. But this time, Ethan wasn't letting Connor skate away from the problem. The cops said the vandal had pushed the rock-laden cart past dozens of glass-plated targets before ramming it though Riptide's door. And he wasn't an alky in search of a bottle, because an alky would have filled up the cart and taken it with him. Instead, he'd fled.

Someone was trying to send Connor a message, and Ethan wanted to know what it was about.

Ethan's shift ended with no sign of Connor, who still hadn't returned Ethan's calls. So Ethan grabbed a pint of Keith's and slipped into a chair at an out-of-the-way table, where he could keep an eye on the back door.

An hour passed. And then another.

It was after eight when the back door finally clanked opened. Connor. Head down, he walked briskly to the office door, unlocked it, and slipped inside. An ostrich headed for the sand. He hadn't even glanced toward the front, which meant he'd gotten Ethan's messages and knew the glass had been replaced.

Ethan finished his beer, and was about to confront Connor, when Garvin and Joey arrived.

Ethan settled back in, pulled on his ball cap, and tugged the peak down low. The thugs spent too much time checking out the front door and surrounding area not to have also known about last night's vandalism.

And if Connor was paying attention, he'd have seen the men's arrival through the two-way mirror in the office.

Ethan slouched down, busying himself with his phone. He knew Joey would be scanning the tables, so he kept his face in shadow. The men passed a few tables over and started down the hall to the office. They didn't knock, just walked right in.

Ethan stood and shuffled close to the wall, out of sight from the two-way mirror. He stepped down the hall and paused at the office door. Raised voices thudded out.

"Wouldn't have happened if you'd increased security—like we suggested." Garvin.

"Trident's security was increased a month ago. At an outrageous price. A lot of good it did. We should fire them is what we should do."

"You're under contract."

"Yes, sadly. We have security cameras and staff on site eighteen hours a day, and an hourly drive-by when we're closed. No other business in this area has as much security. There is no way to justify another gouging increase." Connor.

"You don't have to explain shit." Garvin again.

"Of course we do. We don't operate in secret. If our accountants see unreasonable increases, they'll want answers."

"We disagree—"

Ethan knocked on the door.

Joey opened it. "What do you want?" he said, blocking the way.

Ethan poked his head around Joey's arm. "Connor? You got a

minute?" Connor's hands were on his hips. He stood behind the desk in the alcove at the back of the office. Garvin stood in front of it.

"Does it look like he's got a minute?" Joey said.

Ethan kept his gaze on Connor. "The cops had some questions."

"You heard of a phone?" Joey said.

Ethan dragged his gaze to Joey. He figured they were probably matched in weight, and he'd seen enough of Joey to know he was a fighter, but Ethan had years of dealing with scum like Joey. "I ain't going anywhere. You can step aside or limp aside. Your choice."

Joey snarled and postured, but Garvin intervened. "We're done here. Come on, Joey. Let the ladies chat."

Joey moved out of Garvin's way as he barreled past. Ethan stepped aside, and Joey's glare as he turned to follow Garvin left no doubt that Ethan's challenge would not go unanswered.

Ethan walked into the office and closed the door. Connor's gaze was on the mirror as the men made their way through the bar. Ethan glanced around for clues, anything new or out of place. The liquor boxes remained stacked near the video arcade, the sofas hadn't moved, and the credenza behind the desk and the computer on top of it were unchanged.

Connor didn't turn to Ethan until Joey and Garvin had left the building.

"What's going on?" Ethan said.

"Nothing that concerns you. What'd the cops want?"

"They want to know why someone would smash the front door and not help themselves to even one bottle of booze that was sitting right there in front of them."

"How the hell would I know?" Connor said, his temper getting the best of him. "You interrupted a business meeting for that?"

"*A*, that was not a business meeting. It was a shakedown. And, *B*, those two aren't businessmen. They're thugs."

"You're out of line, Ethan. Mind your own business."

"This bar *is* my business. And whatever those two are up to is going to shut this place down." His words landed like a slap to Connor's hysteria.

Connor calmed himself, sat down, picked up a pen. "Your job is day manager. 9:00 a.m. to 6:00 p.m. Stick to that. Let me handle this."

Ethan stood his ground and folded his arms. "You're not handling it, Connor. They're walking all over you. What do they have on you?"

"Leave it alone, Ethan. Please. You get in their way and you're going to get hurt."

"You're worried about my health? I can handle Joey." Ethan took a breath. Put his hands in his pockets. "Why are you shutting me out?"

"Garvin's organization has a hundred Joeys. Can you handle a hundred, Ethan? You may be a tough guy, but this is beyond you."

"So call the cops. Get some help."

Connor leaned back in his chair and let out a derisive laugh. "You don't think, if it were that easy, I'd have already done it? You know shit about this. Stay out of it."

7 | Jane

Sadie was on her second glass of wine when Jane left. Back in her own apartment, Jane turned the deadbolts. She texted Ariane, half hoping she wouldn't respond. Not that Ariane would give her an *I told you so*. But now that the dreams had returned, Jane would have to face the fear again: fear of waking in strange places, fear of not knowing what awaited her. For all of Ariane's knowledge, she couldn't help her in the moment. No one could.

Jane's phone rang before she made it the five steps to the sofa. "You were right, Ariane. The dreams are back."

Jane unpacked the events of the previous night and sent her the photo Ethan had taken. Looking at it again, it struck Jane that the glow was ghost-like. No longer blood marks, but ghost marks. "What do you make of those markings?"

"Interesting. Makes me wonder if the protection they offered as blood marks continues."

When Jane had borne the chain of blood-red marks, anyone who tried to take her life paid with their own. Sadly, that had happened more times than she cared to think about.

"You know what else is interesting?" Jane said. "In the medical journal, the one with the photos taken of me when I was a kid? The blood marks in those photos disappeared when my marks vanished. But the marks in Ethan's photo are still there, even though they're not visible on my skin."

"That adds weight to the idea that the marks still protect you."

Jane hadn't known about the blood mark's protection. It was Ariane who'd enlightened her before her last birthday. Protection was the only redeeming feature of the horrible red marks that had wrapped around her body and defined the first twenty-five years of her life.

"One of the marks looks different now," Jane said, absently stroking the back of her left hand.

"How so?"

"It's round. Bigger. Touching it makes me feel disoriented, sick to my stomach."

"Do you have a photo of it?"

"No, but I can sketch it. And there's more," Jane said. "In my dream, I was afraid to touch anything, even to pick up a sheet to cover myself."

"You remembered."

"But I didn't remember why I couldn't touch anything. There are blanks in my memory when I'm dreaming. And did you miss the bit about me needing to cover myself? Because I was naked. As in no clothes. Talk about awkward."

"You also made a breakthrough. You woke yourself."

Jane had woken herself twice before. Both times, she'd been highly agitated. This time it was the result of jarring pain. "By hurting myself. Not sure that's a workable option. And that knowledge is only useful if it doesn't fall into one of my memory gaps next time I'm under."

"Don't discount the progress you're making. Children don't learn to walk in a day. They walk, they fall, they get stronger, and walk again. Eventually, they stop falling. You will too."

Jane wanted to believe Ariane, believe that she would learn to control the dreams, to come and go of her own volition and not at the whim of an ancient directive.

"In his diaries, Pedro references something similar," Ariane said. "Bear in mind it was a different era; he died in 1877. It was a time when people believed Witnesses were blessed by the gods. Pedro believed that every time he had a vision, he got closer to an injustice. And if he got retribution for the person who was wronged, and set it right, the gods would bless him with another advantage. That's how he explained it when he gained the ability to hear in his vision state, and when he first felt the earth beneath his feet."

"It's progressive, then," Jane said. "These memory gaps could go away."

"It's possible. As far as I've read in his diaries, Pedro is at the point you were when you first realized the people in your dreams could see your ethereal form."

Pedro was the only other person in the world Jane could relate to, and he'd been dead for more than a century. "Please read faster. I have to know if he learned to control the visions." Jane also wanted to learn how to escape the dreams entirely, but Ariane wouldn't have approved.

"I'm reading as fast as I can. There are dozens of volumes, and his handwriting is atrocious."

"Can the old families help you?"

"They can read the diaries, if that's what you mean, but they're not trained researchers. As you pointed out, Pedro's abilities progress in a linear fashion. It's important I understand the progression so I don't miss anything."

"What about Nate? He's fluent in Spanish and trained." Nate Crawford was the professor who'd recognized Jane's blood marks as Incan. The pattern was the same as a print that hung in his office at UBC—and the same as the pattern found on an ancient ribbon that protected Ariane's Peruvian home. He'd known Ariane for years—they'd studied together in Cusco. When he'd told her about Jane's marks, she'd flown all the way to Vancouver to see them for herself.

"Ha! Funny you should mention Nathaniel. He's coming to visit. I don't know who's more excited, me or my mother. She's already set aside a day to make *picarones*." The not-too-sweet Peruvian donuts were a favourite treat of Nate's. Jane liked them too. She'd tasted one when Ariane made them for Nate the previous fall during her visit to Vancouver.

"Lucky Nate." It was obvious to Jane that Nate and Ariane's relationship had turned some kind of corner on her last visit.

"Ariane, do you think Huan's the person I'm supposed to find retribution for?"

"That is difficult to know."

"I suppose. It usually takes more than one dream to figure it out. I can always hope, though."

"Trust the dreams, Jane. They tell a story. Let them unfold and reveal the events you are meant to witness."

"You say that as if I have a choice in the matter."

"You may not choose who or what you witness, but I believe you can learn to control your body when you dream. You must. The alternative is too dangerous."

The alternative was inadvertently changing history. Case in point: putting Pieter in Buddy's wheelchair. And according to Ethan, the new Buddy was not a boon to society. More like a blight on civilization.

"Did Pedro have blood marks?"

"No. He would have mentioned it. I don't believe the two phenomena are connected, other than they're both Peruvian. Whatever makes you *una testigo*, a Witness, you inherited from your mother. It's in your DNA.

The blood marks were the result of a ritual, protection from the Yupanquis' offering bowl. Rosa and the old families will be so pleased to hear you're dreaming again."

"They'll be the only ones. Maybe they'd like to chip in for a pair of chainmail pyjamas and a sturdy pair of slippers."

The next day, Jane had a terrible case of nerves as she arrived at the Vancouver Law Courts downtown. Her apprehension about dredging up what had happened to her was part of it, but the bigger part was not knowing how the secrets she kept would play out. Not that she planned on revealing the nature of her dreams, but they were intricately bound up in what had happened. And though she hated to admit it, she felt intimidated by the officiousness of the building, with its towering glass-and-steel atrium and the power-suited professionals scurrying about with purpose.

Expecting a metal detector, Jane left her knife with the bike, but she had only to give her appointment details to the uniformed sheriffs at the front door to gain entry. She found Monica's office, where she was greeted by a receptionist and took a seat. Moments later, Monica Fowler came out and introduced herself. Jane had expected a shark, a beady-eyed predator. Instead, she met a classy aunt with a welcoming smile, a warm handshake, and soft blue eyes. Wavy hair streaked with grey fell to the shoulders of her navy suit.

They walked down a carpeted hall to her office. "Can I get you anything?" Monica asked. "A coffee? Tea? Glass of water?"

Jane declined. Monica invited her to take a seat at a round table that sat in front of a bright floor-to-ceiling window, suggesting they'd be more comfortable there.

"As I mentioned on the phone, this is an informal meeting. We won't be discussing the case today, just getting to know one another and answering any questions you may have about the process."

Monica went on to explain that Jane would be referred to as the complainant and that they'd use her legal name, Joyce Walker. She wondered if Monica knew that Joyce was the name of the train station where she'd been abandoned. Hearing it felt like a slap in the face; an unpleasant reminder of the system she'd grown up in.

Monica, on the other hand, would be referred to as The Crown, or Madam Prosecutor, but it was okay to call her Monica in her office. The accused would be in the courtroom, seated in the defence box.

"I thought they'd be tried separately."

"Not in BC. It's important you understand that you will be expected to recount exactly what happened to you. You must answer truthfully all questions, mine as well as ones from the defence. Will you be able to do that with the accused in the courtroom?"

Jane would never be able to recount exactly, nor answer truthfully, but she knew she had to go through the motions. "Do I have a choice?"

Though Monica's demeanour came across as relaxed, Jane had the sense she was being studied, her every reaction gauged, from the tone of her voice to the pace of her words. Monica's smiling eyes took in Jane's posture, her hand placement, the tilt of her head.

"Not about them being in the room. But you don't have to see them. We can ask for a screen."

Jane took a moment. "No. I want them to see me."

Monica paused then nodded. Jotted a note on a pad. She went on to explain that she would be developing questions, as would the defence, to paint a picture of the events for the jury. Monica would review her questions with Jane prior to court, but she could only guess at the questions the defence would ask. She reminded Jane, for the second time, that she was not Jane's lawyer.

"Anything you disclose to me about the case, I am bound by law to pass to defence immediately. You mustn't lie. You have to be truthful and tell me everything."

Jane nodded, knowing she was already lying. She couldn't imagine telling this intelligent woman, who Jane suspected was also streetwise, that on occasion she manifested in her dreams and changed history.

"Have they pleaded yet?" Jane asked.

"No. They'll be given every opportunity, but they may choose to wait until the last minute. It's their prerogative."

"It feels like the law is stacked in their favour."

"Yes, I hear that a lot. But consider that we're asking the court to take away their freedom, possibly for years."

Monica stood, signalling the end of the meeting. "Before our next session, I'll send you a copy of your police statement to refresh your memory. You were in hospital when you gave it, soon after your ordeal. You may find you'd forgotten to mention a detail or two, or you may need to clarify something. It's also possible the person who transcribed your statement made an error. Take your time reviewing it. It's important we get it right."

Jane couldn't remember the specifics she'd included in her police statement, but there were more than a few details she'd left out. As she left the building, what made her heart race wasn't the missing details. It was Monica and the keen edge of her pickaxe as she dug into the mountain of Jane's lies.

8 | Sadie

At the end of each section of the course, Sadie had to successfully complete a real-work simulation to ensure she could apply what she'd learned. Today's simulation involved inputting batches of invoices, cheques, and some mystery items into an online ledger. The school allotted a set amount of time. If you didn't know your shit, you couldn't get the batch done before the screen locked you out. If that happened, you couldn't try again for a week, giving you enough time to repeat the coursework.

Sadie hadn't been locked out today. Something to celebrate! And there was no better excuse for day drinking. She poured herself a glass of wine, surprised that it drained the bottle. She half convinced herself the bottles were getting smaller.

When her glass was empty, Sadie wandered back to the computer and clicked in the course outline to see what came next. Intro to Cost Accounting. Didn't look too challenging, Sadie decided. No need to read ahead.

An unprovoked image of Mike surfaced in her mind, complete with the look of shock on his face. Was there any chance he'd come around? She swallowed her pride and texted him.

When he didn't answer, she decided to take a break. She'd earned it. And she'd been so disciplined yesterday on Fourth Avenue. She would treat herself to a trip downtown. A cheap meal out wouldn't be too big a strain on her budget.

When Sadie returned a few hours later, she dropped her bags on the floor, feeling a little sick to her stomach. Sadie's cheap dinner was the least of her day's expenses. During the drive home she'd run through her justifications for each of her purchases, and they had nothing to do with Mike. The boots would replace an old pair she was pretty sure leaked the last time she wore them. And they were on sale, so there was that. The jeans were fifty percent off. Sure, she didn't need another pair, but she would donate an old pair that never did fit her right to the Sally Ann. And the purse? Well, that might have been a mistake even if it did come from her favourite consignment shop. But three hundred dollars for a Hermès! Sure, it was a bit beat-up, and the lining had a tear that had been badly repaired, but Hermès bags were heirlooms, collectibles. She'd use it for a month or two and then sell it for as much as she'd paid for it, probably more.

The bottle of wine was definitely not a mistake. She opened it immediately and poured a glass. But thirty minutes later, staring at the bags that still lay by the door where she'd dropped them, she felt the weight of what she'd done. She'd blown a hole in her budget. If she didn't fix it, she'd run out of money before she finished her accounting program. *Shit!*

She sat at the computer and tapped the space bar, waking the screen. Tomorrow, she'd look into selling the Hermès bag. And if she didn't sell it for as much money as she'd spent today, she'd return the other items. As tired as she was of feeling broke all the time, she reminded herself that it wouldn't be forever.

Her gaze slid to the Teacher's Pet icon on her home screen.

9 | Ethan

Ethan had let his temper get the better of him last night. He'd stormed out of Riptide, furious with Connor for not bringing him in on whatever Garvin and Joey were up to. Connor was delusional if he thought he could handle those two thugs on his own. Connor was a good guy: he sponsored little league and a ballet troupe; he gave every employee a day off to volunteer in the community. But Garvin and Joey didn't know Connor, and even if they did, they didn't respect *good*. They didn't care about Connor or Riptide. They were a means to an end.

And today, Ethan was going to piece together whatever that end was.

At eight in the morning, he unlocked Riptide's back door and headed straight for the office. Connor wasn't a complicated guy. When he changed the QuickBooks access, he'd have written down the new password somewhere. Ethan started a methodical search of the desk. He didn't have to look far; the new password was scribbled on a sticky note in the front of the payroll file.

After he'd logged in with Connor's credentials, Ethan ran a report of all the transactions that had been entered in the past six months. Two items jumped out at him: large payments to Trident, the security firm whose name Ethan had heard for the first time last night; and a remarkable increase in Riptide's revenue.

Ethan checked the regular orders. They were still bringing in the same amount of alcohol and food, but their dry goods order had shot up, along with their disposables. He'd been in the storage room off the kitchen the day before. There was nothing unusual on the shelves. The paper towel, toilet paper, and napkin supply looked healthy, but not out of the norm.

He jumped at a scrape from the bar area. But there was no movement beyond the mirror, just his nerves and the sounds of an old, empty building settling its bones.

Digging deeper, he discovered it wasn't all the revenue that had increased, just the cash side. Credit card sales were in the range they'd always been.

He mulled over his findings. Riptide's cash receipts were up—way up. Invoices for goods they didn't have on hand were up. That, and there were the inflated payments to Trident Security, a company Ethan knew nothing about and had never seen on the premises. He could think of only one reason for the changes: money laundering. Which made perfect sense, considering the cash-heavy organization Garvin and Joey were messed up in. They just had to dump the cash into the bar's till, and it would come out sparkly clean when Riptide paid them for goods and services never rendered.

But why would Connor go along with them? Put Riptide in jeopardy? Never mind the jail time he could face if he was caught. Whatever Garvin's organization had on Connor, it was serious. Was Connor's pride holding him hostage as well?

Ethan started at another bang, but this one wasn't the building talking. It was the back door. Ethan quickly shut down the computer and scooted out from behind the desk. He stood behind the closed office door and breathed a sigh of relief when the footsteps continued down the hall. Through the mirror, Ethan caught a glimpse of the cook heading to the kitchen. Ethan slipped out of the office and back to his apartment.

He came back at 10:00 a.m. and worked his normal shift, all the while sorting through what he'd learned and pondering how best to broach the subject with Connor. Ethan finally felt armed with enough information to confront him, but Connor didn't show during Ethan's shift. When the new night guy took over behind the bar, Ethan poured himself a been-there-done-that beer and settled at the same table where he'd waited before. Connor was bound to show eventually.

Ethan had barely settled in when Garvin sauntered in through the front without his sidekick. He waddled up to the bar and exchanged a few words with the new guy. The familiarity between the two made it clear that they knew one another. The dots aligned; Garvin had replaced Ethan with his own man, someone who would support the new business model and look the other way. Had Connor known? Ethan wanted to believe he hadn't, but the bitter taste in his mouth wasn't the beer.

Garvin slapped the bar with a nod and a laugh and continued along the line of barstools toward the hallway entrance. But unlike the last time, when Garvin turned in his direction, Ethan didn't try to hide.

Garvin spotted him and they locked glares. "What are you doing here?"

"Taking a load off. You?"

"None of your fucking business." Garvin stabbed a stubby finger at Ethan's beer. "You pay for that?"

Ethan dismissed the comment with a shrug. "I know the bartender. Looks like you know him, too."

"Your shift's over. Get the fuck out of here."

"Does Connor know you and his new bartender are buddies?"

"Did you not hear me?"

The fact that Garvin wasn't gloating led Ethan to believe Connor hadn't known. The lump of bitterness that had been choking him dissipated. "I'm curious, Garv. How did you and I get off on the wrong foot?"

"There were no feet involved, smartass. I know your type. Gym rat punk. Thinks he's hot shit, smarter than the rest of us."

Ethan pointed at himself. "Punk? Me?" He felt incredulous having those labels applied by the biggest punk in the bar.

"I notice you're not denying the rest of it. Go home, Ethan. If your girlfriend shows up, I'll let her know where you are."

Alarm bells went off in Ethan's head. "My girlfriend?"

"Yeah. The pretty little brunette." Garvin leaned in. "Jane, right? Maybe I'll buy her a drink."

Ethan clamped his mouth shut. Provoking Garvin suddenly lost its appeal.

"What? Your little dick afraid of the competition?" Garvin said, grabbing his crotch. When Ethan made no retort, Garvin said, "That's what I thought." He turned and headed down the hall to the office.

Ethan downed his drink and left by way of the front door.

Back in his apartment, he watched Riptide from his window. The bulb over the rear exit was burned out again.

After closing, Garvin left by the back door. Even though he could only see his silhouette, Ethan recognized the shape of the night deposit bag in his hand.

10 | Jane

Jane arrived early to work and started her daily watering routine, which wasn't nearly as time-consuming as during the summer when the plants needed watering twice a day.

Anna came in an hour later with what Jane had come to consider her entourage: Pieter, Reyna, and Anna's brother, Lucas. Lucas Bakker was a horticulturist and Anna's partner in the business. He and Jane did the heavy lifting, and Anna took care of the books and the orchids.

Lucas helped Reyna settle Pieter in his room, which had been converted to meet his special needs. Anna went straight to the office.

"Morning," Lucas said, seeing Jane wind the heavy watering hose back in place. If he or Anna had noticed she'd come in early, they didn't mention it.

Anna came out of the office with the cash drawer in one hand and her cane in the other. She glanced over at the floor where Jane had just finished watering.

"Clean that up before someone slips and falls," she said before Jane could even say hello.

Jane held her tongue. Every day for eight years now she watered, and afterwards, every day, she squeegeed the floor. That Anna felt the need to remind her was irritating to say the least.

Still, Jane couldn't know the hardships Anna had suffered, the nagging pain her leg caused her. If she was short with Jane, it was a result of what Jane had done.

At lunch, Jane left for her appointment with Katerina Vasco, the portfolio manager at the investment firm that handled her inheritance. The firm's offices were in one of the Bentall Towers. She removed her helmet and looked up at the black glass buildings. Their rent had to be astronomical.

The receptionist behind the teak counter advised Jane to take a seat. "Ms. Vasco will be out in a moment."

Jane had barely settled into a deep blue chair when Katerina rounded the corner in a perfectly fitted grey suit.

"Jane. Good to see you," she said, approaching with her hand extended and a warm smile.

Jane stood, clutching her helmet, and shook her hand.

They walked a carpeted hallway to her office. "Can I get you a coffee? Bottled water?" she offered as she closed the door behind them.

Jane declined, and the woman took her seat behind the desk. The view of Vancouver spread out behind her in a panorama, where a dazzling array of glass towers played peek-a-boo with the Pacific Ocean and snow-capped mountains.

"We got a package from the lawyers yesterday. The Morrow-Walker Charitable Foundation's paperwork has been filed. They expect the society's registration and charitable status will be approved within three months."

"Thank you."

"But that's not why you're here. What can I do for you?"

Right down to business. But Jane guessed clients expected that when they were charged by the quarter hour. "I've a good friend, Sadie Prescott. She's taking an accounting course and needs to find a company where she can do an internship. I wondered if you would consider hiring her here?"

"I'd certainly be willing to talk to her about it, to make sure it's a good fit for our accounting department. Of course, she'll have to pass our background check and provide references, but I'm sure that won't be a problem if she's already in the program."

It wouldn't be a problem, or so Sadie thought. But that was only if the lawyers in the Crown counsel's office didn't have any special arrangements with the police. "Thank you. I'll give her your number."

When Jane returned to work, Anna made a point of looking at her watch.

"Sorry. I'll make it up," Jane said, rushing to her locker.

After work, Jane dumped her helmet in her apartment and walked down the hall to tap on Sadie's door.

"I have news," she said when Sadie opened the door, but one look at Sadie's face changed Jane's focus. "Everything all right?"

"Why do you ask?" Sadie said.

"'Cause your eyebrows are stuck together. I can't tell if you're pissed off or just confused."

Sadie rubbed her face. "Pissed off, I guess. But only with myself. Come in."

"What happened?"

"You know how I did so well not caving into temptation on Fourth Avenue the other day?" Jane nodded. "Well, I had a major fail yesterday. I should never have gone downtown."

Jane looked around the small apartment and noticed a few bags on the floor by the door and a newish handbag on the desk. "What's the damage?"

"Nothing I can't fix. I just have to sell that purse," Sadie said, nodding toward the misbehaving handbag. "It's a Hermès," Sadie added, as if that label would clear up Jane's confusion. "Really, Jane?" She rolled her eyes. "A Hermès. Everyone knows Hermès."

"I thought they made scarves," Jane said. She'd always thought of clothing as something that either did or did not cover her blood marks, a mindset that never did align with Sadie's sense of style. Jane walked to the desk and picked up the bag, examining it. "What makes it so special?"

"We just covered that. It's a Hermès." Sadie returned to her computer. "It's worth a lot. That handbag, when it was new, would have cost twenty grand."

"For a purse?" Jane said, incredulous. She set the handbag down like it was made of fine crystal. "For that kind of cash, I could buy two motorcycles. New. Loaded. Hell, I could buy a Fat Boy like Ethan's and have change left over."

"Or," Sadie said, framing the bag with her hands, "you could buy one genuine Hermès handbag to hand down to your children and your children's children. I've listed it on Craigslist and Kijiji."

"How about Marketplace?"

"Thanks. I forgot that one." Sadie took her seat and bent over the keyboard. "I told Mike," she said, still typing.

Jane took a cautious breath, wanting to be excited, but Sadie kept her head bent, not meeting Jane's gaze. "How'd he react?"

"He walked out. Hasn't returned my texts."

Jane exhaled in disappointment. "I'm sorry."

"Nah, it's okay. It won't be the last time that happens." Jane moved to Sadie's side as she finished her Marketplace listing. Sadie finally looked up, a firm set to her jaw. "I've got to get used to it."

Sadie was trying to brush it off, but Jane could see how much it hurt her. "To the right guy, it won't matter," she said, and squeezed Sadie's shoulder. "How about some good news?" Jane fished a business card out of her pocket and set it down by the laptop.

"What's that?" Sadie asked, pausing to look.

"I saw Katerina today. Asked if they would consider hiring you for an internship." Jane took her usual place in the beanbag chair.

Sadie picked up the card. "What'd she say?"

"You're sure you can pass a background check?"

"My juvie record's sealed, so yeah. What else do they need?"

"She mentioned references. She's expecting your call."

Sadie perked up, but Jane didn't want to leave her just yet. Not with Mike's rejection so fresh in her mind. "Want to watch a movie?"

They sat on the floor, reclining against the beanbag chair with Sadie's laptop propped on a pillow between them.

Sometime later, Jane jerked awake. She said her good-nights to Sadie and wandered back to her own place to crash.

Visiting Dream

Jane wakes in a parkade, her bare feet in a puddle. It smells of oil and stale exhaust. Her back is to a wall between two cars. There are no windows, but a sign on a nearby concrete pillar points out the Davie Street exit. She's in downtown Vancouver.

Squealing tires draw her attention to a car coming down a ramp. She ducks and drops to a squat in the shadows. She's wearing her nightshirt. *Thank heavens.* Her form is again translucent, but her pale skin looks alarmingly bright. Her gaze drifts to her right forearm. She's mesmerized by the white markings. She runs a finger across the newly round mark on the back of her left hand. Her vision blurs. She lifts her finger, and the nausea calms.

A car door opens. Voices drift over, male, two of them. She creeps along the wall, closer to the voices. The tags on the licence plate of the car she hides behind expire next year. She takes a quick inventory. Of the licence plates she can see, one expired the previous November, and the other two are set to expire in March and June of the current year. *It's sometime before November last year.*

A car door closes, and the car continues on. In the distance, she hears the squeal of its tires, ascending this time.

In the quiet that follows, she closes her eyes. She's in a visiting dream. The fact that she knows it, and is aware that she's here to witness something, washes over her with relief. But there's another detail she's supposed to remember. What? Minutes tick by.

More squealing tires. Another vehicle approaches, then stops. It's close. She hears a man's voice. A car door opens, and a soft dinging ensues—the driver's left the keys in the ignition. She peers out from behind the bumper. A man in a ball cap walks toward a shiny black truck with silver running boards. The blackened driver's window retracts, and Jane catches a glimpse of the driver. Though he's wearing a beanie, she recognises Garvin. Beside him, Joey scans their surroundings through the windshield. As Joey's head swivels in her direction, Jane yanks herself back behind the car's rear end.

She steadies herself on the bumper but quickly removes her hand. *Don't touch!* In her mind's eye, she sees Pieter. She wants to cry out but holds it in with a whimper. That's what she was supposed to remember. Touching is dangerous. She takes a calming breath. But the exhale is tinged with a niggling doubt. There's more to it, more that she was supposed to remember.

The voices aren't raised. Jane can't make out their words. The car's door closes, and the vehicle leaves, retreating up the ramp. The truck remains. It's quiet again, and Jane waits.

Someone approaches on foot, accompanied by a steady thump, thump. She shuffles to the other side of the car she's hiding behind, out of Joey's line of sight. Huddling in a tight ball, she peers out to see who's coming. The footsteps belong to a young boy, twelve, maybe fourteen. He's slight. When he gets closer, she recognizes it's Huan from the slum apartment. One hand bounces a black basketball, the other is in his pocket. His eyes dart from side to side. He's afraid but trying to look tough the way street kids do.

She scoots to the other side of the bumper and examines her hand again. It's ghost-like. She peeks out. The boy walks up to the shiny truck, his ball now under one arm. But the driver's window doesn't open. Shouts erupt from inside. The boy backs up, unsure. Joey emerges from the truck's passenger seat with a scowl on his face. He slams the door. The boy turns, alarm on his face, and breaks into a run. Joey charges after him. Jane follows in a crouch, taking a parallel path behind the row of vehicles against the wall.

The race ends abruptly. Jane stops short. She's too close and quickly retreats to put a car between them, keeping an eye on the boy through the vehicle's windows.

"Let me go!" Huan shouts.

Joey has got the boy by the tail of his coat and spins him around so his back smacks against a pillar not more than ten feet away. His basketball drops and rolls away. She has a clear view of both of them, side on. Joey quickly pats down Huan and then stands back with his hands on his hips, shaking his head in disappointment. If he turns to the right, he'll see her. She slinks lower.

Huan is defiant. "Louie's going to kill you for putting your hands on me."

"Why are you doing Louie's dirty work? I thought you were a smart kid."

"Louie's smart too."

"Yeah? Did he tell you juvie's a party?" As Joey talks, he twitches in tune with the sounds of the garage, like a predator.

"I'm too young for juvie."

"Louie's using you, kid."

"What's it to you? I got the cash."

Joey sticks out his hand, palm up. "Hand it over."

The kid reaches into his crotch and pulls out a roll of bills. He smacks it into Joey's hand. Joey doesn't even look at it, just tucks the roll into his jacket pocket. He turns his head in Jane's direction. She drops out of sight.

"Get out of here."

Jane hears a struggle, and then what sounds like Huan hitting the floor with a grunt. "Seriously? You're boosting my cash?" The kid's voice. She peers under the car and sees the boy push himself off the ground with his hands.

"I don't deal with kids who got no skin in the game. Tell Louie to come see us next time. Until then, I'm holding his bankroll."

"Come on, man. He's gonna kill me."

"Good. But if he don't, you tell him Garvin and me don't want to see your sorry ass again. You got that? Now get the fuck out of here."

Jane glances under the car again and sees the kid's feet turn and walk away. Huan scoops up his basketball, and then the footsteps speed into a run. "You're an asshole," the kid shouts from a safe distance.

Jane hangs her head. This is what she was supposed to witness? Joey and Garvin dealing drugs and stealing some kid's money? The annoying inkling that she is forgetting something returns.

She becomes aware of the silence around her. She rises on her haunches and dares a peek through the window, but Joey isn't near the pillar. She turns to see if he'd walked back toward the truck, but he isn't there either. And then she turns around and sees him creeping along the wall, coming straight for her hiding place. She dashes to the front of the car, keeping it between them. But he sees her. The expression on his face is confusion. Keeping low, she breaches the front of the cars, runs past the ramp, and scoots behind the first car on the other side.

She has to get out of there. It hits her then, what she's forgetting: she has to remember how to get out of there. Not the parkade—out of the dream. She closes her eyes and concentrates, but all that does is make her aware of Joey's slow approach. He's looking right at her. She rises again and starts for the next car over, but she doesn't see the trailer hitch. She smacks her shin into it and screams in pain.

Jane lurched awake with a cry in her throat. She bent her injured leg to her chest and rubbed the lump. *Damn, that hurt! Who puts a big-ass trailer hitch on a compact car?* She turned on the lamp and pulled down the sheet. There was definitely a lump, and it was already turning colour. Did being a ghost have no benefits?

At least she was wearing clothes this time, even if it was just a nightshirt. Next time she'd be fully dressed, right down to her boots and her trusty boot knife.

And she wasn't mistaken about Buddy having recognized her the day she plowed into Garvin and him at Riptide. Buddy may not have put it together yet, but he'd seen her before their encounter at the bar. He'd seen her in that parkade.

Her shin needed ice. She padded to the kitchen and twisted the ice cube tray, emptying it into a tea towel.

It was the first night she'd woken from a dream to an empty apartment. Not that Sadie could ever do much for her when she was stuck in a dream, but it had been reassuring to know she was there watching over her.

She'd had no dreams for months, and now two in quick succession. *Nothing like easing into it*, she thought with bitterness. She never imagined she'd wish for the good old days when her dreams were sporadic and she was invisible.

On her way to the sofa, Jane checked the locks. They were bolted. Silly to check, but the dreams always reminded her how vulnerable she was, even if she didn't like admitting it. She sat on the sofa and gingerly applied the ice. It was 5:00 a.m. She wouldn't have another visiting dream—she'd not had two in one night since she was a kid—but she didn't think she could get back to sleep.

At least now she knew her connection to Huan was Buddy. Huan had to be the reason for her dreams. She'd also pieced together that Louie was the name of the beefy guy living with Huan.

There were leaves on the trees when she'd dreamed of Huan in the apartment. Given Joey's reaction to him in the parkade, muling drugs wasn't something Huan did regularly, so the episode in the underground garage had to have happened later that night. Everyone had been wearing jackets, so it was cold out. The licence plates indicated it was November at the latest, but the leaves were still on the trees outside Huan's apartment. Last September or October, then.

Ethan was right about Joey. He was a drug dealer and a low-life thief. Jane felt sympathy for Huan. Knowing the scum he lived with, he'd probably get a beating. Joey had to know it, too, which made what he'd done even worse. The Buddy she'd known would never have done that. He'd never deal drugs either. How could this version of Buddy have turned out so differently from the kind and gentle Buddy she'd known? The Buddy with the larger-than-life smile and laughing eyes? It was one more reminder of the damage she'd done. The world was definitely not a better place with the new Buddy in it.

11 | Sadie

Sadie was relieved that Jane hadn't offered to bail her out. Her pride remained intact, but the spendthrift in her was disappointed. Jane had always been Sadie's financial safety net. She'd even shared her orphan's payments when they were kids. But after Jane's abduction, when they'd moved into separate apartments, the deal was that they would learn to live independent of one another.

The fact that Jane was now loaded had no bearing on the situation, since Jane was intent on using the money the Walkers had left her to do good deeds in their name. Which was commendable. But not taking a dime for herself was simply Jane's misguided version of penitence. And she wasn't even Catholic. Sadie still shook her head when she thought of it. Jane didn't have to live in a crappy basement apartment; she could buy a penthouse downtown if she wanted to. Sadie thought the people at the investment firm might try to talk sense into her, but they were happy to go along with her charity idea.

After midnight, Sadie refreshed her screen one last time before going to bed. Still no sale on the purse, though someone had requested she post a third-party evaluation as to its authenticity. She would research how to do that if it didn't sell by morning.

At 10:00 a.m., the purse still hadn't sold, and everyone who'd seen the initial request for an evaluation was piling on, wanting proof that it was the genuine deal. She was hooped without some kind of authentication. And now she'd lose another day of studying to get the damn thing evaluated, which would cost her even more money she didn't have.

She decided to cut her losses and just return it, along with everything else she'd bought. She loaded the shopping bags in her car and drove straight to the consignment shop.

"I know you're a regular, Sadie, but this is consignment. You know the terms. No returns." The clerk pointed to the two-foot sign on the wall behind the sales counter. "But we can take it back on consignment if you'd like."

And take another forty percent cut? "Thanks anyway," Sadie said, and she sulked back to her car. Why didn't men work in consignment shops? Sadie knew without a doubt she would have been able to sweet-talk a man into taking the bag back, consignment or not.

Her next stop was the shoe boutique on Robson. She put on her brightest smile and went inside, tossing her blonde curls in a sexy offensive move as she sashayed to the desk. But there wasn't a man in sight—not even a gay or bi woman on whom she could turn her charms. Ten minutes later she was back on the sidewalk, wondering if the goddess was conspiring against her. Apparently, having *Final Sale* stamped in red all over the bill meant they could refuse to be even a teensy bit flexible.

She hit the trifecta at the jeans shop. "Sorry miss. The half-off specials are always final sales. It's right there," she said, pointing to the sign on the rack that said so.

Sadie headed directly to Starbucks and ordered a skinny latte. While she waited for her order, she looked up how to get a handbag authenticated. She took her coffee to the window bar and dialled Maynard's Auction House. The receptionist said they normally did larger estates, but they'd have someone get back to her.

She dialled a second, smaller estate sales company. They only charged two hundred for an evaluation, but they'd be happy to refund the fee if she had the genuine article and sold it through them at a forty percent commission. Bloody thieves.

Sadie came up with a better option. The pawnshop on East Hastings would know what it was worth, and they didn't charge for an evaluation.

She finished her coffee and headed back to her car only to find a parking ticket tucked under the windshield. It seemed her shit day could indeed get shittier. Cursing, she tossed her bags in the trunk and the ticket in her glovebox, and drove to the pawnshop. It was in her and Jane's old neighbourhood. Their former rooming house was a block and a half away. She locked up and sent a prayer to the goddess that her car would still have all its wheels when she got back.

A gravelly voice called her name. Sadie recognized the street worker. She was hooked on heroin, which kept her in the business.

Jules teetered over in sky-high stilettos and a micro-mini. "Say, you got a hit on ya?"

"Sorry, Jules. Not today," Sadie said. "You check with the dealer over on Pender? He might spot you."

"Nah, used up my luck with him."

Sadie noticed the woman shivering. She took off her scarf and handed it to her. "Stay warm, Jules. Or sell it. You'll get a few bucks for it in the right neighbourhood." She dug in her pocket, pulled out a fiver, and handed it to her.

"You're a good girl, Sadie,"

"Wish I had more."

"Don't we all," Jules said, turning away.

Sadie carried on to the pawnshop. An electronic gong announced her arrival, and soon a grizzled man appeared from a back room, wiping at his moustache and beard with the back of his hand. He pushed his belly up to the counter. "How can I help you?"

"Would you be able to tell me how much this is worth?" Sadie said, pulling the purse out of a shopping bag and setting it on the counter.

The man let out a low whistle. But when he picked up the purse and started examining it, the sparkle in his eyes faded. "The stitching's come loose here and here," he said, pointing it out. "The bottom's been broken, so it'll never sit straight, and the lining's been torn and repaired by an ape. I'll give you a hundred for it."

"Is that all? My grandmother will be so disappointed," Sadie said, shaking her curls, pouting just enough. "She gave it to me before she went into the home in Calgary. Said I could sell it to buy a ticket to see her before she died. She bought it new, said it was worth thousands of dollars. Are you sure you can't offer a little more, say five hundred?"

Sadie looked up at him with baleful eyes, and her heart leapt when he pulled the purse back to look at it again. After opening it up, he unzipped the inner pocket. "What's your grandmother's name?"

Shoot. This sounded like a trick question. Sadie dug deep. "Myrtle," Sadie said. "Myrtle Prescott."

"It looks like Myrtle lied to you. This purse belonged to V.R. Wright. Says so right here." He pointed to the name on the tag inside.

Shit! Sadie hadn't given any thought to the stupid tag. "Surely it's worth more than a hundred dollars. How about three?"

"Not a chance, lady. If there's nothing else, my lunch is getting cold."

Sadie felt utterly defeated. The charm that had worked so well all of her life had abandoned her when she needed it the most. Looked like the *use it or lose it* motto was working overtime.

12 | Ethan

Ethan was awakened by raised voices coming from the alley. He rolled over and glanced at the window blind. A rippling glow leaked around the edges. He leapt out of bed and raced to the window, yanking up the blind.

Fire! Flames licked up the stuccoed wall around the back door to Riptide.

A siren wailed as he threw on his clothes. He dialled 911, grabbed his fire extinguisher, and raced down the stairs. But the firefighters beat him to it. They had the flames out by the time he arrived. He introduced himself as the manager and let them in by the front door to check the damage at the back.

"We knocked it down before it could take hold," the captain said.

The damage was minimal and contained to the exterior. The back wall would need to be sealed and repainted. They'd gotten off light.

"The pile of debris the arsonist lit up came out of the dumpster. You might consider putting a lock on it," the captain said, as he followed Ethan back outside with his crew. "You'll get a copy of the report when the investigation is wrapped up. An inspector will be by first thing tomorrow. If your security camera caught anything, he'll want to see it."

Ethan thanked them and went back inside to call Connor. It went to voice mail. He then checked the security footage, which was, as he'd suspected, useless.

If it hadn't been the middle of the night, he would have called Jane.

It wasn't until he'd returned to his apartment and stood staring out the window at the blackened wall that he remembered the burned-out light.

The second burned-out light in as many days.

The fire at Riptide felt like an omen. It had stolen his sleep. "Sorry to call so early," Ethan said, when Jane answered his call at six in the morning. He knew she woke early to get to the nursery for seven.

"I was awake."

He lay back in bed with one arm under his head and pictured her legs tangled in the sheets, her hair spilled on the pillow.

"There was trouble at the bar last night."

"What happened?"

"More vandalism. Someone set a fire at the back door."

"Jesus. Anyone hurt?"

"Thankfully, we were closed."

"Much damage?"

"The fire captain didn't think so. Maybe it's because I'm tired—I was up half the night—but this vandalism doesn't feel random." He told her about the broken light over the back exit door, and the nagging fact that no other businesses had been hit—or targeted by the window-breaking vandal. "I'm going to drive out to Connor's house this morning. Find out what the hell is going on."

"I'll stop by later and see what he had to say."

"For lunch?"

"It's a day off."

"I'm sorry. I'd forgotten, or I wouldn't have called so early."

"You didn't wake me. I dreamed again. It was Garvin and Joey this time. Last fall, I think. They were dealing drugs out of a parking garage somewhere on Davie Street. Remember the boy from my earlier dream, Huan? They stole a roll of cash from him."

"Sounds like something they'd do."

"Poor kid's going to catch a beating for it. You were right about Joey. He's a piece of crap."

"Yeah. I'm not happy to be right about that. Why are you dreaming about them?"

"That's what I need to sort out. It might be that I'm supposed to help Huan. I'll ask Hunter if he can help me find him, see if he's okay. Maybe there's something I can do for the kid."

Ethan had met Hunter Bishop last year through Ariane. He was a Vancouver-based private investigator Ariane hired when she needed someone who wouldn't raise an eyebrow if the work involved abnormal or unnatural details. Anything connected to Jane's dreams or her strange blood marks fit that criterion.

And though Hunter had Ethan's respect—the PI had located Jane when she'd been abducted—Hunter was still a man. An interesting, competent, and good-looking guy. Who happened to be single.

"I can help you find him," Ethan said. How hard could it be? Jane knew what the building looked like.

"You've got your hands full with the vandalism and Connor. And Hunter told me to call him if I needed anything."

"He's probably busy, though. How about we start looking tonight?"

"You got a problem with me calling Hunter?"

"No. I just think the guy's probably booked up weeks in advance."

"He's good, so that could be the case, but I won't know unless I call."

Jane was certain Hunter's interest in her was all about her dreams, but Ethan thought otherwise. He'd asked Hunter outright if his interest was personal. Hunter said it wasn't, that he just found Jane's dreams fascinating. Hunter wasn't scared off by weird shit like that. And he was the kind of guy you could take at his word. But that didn't mean Ethan wouldn't check in.

"Let me know what he says."

Ethan left a message with Fanny about the fire, asking her to open as usual. Business was slow in the morning hours and Fanny could handle the bar and serving for an hour or so, but he didn't want to push his luck. Servers with Fanny's experience were rare. He then got on his Harley and headed to Deep Cove. He'd had enough of Connor's avoidance tactics.

His first rap on the door went unanswered. That's what polite got you. His second rap threatened to break the door down.

Connor whipped it open. "It's Sunday, Ethan. What the hell are you doing here?" He looked like he'd just crawled out of a gutter.

"We need to talk." Ethan pushed his way inside.

Connor made an effort to protest, but soon hung his head and closed the door. "Come in," he said with a sarcastic bite. He started down the hall. Ethan wiped his boots and followed. They ended up in the kitchen. "The coffee's fresh. Want a cup?"

"Sure," Ethan said, and took a seat at the breakfast bar.

"Who's covering Riptide?" Connor asked.

"Fanny. I'll relieve her when I'm done here."

Connor nodded, pouring their coffees. "I got the photos of the back entrance. The fire won't stop us from opening, so why the visit?"

"Who owns Trident Security?"

Connor jerked his head back. "How would I know?"

"I figured you must have a stake in the company since you're paying them five times what we used to pay SSR for the same service."

"You nicked my password?"

"I may have stumbled across it."

"Damn it, Ethan! I don't know how many different ways I can say it: stay out of this." He pushed a mug toward Ethan and leaned back against the counter, arms stretched out on either side, fingers drumming.

"By 'this,' do you mean paying a bogus company for security that's clearly not working, or do you mean allowing Garvin's organization to launder cash through Riptide?"

Connor's expression morphed from righteous indignation to resignation. He took his mug and walked to the patio doors, looking out at more barbecue gear than the bar owned. "I'm trying to help out my partner. He's in trouble."

"Riptide's co-owner?"

"His name's Norman Walsh. We graduated from Dalhousie together." Connor's shoulders slumped. "Last fall, he ran up a gambling debt. Instead of paying it off like a sensible person, he made a deal with a guy at the casino. A guy he thought he knew. This guy told Norm he used to make a lot of money trading cash for chips. But after the Cullen Commission, the guys with the cash got nervous about casinos."

Ethan remembered when the Cullen Commission hit the news. It had exposed the extensive money laundering schemes used by drug gangs and drew renewed scrutiny from every level of government and law enforcement.

"Norm's buddy said they only wanted to wash five grand a couple times a year. Norm didn't think it was too big an ask, so he showed up and dribbled the cash into Riptide over a two-week period." Connor turned to Ethan. "I didn't know about it. No one noticed. Not even you. But after he'd done it once, they had him in their pocket. They have him on film accepting the money and agreeing to launder it. If he doesn't cooperate, they'll leak the footage to the cops."

"He's got to pre-empt them, take it to the cops himself," Ethan said. "Maybe he can make a deal."

"And if he can't? Riptide goes down with him, bankrupting me and putting everyone out of work." A look of determination crossed Connor's face as he walked back to the breakfast counter. "We came up with a different solution. We're going to freeze the bastards out. We've been quietly shopping Norm's share of the business around, looking for a buyer, a new partner. Don't suppose you've got a couple mil lying around?"

Ethan smoothed his finger down the coffee mug's handle. "Finding a buyer could take months. There's got to be something we can do now."

"It's not your mess."

"Trident's one of Garvin's businesses?"

"Not Garvin. The guys he works for."

"You sign a contract with Trident?"

Connor inhaled, shook his head. "Norm did. Suffice it to say he didn't read it. But it's legal. Ties our hands. Now we have to eat their rates for a year. It's killing us. That's why I had to let Jerry go."

This was news to Ethan. "Norm has signing authority? I thought he was a silent partner."

"He is now. A little late, I know, but it's done."

"Does Garvin's boss know?"

"We haven't enlightened him. And Norm has made himself scarce." Connor topped up their cups.

Ethan took a sip and set the cup back down. "Did you know Garvin and the new night-shift bartender are friends?"

"What? No! Ah, shit. I should have guessed—he came cheap, and his timing was too perfect. His references were probably in Garvin's pocket."

"I wouldn't doubt Garvin's topping up the guy's wages to keep him there."

Connor slapped the counter, spilling the coffee he held in his other hand. "They're like fucking rats. Let one of them in, and next thing you know, you're overrun and they're stinking up the place."

"The light over the back door was out before the fire. I'd just replaced the bulb, so someone took it out intentionally. Made it real easy to get in there unseen and get a fire going."

"Wouldn't be anyone on staff. Had to be Garvin or Joey."

Ethan understood Connor's loyalty to a long-time friend, but it had left him trying to wriggle out of a hole with sharp edges. "The damage to the front door? The fire? Trident's looking for even more money."

"Yup. I said no. This is their way of trying to change my mind." He bent and wiped up the spill with a paper towel. "If they keep this up, the insurance deductibles could end up costing more than the increase for Trident."

Ethan assessed Connor. "What about you, Connor? They have anything on you?"

"I guess that depends on how long I can know about the laundry before I report it. It's why I didn't want you doing the deposits, keeping the books."

"I appreciate that, but if Riptide goes under, I'm out a job anyway."

"At least you won't be behind bars." Connor sipped his coffee, thoughtful. "And you'll still be breathing."

13 | Jane

After a bowl of instant oatmeal, Jane contacted Ariane to update her on the latest dream of Huan in the underground parkade.

"We're right about this Witness thing being progressive," Jane said. "I remembered more in this dream. And Buddy—or I should say Joey, 'cause he's definitely not Buddy—must be my connection to Huan, but I still have no idea why I'm dreaming about the kid. I don't know him."

If Ariane had an opinion on Huan, she kept it to herself, and she had nothing new to add from Pedro's diaries. But Nate had arrived in Peru and was already helping Ariane map the progression.

Out of curiosity, Jane had looked up Hunter's rates on his website. His retainer was a thousand dollars. She wondered if he had a friends-and-family rate; she didn't have a thousand dollars. Her savings had barely been enough to replace the clothes her abductors had tossed—which was every stitch she owned—in their attempt to make it look like she'd moved out. She'd also had to replace the bed and other household items Sadie had needed for her own place. In the plus column, Jane now had an Ethan-friendly queen-size mattress and a real bed frame. She even had a bedside table.

Jane knew it drove Sadie mad that she wouldn't dip into the Walkers' funds, and she would if she had to. But hiring a PI hardly qualified.

A smile curved Jane's lips as she remembered the weekend she and Sadie had spent restocking Jane's wardrobe. Sadie had declared herself Jane's personal shopper. For years Sadie had been trying to get Jane interested in clothes. And Jane had to admit, without her blood marks dictating her attire, the shopping had actually been fun.

Jane padded down to Sadie's door and knocked. "You feel like going for a run to the park, do some sparring? It's been ages." They hadn't sparred since her abduction, and she missed it. It kept her sharp and in shape.

Sadie searched the hall behind Jane. "Where's Ethan?"

Jane sighed. Sadie and Ethan had turned avoiding each other into a habitual dance. "He doesn't hate you."

"He also doesn't like me. I thought you two spent your days off together."

"Not today. Take a break. Just an hour."

"Give me ten?"

After they returned from their workout, Jane showered and took a call from Hunter. "Got a minute? I'm at your door. I need to see you."

Jane rushed down the hall. "This is a surprise. What's up?" Hunter put her in mind of a boxer in the ring, focused and intent.

"Ariane called. Told me what's going on."

Jane frowned. "I spoke with Ariane just this morning. She didn't mention it."

"Can we go inside?"

"Sure." Jane led him down the hall to her apartment. It was the first time he'd been there. She gestured to the sofa. "What did Ariane say?" As he peered around the apartment, she followed his gaze and tried to imagine the information his PI brain was processing. Tidy, sparse, nothing of obvious value. That was Jane in a nutshell.

"She mentioned the dreams are back. Tell me what's going on."

Jane recounted the dreams of Huan in the apartment building and again in the parkade. He interrupted for details and took notes on a spiral flip pad.

"I'd love to find him, but I don't have the money for your retainer."

Hunter looked up from his notepad, his expression contemplative. "I'll waive the retainer. For the time being. Besides, it's a waste of your money to send me looking for Huan's place. You know the low-rent neighbourhoods as well as I do. Go for a drive. Be thorough about it."

"All right. What about Joey and Garvin?"

"Sounds like Ethan's got them pegged. They're likely cogs in the Downtown Eastside drug trade. You don't want to get involved in that."

"And if I have no choice?"

She gave him points for pausing. Last fall when he'd been trying to locate her, Ariane had shared with Hunter the nature of Jane's dreams and her narcolepsy.

"Let's hope it doesn't come to that. But I'm curious: you said you always have a connection to the people you dream about. What's your connection here?"

Jane paused. She knew the connection was Joey, but she hadn't shared with Hunter what she'd done to Pieter, or how it had changed Buddy into Joey. She was too ashamed to tell him. "It must be Ethan."

He furrowed his brow. "But you didn't dream about Ethan."

"Not yet," Jane said, shrugging off the guilt along with the deception.

At lunch, Jane headed to Riptide. She was forced to park on the street because the alleyway was taped off and blocked by a fire inspector's vehicle. She peered down the laneway, catching the pungent smell of a sodden fire barrel.

"What did Connor have to say about the fire?" she asked Ethan, as she approached the bar.

"Nothing I can talk about here. I'll fill you in later."

"Garvin's here?"

"In the office with Joey. How'd you know?"

"Recognized their truck. It's parked outside."

Ethan pulled his phone from his pocket. "What make?"

"Chevy. New. Black with silver running boards."

He thumbed through a number of screens and then pushed the phone across the counter to her. "That it?"

It was a live view from one of their security camera feeds. She nodded. "It's the truck they were in at the parking garage."

Ethan took a screenshot of it. "Can't see the plate."

"Finally, something I can help with." She slid off her bar stool. "I'll text you the plate number."

"Stay out of camera range. They've got the same view in the office."

"Order me a burger," she said, making her way to the door. "With fries."

Neither Joey nor Garvin came out of Riptide's office before Jane finished her meal and left. She looked up at the clearing sky. The drizzle had stopped. If the sun popped out, half the city's population would emerge from their dank caves in shorts and sandals to soak it up.

She strapped on her helmet and started for home, but as she passed Positively Plants, unwelcome reminders of a miserable Anna, a confined Pieter, and an indifferent Lucas invaded her thoughts. Instead of heading home, she pointed her bike north and rode toward the mountains.

She craved an escape, and a full-throttled run on her Rebel would do the job. She tolerated the traffic on Georgia Street and crawled over the

Lions Gate Bridge, but as soon as she hit the on-ramp to the Sea to Sky Highway, she poured on the speed. She loved the anonymity her helmet afforded her, and the freedom of the Rebel.

But not even the tug of the wind could shake off the anchor that was Positively Plants. A thought she'd been avoiding could no longer be denied. She hated her job. And now that the thought was out there, she couldn't take it back. All Jane's efforts to regain the close relationship she used to have with Anna and Lucas were in vain. They were different people now, shaped by events Jane had caused.

She considered quitting, but she hated giving up, walking away. There had to be something she could do to bring happiness back for them. She passed a plodding Dodge Caravan and opened the throttle on the straight stretch of road ahead of her. Besides, she needed the job. How else was she going to pay for Hunter?

By the time Jane reached Squamish, her troubles felt lighter, and she was able to think again. All her extra efforts at the garden centre hadn't had an impact on Anna, but Anna's biggest stressor was probably Pieter, not work. Jane resolved to investigate Pieter's situation more closely. Perhaps there was something the Morrow-Walker charity could do to make their lives easier.

As for Hunter, he had a point. She could do the legwork as well as he could to find Huan's apartment building. It shouldn't take her more than a few hours to search the likeliest neighbourhoods. The dreams had taken place sometime last fall. Hopefully Huan hadn't moved in the meantime.

A niggling voice in her head wondered what she would do if she found him. She ignored it. Being a Witness didn't come with an instruction manual. After she found Huan, she'd work out what came next.

She made a U-turn at the next exit and wound her way back to Vancouver. Along the way she plotted her route to find the crooked *No Vacancy* sign she'd seen outside Huan's building in her dream.

She started in Chinatown—though it was a long shot, there were a handful of streets along the northern edge she couldn't rule out until she'd scoured them. Afterwards, she continued into her old neighbourhood.

Driving the Downtown Eastside was a trip through her and Sadie's teenage years. She wove her way through familiar streets, recognizing a number of weather-worn faces. If she didn't find the crooked sign, she would work her way east, driving a grid between Prior Street and the waterfront.

When her stomach growled, she stopped for takeout and then resumed her search. By nine in the evening, she'd had enough. She turned onto Jackson Avenue, making one last sweep on her way to Hastings. In the morning, she'd come back and continue the search.

The white signpost with the crooked placard caught her by surprise. She pulled to the curb, ridiculously pleased with herself. She'd found it!

The lights were out in the second-floor window of Huan's bedroom, but the front room window that faced the street flickered with the glow from a television.

She dismounted to check the buzzer panel outside the front door. Some apartment buildings listed names beside the buzzers, but not this one. From the panel, she counted six units on the second floor.

Now that she'd found the building, she would keep coming back until she saw Huan. *And then what?* the niggling voice asked again.

14 | Sadie

Sadie's run-and-spar routine with Jane had left her energized, but she hadn't gotten further than signing into her student dashboard. She stared at the button that would take her to the next module on cost accounting. And then the purse drew her attention, just as it had the five other times she'd sat down at the table.

The whole time she'd been out with Jane, she hadn't thought about money once, and now it was consuming her again.

She could sell her car, she supposed. Buy something cheaper. She wouldn't have to do it right away. Before next February for sure, maybe January.

She'd already built an internship's minimum wage into her budget, so the job wouldn't help unless she could negotiate a higher rate. But how likely was that given how many students needed positions?

Could she take on a bigger course load? Try to finish sooner? No. She was going flat out as it was, taking two courses at a time. She had no brain cells to spare for a third course.

Sadie was simply not built to live on a budget.

She opened a new tab and typed Hermès. Sure enough, custom orders could be personalized with a tasteful monogram. Which confirmed she had the real deal. But the purse had been trashed and relegated to the low-rent district. How fitting that she was the one who'd ended up with it.

Sadie set her phone in front of her and pulled up the Teacher's Pet website. Her finger hovered over the contact link. And then she pictured Cynthia the last time she'd seen her, the day Cynthia had paid her out. "You'll never make it," her former madam had said, handing over the money order as if it were evidence. "You like money too much."

It was true—Sadie did like money. But being a hooker cost too much. The look on Mike's face as he'd digested her devastating revelation surfaced in her thoughts. It was proof enough.

She swiped away the website. Cynthia had warned her, "Once a hooker, always a hooker." She'd said Sadie would never be able to work herself out of a basement apartment with a legit job. But Sadie knew lots of people who got along just fine with legit jobs.

Bookkeepers might not make the kind of bank that hookers did, but they had self-respect. They sure as hell didn't have to worry about clients pulling knives, or their madam's enforcers blowing out their client's kneecaps. A shiver ran through her. Last year, after Jane escaped Rick's kennel, Sadie had caught up to her at Rick's townhouse. Cynthia and her enforcers had just left. Sadie still couldn't shake the memory of Rick rolling by on the gurney, his face raw, blood soaking through the sheet that covered his legs.

She picked up the bag and examined it the way the owner of the pawnshop had. As much as she didn't appreciate his dismissal of her and her bag, she'd learned something about the condition of a handbag. Loose stitching, broken boards—or whatever it was that was inside the bottom panel—were important to a handbag's value. And who was V.R. Wright? she wondered. She'd certainly enjoyed the hell out of the bag if its condition was anything to go by.

Sadie turned the bag upside down to inspect the bottom, and when she did, she heard a tinkling from inside. *Strange.* But she looked inside and found nothing metal that would have made that sound. Not even the handles. She flipped it upside down again and heard the tinkle once more. This time she checked the interior with her hands.

Inside the purse, under the lining, she felt lumps that shouldn't be there.

Sadie grabbed a kitchen knife and sawed through the bad stitching job in the handbag's lining. She squeezed her fingers through the hole and, one by one, fished out three rings.

Her initial excitement fizzled out when she realized the rings were nothing special. One was a plain man's wedding band with an inscription too worn to read. The other two made up a woman's wedding and engagement ring set, also old, and the three diamonds were small—if they were even diamonds. She couldn't tell if the rings were white gold or platinum. Either way, they were hardly worth ruining the lining of a Hermès bag. She checked inside the bag again, but there was nothing else to be found.

The rings weighed next to nothing in the palm of her hand. Probably not worth much for their metal. She checked Craigslist and Kijiji. If they were white gold, similar sets were going for four hundred dollars. More if they were platinum. But only if the stones were real diamonds. And if the rings weren't stolen.

Shit. If they were hot and the owners were actively looking for them, she'd have to hand them over for nothing.

Was it V.R. Wright, the name monogrammed inside the purse, who'd stashed the rings? It would be worth finding out. If V.R. had gone to the trouble of stashing them, she might be willing to fork over some cash to get them back.

15 | Ethan

Ethan brought dinner to Jane's from his favourite sushi place.
"I didn't think I'd like the barbecued eel," Jane said, waving her chopsticks in the air. "It tastes a little like the blackened cod Sadie used to bring home from the restaurant."

Over dinner, Ethan had told Jane about his visit to Connor's place. "I don't understand the connection."

"Probably the caramelized sugars," Jane said.

Ethan looked up from his empty plate. "What?"

"The barbecued eel and blackened cod."

"I meant the connection between your dreams and what's happening at Riptide. Why are you dreaming of Garvin and Joey? They didn't see you, did they?"

She hesitated a second too long.

"Shit. Those two will fuck you up if they think you're a threat to them." The moment the words left his mouth, he knew he'd said the wrong thing.

Jane's features hardened. "I can take care of myself."

"Yes. Yes, I know. But you shouldn't have to."

Jane reached for his plate. "Ariane says the dreams tell a story. Maybe it's Huan's story." She took the plates to the sink. "I drove by his apartment again. Hung around for a while. Didn't see him."

"The kid's a survivor. He'd have to be, living in the kind of situation he does."

Ethan joined Jane at the sink, rinsed out the dishcloth, and dabbed at the sauce he'd dribbled on his shirt. "How is it you never spill your dinner when you're balancing your plate with one hand and eating with the other?"

"Years of practice. A kitchen table was never very high on my things-to-buy list."

After they'd finished cleaning up, he asked her if she wanted to take a drive down Davie Street. "See if you recognize the garage where Garvin and Joey were dealing drugs."

Jane furrowed her brow. "What are you thinking?"

"The more I know about their operation, the more options I'll have to get those two out of Riptide. If I knew where the deals were going down and could figure out their routine, I'd make sure the cops knew about it."

"Wouldn't their boss just send two other gangbangers to replace them? And what if they found out what you'd done?"

"They won't. Come on. Let's go for a drive."

Ethan scooted forward to give Jane room to hop on the back of his Harley. It was spitting rain and chilly, but she didn't complain. Davie Street cut straight across the downtown, from False Creek to English Bay. There were a dozen parking lots in the street's vicinity, but only three were underground. Jane recognized the inside of the parkade right away. The rent-a-cop manning the booth likely made minimum wage. Slip him a fifty and he'd look the other way for an hour or two. There was little risk; no one was going to touch one of the customers' cars with the likes of Garvin and Joey hanging around.

He couldn't say the same for the risk to Jane. If they'd seen her in that dream and then recognized her at Riptide, would they think she was spying on them? He couldn't bring himself to think about what they might do if that were the case.

They went back to Jane's place, and he warmed her up the best way he knew how. Horizontally.

Business was slow the next afternoon. Fanny was talking up the cook when Ethan arrived. It was one of his days off, but he wanted to run a few more reports and get a better handle on Riptide's financial picture before Connor changed his mind about Ethan's access to the books.

He was hard at it when Fanny popped her head in the door. "There's a guy here—"

"It's okay, I got this," a man said, shoving his way inside the office.

Ethan jumped to his feet. "Not cool."

The man turned back to Fanny. "I'm sorry. That was rude. I apologize." He touched the peak of a worn baseball cap. But Fanny wasn't impressed. She stood her ground as the man continued into the office, extending a business card to Ethan, who'd moved to the front of the desk and leaned against it with his arms crossed. The man's rumpled jacket looked like it came fresh from a dumpster. He wore a pack over his shoulder.

Ethan glanced at the man's hand. "What can I do for you?"

The man took the hint and stuffed his card in his pocket. "You're the on-site manager? I'm not selling anything. Just need a minute of your time. Name's Lester Wilde. I'm a reporter." He swung his pack off his shoulder and retrieved a spiral pad and pen.

"I'll head back out, then?" Fanny said.

"Thanks, Fanny," Ethan said, and Fanny left, though reluctantly.

"I'm researching a story on increasing property crimes downtown. Police reports say you've had two incidents in the last week. Can you tell me about them?"

"Who do you work for?"

"Depends on who's buying." He had a Jack Nicholson smile, cocky and a little creepy.

"I can't tell you more than what's in the police reports."

"You use a security company named—" He checked his notes. "Trident?"

"That's right."

"They do your after-hours patrols?"

"Yeah, but they didn't see anything."

"And your cameras out there," he said, waving in the vague direction of the bar. "Didn't get a good shot of them?"

"No."

He bobbed his head. "Guess you'll be making insurance claims?"

"You'd have to talk to the owner. He'll be in tonight."

He flipped through his notes again. "That's Connor Boyd?"

"Yup. Anything else?"

"Are you insured with Metro?"

Ethan narrowed his eyes as he considered how this character would know that. "Like I said, you'll have to talk to Connor. You have a card? Lester, right?"

"Lester Wilde." He dug the creased card from his pocket and handed it over.

Connor sauntered in an hour later and didn't comment on Ethan's presence in the office. Ethan took it as a sign that he and Connor were back on the same team.

"A reporter came by," Ethan said. "Asked about the vandalism. Says he's writing a story about increasing property crimes. He has some questions for you about insurance."

"Good. Publicity might force Garvin's organization to back down."

"I wouldn't bank on it, but I have a plan," Ethan said, motioning for Connor to close the door.

"Not here," Connor said.

"My place?" Ethan said.

"Be there in a minute," Connor said, nodding.

Ethan shut down the program and locked the safe. Connor stayed behind. He rang Ethan's buzzer fifteen minutes later.

"What's wrong with the office?" Ethan asked.

"Garvin's coming in with dirty cash. I don't want him thinking you and I are friendly. What's this?" he said, taking the business card Ethan offered.

"That's the reporter who barged in this morning."

"I know the name. Wilde. He did a piece on renovictions a while ago. Won some big award for it." He slid the card in his pocket. "What's your plan?"

"I found out where Garvin and Joey set up shop to supply their dealers."

Connor frowned. "How did you learn that?"

"It's not important. But if we can find out when their next buys are going down, we have a few options. We can make sure the garage owners learn that their rent-a-cop is being paid off and using their premises for dealing drugs. If it turns out they're in on it, then maybe the cops would take an interest."

"And if the organization finds out who's behind their troubles?"

"It'll be an anonymous tip. Crime Stoppers doesn't take names."

It was Valentine's Day, and Ethan had to admit he was nervous. He didn't think Jane was the flowers-and-chocolates type, but now that he was pulling up to the curb in front of her apartment empty-handed, he wondered if he'd gotten it wrong. He phoned her. "I'm at your door. Want to let me in?"

Despite the lack of flowers, she looked pretty happy when she came to get him.

Inside her apartment, he inspected the new bistro table and two chairs he'd had delivered. "You like it?"

"Love it. I gotta say, you're acing our first Valentine's Day."

"There's one more thing," he said, taking her hand. He pressed a set of keys into her palm.

She stared at the keys long enough to give him pause. Finally, she looked up. "I don't know what to say."

"Say you'll make yourself at home at my place. Whenever you want. You and me? I'm all in."

She searched his face, worry in her brow. "Dreams included?"

He pulled her into his arms. "I'd be lying if I said I was okay with the dreams, but we'll work it out."

16 | Jane

Jane leaned against her Rebel and pulled a bag of Mickey D's takeout from inside her jacket. Thankfully, it wasn't raining, but she doubted anything short of a zombie apocalypse could wipe the smile from her face.

Ethan had loved the Valentine's gift she'd had made for him: a carved wooden sign for the end of the driveway he'd have on his acreage someday. They hadn't been to his Sunshine Valley property since the snow had set in out there, but he told her he was thinking about getting a truck to remedy that situation.

Last night, he'd taken her out to the little Airstream trailer he kept in Burnaby. They'd had barbecued steaks for dinner and afterwards, he'd shown her his latest batch of house designs. Building anything was still years away, but from the first time he'd shared with her his dream of owning an acreage, he'd included her in his plans. He wanted her thoughts on every detail.

He was all in.

They'd made love into the wee hours. She should have been exhausted, but she'd never felt more alive.

She'd parked half a block from Huan's apartment. The neighbourhood felt bruised, as if it had lost a fight. Evidence abounded in cracked windows repaired with duct tape and broken railings on porches built too close to the street.

She'd done her research. If Huan still lived here, his catchment school would be the one three blocks away, and the school broke for lunch at eleven forty-five.

Though it had taken a few days, Jane finally understood her obsession with finding Huan. It was about more than her role as a Witness. It was connected to her past. So often, as a child, she'd dreamed of kids who'd been abused by people they trusted, people who should have protected them. Jane had been too young to help them. All she could offer was sympathy, and that was thrown back in her face enough times that she'd learned to keep her sympathy in check and her dreams to herself.

But she wasn't a defenceless little girl anymore. She'd be there for Huan, help his mom if she could, find a way to get him away from those men.

It was almost 1:00 p.m. when she saw a kid Huan's size round the corner bouncing a black basketball. When he got close enough, she recognized him. He should have been headed back to school, not coming home. The bouncing stopped. He'd noticed her—and the fact that he'd have to pass her to get to the apartment. He looked healthy, so if he'd been beaten last fall, there'd been no lasting effects, at least not physical ones.

"How's it going, Huan?" Jane said, when he was still a car length away.

"Who are you?" he asked, his tone defiant.

"We met once. It was a while ago. You still living across the street?" Jane said, nodding toward his building.

"What's it to ya'?"

"Want to make sure you're okay, is all."

He curled his lip, as if she smelled bad.

"Those men you're living with, who are they?"

He ignored her and started across the street.

"Shouldn't you be headed back to school?" Jane called after him.

Huan looked over his shoulder. "Shouldn't you be sucking someone's dick?"

Jane laughed. Huan was fine. Rude, defensive, and probably skipping school, but perfectly fine. And if she wanted to help him, she'd need to improve her technique.

Anna stopped Jane on her way to the breakroom. "You're late again. This has got to stop."

"It couldn't be helped," Jane said. "And I was here half an hour early this morning." She didn't add *just like most days*.

"Lunch is one hour, Joyce—or Jane, or whatever you're calling yourself these days."

"It's Jane. I'm sorry. It won't happen again." She continued to the breakroom and sat on the bench by her locker. Anna was right: this had to stop. The new Anna had proven completely inflexible. Jane had to quit believing the extra time she put in had any impact. No more early hours.

Jane stayed on the floor until four o'clock and then headed back to the breakroom. Reyna was packing up for the day.

"Reyna," Jane said, standing in the doorway to Pieter's room. Pieter sat quietly, watching a nature program on the flat screen. "Is there anything Pieter needs? Special equipment, perhaps, or more help?"

"There's always something," Reyna said, stuffing her knitting into a bag. "An electric lift would be a treat. There's one at the house, but not in here, and I wouldn't dare ask. Money's tight enough. I can make do with the manual lift."

"They're expensive, are they? Electric lifts?"

"Yes, everything for Pieter is expensive. It's all customized. If I won the lotto, I'd buy him the exoskeleton apparatus they use at the hospital. You know they get him up and walking with that equipment. Pieter gets so excited. He calls it Tall Pieter."

Pieter heard her and repeated, "Tall Pieter," with a big smile on his face.

"Now, Reyna, don't go winding him up," Anna said, having heard Pieter as she arrived. "No Tall Pieter this week, sweetie," she said to Pieter, but he paid no attention and repeated the happy refrain. Jane felt Anna's words like a punch to the gut. She slinked out of there, and guilt chased her home.

After dinner, Ariane called on a video chat. Nate was sitting beside her.

"Hey, Nate. How was the trip?"

"Long, but at least the jet lag's not bad." Lima's time zone was only two hours ahead of Vancouver's, at least until daylight savings kicked in.

"We've got something," Ariane said.

"From Pedro's diaries?"

She nodded. "He had to flee his village after accusing a woman of killing her husband. The woman barely survived the beatings his family inflicted and that was before the criminals she'd been locked up with had a go at her. She would have been put to death had her husband not turned up."

"How did that happen? I mean, he must have witnessed the murder, no?"

"He thought he did. In his vision, he saw the husband scolding the woman and beating her for a transgression—of course, wife beating was acceptable back then. But in a second vision, Pedro saw her wielding an axe and wearing a man's apron that was covered in blood. She was walking through a field, laughing, returning to their home. He thought she was mad. He knew where she lived, and he confronted her. The husband hadn't been seen for weeks."

"What happened to him?"

"Turned out he'd left to tend to his goats. Took them farther afield than he'd done previously."

"Probably avoiding her," Nate said, laughing. Ariane swatted at him.

"Pedro wrote that he felt unworthy and humiliated. He hadn't let the visions play out. If he'd waited, he would have witnessed that she was merely having an affair with the butcher."

"A sin worse than murder in those days, I'd bet," Nate said, and this time he dodged Ariane's swipe.

"Pedro wrote this as a warning for the next Witness, who would have inherited his diaries—had such a person existed."

"I understand his warning," Jane said. "I thought Huan was the focus of my dreams until this afternoon. I found him, spoke to him. He's got a mouth on him, but he's perfectly healthy. Which makes me wonder if Huan's purpose was to lead me to Joey? Or Joey's employers? It's so frustrating! I don't know what it is I'm supposed to witness."

Ariane sympathized, as did Nate, but they couldn't offer any insight. "Pedro may have more to tell us. We'll keep at it," Ariane said.

"Thanks. And thanks for talking to Hunter. He came by to see me."

"He said he would help if he could. He's a good man," Ariane said.

Jane agreed, but good was only one of his qualities. He was also clever and strong. Resourceful. Those thoughts turned her curiosity to his personal life. Was he single? The topic had never come up, not that it mattered. "You didn't tell him about Buddy and Pieter?"

"No. I kept my word. I'll only tell him if he needs to know."

"Thank you. It's not that I don't trust him, I just don't want him to think less of me."

"We have some other news," Nate said, draping an arm around Ariane's shoulder. She looked up at him. "I asked Ariane to marry me."

Ariane and Nate looked so happy together. They planned to be married in Lima and make their home in Vancouver, at least for the next few years. Jane was excited at the prospect of having her close by. Not only was Ariane one of the few people Jane could confide in, but her knowledge on the subject of Witnesses was invaluable.

Jane felt foolish sitting on the edge of the bed, fully dressed, pulling on her boots, but she wasn't going to be caught out again in a dream without clothes, or her knife. She tucked her phone in her pocket and dragged the quilt over herself.

Visiting Dream

Jane wakes inside a restaurant, though it might be a pub. She's cloaked in shadows, alone at a table. Outside is an iron streetlamp with white globes. Gastown. On the other side of the room, a group of men have gathered. Joey's there, and so is Garvin. She doesn't recognize the others. They speak in hushed tones, sombre, right down to their black attire. It must be the middle of the night, long past closing. Chairs are upside down on the tables.

She's dressed, no jacket. Her body is ghostly translucent. She's wearing her bike boots and automatically reaches for her boot knife. She remembers putting her cellphone in her pocket, but it's gone. At least dressed, she has less paper-white skin on display. She slinks down in her chair.

A man behind the bar searches for what turn out to be rocks glasses. He's unfamiliar with the set-up, so he's not an employee. He pulls down a bottle of Johnnie Walker and pours shots into the glasses he's lined up. Another man on the public side of the bar takes the drinks and hands them out. The man behind the bar brings the bottle with him when he rejoins the group, plunking it down on the table.

A well-groomed man of about thirty-five with a light brown complexion stands. He wears a poppy on his lapel, and the buttons on his long wool coat are open. "Garvin, Joey," he says. "We have an unexpected opening. You've been selected to fill it. Congratulations. You're moving out of distribution and into supply." He raises his glass, and the other men do the same. "To our newest buyers." Congratulatory mumbles follow. So, not a funeral.

"Dal will show you the ropes," he says, identifying another man who looks like he could be the speaker's brother. Garvin is sporting a jack-o'-lantern smile. Jane realizes she's never seen him smile before. It's chilling. Joey is also smiling, but his flickers, underpowered. He looks around the room like he suspects his luck might evaporate at any moment.

A round of backslapping follows, and more drinks are poured.

Jane looks down to the back of her left hand. Tentatively, she brushes the newly round mark. Her vision blurs. A wave of nausea hits. She lifts her fingers. The nausea passes. She touches the mark again with just the tip of her finger. Her vision wavers, not quite as badly. She makes a fist with her left hand and traces the mark, counter-clockwise. Her vision swims but then stabilizes. The nausea is back.

"... Congratulations. You're moving out of distribution and into supply." Jane looks across the room. The man in charge is raising his glass. "To our newest buyers." Congratulatory mumbles pour out, and then the backslapping starts. Drinks are poured.

Jane glances down at her hand. *Did that just happen?* Once again, she draws a counter-clockwise circle. This time she glances up as she draws it. The room swims in a blur of movement.

"... Congratulations. You're moving out of distribution and into supply." The man in charge raises his glass. "To our newest buyers."

Nausea hits Jane like a wallop to the back of the head. She lurches forward and throws up.

Jane woke with the burn of bile in her throat. Her stomach was cramped. She raced to the bathroom in a cold sweat and threw up again. After her stomach settled, she rinsed her mouth, put the lid down, and sat on the toilet. Her whole body shook. When the shakes subsided, she crawled back into bed and pulled the covers tight.

"Holy crap," she whispered, rocking herself.

At six in the morning, she found her phone buried in the sheets. She left Anna a message that she was sick and wouldn't be in to work.

Then she called Ariane.

"Something's happened," Jane said, and the events of the previous evening tumbled out.

"This is"—Ariane cleared her throat—"unexpected."

"Unexpected? I have a rewind dial on the back of my goddamn hand! Un-freaking-believable wouldn't begin to describe it!" She thumped her fist on the mattress.

"Why are you yelling at me?"

"Oh, shit. I am. I'm sorry. I'm just . . . I can't . . ." Jane threw off the blankets and sat up. "Crap. I don't know what to do."

"This mark, it's powerful. It could be the key to controlling your dreams—the very thing you've been searching for. Next time you dream, you must experiment with it."

"I suppose I could." She held her hand to her head, not that it helped release the tension. "If I can stand the nausea. And if, in the moment, I can even remember what happens when I touch the damn mark."

"Did Ethan get a photo of it?"

Jane examined the unmarred skin on her hand. "I wasn't with Ethan. I'm sorry I haven't gotten around to sketching it. I will. Today."

"Please do. I have a colleague who studies symbols. She may be able to identify it."

"You won't—"

"No, I know what you call 'the drill.' I won't mention your name."

"Thank you." Jane's narcolepsy was a big enough complication. The fewer people who knew about her dreams, the better. The old families knew that another Witness had surfaced, but only two of those families knew Jane's identity. She trusted Ariane's grandmother, Yessica, but the other family, Rosa's, she wasn't so sure of. They seemed to be a little too focused on their own agenda: getting the offering bowl back. Rosa was Maria Yupanqui's sister. Maria had been disowned by her family after she'd taken up with Rosa's husband. The pair had fled Peru with the family's heirloom: a bowl, which Maria and Jane's mother had later used in a ritual that resulted in Jane's blood marks.

"Any news from Pedro's diaries?"

"We're making steady progress. But Jane, he's not like you. He doesn't have blood marks. We're in uncharted territory."

Jane liked that she'd said "we" in relation to the steady progress. But not so much the "we" in relation to the uncharted territory.

At ten in the morning, immediately after sending a sketch of the round mark to Ariane, Jane texted Ethan. *I need to see you.*

Thirty minutes later, Ethan arrived. She wrapped her arms around him and held on tight.

"What is it?" Ethan asked, stroking her hair and holding her close.

She pulled back and glanced up at him. "Riptide isn't the only bar Garvin and Joey are using. You're not going to believe what happened."

"A dream?"

They sat on the sofa and Jane told him the whole story. He held her hand and examined the skin on the back of it. No trace of the mark remained, and touching it had zero effect.

"So Garvin and Joey are no longer dealing drugs?"

"Not if I understood their boss. They've moved up the food chain." Jane shifted to look at Ethan more directly. "Why do you look disappointed? You weren't still thinking you'd catch them dealing, were you?"

"It was the most promising opportunity we had to get rid of them. Looks like we'll have to move on to Plan B."

"Plan B?"

"Connor finally told me what's going on." Ethan then explained about Trident, the money laundering, and Plan B.

Jane paused, wondering why Ethan hadn't told her this news last night.

"What is it?"

"Nothing." She shook off the question. "You sure Connor's not involved?"

"Positive. Connor's not a deceptive guy. The relief coming off him when he told me about it was visible. I could have picked it up and chucked it out the door. He's back to his old self."

"I'm glad," Jane said. Her smile faded and she hung her head, staring at the battered trunk and thinking about Anna, who would never be going back to her old self. Nor Pieter.

"I'm headed over to Riptide. Want to come with? I'll treat you to lunch."

"On your day off? I thought you wanted to go to the gym."

"Already been. And now that I know what's going on at Riptide, I need to run more reports. Get a better handle on what's been happening with the books."

"I've got some time. What can I do to help?"

"Don't you have your own mystery to solve with Huan?"

"I almost forgot: I found him. Talked to him. He's okay."

"You don't sound very happy about it."

"I am. It just makes me think the dreams aren't about him. Just like the dreams I had of my mom weren't about her. I couldn't do anything for her. She was leading me to Rick. I think Huan is leading me to Joey."

"Joey is dangerous. You need to steer clear of him."

"I don't like it any more than you do, but it's not like I can pick and choose who I dream about."

"Then walk away. Just turn around and leave. Let the cops deal with Joey."

Jane considered if dreaming of Joey was karma. "If it weren't for me, Joey wouldn't exist."

Jane knocked on the office door. She'd given Ethan a head start to get his reports ready. He called for her to come in and looked up when she opened the door. She caught that smile again, the one just for her that made her insides quiver.

"All done?" She drifted to the arm of the sofa and sat down.

"Almost." He turned his attention back to the keyboard. When he'd finished what he was doing, he tested the balance of the chair, leaning back with his jeans-clad legs stretched out front. His gaze slid down her body in a promise she could hardly wait to take him up on.

All too soon, his attention darted to movement in the bar area. He straightened, all playfulness gone. "That's the insurance adjustor. I've got to talk with him."

Jane followed his gaze through the two-way mirror. She stiffened. "Shit! The man walking toward the bar?"

Confusion clouded his face. "You know him?"

"He was there in my dream when Garvin's boss was handing out promotions in Gastown. They called him Dal. He was supposed to train Garvin. Drug buying 101. Guess even drug dealers need mentors."

Ethan frowned. "Him?" he said, pointing. Jane nodded. "You sure?"

"Positive."

17 | Sadie

"Have you changed your mind?" the sales clerk at the consignment shop asked, when Sadie approached the counter. "Want to resell the handbag?"

"No, but I need your help." Sadie showed the woman the hole in the lining and the rings she'd found. "Whoever consigned the handbag might want them back. Do you have their phone number or an address?"

"We're not allowed to give out that information." The clerk grimaced, as if it pained her to say it.

"I won't let on where I got the info. Promise."

The clerk darted a nervous glance around the shop. "I could get fired."

Sadie opened her palm again, revealing the rings. "These look old. They were probably worn for years. I'm sure someone's looking for them." Sadie picked up the man's band and feigned searching for an inscription. "A widower or widow. Maybe their family. I just want to help them get these rings back." Sadie blinked up at the clerk.

The sales clerk leaned close. "You won't tell anyone?"

"No. Absolutely not. If someone asks, I'll say I found the contact info on a slip of paper in the lining."

The clerk straightened with a smile then slid to the computer and surreptitiously clicked away at her keyboard. She scribbled down the information on a scrap of paper and pushed it across the counter. "Let me know what happens, would you? It would make a great TikTok for the shop."

"I sure will." Sadie glanced at the name. It wasn't V.R. Wright. The name was Brigitte Monet, and she lived in West Van, one of the wealthiest neighbourhoods in the city.

Back in her car, she dialled the number. A woman answered with "Stafford residence." She advised Sadie that Brigitte no longer worked there and that no, she had no forwarding phone number or address. Sadie hung up and slumped in the driver's seat. Just her luck. Brigitte wasn't loaded, she was just the help.

The woman on the phone sounded curt, as if Brigitte was persona non grata. Why? Sadie's intuition sparked, and she called the number again.

"I don't mean to bother you, but my instincts tell me someone living at the Stafford residence may be missing a valuable or two."

The woman didn't confirm Sadie's suspicion, but she took her name and number and said she'd pass along a message to Mrs. Stafford. Though the woman dug for more details, Sadie didn't give them. She wanted to hear Mrs. Stafford's reaction to the news of the rings first-hand. It would give her an idea of how much of a finder's fee to ask for.

Sadie perked up. She felt she had a good chance of recouping some of the money she'd spent. And if the reward didn't cover the cost of the purse, there was nothing stopping her from re-consigning it. She couldn't be the only one willing to pay for a deeply discounted Hermès bag.

She drove off with a sense of satisfaction, and the worry about having blown her budget melted away. As she passed the Hotel Vancouver, she spied a parking spot on the street. A sign from the goddess! She snagged the spot, put an hour on the virtual meter app, and headed inside. The hotel wasn't one Cynthia used for her clientele, not that it guaranteed she wouldn't run into a former client, but Sadie had always loved the feel of the place. Mingling with the upper crust came naturally to her. It's why Cynthia had thought Sadie would fit into her stable in the first place.

Sadie sauntered up to the bar and ordered a glass of Prosecco. "I'll be sitting over there," she said, pointing provocatively to an empty table. The cute bartender reacted with a sweet smile. Maybe she hadn't lost her charm after all.

Once settled at the table, she silenced her phone and set it beside her, not wanting to miss Mrs. Stafford's return call. She glanced around the opulent room. She loved that for the price of a cocktail, she could belong here for an hour or two. A business meeting was going on at one of the tables. She could tell by the laptops and ties. A woman with a couple of kids sat at another. She was dressed in Lululemon and distracted by her phone. The older child, a boy, ran a toy car along the tabletop, accompanied by excited outbursts which the mom half-heartedly shushed.

The bartender delivered Sadie's Prosecco, a small bottle that he opened at the table and poured with a flair Sadie appreciated. She savoured a sip with her eyes closed and then checked in with Instagram.

"Are you celebrating something?" a man's voice said.

Sadie looked up. Smiled. "No, but I will be." He was handsome. Bespoke jacket. Probably looking for a free hookup to fill a lonely night on a business trip.

"That sounds intriguing. May I join you and you can tell me all about it?"

Turned out he was visiting from Chicago. His business was so boring he didn't want to bother her with details. If only he knew how very many times she'd played that game. Business wasn't boring—he just didn't want her to know the name of his company. A place where she could find him. He was probably happily married with two-point-one kids back in Chicago. An amateur.

She let him talk her up. It was nice to have company, but he was wasting his time. He was exactly the type of gig for which she used to get paid a thousand dollars. The most she'd get out of this guy was a second tiny bottle of Prosecco that she didn't need. He offered, as she knew he would, and when she turned him down, he instead paid for the drink she'd just finished.

As she drove home, she wondered what kind of man would be able to see past what she used to do for a living. Someone familiar with the trade? A former john, perhaps? Someone more open-minded than Mike, that's for sure. She could lie about her past, but it was one of those lies that was inexcusable. She might as well stamp an expiration date on the relationship. Because no matter the investment of time or emotion, it would blow up if—and more likely, when—the truth surfaced.

18 | Ethan

Ethan slapped on a happy face and returned to the bar to greet Dal, the insurance adjustor. He'd promised Jane a rain check on lunch. She'd stayed behind in the office and would slip out the moment Ethan distracted Dal.

"Dalton Reddy?" Ethan said, approaching him with his hand extended. "Ethan Bryce, Riptide's manager. We met briefly when you came by after the vandal smashed through the front door."

"Ah, yes," Dalton said, shaking Ethan's hand. "Good memory. I'm looking for the owner, Connor Boyd?"

Ethan walked past Dalton, forcing him to turn around, away from the hallway that led to the office and back door. "He doesn't come in until six tonight. How can I help you?"

"Connor reported that there's been a fire. If you could show me where?"

Jane had already made her way out of the office and into the bar. She immediately turned away from Ethan. "It's this way, at the back door," Ethan said, taking the lead.

Dalton produced a spiral pad and began scratching notes. He pulled a measuring tape from his pocket and measured the door, then pulled it open, stepped through, and stood back, shaking his head as he took in the scorching. "Most of this wall will need to be replaced, along with the door."

"The fire captain said the fire hadn't made it into the wall. Why replace it?"

"Just be thankful the insurance covers it. I'll send the name of an approved contractor." He handed his card to Ethan. "Have Connor call me."

Back in the office, Ethan dialled Connor. "The insurance adjustor just left. Dalton Reddy. He also goes by Dal. You know him?"

"Never met him. Never had a claim until the front door. Why?"

"He's crooked. Might be involved with Garvin's organization."

"Whoa. That's a leap. What's going on?"

There was no way to explain Dalton's connection to Garvin's organization without sounding like a lunatic. "Says a big chunk of the wall needs completely replaced, along with the back door."

"How is that crooked?"

"The captain said the fire didn't get inside the wall. The stucco is scorched, nothing more. The door isn't even warped. I'd bet my Hog he's either getting a kickback on the repair or Riptide's going to be paying a big fat bill for a skinny little fix."

"I know we're on edge, Ethan, but assessment is this guy's business. Maybe he saw something you didn't."

"Maybe," Ethan said, but he was convinced the only thing Dalton saw were dollar bills going into his bank account. "He wants you to call him."

Ethan hung up. He barrelled out of the office, distracted by his conversation with Conner, and nearly knocked Fanny off her feet. He grabbed her forearm to steady her and apologized.

"Do you have a minute?" she said.

They went back to the office and Ethan closed the door. "What's up?"

"Joey was asking me about Jane. Wanted to know her last name, where she lived."

"Shit." Ethan ran his hand through his hair. "When?"

"Yesterday. After you left. Thought you should know."

"Thank you."

Fanny nodded and crossed her arms. "What's Joey's connection to Connor?"

"He's an acquaintance of Connor's partner."

"And Garvin too?"

"They're a tag team. Have they caused you any trouble, anything at all?"

"Not yet. They're good tippers. But their type is trouble. I'd rather they take their business elsewhere."

Connor showed up at Ethan's apartment later that night.

"I spoke to Dalton. He's suggesting—by which I mean demanding—that we increase our security to round the clock."

"That's not the type of crooked I expected, but it plays into Garvin's hands."

"If we don't increase security, he's going to reclassify us as high risk. Our insurance rates will take a double-digit hike, as will our deductibles. You were right. Dalton's involved. I just can't figure out how it happened. I've been dealing with Metro Insurance for years."

"How long has Dalton been working with them?"

"Good question."

"He could be a freelancer. Garvin has access to Metro's policy—it's sitting in the desk drawer. He probably armed Dalton with a copy, set him up to freelance there. Any chance we can get coverage elsewhere?"

"I can make some calls, but what's to stop Dalton from freelancing for whatever company we go with?"

"In other words, as long as we have Garvin underfoot, we're screwed."

"Tell me again about Garvin and Joey setting up shop somewhere to supply their dealers."

"It's too late for that. We missed our chance. Garvin and Joey have been promoted. They're buying now."

Connor raised his hands like two big stop signs. "Where the hell are you getting this information?"

Ethan scrambled for an explanation. No way was he putting Jane's name out there. "I heard a kid at the gym talking about it. He knows one of the neighbourhood dealers. I followed up. He wasn't bullshitting."

"Who's the kid?" Connor said, his expression challenging Ethan's story.

"Huan. Don't know his last name. Says Joey stole a roll of bills from him."

"All right," he said, seeming to accept Ethan's word. "We can't get them dealing. Any chance this kid knows where they do their buying?"

Ethan shrugged. "Don't know."

"So all we've got is Huan, no last name, who might know something, might not. Our options aren't looking great."

19 | Jane

Jane felt uneasy leaving Ethan to deal with Dal, the insurance adjustor whose side gig was training drug dealers. It hadn't taken Garvin's organization long to get its tentacles into every aspect of Riptide's business. How long until they got rid of Connor and Ethan and took over?

She skirted Positively Plants on her way back to the apartment. Having Anna spot her out and about when she'd called in sick would not go over well.

Jane's need to punch something had grown steadily since she'd awakened sick to her stomach. And now that she was dreaming again, she felt a pressing need to double down on her fitness.

Jane changed and headed out for a run. It was drizzling again. Douglas Park was deserted. She ran laps and practised her knife skills, hitting every target: the first base line, the left post of the park sign, the right post of the scoreboard, the Doritos wrapper blowing across the lawn.

On the way home, she detoured to pick up groceries. The door to her apartment was unlocked when she got there.

"Hey, Sade," Jane said, as Sadie stared into Jane's cupboard.

"Ran out of coffee. Thought I'd try that licorice tea you like so much." She looked over, took in Jane's attire. "You go running again?"

Jane untied her sneakers. "I would have called, but I know you're studying. Needed to shake off some frustration. I've got another meeting with Crown counsel this afternoon."

Sadie shimmied, as if a shiver had gone up her spine. "Okay, you win. Crown counsel beats the hell out of my issues with boredom any day. I started the cost accounting module." She exaggerated a yawn. "Need caffeine. This isn't herbal, is it?" she said, reading the package. "Aren't you supposed to be at work?"

Jane peeled off her hoodie. "Yeah. Called in sick. That's caffeine free. Try the chai."

"Because of your meeting?"

"No, I booked the meeting for after work."

Sadie reached back into the cupboard. "Nice table, by the way. Didn't know you were looking for one."

"I wasn't. Ethan gave it to me."

"Aw. How'd your Valentine's dinner night turn out?"

Jane pulled his keys from her pocket and dangled them.

Sadie looked up. "Are those— He gave you his keys!"

Jane nodded. "He said he's all in."

"Shit, girl. He's serious about you."

"Yeah," she said, smiling. "We have a great connection. The keys caught me off guard, though. I'm not sure he's really thought this through."

Sadie rolled her eyes. "You're an idiot. Of course he has. And those are keys, not an engagement ring."

Jane put her hands on her hips. "I meant in connection to my dreams. He's said—more than once—he wished I didn't have them."

Sadie quirked an eyebrow. "Hmm, where else have I heard those exact same words? Oh, yeah. From you."

Jane flopped on the sofa. Sadie sat on the armrest, the box of tea in her hand.

"Give him time. He'll get used to your dreams. I did."

"I hope you're right," Jane said, and she told Sadie about her latest discovery with the mark on her hand.

"A time dial? Damn, Narc! I didn't think that shit could get any weirder. Wrong again. What's Ariane say?"

"She's not come across anything like it."

Jane filled Sadie in about what had happened at Riptide with the insurance adjustor. "I'm afraid that Connor's in serious trouble and taking Ethan down with him."

Jane had the same uneasy feeling approaching the Law Courts building as she had the first time. It was worse now that she knew how astute Monica Fowler was. She wouldn't be easy to fool.

"Have you had an opportunity to review the statement you gave to police?" Monica asked, suggesting they sit in the guest chairs facing the desk this time. "Before you answer, I want to remind you that I am obliged to disclose to defence any changes to your statement or new details about the case."

Jane nodded her understanding. She clarified a number of minor points, which Monica jotted down.

"As I explained previously, the police prepared a written narrative based on the evidence and statements they collected. It's their interpretation of what happened," Monica said. "I wonder if you could clarify a few small points. Sadie said that Andrew supplied her with an app for her phone, the same app she later sent to you. She suspected, after the fact, that this app's purpose was to track her and your movements." She looked up for confirmation.

"Yes."

"We're trying to establish the existence of this app, but without either phone, we're having difficulty. Did the app have a name or any identifying information that you can recall?"

"No." Jane shook her head. She and Sadie called it the stalker app, which was accurate but not very marketable.

"Okay. We won't get any traction there. Moving on, Sadie indicated that she had been dating Roderick's alter ego, Rick, for approximately two years, but that she'd never brought him home to your apartment and that you'd never met him prior to the kidnapping. Is that right?"

"Yes." *Technically.* Interacting with the man in a dream didn't qualify as meeting him.

"Given that you didn't know him, do you have any idea why he targeted you?"

Several. "No." She plucked a fleck of fluff from her lap. "I'm curious though. What did he say?"

"He's not shedding any light, but that's normal. Defence isn't under any obligation to share information with the Crown. Tell me: why would Sadie, whom you describe as being as close as a sister, not want you to meet the man she'd been seeing for over two years?"

Because she never introduced her johns. Jane raised her shoulders in a questioning shrug. "I guess she wasn't serious about him."

"After two years?" Monica said, arching a perfectly shaped eyebrow. Jane shrugged. Monica continued. "Sadie also stated that Rick told her he was a professor, and that you were the one who advised her Rick was a psychiatrist. How did you come to learn that?"

Answering Monica's questions felt like a game of chess. Jane found herself pausing to consider Monica's next move before she answered. "Sadie mentioned that he could be controlling at times. We watch out for one another. I looked him up."

"I see. All right." Monica picked through her papers and pulled out a new one to put on top. "Switching topics, you said in your statement that Rick believed you could kill his brother, Michael. Did he explain himself?"

"No. He'd given me back my boot knife. I think he assumed I'd use it."

"Then . . . he planned on releasing you from the kennel?"

Jane felt Monica tugging at the carpet under her feet. Though Monica hadn't said as much, Jane sensed her skepticism. She'd warned Jane to be honest with her, warned her that there was no case without Jane's testimony, and that the prosecution would be jeopardized if she wasn't truthful. Jane didn't like lying to her, but she saw no way around it.

"No. He believed I could do it while I was sleeping. In a dream state."

"Why would he think that?"

Jane had to give her credit for not missing a beat. "I don't know. He didn't explain." And if the delusional label was floating around, Jane wanted it to land on Rick, not her.

That night, Jane lay on her bed fully dressed and tugged the comforter over her boots. She resented her dreams for effectively ending her ability to snuggle in Ethan's arms after he'd blown her mind in bed. He might have been all in, but the boots-in-bed thing was an unwelcome reminder of her dreams, and on those, he was decidedly not all in.

In their months together, they'd never exchanged the *love* word. Strange how that little word held so much power. Were the keys his way of telling her how he felt about her? And why did loving Ethan make her feel vulnerable, whereas loving Sadie made her feel strong? She knew the answer immediately: because she'd never lose Sadie. Her love for Sadie was deep-rooted, an oak that had survived seasons of storms. Her love for Ethan was still a sapling, vulnerable and untested.

Tonight, rather than trust her phone would stay put in her pocket, she shoved it down her sock, secure in her boot. Not that there was any logic to this Witness business, but she couldn't imagine a reason why the phone wouldn't travel with her in her visiting dreams. Her clothes did. Her knife did.

Visiting Dream

Jane wakes in Riptide's office, her back to the wall opposite Connor, who is sitting behind the desk absorbed in something on the computer screen. Through the two-way glass, Jane can see that it's Jerry who's tending the bar.

Her body is translucent, but at least she's dressed. She glances about for better cover and slinks slowly along the wall to the Pac-Man arcade game. She watches for Connor to look away, and when he does, she scoots to the other side of the old machine and breathes a sigh of relief when she's tucked into its shadow.

Her boot knife is in place, but the phone is gone. The clock behind the desk reads 2:00 p.m. A minute passes. She studies the mark on the back of her left hand. She strokes it and her stomach flips, reminding her of its nasty side effect. It also reminds her that she's supposed to test the mark. Ariane asked her to. She's pleased that she remembers.

There's a knock on the office door, and it opens. Connor looks up and smiles. "Norm. Good to see you, man." He stands and greets Norm with a handshake and a man's half-hug. "What brings you by? Or are you just looking for a free drink?"

Norm shifts from foot to foot. "You're looking good, Con. Riptide treating you well?"

"Yeah. You saw the quarterlies. Revenue's up, and that's always a good thing. Have a seat." He gestures to the sofa and returns to the credenza behind the desk. "Scotch?"

"Sure." Norm wipes his palms on his thighs, looks around the room, and sits down.

Jane holds her fingertip to the mark and her vision ripples. When her vision stabilizes, she slowly traces the mark in a counter-clockwise circle. The room swims. Jane gags and swings her hand to the wall to brace herself.

". . . brings you by? Or are you just looking for a free drink?"

Norm does the antsy foot shift. "You're looking good, Con. Riptide treating you well?"

"Yeah. You saw the quarterlies. Revenue's up, and that's always a good thing. Have a seat." Connor returns to the credenza. "Scotch?"

"Sure." Norm wipes his palms on his thighs, looks around the room, and sits down.

Jane feels a wash of wonder. She rides out the nausea.

"How's Sally, the kids?" Connor says, pouring their drinks.

"Good. All good."

Connor returns with the drinks and hands one to his friend. They clink glasses. "Cheers." Connor takes a sip and sits opposite Norm. He studies him. "You okay?"

Norm forms a twitchy smile. His gaze darts to the clock behind the desk. "I've been better." His brow is beaded in sweat.

Connor leans forward. "What's going on?"

"Ulcers again." He places his untouched drink on the coffee table. "It's the stress. I've got to take a break. Might be gone awhile."

"Sure thing. We've got this place covered. Take as long as you need."

Norm glances at the clock again. "I want you to meet some friends of mine. They'll check in for me while I'm away."

Connor furrows his brow. "What friends? And why would they need to check in?"

"I'd just like them to be here. Lend a hand."

Connor sits back, swirls his drink. "It's not that I mind, Norm. You have every right to be here. But you've never shown an interest in the day-to-day before. Is there a problem with the financials?"

"No. Not at all. You said yourself, revenues are up. I just want you to meet these guys. Let them be my eyes and ears while I'm gone."

A deep crease digs into Connor's brow. "But I've always been your ears and eyes around here. What's going on?"

"You do too much. I need to contribute more, is all. It'll help with the stress. Knowing they're helping out."

Connor tilts his head with a question on his face. "Why don't I know these friends of yours?"

Norm laughs, but it sounds forced. "What's that say about me, that you think you're my only friend?"

Connor looks to his drink, smiling at his friend.

"Do this for me," Norm says. "I'll rest easier."

Connor exhales. "Yeah, sure. Anything I can do to help. Where are these guys?"

Someone taps on the door. "That's probably them now," Norm says.

It's a bloody party, Jane thinks, hoping no one wants to play Pac-Man.

Norm is halfway out of his seat when Connor waves him back down. "I'll get it." He opens the door, and Garvin and Joey step inside. "You must be Norm's friends," he says and introduces himself, shaking their hands.

Connor pours more drinks, and while the men get acquainted, Jane watches Norm. He's oddly distracted by the clock, sneaking glances at it like he's late for a meeting.

Jane's nausea settles. She places her fingertip on the mark again. This time she slowly traces a clockwise circle. The men's movements speed up, their voices pinch, and then the room blurs and the floor drops out from under her.

Jane woke in her bed, heaving. She didn't make it to the bathroom. It wasn't until the nausea had passed and she was sitting on the toilet lid that she realized what she'd done. She examined the back of her left hand. Once again, Ariane was right. The mark was the key she'd been hoping for all her life—her get-out-of-jail-free card.

Excitement bubbled up in her. For the first time in her life, she was in control. Free. For once, she didn't even mind that she was dressed and felt grungy. She reached into her boot. No phone. That was another question answered. Technology didn't travel.

She found the phone tangled in the bedsheets. It was too early to call Peru, so she texted Ariane what she'd learned about the mark and told her she'd connect with her later.

Jane knew she should try to get some more sleep, but she was too excited. As she wiped up the vomit, she considered the new possibilities. Would she be able to jump out of any dream? At any time? That could mean the end of her dreams altogether. Or would the Witness gene kick in and plop her into the same dream, time and again, until she'd seen what she was supposed to witness?

It made her wonder if she'd pre-empted tonight's dream by jumping out of it early. Had she missed something important? After all, she hadn't learned anything new. Maybe the thing she was supposed to witness had occurred after she'd jumped out.

20 | Sadie

When Mrs. Stafford finally returned Sadie's call, she put the accounting lecture on pause.

"Are you familiar with the name V.R. Wright?" Sadie asked.

"Yes. What is this about?"

"I recently purchased a Hermès bag from a downtown consignment shop. I found three wedding rings hidden in the lining. Wondered if you knew anything about them."

"Have you got a photo of the rings?"

Sadie snapped a photo and sent it. The line was quiet for a long pause.

"The V is for Valerie. She was my mother. Those are my parents' wedding bands. We thought we'd lost them."

Sadie fist-pumped. She learned that the rings had gone missing from the care home where Mrs. Stafford's mother had lived before she died. Mrs. Stafford, whose first name was Georgina, feared they'd been stolen.

"I'm so glad I found them," Sadie said. "I'm a student on a pretty tight budget, but once in a while, I find something like your mom's purse. Figured I could fix it up and resell it. Make a few bucks. You wouldn't believe how expensive textbooks are."

"I'm grateful you didn't sell it."

"I tried—before I found the rings, of course. It's just that the purse is in worse shape than I thought. Beyond repair. I'm afraid I'm out what I paid for it."

"Perhaps I can help with that, Sadie . . . Prescott, right?" she said, as if reading it from the phone message.

"Yes."

"I'd be happy to pay you for the purse and a finder's fee for the rings, if you'd be amenable."

Sadie sighed. "That would be a tremendous relief."

"Wonderful. Does fifteen hundred dollars sound fair? I can send someone to collect them when it's convenient for you."

Fifteen hundred dollars sounded like a mani-pedi and lash extensions in her future. Sadie made the arrangements and then leaned back in her chair, happy that her finances had a new healthy glow. She'd have to redouble her commitment to stay out of the shops until she graduated—and got a job.

That thought sent her looking for the card Jane had given her from the investment firm. It poked out from under her laptop. Katerina Vasco, Partner, CFA, CFP. Sadie decided to call while she was still riding the high from her chat with Georgina.

Katerina invited her for an interview. She had a thirty-minute opening later that afternoon. Sadie raced to get ready.

But her conversation with Katerina did not go as she'd expected. Why had she thought she'd be a shoo-in? Katerina was no slouch, starting the interview off with a no-nonsense tone and a kill-switch question. Sadie didn't miss a beat. She smiled brightly, reassuring Katerina that she'd be happy to get a criminal record check.

The standard questions followed: Where had Sadie grown up? Gone to school? How did she know Jane? Katerina took time out to offer her sympathy for growing up in the system, but the reprieve was short-lived.

Soon after, she drilled Sadie about her work history prior to starting the accounting program.

Sadie knew Jane's reputation was also being weighed.

"I waitressed, mostly at Lodestones." And no, she didn't have a reference. "I had an opportunity that required I quit without notice."

"What kind of opportunity?"

The teensy lie slipped out. "A personal assistant to a man who turned out to be a criminal. He's in jail now." No biggie—an escort was a PA of sorts.

Sadie wondered how much of the story Jane might have already mentioned as Katerina took down the details. Sadie had no doubt she'd check up on every one.

"—but I do have references," Sadie said, offering a confident smile. "I've worked at other restaurants, just not for as long as I was with Lodestones." After Jane had warned her that she'd need references, Sadie chatted up the manager at the Greek restaurant on Fourth Avenue. Though he'd been leering at her at the time, he'd offered her a reference and a work history if she found herself in a bind. This felt an awful lot like a bind.

21 | Ethan

Jane called. She wanted to come by for lunch, but Ethan put her off. After Fanny's revelation, he didn't want her anywhere near Riptide. He told her he'd bring dinner to her place instead and spend the night.

He wondered at Joey's curiosity. Was he attracted to her? Or had he seen her in one of her damn dreams? Regardless, there was no need to tempt fate. She may have been good with a knife, but Joey was more of a gun type. And guns trumped knives every time.

When the lunch crowd thinned, Ethan went to the office and logged into the accounting program to check on the night deposits. Cash was now triple what it had been before Garvin and Joey had showed up. At that rate of increase, they'd be cleaning six times their legit cash intake by the summer. Someone was going to notice. If it wasn't the bank, it would be their accountants.

He phoned Connor, who told him to take a break and meet him at Ethan's apartment.

"What happened to you?" Ethan said, opening his door. Connor limped into the apartment sporting a black eye.

"Joey." He handed Ethan an envelope.

"What's this?" Ethan said, opening it.

"An invoice for a restroom reno."

"At Riptide?"

Connor nodded. "Same company that'll be doing the repair on the fire damage. Joey dropped it off last night. His organization finally figured out that Norm's not in the country and won't be signing any more contracts."

Ethan looked at the invoice and whistled. "That's some reno. Must come with platinum toilet seats."

"I told him we weren't renovating. Gave it back to him." Connor lowered himself gingerly to a chair at the table. Ethan sat opposite him.

"Joey didn't take it so well. Told me to pay up and stop pretending I didn't know what was going on."

"Did he enlighten you?"

"In great detail. If I do what I'm told and keep my mouth shut, they won't turn Norm in. Otherwise?" He shook his head.

"They're willing to jeopardize Riptide?"

"They're betting I choose Norm over Riptide." Connor massaged his ribs. "Joey also didn't appreciate me pointing out the fault in his logic."

"What—that either way, you lose Riptide?"

"I wouldn't doubt Joey recorded our conversation. That's their proof that I know about the money laundering. Which means my clock's ticking. Either I do what he says and incriminate myself, or I go to the police."

"If you pay this invoice, they've got you. You'll never be free of them."

"And if I go to the police, Riptide will get caught up in an investigation. If they shut us down for any length of time, it'll bankrupt me, to say nothing of having to worry about a return visit from Joey. It's a lose-lose proposition."

Ethan leaned forward. "Not if we have a bargaining chip."

"What do you mean?"

"Paying this invoice isn't an option," Ethan said, tossing it to the table, "but you have some time to come up with the payment. A week, maybe two. We can stall them on the fire repair."

"What's the point? Just like the restroom, they won't do the work, just give us an invoice."

"The fire damage is too public. They'll have to paint it at least."

"Tell me about our bargaining chip."

"If you had something extra to offer the police, something that takes down Joey and Garvin and their organization, they might let you stay open while they investigate."

"Something extra? Like what?"

"We put a GPS tracker in their truck. Find out who they're getting their drugs from, and where."

"That's illegal."

"And what they're doing isn't? I don't plan on enlightening them. I just want to track them long enough to get addresses and maybe some photos: proof of their connection to the addresses. Then we hand over our intel to the police and let them do the rest."

Though Connor remained skeptical, he had little to lose, and he agreed with Ethan that they had only a few days, maybe a week, to work with. The research was surprisingly quick. The internet was a beautiful thing. For less than two hundred bucks, Ethan found what they needed in an electronics shop in Surrey. He downloaded the app to his phone and rode out to Connor's place in Deep Cove to show him.

"What if they detect it?" Connor said, handling the small black tracking disk.

"Then you're out two hundred bucks."

"They can't trace it back to us?"

"Nope." Ethan showed Connor the screenshot of Garvin's truck. "Inside the cab is the best place to hide it, but we're not going to get inside without setting off the truck's alarm. Under the frame is supposed to work well, but it's tricky to get the placement right. But see here." Ethan pointed to the Chevy's running lights on the roof and rails on either side. "If we put it up against the rail on the inside, I don't think they'd even notice it. I'll read up on the software tonight and come back tomorrow to test it."

"I know I agreed to this," Connor said. "But it's a big risk for a handful of addresses and photos. It's just information. It doesn't prove anything. And what if Joey or Garvin spot us?"

Ethan set his phone in front of him, the photo of the truck still on the screen. "Risk is relative. You took a big risk investing in Riptide when you bought it. The question is how much risk are we willing to take to protect it?"

Connor inhaled and puffed out his cheeks on the exhale. "The info we find might not be enough to keep Riptide from being shut down anyway."

"That's true. But what's the alternative?" Ethan could feel Connor's roadblocks giving way.

"We don't even know if the police will be interested in what we find."

"How could they not be? They've got a drug gang doing laundry all over the downtown. But if the cops don't want the intel, I know who will. Wilde. Did you ever get in touch with him?"

"Yeah. He told me as a source, he could keep me out of it. Gave him a bunch of names: Trident, Dalton, ProBuilt. Figured that would keep him busy, especially when he learns Trident is just the smelly tip of a very dirty iceberg."

"Perfect. When the cops learn that an investigative reporter is interested in our information, they'll bite. The cops won't want to look incompetent if Wilde turns the drug gang's money laundering scheme into another award-winning story."

22 | Jane

"Good. You're back," Anna said, hobbling into the greenhouse section at the rear of the store. No *how are you feeling, you okay,* nothing.

"Store looks nice," Jane said, referring to the explosion of four-leaf clovers and leprechauns. "Did you buy a tank of helium?"

"I was able to get it done yesterday. While you were off."

Jane sighed. She should just give her notice and leave. "I was sick to my stomach, Anna. Sorry I wasn't here to help."

Anna paused. "Well, best not to bring a bug in here with Pieter so susceptible. When you get a minute, would you pack up the Valentine's decorations and put them away?"

There wasn't a *please* in there, but at least she'd asked.

The day dragged. She was relieved to get on her bike and go home. After she ditched her coat and helmet, she tapped on Sadie's door. "Got a minute?"

"Sure. I could use a break." Sadie stretched her arms over her head.

"Tea?" Jane said as she filled Sadie's kettle. She then settled into the beanbag chair. "I need a new job."

"What happened now?"

"I know it's impossible, but Anna acts like she knows I'm somehow responsible for her accident."

"That's your guilt speaking. It's been months. You need to get over that."

"She's short with me all the time. Impatient. The only one she's kind to is Pieter."

"You are not the reason she's cranky. That's on her. But letting her walk all over you? That one's on you."

"You think I should quit?"

"I think you've tried really hard. You've put in extra hours for free, been nice to her when she's been a bag to you, and you haven't complained once about anything, not even her obnoxious behaviour. What's left for you to try?"

Jane stood and walked to the squat window behind Sadie's desk. "Ethan's coming over later. He's going to spend the night."

"You're changing the subject."

Jane spun around. "Because I don't know what to do."

"Yeah, you do."

"It feels like giving up. You and I?" Jane said, gesturing between them. "We don't walk away from a fight."

"It's a job, not a fight. You're not giving up, you're moving on. Isn't *don't look back* what we've always said?"

Jane's phone chimed. A text. "Shit. Ariane. I almost forgot. I've got to call her."

"Why? What happened?"

"The mark on my hand—it does more than shift time." Jane told her about her latest dream and the revelation that the mark was her ticket out of dream hell. Sadie said a few *hell-yesses* and took the news in her stride. Years of hearing about Jane's dreams had conditioned her to crazytown.

Back at her apartment, Jane recounted the dream's revelations to Ariane.

"That's remarkable. It's almost as if your new marks are melding with your Witness gene, becoming one. I'd like to have your blood drawn, check your DNA."

When Jane was in the hospital after her abduction, she'd reluctantly agreed to give Ariane a sample of her blood on the condition her name wasn't attached to it in any way. She didn't trust her DNA profile wouldn't get leaked to someone who might want to find her and do further tests.

Sidestepping the DNA question, Jane expressed her concern that she'd jumped out of the dream too early. "What if I missed a critical clue? Will I end up back in the same dream, or is that clue gone forever?"

"Your next dream may hold the answer," Ariane said.

Jane would have asked Ariane to weigh in on ending all her dreams the moment they started, but Ariane had made her feelings known many times: Witnesses didn't shirk their responsibilities—their role was sacred. They used their abilities to restore justice. Yadda ad nauseum.

Justice was something Jane had been mulling over a lot. "At work today, I was thinking—if I dream of Mary again, at the hospital, I can use the mark to rewind what I did. Bring Buddy and Pieter back."

"I don't think that's possible. History settled into a new pattern the moment you interfered. Further interference would only alter history again, into who-knows-what pattern."

"What if history just went back to what it was supposed to be?"

"Are you the one who determines that? What about all the lives that would change for the worse?"

"But it was just six months ago. How much could have changed?"

"For you, it's been six months. For Pieter and Buddy, it's been years. Their entire lives."

Jane fell silent. What if Ariane was right? Could fixing her mistake make things worse? She might still lose Buddy and Pieter and end up hurting a different mix of people.

"You have to forgive yourself, Jane."

Ariane's words reminded her of Sadie's advice and their mantra: *never look back*. Jane would have to work on that.

"I'm starving," Jane said when Ethan arrived.

"Me, too." Ethan's kiss hello quickly dipped into sensual territory with a greedy tongue and a groping embrace. Jane pulled back to catch her breath. "Oh, you meant hungry for food?" A sexy smile tweaked the corners of his mouth. "We'll continue this later." He kissed her one more time and made his way to the kitchen to drop the bag of takeout on the counter.

"Nice," he said, glancing at the table. Jane had used one of Sadie's scarves for a tablecloth and dressed it with a borrowed candle. She'd folded paper towels for napkins and tucked them under the cutlery. She'd even put out wineglasses.

"I see Sadie's back in business."

Jane looked up. "What are you talking about?"

"I just watched a brand new Range Rover pull up outside. A suit got out, and unless it was you who let him in, it had to have been Sadie."

"She's not turning tricks. She wouldn't. He must be here for another reason."

Ethan arched an eyebrow. "What else would a well-dressed businessman be doing at Sadie's place?"

"I don't know. But it's not a gig." There was no way Sadie would go back down that dead-end road.

"What makes you so certain?"

"You've seen her place. If she was hooking—which she isn't—she wouldn't be working from home."

"Go ask her."

"I'm not spying on her. I trust her." Jane thought back to her discussion with Sadie about the Hermès bag that was worth a small fortune. Just how much had she paid for it?

"All right," Ethan said, raising his arms in surrender. "I hope you're right."

"I am. What's for dinner?"

Over a heaping plate of pad Thai, Jane told him she was considering giving her notice at Positively Plants. But when it came to talking about him, he was unusually quiet.

"Something happen at Riptide today?"

Ethan swallowed and took a sip of the beer he'd opened. He nodded. "Yeah. Joey took a swing at Connor."

"Why? Is he hurt?" Connor was sweet, but more marshmallow than hard candy.

"He'll survive. He's not a fighter, but he'll choose his words more carefully with Joey in future." He told Jane about Joey's latest demands. "Connor's partner screwed up, and there's no fixing it. Joey's banking on Connor protecting Norm, but that means losing Riptide. He won't do it. He may still lose Riptide, but if he doesn't come clean to the cops, he's going to lose it anyway, and he doesn't have much time."

"What can we do?"

Ethan placed his fork carefully beside his plate. "Don't take this the wrong way, Jane, but you can do nothing. Joey's volatile, Garvin's unpredictable. That's why I blew you off at lunch. I don't want you coming around Riptide anymore. Not until Joey and Garvin are out of there."

"You know who else is dangerous, Ethan? Me. I can help."

Ethan reached for her hand. "You're the most capable woman I know. But even if Joey hasn't recognized you from one of your . . . dreams, I wouldn't put it past him or Garvin to target you. Threatening you would be a surefire way to get to me or Connor. It's not worth the risk, or the worry. It's better all around if you avoid Riptide for a while."

Though the threat was remote, Jane understood his concern. And the tender touch of his hand spoke volumes about where his heart was.

She could help by not adding to his worry. Besides which, Joey *had* seen her, and so had one of the men from Huan's apartment. "Okay. I'll stay away."

She straightened the cutlery. "Something happened in my last dream. The mark on the back of my hand—it doesn't just rewind a dream. When I trace the mark clockwise, it jumps me out of the dream entirely. It's my escape valve. Or I hope that's what it is."

"You hope?"

"I've only tried it once. But if it works, the next time I get into trouble, or someone sees me, I can get out of the dream."

"If you can get out, why not get out right away? End the madness altogether."

"Believe me, I've thought about it. A lot. But I'm a Witness. There's no denying it, no fighting it. I'm supposed to see things. If I tap out of a dream as soon as it starts, I could be in for a starring role in *Groundhog Day*."

"Or you could just get out of the damn dream."

Later that night, Ethan lay in her bed with his fingers laced behind his neck, watching her undress. Emboldened by his lusty smile, she sashayed to the end of the bed and crawled up his body. He was playful in bed, laughing almost as often as he sighed in pleasure. She loved that about him.

After they made love, he spooned against her back and drifted off to sleep. She waited until his breathing slowed to a steady rhythm, and then she extracted herself. He didn't wake.

She closed the bedroom door and padded to the living room. As much as she hated leaving their warm bed, it couldn't be helped. She dressed in the clothes she'd stashed in the trunk she used as a coffee table, tugged on her boots, and lay down on the sofa.

She hadn't slept on the sofa since Sadie had moved out. Back then, with only the one single bed in the apartment, whoever got home last got the sofa. What was Sadie up to? she wondered, thinking of Ethan's earlier reference to a well-dressed man in the building. Jane didn't doubt Sadie was out of the business, but that didn't mean Jane shouldn't check in with her, make sure she was safe. She sent her a text and moments later got her response: a sleepy-faced emoji. Relieved, Jane put her phone away.

Damn these dreams for robbing her of a warm bed! But if she

dreamed right away, she might be able to rejoin Ethan and they could make love again in the morning. She yanked a blanket over her shoulder and rolled onto her side.

She no longer believed her dreams told Huan's story. Not that she wouldn't try to help him, but with Joey and Riptide front and centre in her dreams, how long until Ethan was dragged in? She understood Ethan's concern, but she feared he was part of whatever she was meant to witness. He couldn't expect her to stand on the sidelines.

It was still dark when she woke. She hadn't dreamed. She pulled off the blanket and sat up, rubbing her eyes and yawning.

"You're awake."

She jumped at Ethan's voice. Turning, she saw Ethan dressed and sitting at the table. "How long have you been up?"

"Twenty minutes. You weren't in bed. I came looking for you."

Jane checked the time. "It's early. I've got coffee if you'd like."

"Why are you sleeping on the sofa—in your clothes?"

"I thought I might dream," she said, tugging off her boots. "Wanted to be ready." She sauntered into the kitchen to put the kettle on.

"Ready? What does that mean?"

Jane turned and rested her butt against the edge of the counter. "It seems that whatever I'm wearing when I fall into a dream is what I'm wearing *in* the dream."

Ethan's brow creased. "So in your dream the other night at my place, you're telling me you were in that apartment—"

"Naked? Yeah."

"And in the parkade?"

"Nightshirt. Bare feet. But from then on, this." Jane indicated her hoodie and jeans. "And my boots. My knife."

"Jesus, Jane. When were you gonna tell me this?"

"I'm sorry. I should have mentioned it earlier. It's just . . . I'd already sprung the rewind dial on you, and I know how much my dreams bother you. I didn't want to pile on more."

"That doesn't mean you don't tell me."

"I haven't known for long. Still getting used to it myself. I hate dressing for bed. Hate sleeping in my clothes." She pushed off the counter and sidled up to him, raking her fingers through his hair. "I'd rather wake naked with you any day of the week."

23 | Sadie

Sadie got a late-night text from Jane. *U OK?*
She stared at the screen, wondering what had gotten into her. Maybe an old habit was resurfacing? They hadn't checked up on each other since they were roomies. Since Sadie had left the business.
She replied with a sleeping happy face.
Jane sent an eggplant. Yeah, she was more than fine.

The next day, Sadie got straight to her coursework. She'd left Georgina Stafford's cash in a stack right where the Hermès bag had sat. It was motivation—and a reminder.

Further motivation had arrived in the form of an email from Jane's investment firm. Katerina Vasco had passed Sadie's name on to the accounting department, and would she be available to come in for a second interview? She'd lose another half day of studying, but it would be worth it if she could snag an internship.

Sadie sat opposite the department manager, a representative from their HR department, and the woman who would be supervising Sadie's work should she get an intern position. They were all welcoming smiles and handshakes, but made it clear the interview was a favour. Sadie straightened, unwilling to let them think she'd gotten in the wrong lineup, snagging a VIP seat when they thought she should have been in the nosebleed section.

When they got down to business, it felt like a tag-team interrogation. They repeated Katerina's questions, piled on a slew of new ones, and topped it off with a repeat of the section she'd taken in class on fiduciary responsibilities.

"Given the situation with your former employer and his incarceration, we'll need you to complete a criminal record check. We'll also do a credit check and will need two letters of recommendation. One from a paid position. I would suggest the other one come from the program director at your school. Failing that, we'd accept one from your bank or a landlord who has known you for two years and can vouch for your character."

An hour later, Sadie stood outside the Bentall Centre, feeling wrung out.

"Sadie?" It was Cynthia, straight out of Vogue with thigh-high boots, a cashmere coat, and perfectly smoothed hair. Everything about her—makeup, nails, posture—whispered money, and lots of it. "It's been ages. What brings you downtown?"

Sadie hadn't seen her since the day Cynthia paid her out. "An interview. It's for an internship."

"Ah, yes. Your studies." She nodded, assessing Sadie from hair to heels. Even wearing her best threads, Sadie lacked Cynthia's polish. "Would you like to go for a drink? My treat."

Sadie straightened her shoulders. "I'm not coming back."

"I'm not asking you to. But you look like you could use a drink."

Amen to that, and what could it hurt? They walked over to the Cactus Club.

"Martini?" Cynthia asked Sadie when the server arrived. She ordered for both of them.

"Tell me about school. How are your classes going?"

"What is this? Research for Teacher's Pet?"

Cynthia laughed. "So cynical. We've known each other for years. I'm genuinely interested."

Sadie caught herself. "Yeah," she said, and smiled apologetically. "I guess I am cynical." She told Cynthia about the college, pulled the program calendar up on her phone, and Cynthia scrolled through the course listing. "All the work is done online. Except for the exams. Those I have to take on campus."

Their drinks arrived, and Sadie asked how the girls were doing. She knew most of them. Cynthia was proud of her girls and spoke respectfully of them. She'd always had class that way. It was one of the reasons Sadie had agreed to work for her.

As they parted ways on the sidewalk, Cynthia grasped Sadie's elbow. "I'm glad your studies are going well, but if it falls apart, call me." Cynthia flung her scarf over her shoulder and walked away.

And there it was. Sadie laughed and shook her head, partly because Cynthia was predictable, but partly because of what it said about her that she took *call me* as a compliment—it meant Sadie was still marketable.

24 | Ethan

Ethan got to Connor's place first thing in the morning to test the tracker with the software. The colouring of Connor's shiner had gotten worse, but his limp had improved. Ethan set the tracker on the dashboard of Connor's SUV but didn't secure it. He'd need an alcohol swab for that, and he didn't want to compromise the tracker's adhesive pad ahead of its intended placement on the truck.

Connor drove while Ethan familiarized himself with the software's operation.

"The program will mark out its movements?" Connor asked.

"Yeah, and it spits out the coordinates of any place the truck stops for more than five minutes. The duration's adjustable."

Satisfied with their understanding of the app, they returned to Connor's kitchen and sketched out a plan. After they established the truck's routes, they would identify the businesses involved, and then get dashcam footage of Joey and Garvin coming and going. Nothing illegal in that, but it would be valuable to a police investigation—and with a little luck, enough currency to buy Connor's way out of the jam he'd gotten himself into.

On Ethan's return trip through the downtown, while stopped at a light, he spotted Sadie. She was all decked out—come-fuck-me heels on boots up to her ass and topped with a leather miniskirt. And the woman she was with was Cynthia, her former madam, looking even more expensive. Apparently she was Sadie's *former* madam no longer. Jane would be crushed. He slipped his phone out of his pocket and snapped a photo. Though he doubted it, he hoped Sadie had the decency to tell her. He sure as hell didn't want to be the one.

Connor arrived at Ethan's apartment later in the afternoon with the supplies and equipment they needed.

"It's the biggest one I could get," Connor said as Ethan unrolled the map of the Lower Mainland. Connor helped him pin the map to the wall above the kitchen table.

Connor took a seat and set up his laptop. In minutes, he had Riptide's security footage on the screen. "It's all yours."

Ethan spun the computer around and downloaded the tracking software. He pulled out his phone and found the list of places he'd jotted down where he knew Garvin and Joey might go: Riptide, the bank, Trident, the parkade. "Do you know any others?"

"Yeah. My place."

Ethan added it to the list. "What's the name of the company on the invoice for the restroom reno?"

"ProBuilt something or other."

"Look them up. Give me an address."

Ethan grabbed a highlighter and put a dot on the map at all the addresses they'd identified. "Now all we gotta do is get the tracker on the truck," Ethan said. "When do you expect Garvin?"

"Anytime after six o'clock. I'll ding you when he arrives."

"Okay," Ethan said. "You keep him busy. I'll install the tracker and text you when it's done."

It was late when Ethan got the text from Connor. He located the truck on Riptide's security screen and turned that camera off. He then tucked his phone in his pocket and took a stroll. Once he was sure no one was inside the truck, and no one was nearby, he leapt into the truck bed and set to work.

Thirty seconds later, he was back on the street. He pulled out his phone and turned the camera back on. He texted Connor a thumbs-up and returned to his apartment. The tracker blinked on the screen.

From his window, Ethan spotted the cube van Connor had rented. He'd snugged it up to the scorched wall to act as a stumbling block in the event ProBuilt showed up to paint over the fire damage. Ethan kept an eye on Riptide's back door, waiting for Garvin to leave and hoping like hell the thug wasn't taking his turn pummelling Connor.

When Garvin finally left, night deposit in hand, Ethan sprinted for the computer. On the screen, he watched Garvin get in his truck without a glance at its roof and felt a shot of relief. He switched to the tracking program, and when the truck's arrow started moving on the screen, he fist-pumped. They'd done it. The first phase was complete.

Connor showed up within minutes, and together they watched the arrow travel. It stopped outside the bank, stopped briefly in East Van, and carried on to an address in neighbouring Mount Pleasant. Then they lost the signal.

There was still no activity the next morning when Ethan left for work. He checked the app obsessively, fearing Joey or Garvin had found the tracker. But at noon, the little arrow reappeared. He phoned Connor with the news.

"Maybe they overnighted in an underground parkade," Connor said.

"Could be one of them lives there."

When Garvin showed up at Riptide, Ethan checked the security camera feed. The tracker looked undisturbed. In a few days, he and Connor would have enough data to anticipate their route, follow them, and get the photos they needed for their I-was-there T-shirts.

25 | Jane

Jane peered over the shoulder of the woman in front of her at the hardware store's service counter. She'd zipped down to Davie Village during her lunch hour to get a set of keys cut, but it looked like noon was a popular time to hit the shops.

She'd gone back and forth about giving Ethan her keys. It wasn't that she didn't trust him, but they'd been dating for only six months. What finally swayed her was that her apartment was more secure than his. She'd be spending her nights there, and she wanted him to join her as often as possible. Giving Ethan his own keys would be more convenient for both of them.

After she'd waited her turn and paid for the keys, she had one more stop to make. She checked the time. Getting back to work within the hour would be a squeaker, but she could do it as long as she wasn't delayed. Normally, she'd make up the time by tacking it onto the end of her shift, but not today; she had a meeting right after work with Monica Fowler at the Law Courts building.

She parked in front of Ethan's building, grabbed the six-pack she'd picked up, and jogged up the front walk. He'd be at work, but he'd said to use the keys anytime. Hopefully, he'd be pleasantly surprised when he opened his fridge after work and found her keys dangling from the neck of a Corona bottle.

As she climbed the stairs to the third floor, she had second thoughts. Maybe she should have given him a heads-up the first time she used the keys. But a moment later, she was at his door and out of time for second thoughts. She slid the key in the lock and opened the door.

Jane froze.

Connor stood at the kitchen table and whipped around. "You startled me." He waved her in.

"Sorry. I'm just dropping this off," Jane said, raising the six-pack. She winced at the bruising around his eye. "You okay?"

Connor set his jaw. "I'm fine."

Jane glanced around the studio apartment. "Ethan not here?"

"He's at Riptide." Jane paused. Did Ethan hand out his keys to everyone?

Connor turned back to the street map of Vancouver that had been tacked to the wall behind the kitchen table.

She dropped the six-pack beside the fridge and approached a laptop that lay open on the table. She hadn't seen it before. "What's all this?"

"Ah, it's . . ." Connor waved a highlighter around. "A project we're working on."

An app that looked like a GPS map lit up the computer screen.

"This have something to do with Garvin and Joey?"

Connor turned to face her. "What do you know about Garvin and Joey?"

"I know Joey gave you that shiner. I know his organization is threatening your business."

Connor's friendly smile slipped. "I didn't realize Ethan filled you in."

She looked pointedly from the map to the computer. "Clearly, he didn't. What's this project you two are working on?"

She leaned in to study the computer.

"You'd better ask Ethan."

Jane realized what she was looking at and straightened. "You're tracking them. You think you can find where they do their drug deals?"

Connor reached over and closed the laptop. "I really think you should talk to Ethan."

"You're right. I will." Jane turned on her heel, pulled the keys from the Corona bottle, and dropped them back in her pocket. She put the six-pack in Ethan's fridge and rode back to work.

Anna was waiting for her with a scowl. "You're late again. This time, I'm docking your pay. And you can consider yourself on notice."

The threat barely registered. Jane was more concerned about what Ethan was getting himself into.

After work, Jane parked on the street outside the Law Courts building. She sat astride her Rebel, contemplating which curve balls Monica would throw at her today.

The receptionist walked Jane down to the Crown counsel's office. Monica remained behind her desk and, with a sweep of her hand, invited

Jane to sit in one of the chairs opposite. Jane glanced at the "more comfortable" small table in the corner. She was coming to believe that sharks weren't beady-eyed fish but blue-eyed, soft-spoken women.

"Let's continue where we left off, shall we?" Monica said, straightening the loose papers in front of her. She offered Jane her warm aunty smile. The one that said *trust me*. Jane took the designated seat.

"The police report indicates that you asked your landlord's permission to install a steel door with double locks. Why?"

Jane frowned, wondering where this line of questioning was going. "A precaution. Sadie and I have lived in some sketchy places."

"Can you expand?"

"We grew up in group homes. They could be rough. We lived in a few Downtown Eastside rooming houses." But Monica's question felt a little too much like blaming the victim. "Why is this important?"

"It might not be. But defence has the information about the unusual door. I'd like to be prepared in the event they try to make something of it."

"Like what?"

Monica's smile slipped. "I wouldn't know. But defence will do what they can with it."

She looked back to her notes. "Your boyfriend, Ethan, said you'd mentioned the name of the kennel, Highland Breeders. You'd named it days before you were abducted. How did you come to know the name of Rick's family's kennel?"

Jane felt the blood drain from her face. Ethan hadn't mentioned that he'd included that in his statement. *Shit!*

"As difficult as it is, Jane, you must be truthful."

She sucked in a breath, considering her answer. "It came to me in a dream. Just the name. It had nothing to do with his family's kennel. Ethan and I were talking about the future, what he'd do for work when he lived on his acreage. The dream was fresh in my mind at the time. I suggested he open a dog kennel."

"You dreamed it? That's quite a coincidence." Monica set her pen down and steepled her fingers. "Did you know, or had you met, Rick before you were kidnapped?"

Jane frowned. "Still no. You asked me that question before."

Monica nodded, thinking. "This case is missing a critical element. Of all the people Rick could have chosen to kill his brother, why choose you? You're an unlikely candidate for that job."

"Why does it matter? I mean, with all the evidence against him?"

"Evidence can only take us so far. Rick could say Andrew kidnapped you. That he had nothing to do with it, that he wasn't even aware you were on the property. His fingerprints at the scene are readily explained by the fact that it's his family's home."

Jane sat back in her chair. "You're telling me he could get away with this?"

"I'm telling you our case will be stronger if we can connect him to you, provide a motive for why he targeted you specifically. I'll ask you again. Did you know Roderick or his alter ego, in any capacity, prior to the kidnapping?"

"No!" Jane leapt out of her chair and stalked to the window, fisting her hands at her sides. The bastard was going to walk. She couldn't let that happen.

Monica spoke from her seat behind the desk. "I've been doing this a long time, Jane. I sit opposite tough girls like you every day of the week. You're hiding something from me, and you can't do that. Not if we're going to successfully prosecute this case. What aren't you telling me, Jane?"

Jane stared out the window, contemplating what she could tell Monica that would satisfy her radar and keep Jane on the sane side of her scales. A reliable witness.

She chose her words carefully. "Rick knew my mother. Treated her. There must be records of that somewhere."

"How do you know he treated your mother?"

Jane turned around. "He told me. Said I had her hair. Told me my mother was . . . unstable."

"Unstable how?"

"Suicidal, if you believe the death certificate."

"You've seen her death certificate?"

Jane was walking a tightrope. One wrong step and she'd kill any hope she had of making Rick pay for what he'd done to her. To her parents. If Jane let on that Hunter had dug up that information, it would point to the lie that Jane didn't know her mother's name before she'd been kidnapped. "No. I haven't seen it. Rick told me about it."

"And you don't believe her cause of death was suicide?"

"No. When I was locked in Rick's kennel, he said her wrists were slit to make it look like a suicide. Said it was for the best. He killed her."

"Why would he do that?"

Jane uncrossed her arms and put her hands in her pockets. She'd gone as far as she could. It was impossible to explain her mother's visions, or how Jane knew about them, without revealing her dreams. She looked to the floor. "I don't know."

Monica was quiet again, fitting puzzle pieces together. "I'm still trying to understand why he targeted you. Because you were the daughter of one of his patients?" She looked down to her notes. "Rebecca Morrow. Which brings me back to why. Did he think you held some proof that he killed your mother?"

Monica was uncomfortably close to the truth. She looked at Jane expectantly. Jane returned to her seat, but she had no answers for her.

"You were abandoned at birth with no record of your biological parents. How did Rick know you were Rebecca's daughter?" Monica picked up her pen.

"I asked him the same question. He said a kindly old woman told him. Her name was Maria Yupanqui. She worked at the hospital where my mother died. He called her a meddlesome nobody." Rick hadn't given Jane Maria's name, and he could deny it all day long, but it was a fact that Monica could confirm through employment records.

Back home, Jane walked straight past her apartment and knocked on Sadie's door, desperate for a sounding board, but there was no answer. She returned to her own apartment and flopped on the sofa.

When she'd left the law courts, she'd felt skewered. Monica knew something was off. Not that Monica would ever put together the truth of Jane's dreams—the woman was sane, after all—but Jane couldn't have Monica questioning her integrity. Not when Monica was the one responsible for negotiating plea deals. Jane withered at the thought that Monica might choose a plea deal over her as an untrustworthy complainant.

And why hadn't Ethan told her he'd mentioned Highland Breeders in his police statement? Sure, they weren't supposed to talk to anyone about the case, and they'd tried, but the subject loomed like a bad smell. It was hard to ignore.

She opened her laptop. Connor had likely told Ethan about her visit to his apartment hours ago. He should have called by now. The keys she'd had cut lay on the trunk beside her laptop, a shiny reminder that her trust in Ethan had taken a hit.

After supper, Jane got tired of waiting and called him. He was with Connor, who was driving.

"Can you talk?"

"Sure. What's up?"

Jane told him about her meeting with Monica. "Why didn't you tell me?"

"I don't even remember saying it. How'd you explain it to her?"

"I told her I'd dreamed about it. It's the truth."

He didn't respond right away.

"It's done," he said. "Don't overthink it."

Easy for him to say, Jane thought, having spent the past hour overthinking it. "Did Connor tell you I came by? I saw the map. Who are you following?"

"We're not following anyone," Ethan said. "Just retracing their route, looking at the places where they stopped for any length of time."

"You put a tracker on their truck?"

"It's safer than trying to tail them."

"I have a better idea. Hire Hunter to do this for you."

"We're handling it. Just a couple more days and we'll have what we need."

"I don't dream about nice people, Ethan. I dream about degenerates who do horrific things. Please be careful."

Jane felt out of sorts the next morning. It was a day off work, but Ethan was tied up with Connor and their project. A project Jane feared bordered on a suicide mission.

Her thoughts turned to Huan. She had an idea and phoned her former social worker, Nelson Leonard. She and Sadie hadn't worked with him since they'd aged out of the system, but Nelson occasionally dropped by to check in and see how they were making out.

After the *haven't seen you in ages* pleasantries, Jane asked if his office was aware of Huan.

"Even if we had a file on him, I couldn't talk with you about it. Confidentiality and all."

"I know. But if you don't have a file, put him on your radar. He's living with some nasty characters, and his mom's not doing so well."

Jane jumped on her bike, made a pit stop at a convenience store, and headed for Huan's place. She set the kickstand and waited around for a while, but she drew a few too many curious stares from folks out enjoying the sunshine. She hopped back on her bike and cruised the streets on the off chance she'd run across him. On her final loop before heading home, she rode by the schoolyard, where a motley bunch of kids were playing basketball. Huan was one of the crew. She parked by the curb, removed her helmet, and approached the fence.

Some smartass, who couldn't have been more than twelve, wolf-whistled at her. The kids on the court glanced over. Huan saw her but looked back to his buddies before deciding whether it was cool that he acknowledge her. She must have passed the test. He waved his friends off and strolled over to the fence.

"What do you want?"

"Louie treating you okay?"

"What the fuck, lady? You stalking me?"

"Your mom? She didn't look so good last time I saw her. There's help out there if she wants it."

"Did it look like she wanted help?" He kicked at a clump of grass. "What are you doing here?"

"Just wanted to check in." She reached inside her jacket and pulled out the Spiderman comic she'd picked up. "Got you this."

Though he looked skeptical, he took it from her. "I gotta get back," he said, and turned away, rolling up the comic book and tucking it in his waistband as he jogged back to his buddies.

That night, Jane chucked the new keys she'd had cut into the drawer of the bedside table and checked her phone one last time. Ethan hadn't texted. Her feelings about him were all over the place. She wanted to be *all in*, but a black cloud hovered. Though she appreciated that his intent was to shield her, his protection felt like a straitjacket. He held her at arm's length, not trusting that she could help. She was on the outside, looking in. Excluded, devalued. It was something she and Sadie had struggled with their entire lives. It hurt.

At the same time, she cared about him. He was constantly in her thoughts. Thoughts that made her glow and her insides quiver. It's why she felt anxious about him tracking Joey and Garvin. They were dangerous, unpredictable. Sure, Ethan could take care of himself. He'd misspent his youth in an old-time boxing gym downtown, being mentored by crusty old coaches and cornermen and sparring with wannabe UFC fighters. He'd been steeped in the underbelly of the night club trade. She didn't need to worry about him, yet here she was, worrying.

Did loving someone obliterate the common-sense gene?

Irritated with herself, and peeved about wearing boots in bed, she grabbed hold of the blanket and rolled over. *Dream, damn it, and get this over with.*

Visiting Dream

Jane wakes in a body shop. The smell of chemicals is overwhelming. At one side, a paint booth is lit from inside and a man in overalls and a gas mask is moving to the hiss of a compressor. Vehicles in various states of repair occupy every available bay. Other than gas-mask man, the place is deserted.

She's dressed. She plucks her knife out of her boot and grips it in a translucent hand. Voices draw her attention to a distant office. She tiptoes her way across the debris-strewn floor, lit only by the light coming from the office and the paint booth.

"I saw you, Joey."

"Then you'd better get your eyesight checked."

"I know a cop when I see one. And I know what chummy looks like. What the fuck were you doing? You think it's just your life you're screwing with?"

Jane slinks up to the window and peers inside. Garvin's back is to the door, effectively barring Joey from leaving.

Joey steps aggressively into Garvin's personal space, his face contorted. Jane backs up, fully expecting furniture to explode through the glass.

"Next time you go sneaking around spying on your partner, pay attention. The cop you saw me with? Not a fucking cop. How could you not recognize the weasel from the parkade?"

Garvin's shoulders lift. Jane senses he's puffing out his considerable chest. "My vision's twenty-twenty."

Joey's hands go to his hips. He steps back and hangs his head. *Is he laughing?* He pulls out his phone and swipes at the screen. "Who's this, asshole?"

Garvin's head bends to the small screen. "The weasel. But he's not who you were chumming up."

Joey ignores him and swipes some more. A neon sign on the wall crackles. The sign reads *Tates*. Joey shoves the phone into Garvin's face again. "And this guy?"

Garvin makes a move to take the phone, but Joey pulls it back.

"What's wrong, big guy? You recognize him now?" He shoves his phone in his pocket. "Get a pair of fucking glasses."

Garvin's shoulders slump.

Jane has a flash of memory. She looks to the mark on her left hand, pleased to remember what it can do. She could end this, but has she seen everything she's supposed to? What is she supposed to take away from the dream?

"Why do you have all those pics of the weasel anyway? You got a thing for him?"

Joey's expression hardens. "Don't ever disrespect me." He turns his back on Garvin and reaches for a zippered pouch on the desk. "Knowing what the men you work with do in their spare time is a good habit. Turns out Weasel also works security for a bank downtown."

"That his bank gear?"

"Guess they like their guards dressed in spiffy uniforms."

Garvin grunts. He's relaxed again, his arms loose at his sides.

Joey has the zippered pouch in his hands. He's facing Garvin and his eyebrows are raised, expectant.

"What?"

"An apology is customary after a colossal fuck-up. You know, like accusing your partner of squealing to the cops."

Garvin's pumpkin smile returns. "Sorry, man."

Joey reaches for the door handle. "Let's go."

Jane flattens herself against the wall, slipping back into the shadows as the two men step out.

"When you gonna teach that asshole at Riptide a lesson?"

"Connor?" Joey asks.

"Nah, the punk. Ethan. Guy like that? You can't let his disrespect go unchallenged."

Jane woke feeling rooted to the bed. She was still gripping her knife. She swung her feet to the floor. *Ethan disrespected Joey? What the hell had he done?* Thank god she hadn't spun the dial and exited the dream prematurely. She would have missed the warning.

She undressed, washed her face, and crawled back into bed, safe in the knowledge that she wouldn't have a second visiting dream.

Her thoughts turned to Ethan. He'd still be sleeping, not that her news flash was urgent—the discussion she'd just overheard had happened weeks ago. It could wait.

26 | Sadie

All work and no play, thought Sadie as she leaned back in her chair. She'd powered through the section's lesson in record time and needed a break before she tackled the knowledge test at the end. It would either allow her to move on or stall her for another week.

Thankfully, it was one of Jane's days off. She grabbed her phone, and twenty minutes later, they met up in the hallway and headed out for a run.

Along the way, Jane told her about her latest dream. More of Joey centre stage. And the more Sadie heard his name, the more her curiosity grew. Who was this guy?

They reached the park and started a lap around the track.

"I had keys cut for Ethan," Jane said.

Jane should have been excited about that, but she wasn't. "How'd Ethan react?"

"I haven't given them to him. Something feels off between us." Jane explained about Ethan and Connor tracking the gangbangers who'd made themselves at home at Riptide.

"I had to hear it from Connor. What's that say about Ethan and me?"

"He told you when you asked."

"Only after I phoned him. Makes me question what else he doesn't tell me."

"Do you tell him everything?"

Jane didn't answer.

"Don't be so hard on the guy. He's just following the machismo handbook. Probably has a copy in his sock drawer. 'Gotta protect the little lady, you know,'" Sadie said in her best machoman imitation. It came out sounding more like Groucho Marx.

Jane laughed. "He's not like that."

In Sadie's experience, most men had a little of that going on, like a hangover from their caveman days, and Ethan was no exception. "What's the latest from Ariane?"

"She's full of doom and gloom, warning me about trying to fix things in my dreams. But there's nothing new with the diaries. I'll text her later."

They sparred, and on the run back home, Sadie told Jane about her interviews with Katerina and the team from the accounting department. "I know they checked up on my story. Have you had any blowback?"

"None. And I wouldn't care anyway. You'll always be more important to me than anyone's judgment about our past. When will you know if you got the position?"

"I still have to get a few references together."

They took a detour to Starbucks. Jane said she wanted a chai latte, but Sadie knew it was an excuse to treat Sadie to a cappuccino.

But Sadie beat her to it, whipping out a twenty-dollar bill. "I've got this."

Strolling home with drinks in hand, Sadie told her about Georgina Stafford and the rings she'd found. "You look more relieved than me," Sadie said, laughing at Jane's expression. The fact that Jane shared Sadie's relief felt like a warm hug from the best friend in the world.

When they were in sight of the apartment, Jane grabbed Sadie's sleeve. "Turn around."

They did an about-face.

"Who was that?" Sadie asked.

"His name's Garvin. What the hell is he doing, talking to Mrs. Carper?"

"Who's Garvin?"

"Gangbanger number one. Joey's partner."

"The guys terrorizing Connor?"

"Damn it!"

They turned the corner and watched the black truck from the safety of a cedar hedge. But instead of returning to his truck, Garvin crossed the lawn and approached the building next to theirs. Moments later, he hit the next building over.

"He doesn't know where I live."

"But someone's told him which neighbourhood."

When Garvin finally returned to his truck and drove away, they jogged back to the apartment. Jane buzzed Mrs. Carper, who came to the door.

"That big guy who was just here? What did he want?"

"Probably what you're thinking. But don't worry. I don't know anyone named Jane living here, even if he did describe you to a T." She looked Jane up and down and then peeked out to the street and looked both ways. "Are you in trouble again?"

"That man's dangerous," Jane said. "If he comes by again, don't open the door to him. And if he gets pushy, call 911. Okay?"

Mrs. Carper looked none too pleased, but she nodded. They headed to the side door entrance to their basement units. Sadie followed Jane into her apartment, where Jane filled her in on the goons' latest tactics at Riptide.

"This isn't a swing at Ethan," Sadie said, "but he shouldn't be handling this himself. Connor may be fine to help with the paperwork, but he's a party boy, not a hard body."

"Ethan's going to go ballistic when he hears."

"Well, he needs to hear it. He's put you in that gang's crosshairs."

"Maybe it was inevitable. Garvin and his gang are in my dreams."

"There's no way that goon gets from your dreams to your front door without someone else's involvement. Narc, you know I'm the last person who'd say going to the cops is a good idea, but it's time for Connor to cut his losses. And if Connor won't go to the cops, then Ethan better bloody well do it."

27 | Ethan

Connor pulled into a fifteen-minute delivery zone on Water Street. Ethan double-checked the map on his phone and glanced across the street. This was their second morning retracing the truck's course from the tracker data. Garvin and Joey hadn't taken the same route as the previous day, so they had a handful of new addresses to pinpoint.

"Has to be the pub," Ethan said. The most difficult part of the process was determining which operations the organization was doing business with and which ones they'd just happened to park in front of.

"Or that cafe," Connor said.

Ethan looked to where Connor pointed and noticed a familiar face sitting behind the wheel of a Subaru. "Look who's here."

"You know him?"

"It's the reporter. Wilde. I thought you called him."

"I spoke to him. Never met him."

"Wonder what brought him here? How much has he already pieced together?"

"It'd better not be enough to take public before I can make a deal with the police."

Connor drove back to Ethan's place, where they transferred to the map the info they'd gleaned from their morning run.

"Do you think any of these are drug buys?" Connor asked, reviewing the addresses.

"Won't know until we have a pattern. Their most frequent activity will probably be dropping off cash to clean. I expect the buys will happen less often."

Ethan's phone buzzed. It was Jane. Earlier that morning, he'd agreed to meet her at the Tim Hortons on Fourth Street in the West End. She'd had another dream, but now she wanted him there right away. "Sounds urgent."

"You go ahead," Connor said. "I'll mark the rest of these and lock up."

Jane waved from her window seat at the front counter. She came outside and handed him a coffee. "Let's walk."

"What's the rush. I thought you wanted to grab a bite?"

"Later. First, we need to talk."

He didn't much like the sound of that. She hooked her arm in his and guided them around the corner onto a quiet residential side street.

"What is it?"

"Garvin is looking for me. He knocked on Mrs. Carper's door today."

Ethan stopped short and pulled Jane around. "What the—? She didn't—"

"No. She didn't tell him anything. He doesn't know my address, but he knew what I looked like, knew the neighbourhood where I lived. Did something happen I don't know about?"

"Not a thing. Well, Joey asked Fanny about you, but that was ages ago."

Jane stepped back. "What? You should have told me."

"There was no need. Fanny knows squat. She didn't tell him anything, and she told me right away."

"Did you not think that if he'd asked Fanny, he'd probably asked everyone? Maybe someone overheard you and me talking, and learned I lived in Kits."

Ethan looked to his feet. Kicked a stone to the road. "Sorry. I'm an ass." He reached for Jane's hand. "I thought Joey was taking an interest, that he wanted to ask you out."

His apology didn't soften her expression. And why should it? Garvin was serious business.

"You need to wrap up whatever you and Connor are doing and hand it over to the cops."

"We need more time. A few more days. Come stay with me. You'll be safe there."

"They know where you live. You're an employee, remember?"

"Then stay at the trailer."

"It's a tin can. I'd rather be at my place. Even if Garvin does eventually find out where I live, he can't break down that door."

Ethan straightened. "Wait!" He dropped her hand and pulled out his phone. "There's a feature in the tracker program. It sends a signal if the tracker enters a specified area." He found the feature and showed her. "We can program in your address. It'll warn us if he gets close." He swiped to the map where the tracker had marked the truck's route from earlier. But something didn't add up. Ethan paused. "When did Garvin show up at your place?"

"This morning. Just before I called you."

"Did you see what he was driving?"

"The black truck."

"Damn it." The truck they were tracking hadn't gone near Jane's place. "They have two trucks." He stuffed the phone back in his pocket.

"Or one of them has the tracker in his pocket."

Ethan bent to her. "It's the first thing we check when we see the truck in the video feed. The tracker is exactly where I put it."

Jane turned away, took a couple of steps, and jammed her hands in her pockets. When she turned back around, he saw the determination beneath her calm demeanour. "Joey and Garvin are in my dreams. That's not a trivial thing. Their bosses are in my dreams. Also not trivial. And now Garvin's at my door. You and Connor are messing in their business. Maybe it'll get them out of Riptide, but what if it doesn't? What if it gets you killed? Gets me killed?"

"We're being careful, Jane. We have a few more days before they realize Connor's cheque's not in the mail. We find this second truck, get a tracker on it, and we'll have what we need in days. It'll be over."

"You need help. If it can't be me, then call Hunter or call the cops."

"I promise—it won't be long now."

"That's good, because you don't have long. I had another dream. The next time Joey takes a swing, it's going to be at you." Jane recounted the body shop dream. "What did you do to piss him off?"

Ethan frowned, thoughtful. "Don't know. But if Joey wants to take a swing, I'll be ready for him."

"Careful, Ethan. You might just trip over your bravado and land on your ass."

The next day, Ethan was back behind the bar. Connor had picked up the second tracker and was retracing the truck's route, looking for a twin vehicle. The cube van hadn't been towed, but it had started collecting tickets.

A man in painter's coveralls came through the front doors and paused, letting his eyes adjust to the dim light. He found Ethan watching him and approached the bar.

"I'm with ProBuilt. Here to repair the wall out back. You're gonna need to call the city and get that van towed."

Ethan continued pulling beers. He set a second glass on the service bar. "ProBuilt? Didn't know the owner signed off on that."

"He did. You going to make that call?"

Ethan grabbed a third glass. "What's on the work order?"

Coverall man screwed up his face. "None of your fucking business. Where's your boss?"

Ethan positioned the glass and pulled the tap. "I am the boss. We've got customers. You just painting, or are you going to be making noise?"

Coverall man squinted, gauging Ethan. "Just painting. Won't be disturbing anyone."

"We called the city yesterday. They got the van on their list." Ethan set the full glass down with the others. "Said they'd get to it by the weekend."

"Five days? Jesus, this city's falling to shit." He pulled out his phone and dialled as he walked away.

Ethan looked to the security monitor under the bar. ProBuilt's work van was parked on the street. Coverall man still had his phone to his ear when he came into the frame. He walked past his own van and out of view, reappearing again by the cube van. He plucked a ticket from beneath the windshield wiper and snapped a photo of it.

If coverall man had connections, he could get the van towed within the hour. Time was slipping through their fingers.

28 | Jane

"Not that I don't appreciate the free lunch," Hunter said, "but what's up? You find that kid?"

After Ethan's fruitless night of searching for the second truck, Jane had organized for Hunter to meet them at her favourite falafel place on Burrard Street. Ethan rushed in, spotted them, and trotted over.

He shook Hunter's hand and took a seat. "Sorry I'm late."

"Hunter just asked me if I'd found Huan." She turned to Hunter. "I did. Talked to him. He's good. I've asked Nelson—you remember my social worker?" Hunter nodded. Last year, when they were searching for her birth parents, she'd sent Hunter the case file Nelson had put together on her. "Nelson said he'd keep an eye on him."

"Glad to hear it," Hunter said. "So why the lunch?"

"The dreams aren't about Huan," Jane said. "He was leading me somewhere else. Last time we talked, I told you about the drug dealers who were dealing in Davie Village."

"From your dreams?"

"Yeah, but the dreams have spilled over. I've met the dealers. Garvin and Joey. They're blackmailing one of Riptide's owners and threatening the other."

Ethan filled Hunter in on the extortion and money laundering.

"Connor's got some decisions to make, and fast," Hunter said, turning to Jane. "Are you dreaming about the extortion, the laundering?"

"Not specifically. I see the players, and where they're operating. I have a sense of who the top guy is. I'd recognize him."

"I've got a tracker on one of the dealers' trucks," Ethan said. "But we just learned they're using a second identical truck that we haven't found yet."

"And Garvin's been knocking on doors in my neighbourhood, looking for me."

Hunter rubbed his stubble. "Garvin looking for you is a problem.

Your only value to him, that I can see, is leverage to pressure Ethan. Feels like a long shot. Waste of his time. Unless we're missing something." He turned to Ethan. "What have you got so far?"

"A string of businesses that are probably laundering for them. A crooked insurance adjustor. Two companies that issue fraudulent invoices to pull in the cleaned dough. Names and addresses. No photos. Not enough to get Connor a free pass or to get his partner off the hook."

"Forget about the partner. He's punched his own ticket. And I don't need to tell you how much of a risk Connor took not going to the cops right away. This plan of yours might earn him some goodwill, but he's just as apt to pull you down with him. Can you trust him?"

Ethan started to protest, but Hunter stopped him. "Think about it. Everything you know about what's going down at Riptide you heard from him."

"Connor's telling the truth," Jane said. "I dreamed about the day Norm introduced Joey and Garvin to him. Connor was surprised. Pissed off, even. Norm looked nervous as hell. Kept glancing at the clock like he couldn't wait to get out of there. Gave Connor a bullshit story about having an ulcer, being stressed out, that Joey and Garvin would keep an eye on his interests, help out."

"When did you have that dream? You didn't tell me," Ethan said.

She frowned, thinking back. "Sure, I did. A few days ago. The mark on my hand?"

Ethan nodded, remembering. "You left a few things out."

Jane quirked a shoulder. "The rest was old news. I don't even know why I had the dream. But the dreams are still coming, so whatever I'm supposed to witness isn't over."

Hunter continued to rub his chin. "What's your gut telling you?"

Jane touched a balled-up fist to her lips, considering the direction the dreams were taking her. "That I should pay attention to the boss. He's driving the train, giving the orders. What do you think?"

Hunter pursed his lips, straightening a napkin. "Joey and Garvin are expendable, easily replaced. I agree with your gut. Aim higher. Try to pin something big on the guy at the top, and make sure he doesn't see you doing it."

"I don't know who the boss is, but his second-in-command is a guy name Dal," Jane said.

"He's also the crooked insurance adjustor," Ethan said. "His name's Dalton Reddy."

"All right," Hunter said. "Connor doesn't have much time. And neither does Jane. I can help you find the second truck and look into Mr. Reddy, but you have to understand that you may not get the intel you want before these guys force your hand. When that happens, you go to the cops with what you have and pray it's enough. Agreed?"

Ethan inhaled a deep breath and let it out in a rush of reluctant acceptance. "Agreed."

"You should know, even if you get these players out, gangs are like Hydras. Cut off one head and two grow back. You can hope the cops' investigation dumps enough poison into Riptide's well to deter the next gang, but don't count on it. Show me the photo of the truck."

Jane pulled the photo up on her phone and handed it to Hunter. He enlarged the licence plate. "They probably bought the units from the same dealer, same day. I'll find the second plate. Get an address. Email that to me, would you?"

Jane returned to Positively Plants preoccupied with Hunter's warnings. He hadn't spelled out what *forcing their hand* included, but Jane knew Garvin finding her was at the top of the list. The thought made her shiver. Even if Ethan found the second truck, they had to step up their surveillance, get the photos they needed to go to the cops. She knew she could help, but Ethan wasn't asking.

Jane was on her way to her locker when Anna called out to her from inside the office. Jane backtracked and poked her head in the door.

"Come in. Sit down," Anna said. She had her elbows on the desk.

Crap. Was she late again? She hadn't checked the time. Jane lowered herself to the chair.

"This can't go on." Anna picked up a pen and held it in both hands, turning it in her fingers. "Ever since your ordeal last fall, you've been taking advantage. I know it was terrible, what happened to you, but I've given you plenty of time, ample warnings."

"I know. I'm sorry. There's just a lot going on right now." More than she could possibly know.

"We all have a lot going on, Jane. It's no excuse for disrespecting our time—my time. Fifteen minutes here, twenty minutes there. You take personal calls, you're distracted. It all adds up. We need someone we can depend on."

Jane's face flushed at the insult. She resented Anna's callousness. "You've been depending on me for eight years, Anna. I can count my sick days on one hand. Sure, the last few months have been rough, but give me a break. You know what I went through. Please."

"I've been giving you breaks for six months. Pack up your locker and go home."

Jane's anger flared. She pressed forward. "Are you serious? You're firing me!"

"With cause, but in light of your years with us, we're paying severance. We didn't have to." Anna pushed an envelope across the desk.

"I arrive early almost every day. I've more than made up any time I've taken." Jane had worked there since high school. She bit back the angry words that threatened.

"I've also included your accumulated vacation time. I wish you nothing but the best, Jane." Anna's smile was insincere at best. "Perhaps a new job is just what you need. A fresh start somewhere else."

Jane slouched back in the chair. She felt a disconnect, as if she'd stepped into an alternate universe. She stared at Anna, considering her words, her forced smile. Anna, who used to be a friend, was firing her. From the job she loved—no—the job she used to love. She dropped her gaze to the envelope with her name written on it.

"Jane," Anna said, shaking Jane out of her stupor. "Take your cheque, clean out your locker, and go home."

Jane reached for the envelope and stood, numb. She opened her mouth to say something, but no words came out. What was the proper response to being fired? "Thank you"? "Sure thing"?

"Screw you" fit better. She closed her mouth, turned, and stumbled her way to the breakroom, where she dropped to the bench in front of her locker. The reality of her situation rolled over her in waves. The clammy sweat of shock gave way to disbelief. Sadness followed with an ache in her chest, and then an overwhelming sense of loss and emptiness flooded in.

She opened her locker and stared into it. What use did she have for clippers and a pruning knife? A utility belt?

She changed into her bike boots, grabbed her helmet, and slammed the locker closed. At the breakroom's threshold, she paused. She considered saying goodbye to Pieter and Reyna, but she couldn't do it. The sense of loss she'd felt had been replaced with a hot flush of shame and embarrassment. She slinked down the hall and ran to her bike.

Back home, Jane locked herself into her apartment and curled up on the sofa. Memories of the former Anna flooded her mind. She'd been so kind to Jane. Treated her like a daughter. Pieter had worked side by side with her on his school breaks. During their endless summer watering routines, they would sneak up on one another with a playful squirt. And then there was Anna's brother, Lucas. Never once had he treated her like a girl. He had challenged her to get stronger.

Jane's interference the night Pieter was born had ruined everything.

She had worked a third of her life at the nursery. She'd never had any other job. Sure, there were other nurseries she could apply to, but they were way out in the boonies. She'd have to commute. She'd also be back to minimum wage, and money was already tight; how would she pay the rent? She'd be forced to use the inheritance. Take money from kids worse off than her. The thought of stealing from vulnerable kids raised her hackles. She wouldn't do it!

But what other work was she qualified for? She thought of Sadie's career change and the massive commitment she'd made to the accounting program. In hindsight, Jane's "you can do it" encouragement, sounded like platitudes. Even if Jane could swing going back to school, what did she even want to do?

She might have been there, on the sofa, for an hour or three when her phone rang. It was Sadie, and her voice sounded like a lifeline.

29 | Sadie

"What happened?" Sadie said, the moment Jane opened the door. If Jane's request to bring over a bottle of wine hadn't alarmed her, her demeanour would have. If she'd had a dog, it would have just died.

"I got fired."

"You're shitting me."

Jane didn't react, just padded to the kitchen and pulled two wine-glasses from the cupboard.

"Why?" Sadie asked.

"It doesn't matter. It was never going to work, not after I ruined her life. The new Anna never trusted me. Never saw past my upbringing." Jane set the glasses on the old trunk. "That business with Rick last year only confirmed what she'd been thinking. I'm not dependable."

"That's not true."

"I know. But Anna doesn't. I killed that version of Anna." Jane flopped on the sofa beside Sadie. "Pour."

"What are you going to do?" Sadie unscrewed the bottlecap and filled the glasses.

"I don't know." Jane reached for her glass and immediately took a big gulp. "Get another job, I guess."

They tossed suggestions back and forth: waitressing, lawn and yard maintenance, retail. Nothing stuck.

"Maybe you should take some time off. Get a massage. Something'll surface."

"I can't. Bottomed out my savings replacing my wardrobe, remember?"

Sadie pressed her lips together, but the words pushed their way out anyway. "You're not broke, Jane." She held up her hand to hold off Jane's familiar protests. "You've got this absurd notion about how the Walkers' money should be spent, but you don't even know what they wanted. The charity is your idea, not theirs. There's nothing wrong with spending a little of it on yourself."

It was a discussion they'd had a dozen frustrating times.

"It's not absurd." Jane rubbed the rim of her spotless glass. "And I know I can spend it, but I don't have to. I can work. The kids who need the money can't."

"Fine." Sadie raised her glass to Jane and settled back into the sofa. "When you get evicted, my door will be open. It'll be like old times in the rooming house: tight, but without the critters."

Jane's lips quirked into a smile. "We had some laughs back then, didn't we?"

Whenever Jane spent too much time in her head thinking about Anna and Pieter, she stargazed into the past. "Don't get all nostalgic on me. That building was cockroach central, a rat-infested fire trap."

Jane's smile faded. She swallowed another gulp of wine. Either she didn't want to taste the lovely bouquet of a fine screwcap, or she was on a mission to the land of oblivion.

"I saw Hunter today. He agreed to help Ethan." Jane filled her in on the latest with the search for intel to boost Connor's chances of keeping Riptide afloat after the cops charged in.

"Speaking of Ethan, have you given him your keys?"

Jane upended her glass and held it out for a refill. "Not yet. And just because he gave me his keys doesn't mean I have to give him mine. Besides, he's pretty free and loose with his keys. Gives them to anyone."

"You talking about Connor?" Alcohol hadn't dented her stubbornness. "You don't think that's an exceptional situation?"

"He could have told me Connor had a key. Could have told me about the tracker. Could have told me about Joey quizzing Fanny about me. It's like I'm on a need-to-know basis with him."

"So I guess working at Riptide is out of the question?"

Hours later, Jane nodded off on the sofa. She was a lightweight when it came to alcohol. Sadie stared at the empty wine bottle, wondering if Jane had ever downed three glasses in one sitting. Sadie draped a blanket over her and left the aspirin bottle and a glass of water on the trunk, a kindness Jane had done for her dozens of times. She then locked up and headed back to her own apartment.

Visiting Dream

Jane is outdoors, standing amid the solid trunks of mature maple trees on a strip of green space that abuts a parking lot. It's twilight. She looks across the asphalt to the water's edge and beyond, to the orange and red port cranes that stretch out like behemoths amid a constant mechanical hum.

It's cold, and Jane's dressed, but where are her boots? And her knife? Moisture soaks into her socks. Her body is translucent, enough to remain unseen if she doesn't move into the light, or too quickly.

A BMW X model crawls into the lot and parks. Minutes tick by. Another SUV, a Lexus, pulls in beside it. Moments later, Joey and Garvin's shiny black truck arrives, followed by an Acura MDX. Doors open, headlights dim, and men spill from the vehicles.

Jane recognizes the men who exit the back seat of the BMW. One is the man who promoted Garvin and Joey, and the other one is Dal. Two men step out of the Lexus, and another two men exit the Acura. Jane doesn't recognize them. Joey isn't there.

A gust of wind bustles through the bare tree branches, stirring crunchy leaves on the ground.

The man Jane thinks of as the boss heads to a bench not twenty feet away and at a right angle to her hiding place. Jane slinks back farther into the protection of the trees.

Boss man takes a seat, crosses his legs. Dal walks around the bench and stands behind him and to his right, legs spread. Not casual. Garvin stands, facing boss man to his left. His back is to Jane. The other four men complete a nervous semicircle in front of the bench.

Dal speaks to Garvin. "Where's your shadow? He should be here."

"Joey's taking care of business. We had a buy set up that couldn't be delayed."

Boss man nods. He looks at one of the men Jane doesn't know. "Talk."

Immediately, two of the men start arguing. The other two heave heated insults. It sounds to Jane like a territorial squabble. Acura's men are selling in Lexus's neighbourhood. The argument escalates with aggressive posturing and threats.

The boss man gets to his feet, and the arguing ends abruptly. "You call me out of my home for this?" In one smooth motion, he pulls a gun from his pocket and points it at one of the men. Jane hears a loud bang, and the man crumples to the ground before her gasp comes out. Jane whips her hand over her mouth.

Boss man pockets the gun. "Problem solved. Don't call me again for this petty shit." The four—now three—men who'd been arguing stand slack-jawed and pale.

Dal points to the dead man's partner. "Get rid of this," he says, indicating the body. He then looks to Garvin. "Make sure it's cleaned up properly."

Dal and the boss walk to their vehicle and get in. The BMW pulls out quietly, no rush, as if nothing had happened. As soon as the BMW is rolling, the men from the Lexus jog back to their vehicle and punch the gas, their wheels spitting broken asphalt.

Jane's attention returns to Garvin and the other man. They half carry, half drag the body toward the Acura, then wrestle it into the hatch. Garvin and the remaining Acura man speak briefly before Garvin rushes back to his truck. The Acura races out of the parking lot, and Garvin barrels out behind it.

Jane turns her head in the direction of distant sirens. She stares at the back of her hand, unwilling to touch it. It was bad enough witnessing the murder the first time around.

It took Jane a moment to orient herself when she woke. She was on her sofa under a blanket. Her socks were wet, her feet cold. The empty wine bottle on the trunk explained the thumping in her head. She sat up, willing away the nausea. A weak smile bloomed at the sight of the aspirin bottle. Sadie. She'd thank her later. She pulled off her socks, swallowed two tablets, and lay back down. But she was unable to push away the replay loop of the murder.

30 | Ethan

Ethan paced behind the bar like a caged panther. Only three tables had customers, and he'd long finished restocking. Concern for Jane chipped away at his conscience. She'd been unusually quiet after their meeting with Hunter yesterday. He knew she wanted to help, but if she got hurt on his account, it would kill him.

And though he'd held his tongue, he'd been pissed that Hunter had jumped on her go-after-the-head-of-the-snake idea. She didn't need any more encouragement to do exactly that. It was reckless.

Hunter had, however, found the second truck's owner, not that it added anything to the equation. It turned out to be Tates, the body shop from Jane's dream.

Connor was on the road, retracing the truck's run from the previous night. He'd checked out Tates's lot but hadn't spotted the second truck.

It was after 11:00 a.m. when Connor finished his run. Ethan met him at his apartment.

They stood in front of the map. "I'd bet one of them lives here, and the other here," Ethan said, pointing to two spots on the map. "They're the first two and last two stops most days."

"They mobilize around noon. How about tomorrow, after they're on the road, we visit those addresses? Bet we'll find the truck at one of them. I'll call the temp agency to cover the bar."

"Call them now. I can't keep asking Fanny and the other servers to cover me. We need to step this up."

Ethan left Connor at his apartment to make his call, and returned to the bar to wait for the temp. He was setting a Caesar on the serving bar when activity on the security footage caught his eye. The cube van was moving, and not with the help of a tow truck. Ethan jogged to the front door and spotted Connor behind the wheel. He pulled the van onto the street and parked in the delivery zone.

Ethan met Connor on the sidewalk. "What are you doing?"

"I'm done letting them push me around. Enrico's coming in to power wash the wall and paint it. He'll be here shortly." Enrico was a local handyman they hired on occasion.

"Why now? They see you defying them, and the clock runs out. You're screwed." Ethan jammed his hands on his hips, unable to hide his annoyance.

"First off, they're not going to see shit. Joey and Garvin don't show up here until shift change at 6:00 p.m. Enrico will be done the power wash in an hour and put the van back in place. He'll do the same tomorrow when he's done painting.

"Second, your buddy, Hunter, says Norm is already screwed, so this is me covering my own ass. If I get nailed, I have proof that I resisted their coercion and didn't cave in."

Ethan rubbed his forehead. "They'll leak what they have on Norm to the cops. Riptide will be shut down."

"Maybe. But they need Riptide up and running as much as I do. They might send Joey in to tune me up again, but I'll be ready for him next time."

"Yeah?" Ethan swirled a hand around Connor's colourful eye. "How many guys have you gone head-to-head with? Joey does this for a living. Every day."

Connor's bravado was woefully misplaced, but Ethan's argument would have to wait. He stepped back, recognizing the woman walking toward them. "There's the temp. I'll get her set up and meet you at your car."

Twenty minutes later, on his way to Connor's car, Ethan's phone dinged. A text from Jane. She needed to see him ASAP. He hated to put her off, but it couldn't be helped; Connor was waiting. He told her he was headed out with Connor and he'd call her later. Within seconds, she phoned.

"This is important. I had another dream."

"What happened?" Ethan said, ducking into the alley.

"I witnessed a guy get killed last night. Well, it didn't happen last night, probably last fall or winter. Garvin was there, but he didn't pull the trigger. His boss did."

Even more reason to keep Jane away from Riptide. "You said this happened last fall?"

"Yeah. Leaves were coming off the trees."

"Why don't you come over tonight. Can it wait until then?"

"Where are you going with Connor?"

"To find the second truck. Get a tracker on it."

"Please don't. Go to the cops with what you have."

"It's not enough."

"This guy has killed before, Ethan. He didn't blink. It didn't faze him."

"But it happened ages ago. Take a breath. We're not taking stupid chances. Just driving around. We'll be okay." Ethan heard Jane's frustration in her heavy exhale.

"I'll see you tonight?" he said.

"I hope so."

She hadn't said that with the eyebrow-waggling inuendo he'd hoped, but he was sure she was overreacting. He said his goodbyes and carried on to the car.

Connor drove while Ethan pulled up the tracker app. The truck was already in motion. They headed to the truck's starting point, a townhouse complex in Mount Pleasant. In the back alley, they found the underground parking entrance.

"Any ideas on how we're going to get in there?" Connor said.

"We don't. They'll have cameras," Ethan said. "Maybe he parks on the street." But a tour of the neighbourhood turned up nothing.

They drove to the second address in East Van and encountered the same dilemma: a gated underground garage. They cruised the neighbouring streets, but didn't find the truck.

Thwarted, they moved on to their next goal: getting photographs. Ethan studied the truck's route, anticipating where it would stop next. But their timing was off; they watched as Garvin climbed back in the truck.

The next address they staked out was a dud; the tracker showed the truck going in a different direction. The entire afternoon unfolded like a game of whack-a-mole that ended when the truck pulled in at Riptide after six o'clock.

"I've got to get inside and make an appearance," Connor said. "I'll drop you off around the block."

Along the way, Ethan pulled up the security camera footage. He watched Garvin and Joey exit the truck. Neither paid mind to the cube van, which was back in place.

Connor pulled to the curb outside Ethan's building. "I need those photos. There's got to be a better way to do this."

"I'll look for a pattern tonight," Ethan said. "See if I can determine where they're going to stop tomorrow so we can get ahead of them."

Ethan found Jane in his apartment. She'd been stretched out on his bed, and she sat up when he opened the door. Connor's laptop screensaver was the only light in the room, sending out rainbow colours in lava-lamp waves. He sauntered over to the bed. "Shouldn't you be naked?"

Jane stood. He wrapped his arms around her, but she pulled back too soon. His libido flatlined. She was upset. Ethan flipped on the lights. "How long have you been here?"

"Couple of hours."

"Beer?" Ethan asked, headed to the fridge.

Jane took a seat at the table. "No, thanks." She clicked the computer's spacebar and the security footage from Riptide's cameras came up, flipping across the screen.

He laid his hand over hers. "I'm sorry about your dream, that you saw someone get killed. It must have been horrible."

"It happened near the container port in the east end. I saw the cranes. The thing is, I don't know if this murder is what I was supposed to witness, or if there's more coming. The man who pulled the trigger acted like it was no big deal, as if he were flicking a speck of lint off his Armani."

"You said he'd murdered before."

"I'm sure of it. And I'm more worried he's going to murder again. These guys aren't just dealing drugs and laundering money."

He squeezed her hand and released it. Took a sip of his beer. "It's never just drugs and money. These bastards are comfortable with a gun in their hands. It's why I want you to stay away from Riptide."

"Me? You practically live there."

In the silence that followed, Jane stared at the screen while he studied his beer.

A moment later, Jane pointed to the computer. Her eyes went wide. "Oh my god. That's him! That's the guy who pulled the trigger." Jane lurched out of her chair.

Ethan glanced at the screen.

"He's in Riptide right now!" Jane pointed to the man, transferring her weight from foot to foot like she was standing on a hotplate.

Ethan spun the laptop around. He rewound the footage, zooming in on the man's face, and clicked a screenshot.

Jane crouched by his side and looked up at him, pleading. "You have to stop following them. Go to the cops. What you've got will have to be enough."

"We're almost there, Jane."

She slapped her hands on her thighs and pushed herself up, disappointment leaking out of her pores. "If those men get wind of what you're up to, they will kill you and Connor, too."

31 | Jane

And people called her stubborn? How could Ethan say he understood the danger and then carry on tracking the truck as if he were bulletproof? She knew Connor couldn't help him. Hell, Connor couldn't find the pointy end of a knife. Which meant Ethan was on his own if it came to a confrontation. It was small comfort that he now knew what the murderer looked like.

Jane was too wound up to go home. She rode out to the container port and found the parking lot where the murder had happened. Why she thought she'd find proof of the life lost, she didn't know, but she felt compelled to walk around, search the ground. Finding nothing but soggy leaves and fir cones, she wandered to the spot behind the tree where she'd stood when the boss pulled the trigger.

Her dreams had been progressive, leading her to this spot, this murder. If she couldn't prevent it and couldn't prove it, what was she supposed to do with what she'd witnessed? She heaved her boot into the tree and screamed in frustration. She felt impotent. Useless.

Ethan wasn't going to stop until he had the proof Connor needed. She'd offered to help, but Ethan wouldn't let her. She was so tired of him giving lip service to her competence. She'd taken down a man from inside a fucking cage. She didn't need protecting.

Whether Ethan liked it or not, her dreams had made her a part of this. He may not have given her the addresses she'd asked for, but she knew about the Gastown pub, and she knew about the body shop. Sooner or later, the second truck would show up at one of those places—and it just so happened she had all the time in the world and no place else to be.

She rode to the body shop, pulled to the curb on a residential cross street where she could see the front of the shop, and sat astride her Rebel. Turned out she didn't need all the time in the world. The cold had barely seeped into her gloves when she spotted a black truck pulling into the lot.

She texted Ethan. *Where's the truck?*
Riptide. Why?
Then your second truck just pulled into the body shop.
Her phone rang. Ethan. She engaged the Bluetooth and tucked her phone in her pocket.

"What are you doing?"

"You should get down here before he leaves."

"You're putting yourself in danger."

"I think Joey was driving, but it's hard to tell from this angle."

"Go home. We're on our way."

Jane disconnected, disappointed in Ethan's reaction. Not even a thank you. She looked back to the body shop. Joey was exiting the building. Ethan wouldn't get there in time. Joey looked in her direction and squinted right at her. She wasn't worried; he couldn't see through her visor, and he'd never seen her bike. Unhurried, she rode off, but she didn't leave the neighbourhood. She texted Ethan. *He's on the move.* Then she picked up the truck again a few blocks away and tailed it to a warehouse in East Van.

A *For Sale* sign was affixed to the front of the building. Last season's weed skeletons protruded from cracks in the front sidewalk. The loading dock around the back of the building was tagged with graffiti, as were the stacks of empty pallets that had been kicked over.

She texted Ethan the warehouse location.

On my way.

At least he hadn't lit into her. When she finally saw Ethan's Fat Boy creep up, she didn't stick around. Didn't want to hear him mansplaining why she shouldn't be there.

Back at her apartment, she parked behind the dumpster, cursing Garvin for the necessity, and said a prayer it didn't get knocked over by the garbage truck. She remained vigilant for Garvin as she swung by the front door to collect her mail. Among the letters, she found a surprise: a package from Peru. After she locked herself inside her apartment, she opened the small parcel. On top was a note in Spanish from Rosa Yupanqui, the woman whose family wanted her to locate their offering bowl. A second note, written by a granddaughter, transcribed the message.

My family sends a small token of our appreciation for your efforts. Wear it with our blessings for your protection and long life.

Sweet of them, Jane thought. Inside the box was a leather bracelet embossed with the pattern of her now vanished blood mark, the same pattern that was stamped into the side of the offering bowl. She'd never been much for jewellery, but it was a kind gesture. She left it on the trunk. It was too late to phone Peru. She'd thank them tomorrow.

Ethan dropped by a few hours later. Jane had spent the intervening time stewing in her frustration over his arrogance. He didn't kiss her hello, not that she would welcome it at this point.

"I suppose you're angry with me," she said, slamming the door. Her sarcasm didn't even register with him.

"Thank you for finding the truck, but yes, I'm angry."

She turned away from him and flopped on the sofa. "You have no right to be."

"He could have spotted you. Figured out what we were up to."

"Right back at you—or do you think you have some special ninja skills that I don't?" Jane pulled a pillow into her lap.

Ethan stood by the door with his hands on his hips. "This isn't your fight."

"Are we back here again? You're involved, and I'm dreaming about them, so, yeah, it's my fight."

Ethan sat on the trunk opposite Jane and leaned in. "If they get to you because of your involvement in the shitshow at Riptide, if they rough you up or—god forbid—kill you, how do you think I'm going to feel?"

"Again, right back at you." How could he not see that she faced the same fears?

He shook his head. "I love your loyalty, Jane." He thumped his heart. "But it clouds your judgment."

"What are you talking about?"

"Your loyalty is why you put yourself in harm's way tonight, and to hell with the consequences. When I tell you that Connor and I have it covered, you need to trust that we have it covered."

Jane laughed, not in the fun way, and leaned into his personal space. "You didn't have it covered. I covered it for you."

His nostrils flared. "Yes, you helped, but you blew off the possible consequences. That's what I mean when I say your loyalty clouds your judgment."

Jane threw up her arms. "According to who? You? I took a calculated risk. My judgment is crystal clear."

"Is it?" Ethan stood, knocking the trunk out of place. "It sure as hell wasn't when your loyalty to Sadie nearly got you killed."

Jane jerked her head back at the sting of his words. "Sadie? She has nothing to do with this." A disturbing thought crossed her mind. Was he intentionally driving a wedge between her and Sadie? "Why are you dragging that up again? Sadie and I have moved past it. Why can't you?"

"She's lying to you."

Jane jumped up and crossed her arms. He'd gone too far. "You don't know her like I do. It hasn't been easy for her, but she's changed her life. If she hadn't, I wouldn't have recommended her for an internship at the investment firm."

"You what? Jane!" He stomped to the other side of the trunk, which was now doing double duty as a safety barrier. "They won't hire a prostitute—they can't. And believe me, she's still hooking. What's worse is your friendship puts you in her orbit along with her madam, her enforcers, and all the pimps she's in competition with." The heated words flew out of his mouth like venom, as if stamping Sadie with the prostitute label was the anointed truth that proved the theory.

"What the hell, Ethan?" He *was* trying to divide her and Sadie. That was not going to happen. She wouldn't allow anyone, not Rick, not Cynthia, not even Ethan, to come between them. To judge them. "You're wrong. She's not."

"Your loyalty is preventing you from seeing the truth." Ethan pulled out his phone and swiped like a madman. "Explain this."

He shoved a photo under her nose of Sadie walking across a road. With Cynthia.

"So what? That proves nothing. There's probably a simple explanation."

Ethan dropped his hands to his hips. "You're unbelievable. She might as well have a sandwich board on her back with a menu and pricing."

His words set Jane's face on fire. How dare he?

Ethan picked up his helmet and stormed out.

Jane threw her water glass at the door.

32 | Sadie

"Ethan and I just had a fucking blowout," Jane said, when Sadie answered her knock.

"You mean the honeymoon phase is over?"

"Won't be any fucking honeymoon, that's for sure."

"That's a lot of fucks. What happened?"

Jane noticed Sadie's kimono. "Did I wake you?"

Sadie arched an eyebrow. It was after midnight. But she was awake now. She opened the door wide in invitation.

"You were right about the machismo thing," Jane said, crossing the threshold. "Ethan's got the handbook. Probably a spare copy, too. Might even teach a course in it."

"What'd you fight about?"

Jane paused at the desk, her attention on the stack of cash that Sadie had yet to put away. She looked at Sadie, her expression a combination of hurt and concern. "What's this?"

"The Hermès bag? Georgina Stafford? Where else would I get—" Sadie faltered as Jane's supposition hit. Jane might as well have slapped her. "Jesus, Jane."

"I'm sorry." Jane shook her head. "I'd forgotten. I have Ethan on the brain. Why are you leaving the money lying around? What if the super comes in and helps himself?"

Jane's attempt to cover her suspicion with a ramble failed to soothe the sting. "Once a hooker, always a hooker?"

"I didn't mean that. I'm sorry. I know you're out of the business."

And yet she hadn't hesitated to jump to the opposite conclusion at the first sign of some cash. Sadie hadn't expected that reaction from her best friend. She let Jane stew in her remorse and walked to the fridge.

Sadie sighed and finally shook it off. "Do you want a glass of wine?"

"The mere thought of it makes me want to gag." Jane sank into the beanbag chair.

Sadie laughed. "Yeah. Been there."

"Thanks for the aspirin," Jane said, looking sheepish.

Sadie poured herself a glass of water and took the chair at the desk. "Back to your fight. How big was it? On a scale."

"Beats me. I'm new at this. He walked out on me."

"Sounds serious. What was it about?"

"Mostly? Ethan's ego. He doesn't want me helping with what's going down at Riptide—doesn't want me anywhere near it." Jane told her about finding the truck and following it to the warehouse. "He's so damned pigheaded."

Sadie reined in an indulgent smirk. "I can't say I blame him for being concerned. Joey and Garvin are caricatures straight out of a Hollywood movie."

"I can hold my own."

"Hey, I'm not the one you need to convince. How'd you two leave things?"

"Unfinished. Not good."

"I'm no relationship expert," Sadie said, "but I'd let things cool off for a few days."

"I hope we have a few days. Last night I dreamed of a murder, and tonight, I saw the guy who pulled the trigger on security cameras inside Riptide." Worry etched a deep line on Jane's forehead.

"Doesn't mean the guy's trigger-happy. Any way to prove he offed someone?"

"No. I rode out to where it happened. Couldn't find a damn thing."

Jane vented her frustrations about the dreams she called pointless, about her unfathomable Witness gig, about Ethan's lack of faith in her. Sadie understood her frustration. Ethan was an alpha type. And so was Jane.

After she left, Sadie crawled back into bed. Her thoughts turned to Mike, who was definitely not an alpha. She pictured the look on his face when she'd told him about being a Teacher's Pet. How many other handsome faces in Sadie's future would sport that look? She thought she'd prepared herself, but it still stung.

Why would she subject herself to more of that judgment and rejection? Maybe a relationship like Jane and Ethan's wasn't in the cards for her.

She wondered if Jane and Ethan would be able to patch things up. Whenever she saw them together, she felt the static in the air. They were crazy about each other. But their argument tonight sounded serious, and Sadie knew Jane. She'd never tolerate someone making her feel less. Not since the day her blood marks vanished. No one would ever put her in a box again.

33 | Ethan

Ethan met Connor at an East Van greasy spoon.

"You look like shit," Connor said, pushing a coffee across the table to him. "Did you get any sleep?"

"Not much." He'd spent most of the night rehashing his argument with Jane. He shook his head. How could she be so blind where Sadie was concerned? "You get my text?"

"Yeah." Connor corralled the last of his hash browns. "Thanks for doing that."

"It's a crap shoot, but those addresses are our best shots. Don't wait more than thirty minutes at any one of them. If Garvin doesn't show in that time, move on to the next."

"Can I buy you breakfast?"

"Nah. I'm good. Heard from Hunter, the PI?" Ethan said. "Dalton Reddy's a freelancer. Has a licence."

"Did he find it in a Pringles can? He must have paid someone off."

"Dalton's not stupid, he's connected." Ethan's coffee was cold. He waved the waitress over, and she poured him a fresh cup.

"How'd it go with Jane?"

Ethan exhaled, stared out the window. "Jane's sense of self-preservation is fucked." He wanted to enlighten Connor about the murder, warn him the stakes had been raised, but there was no way to do that without involving Jane or calling his own sanity into question.

"Give her a break. She helped find the second truck, didn't she? Shame we couldn't get the tracker on it, but at least we know where it's parked."

The previous night, after Ethan had called in Connor to relieve him, Connor trailed the truck back to the underground at the East Van address. Ethan was heading back there this morning to pick up its trail and look for an opportunity to get the tracker on it.

"I've been thinking about that warehouse." Ethan took a sip of coffee. "It's an odd choice. Doesn't fit. Even when it was a functioning warehouse, it would have been used mostly for storage, light assembly. It would never have been a cash-heavy business."

Connor pushed his plate aside. "Maybe they have access to a safe in there, somewhere to hold the bills they're doling out."

"Could be. It's also an ideal location for a drug deal. There's a ramp at the back of the building, and a privacy fence. Could drive a vehicle right inside, roll down the door behind it. No one would be the wiser."

"Let's take a closer look tonight."

"No. I'll go. You need to spend some time at Riptide before Garvin and Joey start wondering what you're up to." Besides which, Connor wasn't a stealth model; having him tag along would only double their chances of getting caught.

Ethan parked at a distance from the East Van apartment building where Joey lived. A light drizzle ramped up into rain territory and beaded on his visor. He ignored it, kept his attention on the grated door. Minutes turned into a half-hour, and then an hour. Had he missed him? Just as Ethan was considering his next course of action, Joey finally emerged from the mouth of the garage. He checked left and right then drove off, unaware of the motorcycle that followed several blocks back.

From Ethan's review of the other truck's routes, he knew which of their regular stops were short visits—in and out in minutes—and at which ones they lingered longer. A bar in Davie Village was one of the longer stops, and Joey was headed in that direction. So when Joey slowed as he approached the block in question, Ethan prepared to jump into action. But Joey lucked into a parking spot out front, in full view of the bar's full-length windows.

Ethan hung back and waited. When Joey got back in his truck, Ethan followed. He got his hopes up again when Joey slowed in front of the Gastown pub, another of their typically longer stops. This time, the parking gods weren't smiling on Joey, who had to pull into a spot half a block away.

Ethan secured his helmet to the bike, and the moment Joey disappeared into the pub, Ethan jogged down the block. In one pocket, he gripped the tracker, and in the other, he held a wipe of rubbing alcohol. Five seconds max to wipe and stick. A quick one-two. He was one step away from leaping into the truck bed when Joey resurfaced.

Ethan swore under his breath and walked past the truck.

"Kinda early for a coffee break, isn't it?" Joey said, recognizing him.

Ethan didn't break his stride. "Stay out of my fucking business." He cursed his bad luck and his knee-jerk reaction. Not only had he not put the tracker in place, but he would lose Joey's truck in the time it took him to circle back to his bike. On top of that, he'd lost his temper and antagonized Joey, which was a stupid move. Now Joey and Garvin would know Ethan wasn't at work, and the last thing he wanted was for them to become curious about why.

Later that night, under cover of darkness, Ethan took his Harley to the warehouse. He parked two streets away and walked back, standing out of sight with a view of the building. The front-facing windows, likely an office, had been soaped, a deterrent to curious passersby. Not a thick enough coating to prevent light from leaking out, though, and there were no lights on inside. The place appeared deserted.

He kept to the shadows to get a closer look at the side of the building, and then the rear. Chain-link fencing and a cedar hedge provided cover, but the back door was locked, and the rolling receiving doors wouldn't budge. He'd need a crowbar to get in, which he didn't have, and he wasn't keen on creating damage—a flashing sign that someone had broken in. He jumped off the loading dock across the ramp next to it and carried on down the one side of the building he couldn't see from the street.

Close to the corner, he stared up at a wall-mounted ladder to the roof. The lower rungs were secured with a plate to prevent unwanted access, but it wasn't enough to stop Ethan. Adrenalin flowing, Ethan pulled himself up using the pegs that attached the ladder to the building, jammed his foot in the peg opposite, righted himself, and repeated the process. It took mere moments to rise above the plate and finish his climb on the upper rungs of the ladder.

On the roof, he located the door into the building. It wasn't locked. He took a deep breath and opened it. It squeaked in protest. Ethan quickly jumped inside and eased the door closed again. He turned on his phone's flashlight and headed in, ending up in a mechanical room equipped with large exhaust fans. He cracked the interior door and peered into the warehouse. He was at the midpoint of a catwalk that ran the length of the building with stairs off either end. One set led down to the rectangular block of an office that ran the length of the front wall behind the whitewashed windows. The other set of stairs led to the warehouse floor at the opposite end of the building, close to the roll-up doors at the ramp and loading dock. Below, the warehouse floor was bare except for a heavy-duty gantry crane near the front, a couple of beat-up forklifts on the side, and stacks of empty shipping pallets at the back. The walls were exposed metal supports.

He crept down the staircase at the office end, sweat dripping down his spine. A door into the office space sat a third of the way along the wall. The door had a window in the upper half that revealed the administrative space beyond was unoccupied. Whatever company had used it last had packed up and moved out. A few boxes remained on the floor, heaped with what appeared to be telephone equipment and keyboards. The desks were cleared off and the shelving units empty. He tested the door; it was locked.

He turned back to the warehouse, which was massive. There was room for two transport trucks nose to tail if they came in via the ramp. It was the perfect place for a drug deal. Private. Secure. Ethan jogged to the roll-up doors and examined the metal supports. He could easily install motion-activated cameras to catch every angle.

They'd finally caught a break.

34 | Jane

Jane had taken Sadie's advice to heart. Ethan needed time to cool off. She did, too, maybe more so than Ethan. Regardless, she checked her phone for a text or a call with annoying frequency. She felt scattered. She had too much time on her hands and nowhere to go.

Sitting at her kitchen table, she scrolled through the online job boards. She knew all the downtown landscapers by name, having loaded their trucks over the years. Maybe it was her foul mood, but none of the prospects appealed to her.

Had Anna already replaced her? Jane had convinced herself that the additional hours she'd put in at Positively Plants had somehow helped Anna. Looking back at it now, she admitted to herself that the extra work was for her own benefit, tokens to soothe her guilt. If Jane had respected Anna's rules, she'd still have a job.

A job she'd grown to hate, she reminded herself, but a job regardless.

She stood and paced yet another circuit around the small apartment. The package from Rosa sat on the trunk, a reminder that she owed Ariane a call.

Jane connected with her on a video chat. Before she got into her latest dream, Jane asked Ariane to pass along her thanks to Rosa. "She sent a thank-you gift for my efforts. Sweet of her, considering I haven't located her bowl."

"I believe that's the first time I've ever heard Rosa described as sweet. She'll be pleased to hear it."

They shared a laugh which ended when Jane explained about the murder she'd witnessed. "Hunter agrees that Joey and Garvin are just soldiers, that it's the men at the top I need to target. But how do I do that?"

"You said that the dreams are progressing, leading you somewhere. Perhaps they're not done telling the story."

"Or they are, and I just don't know it."

"It's difficult, yes. So much we don't know."

"Have Pedro's diaries shaken loose any more words of wisdom?"

"It doesn't appear he's able to control his visions, if that's what you're asking, but he's becoming *descarado*—cheeky, as you might say—making frequent mention of exposing his wraith form to his subjects. He's been using that to pull confessions from the guilty and influence the villagers. Nathaniel thinks the power of his influence has gone to his head, but it's been quite effective in exacting justice."

Envy seeped into Jane's pores. "I doubt that would work these days. If someone saw my ghost form, they'd dismiss it, think they were seeing things. Or ignore it." Jane sighed. "The dreams were so much easier to deal with when I was invisible. But ever since my blood marks turned ghostly, I haven't caught a break." Pedro was a lucky man, living in an era when ghosts were something to be feared. "How much longer until you're finished going through his diaries?"

"A few more days, maybe a week. But don't get your hopes up. The entries in these last few diaries have become repetitive with no new phenomena."

"If you learn anything at all, call me, okay?"

"I will. And please keep Hunter safe. Don't let him be blindsided. Once he gets his teeth into an investigation, he doesn't let go. And this one feels dangerous. Tell him everything."

Ariane's concern for Hunter, a hardened PI with the instincts of a street fighter, rang alarm bells for Jane. Ethan and Connor were dancing around the edges of a violent gang. One wrong step and they'd be taken out.

She felt annoyed all over again that Ethan had pushed her away. She wasn't fragile and didn't need his protection. Ethan may not like it, may not understand it—hell, she didn't understand it herself—but her dreams of Joey and Garvin connected her to whatever was going on at Riptide. She might not be the only one who could stop Joey and Garvin, but she was the only one who might find the answer in a dream.

So she would sleep and hope the next dream provided a way out for all of them. Jane lay on her side, thinking there was no such thing as getting comfortable in bed wearing biker boots.

Visiting Dream

It's dark outside, and Jane is standing on a sidewalk near the emergency entrance of an old hospital. She recognizes the red and beige bricks of

St. Paul's in downtown Vancouver. A man dressed in a grey parka comes out of the swooshing doors with a pail in his hands. As he begins scattering handfuls of rock salt on the sidewalk, Jane feels a chill, and it's not from the bitter wind that blows across the icy asphalt. She's been here before.

Parked on an incline, ambulances occupy two of the four bays. Nearby, cigarette smoke wafts from a huddle of patients. She looks to her hands, noting that she's translucent, visible. She keeps her back to the wall, staying in the shadows. Jane rubs her arms, shivers. She's glad she's wearing boots.

A taxi pulls into one of the vacant ambulance bays. Confirmation. Jane's sense of déjà vu solidifies. Jane's not in a dream—she's in a nightmare. And she mustn't fix it, even if she can.

Jane sees the woman lean forward in the back, and the taxi driver take the bills from her hand. The woman opens the car door. It's Mary, Buddy's mom, and she's pregnant. It's the night Buddy is born. The night Pieter is born. The night Jane changed history and turned Buddy into a monster named Joey.

She watches, helplessly, as a canvas-topped Jeep pulls in behind the taxi, sliding on the ice, narrowly missing a collision. The Jeep stops askew, the front driver's side jutting out behind the taxi. Jane knows without looking that it's Anna in the Jeep, pregnant with Pieter. Her husband is driving.

Jane is rooted in place as the taxi driver emerges, swearing at Anna's husband for the near collision.

Jane glances at Mary, who has made her way out of the taxi and starts across the treacherous ice. Jane has imagined this situation a thousand times, and each of those times, all she has to do to fix her mistake, to heal Pieter and bring the good Buddy back, is stand down and not interfere. Let history unfold as it should have, no matter how difficult it will be to watch.

But Mary stops. She's glancing at her arm, her expression perplexed. Jane looks closer and realizes that the version of herself that helped Mary across the icy path is here, a ghostly sheen, guiding Mary to safety. Jane's heart sinks. History has already been changed.

Jane looks down to the glowing dial on her hand. She can still fix this. If she shows herself, she can stop the earlier Jane. She can prevent ruined lives and an aching lifelong regret.

Bracing for the nausea, she traces the dial backwards. Her vision blurs, her stomach cramps. When she lifts her finger, the taxi is pulling into the empty bay. Ariane's warning surfaces in Jane's mind. Doubt pushes in. Pieter's and Buddy's lives have already been lived, have already impacted countless people. Would interfering again only hurt a different set of people?

The taxi door opens. Mary emerges from the passenger side. Did Buddy have children? A wife? How would Jane's actions affect their families? Who is she to make that call? Jane groans in frustration.

The sporty Jeep slides to its crooked stop. The taxi driver leaps out, shouting. Mary is making her way across the slanted asphalt. Anna's husband races around the Jeep to the passenger side, where Anna is now standing, steadying herself on the passenger door frame.

Jane fists her hands, and tears well. She looks toward the open taxi door, the door Mary left open because the earlier version of Jane has already taken Mary's arm, diverting her.

The taxi is rolling backwards, the driver having left it in reverse when he leapt out to shout at the Jeep's driver. The back end of the Jeep swings around, clipping Anna's husband. He goes down, bowling Anna into the Jeep's door, which folds back against the front fender. Anna skitters on the ice, upright until the taxi's door knocks her over. Tears roll down Jane's cheek as Anna disappears, sucked under the car. It is silent but for the screams from the smokers.

Jane woke, choking back sobs. She felt the weight of being powerless, the pain of watching a tragedy unfold—one she'd caused. One she couldn't prevent and she couldn't fix. Was that the dream's lesson?

She got up and changed into her nightshirt. If the dream was meant to force her to wallow in her guilt, she would do it in comfort. She crawled back into bed and stared at her bedroom ceiling. At least she knew now. She would never be able to repair the damage she'd done.

She also hadn't dreamed of Riptide, so she had no solutions to the problems brewing there, not that Ethan had called. And then she remembered she'd been fired. She added *unemployed* to her list of miserable accomplishments.

35 | Sadie

Sadie closed her computer and stretched. She'd been hard at it since this morning's coffee, and she was starved. Sunlight shone across her table, tempting her outdoors despite the chill. Her body ached to limber up. Maybe Jane would join her for a run since she didn't have to go to work. They could pick up lunch.

But Jane was in Squamish, having taken off on her Rebel in an attempt to outrun her troubles. Jane didn't see it yet, but Anna had done her a favour by firing her. Guilt had been the only thing tying Jane to that job, and seeing Anna and Pieter every day only reinforced the guilt. Jane didn't deserve that, and Anna didn't deserve Jane.

Sadie dressed for a run and pulled a twenty from the stack of bills on the table. She'd grab takeout on the way home.

As she locked up, someone pounded on the outside door. She walked down the hall and looked through the peephole. Big bald guy.

Garvin. Fuck!

She shook out her hands by her sides. It'd been months since she'd had to lay it on thick, deal with a gnarly man, but this was something she was good at.

She whipped open the door and stepped outside. "Can I help you?" She moved a few steps away from him and started into a sexy version of her pre-run stretching routine.

He jammed his foot in the door, keeping it ajar. "I'm looking for Jane." His creepy smile was an afterthought. "I'm told she lives here."

"Jane?" She frowned, thinking. "No. No one by that name here." She grabbed her foot to stretch her quad.

He had an envelope in his hand and shoved it toward her. "That's not what her mail says." The asshole had broken into their mailboxes?

Sadie kept her face schooled in innocence. A Teacher's Pet. She leaned forward to look at the envelope. It was addressed to J. Walker. "Oh, that's James. He's at work. Should be back by tonight, though."

Garvin's horse-like nostrils flared. "This Jane chick? She drives a Honda motorcycle."

"Does she?" Sadie shook her curls and shrugged. "No one in this building has a motorcycle. You sure you have the right address?"

He swung around, flung open the door to the basement, and leapt down the steps. He stopped at Jane's door and rapped on it like it had insulted him. Sadie watched from the top of the steps. When his knock got no response, he continued to Sadie's door and assaulted it.

"Uh, that's my place," Sadie said. "If you're looking for James, I can leave him a message."

The big man spun on his heels and stormed back. Sadie held the door open. He was cursing under his breath when he passed her and continued up the path to a shiny black truck. The truck's door slammed, and the truck squealed off.

Sadie walked around to the front of the building and up the steps. The panel on the front of the mailboxes inside the front door had been jimmied. Mail was scattered all over the floor. Sadie picked it up and sorted it into the proper slots, but the front panel would have to be fixed. The landlord would be pissed.

Sadie went back outside and sat on the top step. She dialled Jane and told her about Garvin's visit.

36 | Ethan

Ethan and Connor had wasted another morning in a frustrating search for the second truck. In the afternoon, they'd gotten lucky with a photo of Garvin entering and then leaving the Gastown pub. But that was all they got. It was hardly a smoking gun.

Jane hadn't texted or called all day, and he'd restarted his phone to make sure it was working. He didn't understand how Jane could get so worked up when all he was trying to do was protect her, to peel off her damn blinders. Sadie was Jane's Achilles' heel. He only wished she could see that. But he was done trying to enlighten her, where Sadie was concerned.

Ethan was woken in the early morning hours by a woman who identified herself as a doctor at St. Paul's hospital. "Connor Boyd was admitted last night. He's out of surgery, and he's asking for you." She wouldn't give him any further details, just told him to get there as fast as he could.

The doctor intercepted Ethan at the ICU nursing station. "Mr. Boyd has been badly beaten. He needs to rest, but he's refused sedatives until he's talked to you." She directed Ethan to keep his visit short. "We've administered morphine, so don't put stock in anything he says."

Ethan entered Connor's room and paused on the threshold. His boss was unrecognizable. Gauze covered much of his face, and what wasn't covered was a bloody, bruised mess. His eyes were swollen shut.

When Ethan's feet caught up to his brain's instructions, he wove a course through the equipment to Connor's bedside and placed a hand on his shoulder. Connor stirred.

"It's Ethan. Who did this?"

Connor's lips parted. He whispered something Ethan didn't catch. He bent his ear to Connor's mouth. "Who?"

Garvin's name came out with a groan.

Ethan straightened. He patted Connor's shoulder. "He'll pay for this. I promise. You rest. I'll be back in a few hours." Ethan's mind was already strategizing how to separate Garvin from the flock, corner him, and let him know what it felt like to slip on his own blood, lie in a pool of it, and choke on it as it trickled down his throat. And the warehouse might be the perfect place to execute that plan.

The moment Ethan emerged from Connor's room, a nurse entered in his place, needle in hand. The doctor was waiting at the nursing station.

"Have the police been by?"

She nodded. "Earlier, but they haven't been able to talk to him."

"He looks pretty bad. What are his injuries?"

"Are you family? His spouse?"

Ethan shook his head. "Will he make it?"

"The next few hours are critical."

Ethan headed back to his apartment. He needed to centre himself, move beyond the anger, and think through his options. Strategize with a clear head.

He wasn't inside more than five minutes before the police called. They were at Riptide and had learned from Trident's security people that Ethan was the one to call. There'd been another break-in. He let himself in through the back but was barred from entering the office. Through the open door he saw that it had been torn apart. Discarded latex gloves and bandage packaging lay on the floor near a puddle of blood. Connor's blood. Ethan hadn't realized the beating had taken place at Riptide. A bloodied baseball bat leaned against the wall like a cocky calling card. The constable guarding the office door directed Ethan through to the bar.

It looked like a cop convention. The front door had been propped open and was being examined by a man in a white disposable suit.

One of the men noticed Ethan arrive and waved him over. "You Ethan Bryce?"

"Yeah, what happened?"

"I need to see some ID." The man identified himself as the investigating officer in charge. He glanced at Ethan's ID then handed it to a colleague who snapped a photo of it. "What did Mr. Boyd have to say?"

The ICU doc must have had the cop on speed-dial. "His speech was garbled. I couldn't understand him. Told him to rest."

The officer nodded, unconvinced. "Do you have access to the CCTV feeds in here?"

"Sure." Ethan pulled out his phone. "But there's no coverage in the office." He scrolled to the app and passed it over. The cop flipped through the feeds like he knew what he was doing. He stopped at one and rewound it.

"Perp came in through the kitchen. Must have hidden in there until after closing. Recognize him?"

Ethan glanced at the clip. Army surplus jacket, balaclava, gloves. It could have been anyone. But the bullish gait was Garvin's. "No." He hadn't been carrying a bat. Ethan recalled Connor saying he'd be prepared next time one of the thugs came looking for him, which meant Garvin had whaled on Connor with his own bat.

"Can you tell us what's missing?"

"Not without looking at the night's receipts. If they weren't deposited, they'll be in the office safe."

While they waited for the safe to be processed, the questions continued. Ethan learned the police had elevated the investigation because of Connor's condition. If he died, this turned into a murder investigation.

"Tell us about Mr. Boyd's partner, Norman Walsh."

"Don't know him. He's a silent partner. An old friend of Connor's from their university days."

"The Trident guys say you've had some trouble of late. A break-in. A fire."

"Yeah. And now this." Ethan bristled that all of it had happened under Trident's overpaid watch. Trident's motto should have been "Look the Other Way."

Ethan could end this now. Tell the cops about the money laundering, the coercion. That Joey and Garvin's organization had their hands in every business owner's pocket in the downtown. But did Ethan have enough information to lay the blame where it belonged? Or would his words turn into a noose around Connor's neck? Who knew how many palms the gang had greased? Without solid proof, Joey, Garvin, and their ilk might slip away unscathed. So he kept his mouth shut.

Ethan took a walk around the building while he'd waited for the police to finish their investigation. Though the cube van was back in place, he could see that Enrico had completed the paint job on the scorched wall. Is that what had triggered the beating?

Ethan didn't get Riptide reopened until late in the afternoon. The temp agency took over staffing the bar, and Ethan stepped into Connor's shoes. Fanny brought in a friend to clean the office and put it back in order.

"A cruiser's parked outside," Fanny said, after depositing her friend in the office.

Ethan was seated at the bar. The cruiser explained why Garvin and Joey had made themselves scarce. "Yeah. They said they were going to increase their presence."

"How is he?" Fanny asked.

"Not great. I'm going to see him again shortly."

"Give him a kiss for me, would ya?"

Connor was awake when Ethan arrived, but his eyes were still swollen shut. Ethan had been limited to a ten-minute visit. "The cops were all over Riptide. They're treating it like a robbery gone wrong. Have they been in to see you?"

Connor inched his head left then right. "Did you tell them?" His words came out in a slur. Ethan realized Connor's jaw had been wired shut.

"About the laundry? No." Earlier in the day, while Ethan waited for the police to clear out of Riptide, he'd decided the best way to help Connor was to follow through with his plan. "I'm going to plant the cameras at the warehouse. That has to be where the drug dealing is happening. As soon as I have the proof, I'll hand it over. Does that sit right with you?"

Another wincing move of his head, up and down this time. "I'm sorry for getting you involved."

"Was the beating because you had the wall repaired?"

"A lesson."

"Well, I've got a lesson for them they won't soon forget."

"Not worth it."

"We're in agreement on that point. They're worthless scum. But they will pay for what they've done to you."

"He asked about Jane."

Ethan paused. "What about her?"

"Where to find her. I didn't tell him."

Ethan strode back to his bike, his fists clenched, his rage barely under wraps. He knew what he had to do, but it would be a test of his patience. And while Ethan's attention was elsewhere, if Garvin or Joey so much as breathed in Jane's direction, they'd feel his wrath in biblical proportions.

First, he had to get the cameras in place. Recording proof of the thugs dealing drugs might not be an immediate fix, but it would wield short-term legal pain with the possibility of a long-term KO.

And the minute those cameras were in position, Ethan would set up an opportunity to bump into Garvin and Joey, in turn, a satisfying one, two. It would be his pleasure to put them both in the ICU, though he'd settle for the morgue.

But he couldn't set up the cameras on his own. He needed a lookout, someone he could trust absolutely, someone who didn't flinch when things got rough. He needed Jane.

Which meant he had to get out of her doghouse, if that was even possible. She was pissed at him to the point of avoiding him—he knew that. Not only for questioning Sadie's integrity, but for keeping Jane out of the fray. Ethan was plenty pissed himself. Protecting the people you love was instinct, a no-brainer. Jane did it all the time for Sadie. Why couldn't she see he was doing the same thing for her? Her position on the subject made no sense, was even hypocritical. He'd never known anyone as headstrong.

He took a breath and put a stop to the downward thought spiral. It wasn't helping. If he couldn't convince Jane to help him, he'd install the cameras without a lookout. He wouldn't expose anyone else. The risk for retaliation by those thugs was too great.

Though he was reluctant to admit it, Jane's damn dreams involved her in the situation with Joey and Garvin whether he liked it or not. And now that Joey and Garvin had her in their sights, she deserved an opportunity to help put the bastards away. Jane might not speak with him, but he would try.

He rode over to Jane's and phoned her from the street. That she answered at all gave him hope, but when she opened the outside door, she barred his entry.

"Can we take this inside?" Ethan asked.

"Your apology?"

"I need your help."

"You need to apologize."

"What for?" Ethan stepped back. "Trying to protect you?"

"Is that what you call it? Because it feels to me like you're protecting yourself."

Ethan glanced at the parting curtains in Mrs. Carper's window. "We've got an audience."

Jane looked up to the bay window and forced a smile. When she returned her gaze to him, it was with a firmly set jaw. "Fine." She opened the door with a heavy sigh and let him in.

In the apartment, Ethan set his helmet on the floor. He approached her like a bomb that might go off and stood toe to toe with her. "I'm not going to apologize for keeping you safe."

"Then you can leave."

Ethan hung his head. He was blowing this. "I *am* sorry I walked out. I know you can hold your own. Full stop. But you shouldn't have to."

She shook her head with a derisive laugh. "I've always had to. Do you understand that I have no choice where my dreams are concerned? That whatever is going down at Riptide is part of something I'm supposed to witness?"

He felt like he was risking his life, but he placed his hands on her shoulders. "I don't want that for you."

"Damn it, Ethan! You think I do?" She lifted her arms, knocking his hands off. Shit. This was not going well.

She stomped to the kitchen. "There is nothing you can do to protect me. Not here, not in my dreams. No one can. I'm on my own. But everything you do where Joey and Garvin are concerned, impacts me. And you're keeping me in the dark about it. That blinds me, which is the opposite of protecting me."

Ethan frowned, weighing the truth of her assertions. "That's not what I'm doing. I'm asking you to stay away from Riptide, to not put yourself in their line of sight."

Jane tilted her head like he'd grown a second one. "Not telling me that Garvin had been looking for me? That you and Connor were tracking them? Not trusting that I'm clever enough to remain out of sight of those two assholes?"

"Come on," Ethan said. "You know me better than that."

"Do I?" Jane walked to the sofa and curled into a ball in the corner.

Her words hurt worse than a gut punch. The thought that they were over, took all the oxygen out of the room. He dropped into the other corner of the sofa. The ensuing silence felt like a standoff.

Jane broke the stillness in a quiet voice. "I could blame the problems you and I are having on poor communication, or lack of understanding, or even my stubbornness." She looked at him with a sad smile. "But the real problem is my dreams. You can't be *all in* if you can't accept my dreams. I'm a package deal, Ethan. This thing between you and me has been fun, but maybe it's run its course."

"I don't believe that. You told me you hated the dreams," Ethan said. "Wanted to be rid of them. If that's true, seems to me the answer is to use the mark and parachute out."

"I do hate them. They're terrifying. But I inherited them. They're a part of me, in my DNA. They're not going to stop."

"You don't know that. You haven't yet tried to make them stop."

Jane didn't answer right away. She picked at the seam of her pants, considering it. "You're asking me to change who I am. To change a fundamental piece of myself."

"What I'm asking is for you to challenge that assumption."

She nodded once, thoughtful again. "And if I do try, and the dreams keep coming? What then?"

"You'd do that?"

"If I thought you and I had a chance, I would."

Ethan scooted closer and took her hand. "We have more than a chance. You and I have something special."

She didn't look convinced.

"Listen, if you try and it doesn't work," he said, "I'll stand by you. Hell, I'll don a fucking supernatural cape."

"And you'll stop with the machismo shit? Because me collapsing into your arms begging for your protection is never going to happen. We protect one another," she said, pointing between them. "A two-way street."

"You won't find me riding a white steed. I'm all for equal footing, but I'm still a man. And men put women first. That's not going to change."

A small smile cracked her lips, a real smile. It was all the encouragement Ethan needed. He leaned over her knees and kissed her. He was somewhat relieved that she kissed him back, but her knees formed an effective barrier. She broke away from their kiss too soon.

"You said you needed my help."

He sat back and took her hand again. "Connor's in the ICU. Garvin beat the crap out of him."

She lurched forward. "ICU? How bad is it?"

"He's still critical. Looks like he stopped a bomb with his face."

Jane pushed the pillow aside, her brow furrowed. "Why would Garvin do that?"

Ethan explained about Connor defying the organization's instructions on how to repair the fire damage. "He'd already had one warning. The black eye Joey gave him? That was for questioning an invoice for a restroom reno that never happened. This was the second warning. There won't be a third."

"How can I help?"

"There are a dozen businesses doing the gang's laundry, all cash-heavy operations. But the warehouse you found the other night doesn't fit that model." He told her how he got inside the building, took a look around. "Even if the organization doesn't own the warehouse, they're using it. I think it's where they do their drug buys. Big ones. It's the perfect setting for it."

"And you plan to what? Catch them buying?"

"Just on camera. I figure four motion-activated units will cover every angle."

"You want me to help install the cameras?"

"No. What I need is someone on the outside. A lookout in case the second truck drops by. I've already scoped out where the cameras need to go. But it'll take five to six minutes per camera, thirty minutes in and out."

"All right. I can do that," Jane said, nodding. "When?"

"Tonight."

Jane frowned. "Didn't you say Garvin and Joey operate at night? Wouldn't it make more sense to visit the warehouse in the morning, when we know for sure they're still in bed?"

Ethan took a breather. In his haste to get the bastards on camera, he'd introduced unnecessary risk. He smiled, feeling some of the pressure lift. "You're right, partner. No need to rush."

He reached for her and she climbed into his lap. She wrapped an arm around his neck and traced his lips with her fingers. "What will we do with all our extra time tonight?" she said. This time, she kissed him, and she was in no hurry to end it. She tugged on his bottom lip with her teeth and proceeded to give him a few tantalizing ideas of how they might spend the time, starting with her tongue.

They made love on the sofa and again in the shower. After they dried off, they spooned in bed. He loved the warmth of her breast in his hand. He stroked her skin, soft as rose petals.

"Are you going to tell me the rest of your plan?"

He stilled his hand.

"I know you, Ethan. You won't let Joey or Garvin get away with what they did to Connor."

He remembered his promise to Connor. A promise he didn't make lightly. "No. You're right. Garvin will pay. And so will Joey. And when

I'm done with them, they won't be fucking up anyone else. Ever." Jane stilled beside him. He was grateful she didn't try to talk him out of it.

He must have fallen asleep, because he was woken briefly as Jane left the bed. "Where you going?"

"I'll just be a minute."

When she returned, she was fully dressed, boots and all. She lay on top of the blankets. "I'll try to get out of my dream. I promise. But I need to be prepared." She pulled an old quilt over herself.

Ethan swallowed his objection to her sleeping attire, kissed her good night, and turned over, hoping this would be the last time she'd come to bed dressed.

37 | Jane

Visiting Dream

Jane wakes in an aisle of bowling shoes. Loaded cubbyholes against one wall, a floor-to-ceiling shoe rack down the centre. The smell of sweat mixed with chemical disinfectant is suffocating. Jane's form is translucent. Through the centre wire rack of shoes, an aisle on the other side of the room is visible, identical to the one she occupies. One end of the long narrow space is enclosed with a wall and a closed door. The other end is open to the bowling lanes. She walks toward the light at the open end. Beyond the light, she hears mechanical noises, bowling balls crashing into pins, boisterous voices. The shoe-rental employee, a teenager, sits on a stool on the shoe-room side of the counter. He's streaming something on his phone.

Jane glances at the back of her hand. Her memory is clear. She'd promised Ethan she'd try to get out of the dream. Her finger is hovering over the mark when a figure appears. He lifts the flip-up end of the counter and joins the teenager. "Ring the bell if anyone comes in."

It's Joey. Jane flattens herself against the rack of shoes.

He walks down the adjacent aisle. Jane follows him on her side, watching his back through the shoe rack, hoping like hell he doesn't round the corner into her side of the room. She hears a door open and close.

"You get it?" Joey says. A second man has entered through the back door.

"Special price. Just for you." The two of them laugh like chums sharing a secret.

Jane can't see what's exchanged. She assumes drugs, maybe a gun, but what does it matter? Tools of the trade.

She feels too visible to be this close to them. She reaches for the mark on her hand, braces for the nausea and slowly traces the circle clockwise.

The nausea hits as the men's voices speed up and their movements become comical, jerky.

A flash catches Jane's eye. She lifts her finger and the room swirls to a stop. Was the flash just a belt buckle? Or something more?

The second man is out the door, and Joey is headed back up the aisle to the front. But something about that flash causes Jane to act. She touches the mark again, pushes through the nausea, and traces the circle counter-clockwise.

The second man says, "Special price. Just for you." They laugh, and this time Jane watches for the flash and hears what she's missed.

"Are we ready?" Joey says.

"As soon as you give the signal, we'll flood the place."

"And the secondaries?"

"Covered. All covered. When's it going down?"

"Sunday night. Eight o'clock."

"Good luck." The men shake hands, and the second man turns for the door. As he does so, Jane sees the badge at his belt. He's a cop.

Jane gasps.

The door closes, and Joey heads back up the aisle.

Jane woke in her bed with Ethan beside her, sound asleep. She unpacked what she'd heard. Joey had said, *Are we ready?* We. Was Joey a cop? Nah, he couldn't be. He'd taken a swing at Connor. If he was a cop, he was probably crooked. But why would Joey be meeting with a cop? Again, she questioned, was Joey a cop? And what was happening on a Sunday night at eight o'clock? Was that this Sunday? Or some other Sunday?

She looked over at Ethan, who was sleeping peacefully, completely relaxed. He had looked so tired earlier. Jane knew Ethan felt sick about Connor, who was more than a boss to him; he was a good friend. For days now, Ethan had been stressed, staying up late to monitor the tracker and getting up early to analyse its route, and then open the bar. No wonder he was exhausted.

Jane slipped out of bed. She had all morning to talk to Ethan about what she'd overheard in her dream. Her thoughts flipped back to Joey. If he was a cop, that changed everything. But no need to wake Ethan in the middle of the night and add to his sleep deprivation.

Knowing she wouldn't have a second dream, she changed out of her clothes and into her nightshirt, smiling at the thought of rolling around in the sheets with Ethan come morning.

She set her stack of folded clothes on the trunk next to Rosa's gift box. Next time she spoke with Ariane, she'd ask her how to thank Rosa in Spanish. Jane opened the box and snapped on the bracelet. It was snug but the leather looked pretty badass. She left it on, a reminder to tell Ethan about it in the morning.

She tiptoed back into the bedroom and slid beneath the covers. Her thoughts drifted to the offering bowl as she slipped off to sleep.

38 | Ethan

Ethan woke in the pre-dawn hours. Jane lay eerily still beside him, the marks on her face glowing as if she'd swallowed a spotlight. At some point in the night, she'd changed into a nightshirt, which confused him. Hadn't she said she needed to be dressed for her dreams? These fucking dreams were absurd. And dangerous. He was glad she'd agreed to try to jump out of them.

He used the bathroom and dressed, thinking she'd snap out of the dream at any minute. When she didn't, he went in search of coffee. He found a bag of grounds in her kitchen cupboard but couldn't find the coffee maker. Couldn't even find a drip filter. He improvised using a paper towel and a strainer. It made a barely passable cup. If he was going to spend any time here, which he hoped was the case, he'd have to get a coffee maker.

Forty minutes later, Jane was still comatose, her marks glowing. He sat beside her. Though she was under the covers, she looked cold. Her skin even felt cold to the touch. He pulled the discarded quilt from the floor, laid it on top of her, and tucked the blankets in around her.

39 | Jane

Visiting Dream

Jane wakes in a darkened room. An office. The air is cold. She's wearing a thin nightshirt and her new bracelet. Why isn't she dressed? Her form is translucent, which she is coming to understand is her new normal.

She takes in her surroundings. Lining one wall are floor-to-ceiling shelves stacked with carefully labelled magazine boxes. A telephone and a large printer, or maybe it's a scanner, sits on a long table opposite the shelving.

She wraps her arms around her torso and pads toward what looks like an exterior door. The floor is ice cold. Through the door's window, she sees a vast expanse of snow twinkling under a bright moon. Off in the distance, a lone streetlamp shines a cone of light onto a plowed bank of snow on the roadside. The landscape is bereft of trees. A large drift has blown in against the door. Jane turns the handle, but the door is locked.

At the opposite end of the room, an emergency flashlight blinks in its cradle to the left of an interior door that has been propped open. When she crosses the threshold, the overhead lights flicker on. Motion activated. The room she has stepped into is a much larger space. Ghostly metal shelving lines the walls and fills the room, creating aisles. There are bigger boxes here, but also unboxed items, loose and in trays. Shells, bones, arrowheads. Woven baskets and bowls. Clay cups and plates. Artifacts. She's in some kind of museum storage room.

She looks at her bracelet. Rosa and her family's offering bowl had been in her thoughts when she'd put it on. That's why she's in a museum; her family's heirloom bowl must be here somewhere. Has she chosen this place? This dream? She's curious now.

A glance at the white mark on her hand reminds her that she's promised Ethan she'd get out of the dream. Or was that another dream? The confusion frustrates her. *Focus!* As soon as she finds the bowl, she'll tap out. Jane shivers as she walks through the industrial shelving, searching.

On the end wall, Jane finds a thermostat behind a locked acrylic case. It's set to 10 degrees Celsius, a cold spring day at best. A green light blinks under the label Humidity Control. Farther along the wall is another door. It too is propped open. *For air circulation?* Jane wonders, finding herself in an even larger room, the public side of the museum. Jane's teeth are chattering now, her feet aching. She's drawn to a treadle sewing machine, a mannequin dressed in a dusty black gown with a lace collar. A quilt tacked to a wall gives her pause. She's tempted to wrap herself in it but knows she can't touch it. Touching anything could change the past in terrible ways.

A fox, frozen in time, stares down at her from the top of a display case that holds stuffed birds, reptiles, and insects.

She finds another door, this one to a restroom. There is no water in the toilet. Perhaps the water is turned off? The place must be closed up for the winter. The heat's been turned down low, just enough to keep the pipes from freezing. Not enough to keep her from freezing. Her breath comes out in white puffs.

She hunches her shoulders, curling inward, and cruises the remaining museum aisles. Write-ups beside the displays are labelled with the museum's name: the Lodgepole Heritage Museum. A faded sepia map of Alberta hangs in a frame.

Jane's mother is buried in Alberta. Makes sense that the bowl is still in the province.

She's back at the door to the storage room. Had she missed the bowl? Or was it hiding inside one of the big boxes in the next room? One of the many floor-to-ceiling boxes. Boxes she mustn't touch. And even if she dared to, a search would take hours, and she's already crippled with the cold. Sleep tugs at her.

She cruises the museum's aisles again, passing the quilt that seems to mock her shivering form, and arrives back at the storage room. She pauses on the rough mat that sits just inside the threshold, which is not as cold as the floor, and crouches, wrapping her arms around her knees and her thin nightshirt.

Jane talks to herself. "Send me a sign, Rosa. You got me this far. Don't let me leave this frigid place without your bowl."

40 | Ethan

Ethan returned to Jane's bedroom with a second cup of terrible coffee. Jane was still out of it. Where was she? The only other time he'd seen her like this, she'd come around in twenty minutes. But as he thought about it, he reassessed. She'd been in the dream state when he'd woken that night. She could have been comatose for hours.

He checked the time. They didn't have hours. Garvin and Joey would be hitting the road at noon. Jane and he needed to be in and out of the warehouse by then. After which, Ethan needed to get his butt into Riptide. With Connor out for the count, he'd have to step in and play his part to keep the gang from taking over entirely.

Despite the blankets, Jane's skin was still cold to the touch. Was she in danger? The thought that he could lose her shook him. What if she ran into Joey or Garvin in her dream? Did she have her knife with her? *Damn these dreams.*

He picked up her phone, hoping to find contact information for Ariane, but the phone was locked. The professor's name was Nate, but what was his last name? Ethan found UBC's online directory and searched for Nate, and then Nathan. He got a hit on Nathaniel Crawford. That was it! He recognized his name and felt a wash of relief. But when he dialled the number, he got an out-of-office message. The professor wouldn't be back for a week. Another dead end.

41 | Jane

Visiting Dream

The rough floor mat helps. At least it's not as cold as the tile floor. Jane's shivers dip a notch while she's crouched there with her arms tight around her knees. She's tired and dreads the thought of standing up again, losing the little bit of heat she cradles in her lap, but she feels compelled to resume her search for the bowl.

The sooner she finds it, the sooner she can get out of this freaking place. She stands, and the cold washes her anew, even through her nightshirt, lapping at her stomach, thighs, and the backs of her knees. She enters the storage area. Hundreds of boxes line the shelves. If the bowl's even here, it could be in any of them. She sighs and walks the aisles, hoping the bowl is among the loose items on one of the trays. But it's not. She crouches on another carpet outside the door to the office and hugs her knees to her chest again.

Exhaustion tugs at her. It's the cold. She has to get warm. She rolls on her side and rests. She makes a deal with herself. She'll walk one more circuit of both rooms. If she doesn't find the bowl by the time the cold forces her back to the small office carpet, she'll use the mark to escape.

She braces herself for the cold and stands. With her arms wrapped around her torso, and shivering violently, she walks the aisles of the storage room, not touching a thing, looking carefully at each artifact that's not in a box. She then checks the public side of the museum. There are so many items carefully displayed that with each pass, she sees something new. But she doesn't find the offering bowl. She crumples to the carpet outside the office and rolls on her side into a tight ball.

As much as she hates giving in, quitting, she can't fight the cold. She'll just lie here until her shivering calms down a bit. She stares at the rows of boxes. They're labelled. Maybe there's an index of some sort in the office, in a binder, or on a clipboard. But no matter its form, she'd have to touch the index to use it. Would such a minor infraction cause an unforeseen ripple in history? Surely flipping through sheets of paper in an empty office would be harmless.

Maybe it's enough that she knows the museum's name. She pushes herself upright. Thank god for her get-out-of-hell-free dial. She puts a numb fingertip to the mark on her left hand. She rides out the nausea and draws a clockwise circle.

42 | Ethan

Ethan lay in bed, propped up on pillows next to Jane's comatose form. He checked her every few minutes. She still felt cold, and the marks on her face remained lit from within.

He had a two-hour window before Joey and Garvin would be back on the road. After that, all bets were off as to if or when they might show up at the warehouse. If he wanted to get in and out of the warehouse today, without running into one of them, he had to leave in the next half-hour. It would take him thirty minutes to install the cameras, and then he had to get back to Riptide. The longer Connor's chair sat empty, the more opportunity Garvin's and Joey's boss had to insinuate himself and his organization into Riptide's operation.

He'd found Jane's keys by the front door, so he could have locked up and left, but that felt all kinds of wrong. Even though she'd told him often enough that she was safe behind her locks and her steel door, it felt like abandoning her. He wouldn't do it.

The only way he would get those cameras set up today was by swallowing his pride and knocking on Sadie's door. He wouldn't be abandoning Jane if Sadie stayed with her. Connor's life was already hanging by a thread. It was just a matter of time until Garvin found Jane and did the same to her. Jane would understand. He had to get Garvin and Joey on the run, if not out of the picture entirely. And that meant getting those damn cameras set up as soon as humanly possible.

He checked on Jane one more time. With no change in her condition, he tucked his pride in his back pocket and marched down the hall to Sadie's place.

"Ethan?" She glanced past him, probably looking for Jane.

"Hey. Sorry to bother you. Could you come to Jane's apartment? Stay with her?"

A look of alarm crossed Sadie's face. "Why? What's wrong?" She pushed past him and down the hall.

Ethan followed on her heels. "Nothing. She's just, you know... dreaming? I don't want to leave her there, but I've got to go."

Sadie rushed into Jane's apartment, calling her name. She ran into the bedroom and stopped on the threshold. Ethan nearly bowled her over.

"Jesus fuck." Sadie approached the bed with caution and sat gingerly on the edge of the mattress. "She showed me a photo, but I never imagined—"

"Yeah, it's fucked up."

Sadie snapped her head around. "She can't help it."

"I know." Ethan raised his hands in surrender. "Take it easy."

"How long's she been like this?"

"Since I woke up. Three hours. Maybe more. Is that normal?"

"What the hell is normal? I'll call Ariane. Where's her phone?"

"There, but it's locked," he said, pointing to the nightstand.

Sadie picked up Jane's phone, punched in a code, and unlocked it. He felt a ripple of annoyance that Sadie had Jane's code. *Petty*, he thought, and pushed the annoyance aside. At least now Sadie could call Ariane, who was the only one on the planet who seemed to know what Jane's damn dreams were all about.

Ethan glanced at the time. "I've got to go. Can you stay with her?"

"Where are you going?"

"I've... got to get to work. Which reminds me, I don't know if Jane's supposed to work today. Can you call her boss? Let her know she's sick or something."

Sadie furrowed her brow. "Sure."

"Thanks. I'll come by when I'm done. After work, that is. Sooner if I can."

43 | Sadie

Sadie considered if Jane and Ethan ever talked to one another. Why hadn't he known Jane had been fired? No wonder the honeymoon had soured. She asked Ethan to stay a moment longer and went back to her own apartment to get her phone. Ethan grabbed his helmet, and when he left Jane's apartment, Sadie locked the deadbolts.

The light coming from Jane's marks was freakish. Where was it coming from? Sadie reached a tentative finger and touched the glowing mark on Jane's face. But her wonder curdled. Jane's skin was as cold as ice.

She dialled Ariane. "It's not Jane," Sadie said, correcting her. "It's Sadie. I'm using Jane's phone. I need your help. Jane's in a dream, and she's freezing cold."

"What do you mean?"

"Her skin, it's cold. She's in bed with a stack of blankets on her, but she's so cold."

"Can you warm her? Do you have a hot water bottle? A heating blanket?"

"No. Something's wrong. She's never out this long."

"How long has it been?"

"Ethan said three hours, maybe more."

"Get into the bed with her. Try to warm her with your body. I'll call Hunter."

Sadie burrowed in beside Jane, draped an arm and a leg across her body. She rubbed Jane's shoulder and arm, using friction to stimulate heat. But it was like hugging a slab of stone.

By the time Hunter arrived, Sadie was shivering. She welcomed the opportunity to get out of the bed and warm up. She thanked Hunter and locked the door behind him. He'd brought an electric blanket.

"This way," she said. He trotted behind her, but his footsteps faltered when he got his first glimpse at Jane. Sadie understood his shock.

It lasted only a moment before he swung into action. He threw Sadie the blanket's electric cord.

"Plug that in," he said as he yanked Jane's blankets off. Sadie plugged in the cord and jumped on the bed to help Hunter prop Jane on her side. She held her there while he swiftly laid out the electric blanket. They rolled Jane onto it. He examined her fingers and her toes before he wrapped the electric blanket around her.

"No sign of frostbite in her extremities," he said as Sadie crawled off the bed. "She should be warm soon." He reached for the blankets he'd stripped off her and replaced them, tucking her in. "What happened? How did she get so cold?"

"I don't know." Sadie explained that Ethan had knocked on her door earlier. That he didn't want to leave Jane but had to go to work. Sadie sat on the edge of the bed. "She's been like this for hours."

"Cold like that?"

"I don't know. Ethan didn't mention it."

Hunter turned and left the bedroom, stepping down the hall. "Is she taking any prescriptions? Medications of any kind?"

"Not that I know if," Sadie called after him. She recognized the snick of the mirrored medicine cabinet opening. Moments later, it snapped closed. She heard water running in the bathroom sink.

Hunter returned with wet hands and stuck a finger in Jane's mouth.

Sadie leapt out of her chair. "What are you doing!"

"I don't have a thermometer. I'm checking her core temperature. She's been cold for a while. She should be shivering, but she isn't. I don't know if that's a product of her sleep paralysis or a sign that she's hypothermic. If she doesn't warm up soon, we'll have to get a warm saline drip into her."

"An IV? How? We can't take her to the hospital. Look at her!"

He shook his head. "No hospital. I can take care of it. I was a medic in a former life." Hunter stared at the marks on Jane's face "Does she take vitamins? Use recreational drugs? Hell, drugs of any kind?"

"Jane? Not a chance. Is that what you were looking for in her medicine cabinet?"

"Thought it might hold a clue." He stared at Jane with a furrowed brow.

Sadie slipped a hand under the blankets. "The electric blanket's warming up."

"Good." Hunter turned his attention to the bedside table. He opened the drawer and searched through it. "Something's caused this change," he said, speaking to himself. Sadie caught a glimpse of the shiny new keys to Jane's apartment.

"She had an argument with Ethan. Stupid shit. He doesn't want her to get sucked into Joey and Garvin's vortex."

"Can't blame him there." Hunter straightened.

"Did you know Garvin came looking for her again?"

"Again? I only heard about the first time."

"Yeah. Nearly knocked the door off its hinges." She told Hunter about her encounter with Garvin, the jimmied mailbox.

Hunter sauntered to the doorway and leaned against the door jamb, contemplative.

"What are you thinking?" Sadie asked.

"Why is Garvin so determined to find Jane? He doesn't need her for leverage to influence Ethan. Garvin's not that nuanced. He'd go straight to Ethan."

"Maybe he's afraid of Ethan. He's got a reputation, you know. No one picks a fight with Ethan if they can help it."

"Garvin's not smart enough to be afraid of Ethan. I think something else is going on, we just don't see it yet. Does Ethan know that Garvin came looking for Jane again?"

"I doubt it. Ethan doesn't even know she was fired."

"What? Ah, shit, never mind. Watch her. Call me if she doesn't warm up, or if she wakes. I've got to find Ethan."

"Wait! You can't go to the cops. Jane wouldn't want you to involve them, not even your cop friend. I mean, she's a goddamn night light. They can't see her like this."

Hunter glanced at Jane. "No one's coming here. I'll be back with medical supplies. You have my number?"

"Yeah."

"Call Ariane and give her an update. I'll be in touch. It's time to end this."

44 | Jane

Visiting Dream

Jane endures the nausea and traces the mark's circle on her hand—but nothing happens. The room doesn't blur, the floor doesn't drop out. She lifts her finger and tries again. A new wave of nausea hits and then nothing.

Jane's miracle dial is broken.

What does it mean? Is it a sign that she isn't yet done with the dream? That she needs to look harder to find the bowl? Repeating her search seems like a waste of precious time. How much longer until hypothermia sets in?

She decides to search instead for an index to the box's contents, and to hell with the consequences. Touching a few sheets of paper couldn't possibly be as consequential to history as rummaging through the boxes. Or freezing to death.

She staggers to her feet, and a fresh slap of cold hits her warmer bits. Inside the office, she rakes the shelves for an index. A collection of six binder boxes on the table seems the most likely choice. With a shivering hand, she pulls out the first box, sets it on the table, and extracts the binder.

She flips open the cover and feels a sense of achievement. It's the collection's index. Each line contains an artifact number, a classification code, a description. Several items have more than one date noted. She had hoped the index would be alphabetical and she'd find the offering bowl quickly under B or O. Maybe I for Inca, or P for Peru. Instead, the list is sorted by artifact number, which she assumes experts find helpful but is not intuitive to her.

A number of pages in, she can no longer take the cold standing up, so she carries the binder to the mat, where she once again crouches and draws her knees in tight. Though she's mindful not to damage the pages, her hands shake badly.

When she doesn't find the offering bowl in the first binder, she pulls down the second. Her arms feel too heavy, her eyelids the same, but she pushes through. Sleep constantly tugs at her. She blinks her eyes open. Shivers. Did she drift off? She probably shouldn't do that. Not when she's so cold. She needs to keep moving, even just a little, to keep warm. She moves to the edge of the mat, pushes the second binder into the patch of moonlight shining on the office floor, and flips open the cover.

Her trembling fingers turn another page. The number at the top reads twenty-five, but it doesn't seem right. Had she read that far? Her mind was playing tricks on her. Perhaps she'd drifted off again. She's never fallen asleep in a dream before, but this dream isn't like any other she's experienced.

She pushes through the remainder of the second binder, careful to repeat the page numbers out loud to help her keep on track and awake. She turns the last page and hangs her head. Her eyelids want to close, shutting out the black cloud of defeat that's growing in her chest. She fights it off, struggles to her feet, forcing her heavy limbs to shelve the binder and pluck out another one.

Rubbing her arms, once again she settles on the mat and opens the third binder. Another two inches of paper to read through feels like a monumental undertaking. The moonlight is weak and makes her task difficult. Once again, she curls on her side. Just for a moment.

45 | Ethan

Daytime traffic near the warehouse was busier than Ethan had observed during his nighttime surveillance. He wished he'd given himself more time. He parked a few blocks away and sauntered back, a knapsack of equipment over his shoulder. With his phone in his hand, he looked like any other distracted pedestrian. He checked the tracker app. The truck wasn't active yet.

Adopting a casual air, he was about to turn into the warehouse lot when he faltered. *Shit!* In the time it had taken him to park his Harley and walk over, a Tesla had claimed a parking spot outside the office area. A woman stood beside it with a portfolio under her arm, looking expectantly toward the road.

Ethan walked past, out of her line of sight. He stopped at the first power pole, leaned against it, and bent his head to his phone. But his attention was on the warehouse driveway. His nerves frayed a little more with each minute that passed. Soon another vehicle arrived. Ethan turned back and watched the woman usher a man in a suit through the front door.

Ethan walked into the lot and strolled past the vehicles. The Tesla belonged to a realtor if the corrugated plastic *For Sale* signs in the back seat were any indication. Their meeting was eating into his narrow time window. He headed back to the street to wait for them to leave.

It took a half-hour for them to clear out. His wiggle room was gone. He had to get in and out.

Having determined through the tracker app that the truck still hadn't moved, he approached the driveway again. With a final surreptitious glance around, he slipped into the warehouse lot and disappeared behind the building. He checked the doors, all still locked, then waited a moment more listening for footsteps following him. When none came, he jogged to the roof ladder and started up.

On the rooftop, he reorganized the knapsack, tied it around his waist for easy access, and then made his way inside. He checked the tracker app one more time and then went to work. Ample skylights provided enough lighting for Ethan to navigate.

His first footsteps on the catwalk echoed throughout the building. He stilled. When nothing came of it, he quieted his footfalls. With no one on the outside watching for unwanted company, he felt vulnerable. He didn't want to be inside a moment longer than necessary, so he worked quicker than he would have liked.

He descended the stairs to the warehouse floor and approached the ramp's roll-up door. A strut high on one side was the perfect mounting place to catch vehicles' rear licence plates and the faces of those approaching the vehicles from the inside. He dragged an empty pallet over, leaned it on its edge against the wall, and used it like a ladder. Once the camera was zip tied in place, Ethan pulled out his phone and checked the visual. He adjusted the camera to a wider angle and reviewed his phone again. Satisfied, he hopped down. He looked at the time. Six minutes had passed.

He would mount camera number two farther in on the other side. Ethan dragged the pallet with him. He searched the area, found a suitable mounting place, and climbed the pallet again. Twelve minutes had passed. The third camera he mounted at the far end of the warehouse, near the office.

He headed back up the stairs to the catwalk to mount the final camera at midspan. When he finished with the zip tie, he yanked out his phone to check the image, but the phone caught up on the pack's strap and slipped from his hand. He dove for it as it bounced off the catwalk, but he missed. Ethan cringed at the sound of it shattering on the warehouse floor.

Swearing to himself, he started across the catwalk but pulled himself up short at the sound of the interior office door opening below. Voices in conversation drifted up: a man and a woman. Ethan retreated silently to the mechanical room and slid behind the door.

The realtor and her client had returned to examine the forklifts, but before they reached the machinery, they stumbled upon the remains of his phone. The woman bent to pick up the pieces. "Looks like someone's phone," she said, examining it. She looked up, her brow furrowed. Ethan pressed into the shadows. She tucked the pieces into her pocket and addressed the man. "I'll write the forklifts into the lease," she said, continuing on her way.

Ethan gently closed the door and made his way back to the rooftop. Without his phone, he was blind to the truck's tracker and Riptide's security feeds. He'd screwed himself, and he prayed he wouldn't miss anything in the time it took to fix the mess he'd made.

It was another agonizing twenty minutes before the two vehicles once again vacated the lot, allowing him to leave.

He returned to his apartment to find a note that Hunter had slid under his door. How had Hunter gotten into the building? Probably followed someone in. Jane or Sadie must have given him the address.

Jane.

He quickly jotted down the serial number and password info he needed and left for Riptide.

The cube van was gone. *Towed?* Didn't matter now.

He unlocked the back door, went straight to the phone, and dialled Jane. Sadie answered.

"She awake yet?"

"No. I'm worried about her."

Ethan watched Hunter walk by the bar through the two-way mirror, motioning for Ethan to get out of the office. It wasn't an idle request.

"I gotta go."

Ethan hung up and found Hunter at a table to the side of the room, out of view of the mirror.

"What's going on?" Ethan said, taking a seat. He waved Fanny off.

"I called. You didn't pick up."

"Smashed my goddamn phone. Long story. What have you learned?"

"Something Jane said has been bothering me. Call it a hunch. Have you and Jane talked about her dreams in that office?"

Ethan frowned, thinking. "Don't know. Yeah, probably. Why?"

"I think Garvin's organization knows about her. That she knows things she shouldn't. Things they don't want made public."

"You think that's why Garvin's been looking for her?"

"They might have planted a bug in the office." Hunter passed a wand across the table. "Tuck this in your shirt. Take it inside and walk the room. Every inch of it. Do it slowly."

Ethan did as Hunter directed, and when he got to the wall behind the desk, the wand's ticker stepped up to a steady hum. The sound slowed when he moved either side of the centre; when he moved away from the clock.

Hunter waited near the edge of the bar like a cat on the prowl. "What did you find?"

"There's something in there all right. In the clock. Damn it! Jane knew it, too. She dreamed about it."

"I remember. The day Connor's partner introduced Joey and Garvin. Jane said the guy looked nervous, that he kept looking at the clock."

"The organization was watching him. That's why he was nervous."

"Jane didn't know why she'd had that dream. That's what's been bothering me. There had to be a purpose."

"Shit." Ethan thought back to the many conversations he'd had in Riptide's office since Garvin and Joey had stunk up the place. "I'm sure Connor and I talked about Garvin in there. So they know we're on to them. They'll have seen Wilde. Know he's doing a story." Ethan raked a hand through his hair.

"Lester Wilde?"

"Yeah. He's a reporter. Been digging into property crimes in the downtown."

Ethan considered the position of the clock, and the computer in its field of view. "Ah, damn. They probably know our passwords, have access to the books. They can make it look like Connor and I are involved in their scheme."

And then another revelation struck him. "And they know about Jane." He concentrated, trying to recall what she'd said, and how much they might have heard. "She was in the office when she recognized Dal through the mirror. Named him. Mentioned Garvin's boss and the promotions he'd given out in Gastown. She told me Dal was set up to train Garvin. She called it Drug Buying 101."

Hunter rubbed his face. "Were you aware that Garvin had paid her another visit?"

"No. Fuck! When?"

"Keep your voice down. Two days ago. Sadie said he nearly took down the door. It's time to wrap this up. Go to the cops."

"Damn it!" Ethan turned and shoved the closest bar stool, sending it smashing into its neighbour. He took a breath, put his hands on his hips, and turned back around. "I know where they're doing business. Just planted some cameras. I need a couple more days."

Hunter shifted forward, his voice a hoarse whisper. "After what happened to Connor? You want to see Jane in the bed beside him? Because she's next. She knows too much, even if they don't know how she learned it. She's a threat to them."

"Jane needs this as much as I do. We're this close to getting what we need to take them out."

"You knew you might not get what you needed before they backed you into a corner. Look behind you. That's a corner."

"If I don't get solid proof, Garvin and Joey will still be out there. Still be a threat to Jane."

Ethan took Hunter's silence as agreement.

"You're a PI. Is there any way to get access to the clock's feed?"

"Maybe. If I can find a serial number. But I can't get that without taking a closer look at the camera." He furrowed his brow. "What do you think the feed's going to tell you that we don't already know?"

"Who exactly is watching us, and from where. It's one more piece of intel we can hand over to the police."

But how could they get their hands on it? Ethan knew that even with the office light flipped off, enough light leaked in from the bar through the mirror to make it impossible to hide from the clock's camera. Still, there had to be a way.

And then it hit him. "I can arrange a power outage after hours."

Hunter nodded, thoughtful. "That could work."

Hunter and Ethan took a table and worked out the best approach to getting the clock off the wall without tipping off the people behind the lens.

With closing time still hours away, Ethan's thoughts drifted to Jane. Their fight was fresh in his mind, as was their make-up session. He couldn't lose her now. "What do you think is going on with Jane?"

"Wish I knew. Even Ariane is stumped."

Jane was unbearably vulnerable right now, though he knew she'd kick his butt for even having that thought. He took comfort that Sadie was with her, but Sadie was no match for Garvin or Joey should either one decide to make a return visit.

Though Ethan was certain he needed only a few more days, if the thugs got to Jane in the meantime, it would be entirely his fault for delaying. He had to come up with a way to divert Garvin and Joey's attention.

Ethan drummed his fingers on the bar, pausing when an idea formed. "I might know a way to cool off Garvin and Joey. At least temporarily. Connor gave Wilde a few names for his story, but we have more now. If Wilde takes it public, the organization will have to take a breather."

"I know Lester Wilde," Hunter said. "How about you let me take this one?"

He'd have to thank Jane later for involving Hunter. Smart woman. Ethan borrowed a phone and sent Hunter the list of names.

46 | Sadie

Sadie brought a kitchen chair into the bedroom and sat in it, propping her feet on the bed. She still felt chilled from her attempt to warm Jane and wriggled her feet closer to the warmth of the electric blanket.

She called Ariane with an update. "What do you think's happening to Jane?"

"Her dream has taken her to a place that's cold. What's she wearing?"

"Her nightshirt."

"She told me she wore clothes to bed to be prepared. What happened?"

"I don't know." Sadie leaned forward and touched Jane's face. "Her skin's still cold."

"Try not to worry. Hunter wouldn't have left if her life was in danger."

Sadie's phone dinged. "I've got a call coming in. It's Ethan. I'd better go. I'll call again when there's news."

Ethan was outside. Sadie let him in. "You hung up on me. What's going on?"

"Long story. How's Jane?" He walked past Sadie and into the bedroom. He had a shopping bag in his hand.

"Cold. Was she cold when you left her?"

"What's this?" He'd noticed the dangling electrical cord.

"Hunter brought an electric blanket to help warm her up."

He reached inside Jane's covers. "The bedding's warm, but she's still cold. What the hell?"

Sadie crossed her arms. "What the hell is right. Why didn't you make sure she was dressed? I mean, I get it, she hates sleeping in her clothes. But now she's in a dream somewhere, freezing cold."

"You think clothes would have made a difference when a damned electric blanket hasn't?"

"You could have at least made sure she had her knife!"

He stared at her with a look of contempt, one that asked how she dared question him. What a dick.

"I get it, secret fucking agent man. You don't like me, fine. I don't give a shit. But Jane? Her, I care about. And you're fucking her around."

Ethan rounded on her. "Me? You're one to talk. When are you going to tell her that you're still hooking?"

Sadie jerked her head back. "Is that what you think?"

"You going to deny it?"

Ass. Hole. She curled her lip. "You know nothing, Ethan. Go on back to work." She put *work* in air quotes. "Hunter and I can take it from here."

"You don't get to dismiss me, Sadie. And for the record, Jane is my life. My future. I would never *fuck her around*. I'm doing everything I can to protect her."

"By shopping?" Sadie said, looking pointedly at his bag.

He closed his eyes and inhaled, as if Sadie was testing *his* patience. "I smashed my phone. Had to replace it so Jane can reach me." He marched out of the bedroom.

Sadie had hoped he was leaving, but instead he made himself at home on the sofa and started futzing with his new phone. She went back to her chair in the bedroom, fuming about Ethan around the edges of her concern for Jane.

What if she never woke up? They were supposed to grow old together. Count each other's wrinkles. Have wheelchair races and joust with their canes. Sadie stewed in her gloom.

How dare Ethan judge her? She'd thought he was the open-minded type, but he was taking "once a hooker, always a hooker" to new extremes. This was exactly why she avoided him.

And then another thought occurred to her. What if Jane really loved him? Married him? Jane was fiercely loyal. Her and Ethan being at each other's throats would tear Jane apart.

She stared at Jane's still form, her shallow breaths, and chewed on the worrying thought a while longer. Would confronting Ethan about his assumptions worsen the situation? Eventually, she convinced herself it couldn't get any worse. Ethan already hated her.

She stood, straightened her spine, and walked out to the living room. He was still playing with his phone. Begin with something nice, she told herself.

"Is it working?"

Ethan looked up at her. His expression softened. Maybe he'd reconsidered as well.

"Yeah. The geeks at the phone shop recovered my data. I just had to reload some apps."

"That's great." She chewed her lip, screwing up her courage. "I'm sorry about before. Jane wouldn't want us to fight."

His head ticked imperceptibly up and down. Once. A tick or partial agreement?

"I don't want to fight either," he said. "FYI, she was dressed. Full gear. She must have changed in the night. I'm just trying to help her. She's in trouble."

"I know. Again, I'm sorry. She's in good hands with Hunter. Did you know he used to be a medic?"

A scowl crossed his face. "I don't mean the dreams or whatever the hell is going on in there," he said, gesturing toward the bedroom. "That shit's out of my league. I'm talking about Garvin and Joey. They're coming for her. I'm doing everything I can to prevent that, but you're not helping."

What? This guy was incredible. "Of course I am! I'm here, aren't I?" Maybe it was a mistake to try to be nice to the guy.

"The people you associate with add more risk to Jane's situation."

Sadie felt a wave of confusion. Students? Professors?

He looked annoyed by Sadie's bewilderment. "Jane thinks you're out of the business. She doesn't know you're exposing her to those people. Again."

"I have no idea where that's coming from, but you're wrong."

"Okay." Ethan stood. He grabbed his coat and helmet. "I've got a meeting with Hunter. I'll be back as soon as I can."

Sadie stared at the back of the door in stunned silence. Ethan was impossible. She turned the deadbolts and returned to Jane's bedside. A moment later, her phone dinged. It was a photo from Ethan.

47 | Jane

Visiting Dream

Jane wakes after the sun rises. She's still in the museum. Still cold. Daylight streams in the office window, making the room feel warmer even if it isn't. She listens for voices but hears nothing. The third binder lies open on the floor before her. She leaves it there and searches the building. Through the windows, the snowy landscape is undisturbed. A road curves in the distance. If there's a driveway to the museum, it hasn't been plowed.

She returns to the office, crouches in the patch of light—which she's convinced is warmer—and continues her search of the third binder. Three quarters of the way through, she finds the bowl, or at least what she believes is a description of it. Silver, twenty centimetres in diameter, eight centimetres high. Circa 1550. Unknown origin. Unidentified symbol stamped into its side. Donated by Stanley Trutch's estate in 1988.

The sense of accomplishment that washes over her quickly evaporates as it occurs to her that she still has no way to find the bowl. Its location is probably cross-referenced to its artifact number, but where? Locked inside a computer? Even if by some miracle she finds it, will the bowl travel back to the present with her? If she can escape this unending dream.

She lifts the book to the table and once again searches the shelves opposite for a cross-reference. Empty-handed, she lifts down the fourth binder and searches it. Disappointed, she memorizes the bowl's artifact number and returns the binders, careful to ensure they are in their original positions.

What she's learned should be enough to get her out of the dream. It's happened spontaneously many times before. So why isn't she back home already? What else could she possibly witness inside a deserted museum?

She returns to the edge of the mat, crouching in the sunny spot, and examines the mark on the back of her hand. Her stomach lurches at the touch. She draws the clockwise circle. Nothing. Again, she tries. Nausea and nothing else.

Something is very wrong.

48 | Ethan

Hunter arrived at Ethan's apartment, having just left Jane's place. He'd put her on an IV drip that would help warm her and keep her hydrated. Hunter said her temperature had come up a little, but she was still colder than she should be.

Ethan pulled up Riptide's security feeds and explained to Hunter where the main electrical breaker was located. He showed Hunter how to disable the bar's security cameras, and then how to disable the emergency battery backup power that would kick in automatically.

With a plan in place, Ethan returned to the office. Hunter bided his time in his car, out of sight of the cameras.

Ethan sorted through invoices and packing slips, entering them into the system, business as usual. He kept an eye on the cleaners, and when they'd cleared out, he signalled Hunter.

The place went black. Ethan breathed a sigh of relief that it was dark enough that the camera wouldn't see what came next.

He counted to twenty, enough time for Hunter to disable the backup power. He then threw a towel over the clock, pulled it off the wall, and laid it on its face on the desk.

Hunter arrived using his phone's flashlight and silently went to work.

The clock was an inexpensive plastic model with a two-inch square box that held the timekeeping works and an AA battery. A small hole had been drilled in the number six on the face, barely noticeable, and that's where the organization had mounted the lens, which was wired to a unit the size of a deck of cards.

Hunter took photos of the model and serial numbers printed on the back of the camera unit and followed up with some readings taken with a bug sweeping device.

When he'd finished, he signalled his intent to flip the breaker back on.

Ethan rehung the clock, and after Hunter was out of sight, he removed the towel and retook his seat behind the desk.

The lights came back on. Ethan gave Hunter thirty seconds to exit and restarted the security system and then the cameras.

49 | Sadie

Sadie couldn't fathom how she'd ever slept on that lumpy old sofa in the days when she and Jane shared the apartment. Her night had been restless, laced with worry.

Hunter turned up early to change Jane's IV drip. While he worked, he taught Sadie how to do the next one. He'd also brought a supply of incontinence pads. Fluids in meant fluids out.

"Jane's going to be mortified," Sadie said. As if the dreams weren't bad enough. "I hope wherever she is, it's not with those gangbangers or their boss. If they figure out what Jane saw, the head honcho will kill her, too."

"Too? What are you talking about?"

"Jane witnessed a murder in a dream last week. She told Ariane, so I'm sure she won't mind me telling you. It happened in the east end last fall, maybe winter. Near the container port. Garvin's boss blew a guy away over a territorial dispute. He ordered Garvin to make sure it was cleaned up."

"How close to the port?"

"Don't know." Sadie searched her memory for details Jane had shared about the dream. "Jane said she could hear the cranes. She was in a grove of maples. There was a park bench, a parking lot."

"Did she mention their vehicles?"

"No. Why?"

"Clean-up in these cases usually means driving the body out of town and burning out the vehicle to destroy the evidence. I'll check around."

A few hours later, Ethan came by. Though Sadie was reluctant to leave Jane, Ethan wanted some time with her. And, truth be known, she needed a break. She wandered up to Fourth Avenue and treated herself to a coffee. When she got back to her own apartment, she had a long shower and changed before returning to Jane.

Ethan was propped up on the bed, his back against the wall. He had his phone in his hand and a scowl on his face. He swore under his breath.

"Something wrong?" Sadie asked.

"A camera's slipped. I need to fix it. You okay here?"

"Of course. What camera?"

He leaned over and kissed Jane. "She's still cold."

"Hunter said he'd be back this afternoon."

Ethan crawled off the bed. "I will too. You'll call if anything changes?"

Sadie wondered if he thought she should snap to attention with a salute and a *yes, sir*. He hadn't even had the courtesy to answer her question. She held her tongue, glad to see him leave.

At noon, Ariane video-called her for an update.

"Are you certain Jane hasn't ingested a drug of some kind?"

"Not knowingly. Jane's a control freak."

"Could she have been slipped something? A laced gummy, perhaps?"

Sadie couldn't be sure, and Jane did enjoy wine gums. "Sure, I guess, but if you're looking for a package, there isn't one. Hunter and I have looked in every drawer and cupboard in the apartment."

"What about pockets?"

Sadie put Ariane on speakerphone while she searched Jane's clothes. "Nothing there. But let me check her coat." She walked to the front door and went through her biker jacket. The pockets were empty.

"Look in the kitchen for anything new. Tea or juice. Any package at all that you haven't seen before."

Sadie set her phone on the kitchen counter and went through the cupboards again. She then checked the fridge and freezer.

"Check the garbage bin."

Sadie sifted through it as well. She came up with the wrapping from the parcel from Peru, but Ariane already knew about that. Sadie hung up with a promise to call the moment something changed.

On her way back to the bedroom, Sadie paused. She backtracked to the trunk in front of the sofa and picked up the card beside the empty box, and read it. It was nice of them to send Jane a gift. Funny she hadn't mentioned it to her. She was curious what it was that Rosa had sent. She'd have to ask Ariane. Or better still, Jane. If she ever woke up.

Hunter dropped by in the afternoon, and while he was there, Ariane video-called again. Sadie sensed her frustration that Jane hadn't come around yet.

"What about a new perfume or cosmetics? Maybe a new lotion," Ariane asked.

"This is Jane we're talking about." Still, Sadie headed to the bathroom. "There's nothing here." Sadie ended up back at Jane's bedside, staring down at her still form. "She must be hungry by now. Do you think she can die in a dream?"

"I should be there," Ariane said. "Nathaniel and I should both be there."

"Why?" Hunter said. "There's nothing you can do that Sadie and I can't."

"We could get her to a lab. Run tests."

"Jane would hate that," Sadie said, retaking her seat by the bed.

"How long has it been?"

"Thirty-six hours, maybe more," Sadie said. "Ethan couldn't be sure when it started."

"How long before we have to move her?" Ariane asked of Hunter.

Sadie jerked forward. "You can't!" Jane would never forgive her. She'd lose her for good.

"She'll need a feeding tube and more care than you or I can give her," Hunter said.

"We can't wheel her into a hospital like this," Sadie said, looking from Hunter to the image of Ariane on the phone. "She's a spectacle. Have you seen her?"

"Show me," Ariane said.

Sadie turned the camera to frame Jane's face. "Anyone sees her like this will hook her up to more than feeding tubes."

Ariane cursed under her breath. "We should have insisted on testing her before now," Ariane said. "We might have some answers if we had."

"If she gets hurt in a dream," Sadie said, "would her injuries be visible on her body?"

"Remove Jane's blanket," Ariane said. "Her marks might hold a clue."

Sadie turned to Hunter. "If I have to strip off her nightshirt, you'll have to wait outside."

Hunter reached for Jane's covers, nodding his agreement, and then threw off her blankets.

Sadie mumbled an apology to Jane. She aimed the camera at Jane's face and scanned down her torso to her feet.

"And her arms?" Ariane said.

Sadie readjusted the phone.

"What's that?"

"The bracelet? Is that the gift Rosa sent?"

"Move in closer," Ariane said. "What's it made of?"

"Looks like leather," Hunter said. "It's embossed."

"Get it off her."

Sadie put the phone down and tugged at the closure, but it held fast. "I can't. It's tight."

"Then cut it off her. Get scissors or a knife."

Sadie raced to the kitchen and came back with scissors. As gently as she could, she wiggled one blade under the leather and squeezed tight. Bite by bite, the scissors chewed through the leather.

When it finally let go, Jane gasped.

50 | Ethan

While Ethan was at Jane's, he'd discovered that one of the warehouse cameras, the most important one that could record faces and licence plates, had slipped. It was now pointing at the floor. He'd be at the warehouse right now, fixing it, if it weren't for the tracking app that pegged the truck at that location.

So instead, he sat at a table in Riptide, bouncing his leg like a strung-out addict.

He kept one eye on his phone while he listened to Fanny, who'd latched hold of him the moment he'd walked through Riptide's door.

"He looks terrible, though I'd never tell him. Who would do such a thing?" Fanny said. She'd visited Connor in the hospital and was still visibly shaken by the extent of his injuries. "At least he's out of ICU. Have the police figured out who did it yet?"

"Don't know," Ethan said. He'd given some thought to whether Garvin would try to finish what he'd started with Connor but figured he would have killed him after the beating if that was his intent. The organization was probably waiting for him to get well enough to return, cowed and compliant.

"I wouldn't put it past one of Garvin and Joey's crew. They're trouble, that lot. Is there nothing you can do to get rid of them?"

"I wish I could, Fanny. I don't like them any more than you do. They haven't been mistreating you, have they?"

"Nah, but they're smug bastards. Haven't even asked how Connor's doing."

The truck didn't clear out of the warehouse neighbourhood until after three. In all that time, the cameras that were functional hadn't picked up any activity inside the warehouse, which puzzled him. He leapt on his Harley, hoping like hell he hadn't missed a deal that had gone down in the office instead of the warehouse. He hadn't pointed a camera at the interior office door, but he would now. He'd be pissed if the risk he'd already taken had been for nothing.

But he refused to think the worst. Jane was worth the risk, and so was Connor. He had to get that camera fixed so he could get the proof he needed to put Garvin and Joey away.

On the drive over, he kept hyper-alert for the second truck, but he didn't see it. He dismounted and checked the apps one more time. Then, with his knapsack over his shoulder, he walked the few blocks to the warehouse. The parking lot was empty. He took a circuit around the building, tested the doors—still locked. Convinced no one was hanging around, he climbed to the roof.

After he'd secured his phone, a handful of zip ties, and the few tools he might need, he headed inside. He took his time, listening for sounds of activity, and hearing none, crept down the stairs to the receiving end of the building. When he was in camera range, he checked his phone to be sure the other cameras caught his image. They did, so they were working. If he'd missed something incriminating that had taken place in the office, there was nothing he could do about it.

He grabbed the same pallet he'd used previously and hauled it over to the misdirected camera. His hands were over his head, securing a new zip tie when the man door beside the roll ups banged opened.

"If it isn't Ethan Bryce. What brings you by?"

Garvin.

Fuck! Ethan jumped from the pallet and landed in a crouch.

"I thought you were a smart guy, Ethan. But only someone dumb as a brick would leave his SIM card on the floor of a building he'd broken into. Not too bright, are you?"

The bastard must have been lurking in the shadows outside waiting for him. A second man Ethan recognized as one of their crew entered next and skirted out to Garvin's left.

"Thank you, by the way, for the cameras," Garvin said, nodding to the one he'd just fixed. "We'll put the digital recording of you breaking in here to good use."

Any chance Ethan might have had of getting these guys away from Jane, away from Riptide, had just blown up in his face. There was only one way out for him now, and it was through them.

Ethan straightened and looked Garvin's sidekick up and down. He turned his attention back to Garvin. "You break up with Joey?"

"He'll be here soon. Says he wants to teach you a lesson."

Ethan would have to take out Garvin's mate first. The man moved like a strutting cock, but he wouldn't meet Ethan's gaze. He was scared, lacked confidence.

"I assume you got yourself a new phone? We'll take it," Garvin said, and nodded to his cohort to fetch it.

The idiot extended his hand. *Perfect.* The man had no time to look surprised before Ethan's arm flew out. He grabbed his wrist and twisted, pushing back until he snapped the idiot's arm. The man crumpled to his knees with a scream, cradling his broken limb. One kick to his shoulder put him on his back. Ethan pressed a boot on his throat and glanced at Garvin, who stood twenty feet away.

Garvin shook his head from side to side, unaffected by the man's choked cursing. "What'd I tell you about approaching him like that?"

Ethan moved quickly to cover the distance to Garvin but pulled up short at the sight of a gun in Garvin's extended arm.

"Put your phone on the floor."

Ethan inhaled. He'd have to bide his time until he got some leverage. If he had time. He set his phone on the concrete.

"Kick it over here."

Ethan did as instructed.

Garvin turned to his mate, who'd stumbled to his feet, still clutching his arm. "Pick it up." Grimacing, the man bent to the phone and handed it to Garvin, who pocketed it.

Garvin used his gun like a pointer, directing Ethan to move toward the front of the building. When they got close to the gantry's I-beam support, which was twenty feet back from the office wall, Garvin told him to stop.

"Sit on the floor and straddle the I-beam. Hands out front, either side," Garvin said.

Ethan stared daggers at Garvin. Seated, Ethan couldn't use his legs as effectively. Garvin wasn't as stupid as he looked. If the bastard wasn't holding a gun, Ethan would have had him on the ground crying like a baby by now.

Damn him!

Ethan sat on the floor at the base of the gantry support and held his arms out.

"Think you can manage this?" Garvin said, handing his gun to his cohort. "Keep it on him. He tries something, shoot him."

Garvin produced a zip tie, squatted, and secured Ethan's wrists. He snugged on a second tie for good measure. He patted him down, taking his keys and going through the pockets of his biker jacket. When he stood, he reached out his hand to his idiot partner for the return of his gun.

The moment the gun changed hands, the partner walloped Ethan with a boot to his back. Sharp pain radiated out in every direction, lighting his back on fire. The fucker followed up with a stomp to his thigh. Ethan grimaced and absorbed the excruciating punishment with a grunt. The injured man let out a stream of curses, and Ethan knew if his arm hadn't been broken, Ethan would have suffered considerably more damage.

"What's the code?" Garvin said, holding Ethan's phone.

Ethan spat it out.

Garvin furrowed his brow, concentrating on the phone. Ethan knew the minute he found the tracking app. His eyes went wide. He glared at Ethan. "Do you have any idea who you're fucking with?"

Ethan remained silent.

"It's time you got your hands dirty, my friend."

51 | Jane

Jane heard Sadie before she saw her. She blinked hard and Sadie came into focus, hovering over her. Her voice came up from the bottom of a well. Jane closed her eyes again and curled into the heavenly heat of the blankets. She drifted away, safe in Sadie's presence.

When she next surfaced, Sadie was still there, sitting in a chair beside the bed. Jane cleared her throat, startling her.

"She's awake," Sadie called out.

Jane felt the pinch of an IV in her arm and gazed up to the floor lamp from where a bag of clear fluid hung.

Sadie leaned over her, hugged her fiercely. "Don't you ever do that to me again."

Jane smiled at Sadie's mock sternness and turned to see Hunter waltz into the bedroom.

"What happened?" Jane asked.

"What do you remember?" Hunter asked.

Jane had to concentrate. "I was in a museum. The Lodgepole Heritage Museum. In Alberta, I think."

"Let me take that out," Hunter said, crossing behind Sadie. He reached for the IV line. Plastic clicks followed. "What else do you remember?" He pulled the tape from her arm and pressed a cotton ball to the base of the needle before he removed it.

"It was wintertime, snowy outside. The building was closed. It was freezing in there."

Hunter nodded. "So that's why," he said, looking knowingly at Sadie.

Sadie answered Jane's puzzled expression. "Your skin has been really cold."

"I tried to get back, to get out of the dream, but I couldn't no matter what I did." She ran her fingers over the back of her left hand. "The dial's broken."

"Maybe just jammed." Sadie showed her the bracelet. "You came to when we cut this off you."

"Rosa's gift?"

"Ethan said you went to bed dressed, but when he woke, you were in your nightshirt and wearing that bracelet."

Jane furrowed her brow in thought. "Yeah. Ethan was here last night. We sorted out an argument. He wasn't happy about me coming to bed dressed, but hell, I'm not happy about that either. I remember dreaming about something. It was important, but it's... fuzzy. A bowling alley? It'll come back to me. The museum was a second dream. I haven't had two dreams in a row since I was a kid."

"Why the museum?" Hunter asked.

"It must have been the bracelet. When I put it on, I'd been thinking about Rosa and her family's offering bowl. I found it, too. The bowl. It's in that museum."

As she watched Hunter wrap the IV line around the near-empty bag, another thought occurred to her. "Why am I on an IV?" She glanced around the room, noticed the chair Sadie was sitting on, the empty pop cans on the floor, the coffee mugs and chip wrappers on her bedside table. "How... long have I been out?"

Jane curled on the sofa, her hair still wet from the shower. Sadie had made her noodles, and she was feeling stronger. She'd spoken with a much-relieved Ariane, who was furious with Rosa, flinging around words like *callous* and *purposeful* in reference to Rosa putting Jane's life at risk. Rosa's defence was that she was merely helping Jane dream in the hopes she'd find their family's ritual heirloom. Rosa had designed the bracelet herself, had it embossed with the same ritual marking that graced the offering bowl. It was the unbroken circle of the bracelet that had trapped Jane in the dream.

Hunter sat at the kitchen table, scrolling through his phone, while Sadie finished washing up the dishes. She brought Jane a mug of tea and sat beside her.

"Who's the card from?" Sadie asked.

She'd brought in Jane's mail. "Reyna. Pieter's care aide. She's thanking me for Pieter's equipment." Jane handed Sadie the card to read. Reyna had figured out that the power lift and exoskeleton had come from Jane. They were the exact pieces of equipment she and Jane had talked about.

"Classy move, Narc," Sadie said.

Anna had sent her thanks to the Morrow-Walker Foundation, not making the connection that Walker was Jane's surname.

"It was the least I could do."

Jane tried again to call Ethan. He hadn't replied to the message she'd left him earlier. She didn't think they'd had another argument, but she couldn't trust her memory. "Ethan's not answering."

"He'll call." Sadie set Reyna's card on the trunk. "While we're on the subject of Ethan, he and I had . . . words."

"About what?"

"He doesn't think I'm clear of the business. Sent me this." She showed Jane the photo of her walking alongside Cynthia.

"Yeah, I've seen it. I told him you'd have an explanation, but he wasn't in the listening mood."

"It was the day of my internship interview. I just bumped into her. We went for a drink—that's all. I'm not working for her."

"You don't need to explain anything to me. I trust you. I know you're out."

"Then how do I convince Ethan? I don't want to fight with him."

Jane considered Ethan's frame of mind with Connor being in hospital, Riptide threatened, and her trapped in a dream. "He's under a lot of pressure right now. I'll talk with him, make him understand."

Hunter spoke up from the kitchen. "Sadie, didn't you say Ethan would be back this afternoon?"

"Yeah."

"He's not answering his phone," Jane said.

"He had to get a new one," Sadie said.

Jane frowned. "Why? What happened to the old one?"

"He didn't say," Sadie said.

"Did he tell you where he was going when he left?" Hunter asked.

"Said something about having to fix a camera?"

"At the warehouse?" Jane felt a pang of guilt. She'd agreed to help him, and now it looked like he'd had to do it himself. Without a lookout.

Sadie shrugged. "Don't know where."

"When'd he leave here?" Hunter asked.

"Noonish."

Hunter punched a number into his phone. "Ethan Bryce, please." A pause. "May I speak with her?" Another pause. "Hi, Fanny. I'm a friend of Ethan's. When he left Riptide, did he say where he was going?" A pause. "When did he leave there?" Hunter thanked her and disconnected.

"He left Riptide at three o'clock. It wouldn't have taken him two hours to reposition a camera."

"Maybe he's having trouble with the Harley," Sadie said with a grin, mocking his ride. And then her smile slipped. "Shit. Or he had an accident." She shot an apologetic glance at Jane, pulled out her phone, and stood. "I'll check the hospitals."

Hunter scraped back his chair. "Jane, where was Ethan installing the cameras?"

"A warehouse in East Van." She pulled up the address and swung her legs off the sofa. "I'll text you the location."

A look of alarm crossed Hunter's face. "Where do you think you're going?"

Jane cocked an eyebrow at him. "With you. I'm not an invalid."

"You've been comatose for two days. You're not fit. Not yet." He rested a hand on her shoulder. "I'm just driving over there to see if I can find his bike. Rest up. I'll call when I find him."

"I can't stay here and do nothing. Garvin's boss has killed for a lot less than what Ethan was planning to do. I'm supposed to have his back."

Hunter squeezed her shoulder. "I know you want to help but be reasonable."

"There must be something we can do," Sadie said.

Jane admitted she didn't feel one hundred percent, but she had Sadie, and even if she weren't quite in fighting form, they were still a kickass team. She looked up at him. "What she said."

"All right." Hunter walked to the door and opened it. "But let's be smart about this. If Ethan's in trouble, it's going to take more than you and me to get him out. We'll need backup. I'll need you to convince Porter Bicks to haul ass over there."

"Porter Bicks?"

"My contact at the Cambie and Second police station. You'll recognize him. He's the cop I called after you escaped that cage last year. Give me time to get to the warehouse, check out the neighbourhood. Say twenty-five minutes? I'll check in. When I do, be at the station ready to fill Porter in on what's been going on at Riptide. Give him Garvin and Joey's names; he's sure to know who they are."

"Okay. And then I'll meet you at the warehouse."

"Let's hope I find Ethan with a flat on the side of the road instead." He offered a reassuring smile before he left.

"I'll drive," Sadie said. She had her phone to her ear as she headed down the hall to her own place. She returned a few minutes later, keys in hand. Jane was waiting for her.

"Ethan hasn't been admitted to any of the local hospitals."

Sadie parked on Second Avenue. "Never thought we'd be walking into a cop shop voluntarily." They climbed out of the car, and as they approached the building, Jane slowed to a stop. She stared at the sign. *Police Department. Cops.*

Sadie looked back at her. "What is it?"

"Shit." Jane spun around and walked a few steps in the other direction.

Sadie caught up to her. "What?"

Hands on her hips, Jane took a deep breath. "I remember my dream. The first one. In the bowling alley."

Sadie raised an eyebrow.

"Joey's a cop."

"Garvin's partner?"

"Goddamnit! I was going to tell Ethan this morning—yesterday morning. I would have, but he'd been so tired. I hated to wake him—" She stilled. "What day is this?"

"Sunday. Why?"

Jane checked the time. "Something big is going down on a Sunday at eight o'clock. That's tonight. Did Ethan know about it?"

"He didn't say anything if he did."

"He was going after Garvin and Joey. Delivering street justice for Connor. If Ethan knew for sure where to find them and when, he might have planned to be there, to pick one of them off."

Sadie shook her head, dismissing Jane's thought with a frown. "No. He would have told you if he was going to do that."

"I was playing corpse. Remember?"

"Then he would have told Hunter. Ethan's not stupid."

Not usually. "He is when it comes to me. He knew Joey was asking about me, that Garvin had gotten close enough to talk to Mrs. Carper." Jane felt a bubble of panic rising in her chest. She knew if Ethan was provoked, if he was angry enough, he could inflict serious bodily damage. He could kill them. "I have to find Ethan and stop him." Jane pulled Sadie's arm and started back to the car. "We've got to get to the warehouse."

Sadie dug in her heels. "No. We wait for Hunter's call. They might not even be at the warehouse."

"If Ethan beats the shit out of Joey, he's going to jail."

"Text him."

Jane pulled out her phone. She typed *Joey's a cop* and hit *send*, praying he got the message before he inflicted any damage.

"We need to think this through," Sadie said. "If Joey's a cop, then he knows what's going down tonight. He's embedded in the organization, working them. He has to know Ethan's not involved."

"And what if he thinks he is?"

"Then even more reason for us to go back to the cop shop. Warn Hunter's contact and Joey. Save Ethan from himself."

52 | Ethan

Garvin and the broken-winged idiot disappeared into the office. The office door's window had been covered, blocking Ethan's view inside. He bent his legs and inched his torso back until he could get his legs under him. He then pushed up and struggled to his feet. He stretched out his quad to ease the charley horse from the kick to his thigh. They'd made a mistake not securing his legs.

He pulled his wrists to one side to get a look at Garvin's zip-tie job. Zip ties were easy enough to get out of using momentum and swinging your arms from above your head. But with two ties, he couldn't do it. After a dozen attempts, he'd only aggravated the situation, causing his wrists to swell and the zip tie to dig deeper.

His back ached where he'd been kicked. His thoughts turned to Jane. Had she regained consciousness? He had no illusions of who he was dealing with here. If he couldn't find a way out, he might never see her again. The loss felt like a lump that threatened to choke him. He swallowed it down. He needed to be clear-headed right now, not distracted by what-ifs.

He heard voices, cars coming and going, the outside office door opened and closed. The skylights darkened as the short March daylight hours waned. It had to be close to five in the evening.

Garvin returned and gave Ethan the once-over. Ethan stood close to the gantry I-beam, hoping Garvin would misjudge how much reach he had. Garvin moved to Ethan's side, but he wasn't a total imbecile; he stood out of kicking range even with the hidden reach.

Ethan recognized the next man to step through the office door. It was the man Jane had identified on the security feed as the murderer from the waterfront. The boss. He looked the part of a gentleman in a three-quarters wool coat. Dalton Reddy followed, also dressed well, as if he had dinner plans at a high-end restaurant. The injured man wasn't with them. The boss settled at a distance from Ethan, his back to the front wall, and nodded to Dalton, who stood between the boss and Ethan. Where was Joey?

"How's the insurance business, Dal?" Ethan said, peeking around the gantry leg.

"Tell us about Jane Walker."

Ethan hid the shock he felt at hearing her name. He schooled his face in nonchalance. "What about her?"

"She seems to have extraordinary access to our organization."

How much did they know? Ethan quirked an eyebrow.

"We have your phone. We know where she lives." A smug smile crossed Dalton's face. He pulled Ethan's phone from his pocket. "Found an email receipt in here for a furniture delivery to her address in Kitsilano. You can tell us what you know, or we can get it from her. Which would you prefer?"

Ethan had been right; the clock's camera in Riptide's office had caught Jane talking about her dream of them in the Gastown Pub, the promotion, the drug buying. He had to redirect these goons.

"Are you referring to Jane thinking she's psychic? You don't believe that shit, do you?"

"You seem to believe it."

Ethan gave them a knowing smile. "She's a woman, she's hot, and I like getting laid. I'd believe she was Marilyn Monroe if she wanted me to."

Garvin snickered, but Dalton wasn't fooled, and neither was their boss.

"She knew my name. She called the man behind me 'Garvin's boss.' And somehow she knew I was assigned to train Garvin. I'll ask you again—how is she getting her information?"

"Hey, man. I don't know. Maybe she *is* psychic."

"She couldn't have been inside the pub when we met that night. We'd cleared the place before our meeting. Which means she planted a camera. As curious as I am to know when she managed that, we're more interested in why. Why would she do that, Ethan? Who's she working for?"

"You think she's working for the cops? Jane? You don't know much about her if you think she's working for the cops. She hates cops."

"Our competition then?"

"No way. She doesn't do drugs. She'd never work for one of your organizations."

"Then the only one left is you. She working for you, Ethan?"

"Me?" Ethan jerked his head to the side, dismissing the remark. "I have no interest in your business."

"Is that so? Then how do you explain the apps on your phone? You're tracking one of our trucks." He glanced around the warehouse. "Took the time to put up these cameras. What were you planning, smart guy?"

Ethan was fucked. Before he could decide if it was better to tell them or keep silent, Garvin punched him in the back of the head. His face bounced off of the steel gantry support. The taste of copper pennies filled his mouth.

"You were saying?" Dalton said.

Ethan blinked blood out of his eye. "I knew what you were doing to Connor, so I did what you would do if you knew someone was fucking your friend up the ass."

Garvin punched him in the ribs. Ethan cried out, nearly crumpling to his knees. Garvin hit like a piling ram.

"What were you thinking, Ethan? That you'd implicate us? In what?"

Ethan gulped shallow breaths, breathing through the pain. "Buying drugs."

"You were going to turn the footage over to the cops?"

"That was the plan."

"I see." Dalton turned and walked to where his boss stood. They conferred. Garvin stayed put.

Dalton came back with a declaration. "You're working for us tonight. And after you complete the purchase of a very large quantity of drugs—on camera—we'll expect your complete co-operation at Riptide and elsewhere."

A phone in the room dinged. Dal pulled it from his pocket. It was Ethan's phone, which meant the ding was a text message coming in.

"Well, well," Dal said. "This is interesting."

53 | Jane

Jane and Sadie presented themselves to the uniformed cop at the front desk.

"We need to talk to Porter Bicks," Jane said. "Is he here?"

The uniform checked a clipboard. "He expecting you?"

"No. Tell him Hunter Bishop sent us," Jane said.

Sadie added, "It's an emergency."

"Nature of the emergency?"

Jane resisted rolling her eyes. "A man's missing. We have critical information."

"Your names?" She wrote them down. Jane bit her tongue, annoyed at the delay.

"Hurry," Sadie said. The woman cocked her head. "Please."

"Take a seat."

Sadie sat, mumbling under her breath about the speed of slugs.

Jane remained on her feet, transferring her weight from one leg to the other.

They looked to the man who bustled into the reception area. It was Hunter's contact, all right. Jane recognized the moustache and matching eyebrows.

He offered Jane his hand. "Good to see you again, Jane. Walker, right?" Jane nodded.

He turned to Sadie. "Sadie Prescott?"

"We're in a bit of a hurry," Sadie said, holding her phone like a stopwatch.

"Follow me." He grabbed the visitor's badges the uniformed receptionist had set on the counter. "Put these on." Jane and Sadie fumbled with the badges while rushing to keep up with Porter as he continued into the building. Halfway down the hallway, he opened a door and ushered them inside a small box of a room. A desk was shoved up against one wall. He waved them to the stationary chairs and took the rolling one, then shuffled through the desk drawers, coming up with a pad and pen. He spun around to face them.

Jane's phone rang.

Porter cocked an annoyed eyebrow.

"It's Hunter," Jane said, quelling Porter's admonishment. "We're with Porter," she said into the phone.

"Let me speak with him," Hunter said.

"Did you find him?"

"No. His bike is parked a few blocks from the warehouse."

"Shit!" Jane handed Porter her phone and stood, unable to keep still.

Porter listened, scribbling furious notes. He handed back Jane's phone. "I've got to make arrangements. Give me five." He left without another word.

Sadie reached for Jane's hand. "They've got it, Jane. Ethan'll be okay."

Jane had her doubts. Big ones. "Not if he gets to Joey first." The bubble of panic rose again. Jane pulled out her phone and dialled. "Hunter's not answering."

"Probably can't talk."

Jane texted him. *Joey's a cop. Ethan doesn't know.*

She drummed her thumb against her thigh. Sadie tapped her foot. The room grew smaller as anxious minutes passed. Jane glanced around the room, noting the camera in the corner.

Sadie followed her gaze. "Think they're recording us?"

"Yup." Jane started pacing. Sadie skewed her lips, chewing the inside of her cheek. Hunter replied. *The men in the warehouse will be armed, Jane. Your knife is no match. Don't even think about coming over here. There's no shame in staying alive.* She turned it to show Sadie.

"What do you want to do?" Sadie said.

"I haven't changed my mind. I need to get to Ethan. Get him away from Joey."

Ten minutes later, they both jumped when the door opened and Porter walked in. "I understand you witnessed a murder? Tell me what you know."

"Oh no, Hunter did not!" Sadie said.

Jane's anger flared. She jumped out of her chair, took a step toward the door. She didn't have time for Hunter's stalling games. She spun on Porter. "I need to talk to the cop who calls himself Joey Hampton."

"You didn't witness a murder?"

Jane crossed her arms. "Joey's real name is Dylan O'Brien. Can you reach him? It's important."

"Are you telling me Hunter is misinformed?"

"And misguided. Are you able to find Dylan or not?"

Porter leaned back. "If you're withholding information about a murder, you're in over your head."

Jane stared him down.

Porter caved. "He's undercover."

"Yeah. With Garvin Burman's organization."

"He's involved in this business Hunter's tangled up in?"

"Yes. Please. It's urgent."

"How do you know him?"

"He—I can't explain. I just know him."

Porter nodded, thoughtful. He stood. "Give me a minute." Once again, he left the room.

"You think Joey's out there, watching us?"

Jane had a thought.

She looked directly at the camera in the corner. "Buddy, if that's still your nickname, you may not know me, but I know you. You were born at St. Paul's Hospital. You love butter tarts, or you used to. I'm a friend. It's critical that I speak with you."

"Jesus, Jane," Sadie said, a look of alarm on her face. "You just put yourself out there."

"If Buddy's not here in five minutes, we're leaving."

At the four-minute mark, Porter returned. He had a laptop in his hands and set it on the desk facing Jane and Sadie.

"I've filled him in," Porter said.

The figure on the screen was Buddy. He was behind the wheel of a moving vehicle. Jane nearly sagged with relief.

"I don't know you, Jane. I'm not your friend. So how the hell do you know so much about me?"

"It's complicated. And I will explain, but later. Ethan's in that warehouse and I can't reach him. He doesn't know you're a cop—you've got to tell him. Get him out of there before eight o'clock."

"Oh? What's happening at eight?"

Jane crossed her arms. "You know goddamn well!"

"How did you know I was a cop?"

Sadie's patience blew a gasket. She grabbed the laptop and drew it close. "It's not important."

"He wasn't talking to you," Porter said, pulling the computer back and dismissing Sadie. Never a good idea.

Sadie stood. "Let's go."

Porter glared at her.

"It's important to me," Buddy said, sparing a glance at Sadie.

Jane took a deep breath and looked to Sadie. She turned back to the computer. "Saw a badge on the guy you met with in the bowling alley."

"You couldn't have."

"Ethan's going after you and Garvin for what you did to Connor."

"He can try."

"Don't be an ass, Buddy. Ethan's a decent guy. I think you are, too."

"And what about you, Jane? Or your friend there, Sadie. How do I know you haven't compromised our operation? Set me up?"

"If I had, Ethan wouldn't be in that warehouse."

"And we sure as hell wouldn't be sitting here in your house," Sadie added.

Buddy shot her a look. He pulled in somewhere and put the vehicle in park. "Porter, we need to talk. In private." Porter jumped up, scooped the laptop, and left the room.

Jane checked her phone. It was after six. "He's going to come back with another stall tactic. We don't have time. Let's get Ethan out of there."

Sadie pulled open the door. They exchanged a surprised glance. It wasn't locked. They rushed back to reception, slapped their visitor's badges on the counter, and raced for Sadie's car.

54 | Ethan

Dal walked Ethan's phone back to his boss and showed him whatever the message was that had come in. The boss spared a glance at Ethan, then nodded toward the office. He, Dal, and Garvin disappeared inside.

By the time they returned, darkness had fully fallen. Dal flipped on the overhead lights. Garvin resumed his post behind Ethan. Joey sauntered in like an afterthought, shooting a questioning glance at Ethan. His hands were stuffed in the pockets of a baseball letter jacket sporting the Blue Jays logo.

"Ethan's the idiot you've been talking about?" Joey said. "You want *him* to do the buy?" His tone was incredulous.

"Some reason we shouldn't, Joey?" Dal asked.

"This your idea of a test? You're the one who told me we don't spring surprises on our suppliers. Garv and I need time to work the guy. He's real cautious. Won't like seeing a new face."

"You are right, of course," the boss said. "Normally, it would be unprofessional of us to jeopardize our supplier to resolve an internal matter."

Joey shook his head. "Last minute addition like this? He won't go for it."

"That's why I asked Garvin to give him the heads-up," Dal said, but his smile seemed off, forced. Something else was going on here.

"I told him we had to make an unexpected replacement," Garvin said with a knowing laugh. "Said he's familiar with the drill. I would have told you, but I been all tied up."

Ethan found it curious that Joey seemed uninformed, and more so that they were having this discussion in front of him.

"All right, then. Looks like you've got it covered. I've got time to make another drop." Joey headed for the office door. "I'll be back."

"I'd rather you stay," the boss said.

Dal motioned Joey back and nodded in Ethan's direction. "Clean him up. They don't need to know our business."

"We got time," Joey said. "They're not due 'til eight."

"The plan's changed," Dal said.

Joey paused, looking put out. He glanced at Garvin, who shrugged.

"You got snips?" Joey asked.

"He stays here," Dal said. "Use the rags over there." He jerked his head to the side. "Be quick."

Joey raised a questioning eyebrow, but he was a good little soldier. He trotted over to a pile of dirty rags lying where the wall met the floor. Returning, he wiped roughly at Ethan's face, frowned, then spit on the rag and wiped again. Repulsed, Ethan twisted his head out of his grip. He was tempted to head-butt him but knew he wouldn't get away with it.

Garvin's phone dinged. "They're two minutes out."

The boss addressed Ethan. "One misstep from you and . . . well, I'm sure you can figure it out. And then we'll do the same to Jane. Do you understand?"

"Yup," Ethan said. Clear as fucking day.

The boss nodded at Garvin, who disappeared into the office and returned with a duffle bag that he dropped at Ethan's feet. He then moved in and snipped Ethan's zip ties.

Ethan rubbed his wrists. With the number of guns in the room, he saw no way out of there. All he could do was hope an opening presented itself.

"Pick it up," Dal said. Ethan hefted the duffle bag off the floor and their little party marched lock step toward the rear of the building, stopping thirty feet shy of the top of the ramp. "Stay here." Ethan stopped. The boss and Dal stationed themselves by the man door on the far side of the loading dock. Garvin broke off and tugged Joey with him to the wall nearest the ramp. Dal checked something on Ethan's phone and nodded at his boss.

Dal was looking at Ethan when he poked his gun back in his pocket, ready to fire. Dal raised his voice. "Open the bag, Ethan. Pull out a bundle and put it back."

Ethan crouched in front of the bag. It was loaded with bundles of cash secured with elastics. He held one up, dropped it back. He glanced up to where he'd mounted the cameras. Dal must have checked for the cameras' blind spots because he and his boss weren't in range of any of them. Garvin and Joey were, but just from one camera. Ethan and the mystery drug supplier had a camera all to themselves. This was their set-up. Make it look like Ethan was buying the drugs all on his own.

"You'll find a tester in the side pouch. Put it in your pocket."

Ethan reached in the side pocket and removed a metal straw, one end of it cut on a slant and sharpened. A weapon. He tested the edge with his thumb thinking he could take one of them out with it but would likely earn a bullet for his trouble before he could take out anyone else. He put the straw in his pocket, zipped up the bag and stood.

Maybe he could turn the camera to his advantage, look pointedly at each of the pricks, call them silently by name. A lipreader's evidence in his defence? Or another bullet for his trouble? An image of Jane floated through his mind. He'd fucked up supremely. One of these thugs would go after her, and he couldn't protect her if he was on the wrong side of the lawn. She would hate that he just thought that. She would also hate that he let this go down without at least trying to get out of the colossal mess he'd made.

"This is what's going to happen," Dal called out.

Dalton, Ethan mouthed, turning toward him.

"Face forward!"

Garvin, Joey, Ethan mouthed, sliding his eyes in their direction. He searched his memory for Joey's surname but couldn't remember the name Jane had told him.

"The supplier will make certain you're paying what you agreed to," Dalton said. "When he's satisfied, he'll deliver the goods. You're going to test the product, and when you're done, nod your approval to the suppliers, who will then be on their way. You got that?"

Dal didn't wait for a reply. Garvin hit a wall-mounted button, and the rear roll-up door ascended noisily in its tracks.

A Cadillac Escalade drove inside, and the big door rattled back down. The people in the vehicle wore face coverings, unrecognizable.

The front passenger got out and approached Ethan. "You got something for me?"

Ethan handed him the bag. The man walked back to the vehicle and put the bag on the hood. He unzipped it, checked the contents, and then knocked on the hood. The back hatch opened. A back-seat passenger got out and jogged to the rear of the vehicle. He retrieved a box the size of a large microwave, dropped it at Ethan's feet, and went back for a second.

The delivery man stood in front of Ethan, waiting. Ethan bent to the boxes, which were filled with grey Cellophane-wrapped bricks. He punched the straw through a brick and touched the bitter powder to his tongue, wondering if this was the real deal or a total scam. As he stood, he slipped the testing straw in his front pocket. He nodded to the delivery man. The duffle bag disappeared into the vehicle along with the masked men. The big door rolled up, and the Cadillac backed out.

When the rolling door touched the floor, Dal approached, his gun out in fresh air again.

The boss emerged from the shadows near the back wall. "That went well. Garvin, Joey, put those in the office." The two thugs jogged over, picked up the boxes, and started for the front of the building.

"Get moving," Dal said, and with a swipe of his head, he directed Ethan to move back toward the other end of the building.

Ethan stood his ground. "You've got your film. I'm not going to be a problem. Cut me loose."

Dal shook his head and pointed the way with the barrel of his gun. "Not a chance."

Ethan exhaled. Gun wins again. He started forward, considering Dal's words. Not a chance tonight, or not a chance ever? He didn't like the finality of the direction his thoughts were taking him. He slowed, puzzling out how to make the most of the two-men-out advantage he'd have when Garvin and Joey left the room to deliver the boxes to the office.

The boss kept three paces behind and to his left. Ethan hadn't seen his gun so assumed it was still in his pocket, a hindrance that could gain him a second or two. Dal and his gun were an arm's length away on his right. Ethan brushed his hand across the pocket where he'd stashed the straw. Dal hadn't noticed. Good.

The moment Garvin and Joey disappeared into the office, Ethan made his move. He seamlessly removed the straw from his pocket and lunged for Dal, planting it in his left biceps and spinning him around to use as a shield from the boss's gun. But as Dal spun around, he managed to swing his gun up and into Ethan's jaw. Ethan sailed past Dal and before he could make a run for the back door, the boss stepped in his path, gun extended.

"I wouldn't do that if I were you, Mr. Bryce."

"Fucking hell!" Dal said, pulling the straw free and whipping it across the room. He pointed at Ethan, his face contorted in rage. "You're going to pay for that, asshole. Now move it!"

Garvin and Joey reappeared empty-handed just as Ethan arrived at the gantry leg.

Dal raised his gun to Ethan's head. "Hands out front."

Ethan's spine prickled, and not from the boot he'd taken to his back earlier. The coldness in Dal's expression spiked Ethan's heart rate. He put his hands out either side of the gantry support. He was fresh out of escaping ideas.

"Garvin, secure his wrists." The goon approached and looped a zip tie, securing it tightly. Dal stepped close and gave the loose end of the zip tie a vicious yank.

Ethan winced. He would lose the feeling in his hands in minutes, not hours.

Dal projected a punch to Ethan's face, but Ethan saw it coming and jerked to the side. But there was no avoiding the second punch that landed in his gut. Ethan cried out, his whole body feeling the pain.

Garvin snorted out a laugh as Dal shook out his hand, his lip still curled. He pointed to Joey. "Remove those cameras. I want them all down."

The boss turned to Dal. "Take care of Mr. Bryce."

55 | Jane

"This brings back memories, doesn't it?" Sadie whispered, hopping the fence at the back of the warehouse. They'd parked several blocks away and doubled back. Jane joined her, and they crouched between the fence and the cedar hedge. Darkness had fallen.

"See anyone?" Jane asked.

"No. It looks deserted."

"Maybe they parked their vehicles inside." There were two roll-up doors, one on the loading dock and one at the top of a ramp.

A black SUV turned into the driveway. Jane and Sadie pulled back from the hedge just as the headlights raked across their position. The rear door to the warehouse ramp began its trek up. Light from inside spilled out into the loading bay. Jane and Sadie didn't dare move. The SUV drove into the building before the door was all the way open. The door paused for a moment and then rolled back down.

"The licence plate was covered. Could you make out anyone inside the SUV?" Jane asked.

Sadie shook her head. "They had masks." She checked her phone. "It's not eight o'clock. What's this, then? The early show?"

"Or they're just setting up. I'm texting Hunter." Had the cops got the time wrong? Jane clicked out the message and then tucked her phone back in her pocket. "I wish we could have seen who was inside."

"Want to take a closer look?" Jane's phone buzzed. She read the message and scoffed.

"The traitor?" Sadie asked.

"He advises us to leave."

"He wouldn't say that if it were his girlfriend in there."

"Damn straight he wouldn't. Porter said his team won't be here until eight. I can't wait that long, not if Ethan's in there."

"I'm game," Sadie said. "You ready?"

Jane grabbed her hand and gave it a grateful squeeze. "Let's go." Jane slid out from the cedar hedge, darted across the loading apron to the building, and scurried to the corner. Sadie followed. They slinked along the back wall and climbed the loading dock steps. At the top was a door. She pressed down on the handle. Locked. A few steps farther along, they stopped, just short of the roll-up doors.

"I can't hear anything," Jane said.

Sadie grabbed Jane's jacket and hauled her back. "I heard an engine start."

They both started as the big roll-up ramp door came to life. Jane and Sadie glanced at each other, eyes wide. They were trapped. Light crawled out the door, illuminating the dock inch by inch.

Jane spun around, flight beating fight by a long shot. "This way," she whispered. She raced to the end of the dock, grabbed the rail on the side of the stairs, swung herself over, and dropped down. Sadie followed, knocking her over. They scrambled back and crouched against the raised dock in the lee of the stairs. But it wasn't much cover. If anyone glanced out the vehicle's side window, they'd be spotted. Jane's heart thumped against her ribcage.

The dock was still glowing in spilled light when the SUV rolled past. Jane and Sadie held their breath.

"Do you think they saw us?" Sadie whispered. It felt like an eternity had passed as they waited for the big metal door to rattle closed.

"No. They wouldn't have left if they did." Jane unfolded herself from beside the stairs and brushed off her jeans. She inhaled a calming breath and checked to see that she still had her boot knife.

Jane held her finger to her lips. She leapt up the steps and crossed the loading dock to listen at the roll-up door. She couldn't hear anything. It was either well soundproofed, or there was no one inside. She motioned for Sadie to follow her and crossed the ramp, making her way to the blind side of the warehouse. When she turned the corner, she spied the roof ladder's cover leaning against the building. That wasn't Ethan's work. She reached for Sadie, flattening herself against the wall. Ethan hadn't had to remove the guard to get up to the roof. Jane pointed up. Sadie followed her line of sight and nodded.

Jane cupped her hand around Sadie's ear. "Ethan wouldn't have left the guard off like that. Someone else is up there."

"What do you want to do?" Sadie asked.

Jane furrowed her brow. She pulled out her phone again and texted Ethan *Where are you?* When no answer came back, she looked at Sadie and shook her head. "He might not be in there, but I can't leave without knowing."

"If they've left a lookout up there, he's not very good," Sadie said.

"I'll go look." Jane pulled herself up the ladder, glad when she got high enough to get her foot on a rung. At the top, she peeked over the lip of the roof. She didn't see a lookout, but large steel vents and boxy equipment could have obscured them. Had someone simply forgotten to put the ladder guard back in place?

Jane waved Sadie up. "You go that way, I'll go the other." They circled the roof in opposite directions and met at the access door. Jane bent to a knapsack. "This is Ethan's." In it she found a roll of duct tape and a handful of zip ties. "Why leave it out here?"

"Maybe he's holed up inside, waiting," Sadie said.

He was inside. Jane was sure of it. She worried her lip. She wanted to believe Ethan was simply waiting to catch Joey or Garvin alone for some quality payback but feared that couldn't be the case. "He wouldn't have removed the ladder guard, let alone left it there to tip them off. Someone else is in there with him and they have him pinned down." Jane shuddered at the thought that he was trapped. "Let's go in and see what's going on."

Sadie's hand was on the door handle when it burst open from the inside.

56 | Ethan

Joey did a double take. "Whoa. What's going on?"
"Fucking bastard stabbed me."
Blood rushed in Ethan's ears amplifying the pounding of his heart. He raised his hands and slammed them down against the I-beam, but the zip tie didn't break.

Joey strutted back to Dal. "So you're going to waste him?"

Ethan raised his hands again, but Garvin shoved him off balance from behind. Ethan kicked out. Garvin sidestepped quicker than Ethan would have thought possible.

Joey tipped his chin. "What happened to 'he's more value to us alive'?"

The boss turned his gaze on Joey. "As you can see, Ethan's not capable of co-operating. He'll never be an asset. He's been a problem from day one. And we just learned why. Seems he's been working with a cop. He's a low-life snitch."

Ethan took a futile lunge at Dal. "That's a fucking lie!"

"Shut up!" Garvin said. Ethan kicked out, but Garvin stood out of range.

Joey turned to Dal. "How did we not know this? You said your people vetted Riptide and everyone working there."

"We're fixing the oversight," Dal said. "Tonight. After we leak that footage on social media, everyone will know that Ethan Bryce is a drug dealer. He'll become another statistic, another victim of gang violence." He looked at Ethan. "I understand gang shootings are a real problem in the Lower Mainland."

"I'm not a goddamn snitch!"

Garvin slammed Ethan's head against the I-beam, reopening the gash in his forehead. "When we want your input, we'll ask for it."

Ethan bit back his fuck you retort as blood once again dripped into his eye. He thought of Jane, and if he'd ever get out of this alive to see her again.

The boss nodded to Dal. "Show Mr. Bryce how we take care of cops."

"Cops?" Joey said.

Sweat trickled down Ethan's brow, mixing with the blood, and stinging his eyes.

"Slip of the tongue." A slow smile curled the boss's lip. "I meant snitches. Mr. Bryce will serve as an example for our colleagues."

Dal pulled out his gun and stepped toward Ethan, who strained against the zip ties, fighting down the roar in his ears. This couldn't be how his life ended.

"We're not in a rush, are we?" Joey said, looking at Dal as he stepped toward Ethan. "Because I owe this piece of shit a beating, and I'd like to pay up."

While Dal deferred to his boss, Ethan put the I-beam between himself and the gun in Dal's hand.

The boss checked his watch. He looked first at Ethan then at Joey, as if deciding whether the dalliance was worth his time. "Go ahead. Entertain us. But first, give Dal your piece. We'd hate for it to fall into Mr. Bryce's hands."

Ethan felt a wash of relief. One more chance to get out of there alive. He wiped his brow on his upper arm, in an attempt to clear his vision.

Joey hesitated, and then reluctantly plucked his gun from inside his jacket and handed it to Dal, who pocketed it and stood back. Joey approached Ethan, cracking his neck from side to side. "Snip his cuffs," Joey said to Garvin.

"Why the fuck would I do that?" Garvin said.

Joey punched his right fist into his left hand and bounced from foot to foot. "One way or another, he's going down. I'd hate for him to be able to say he had a disadvantage."

Garvin looked to the boss for his approval. The boss tipped his chin. A yes.

Garvin remained in the No camp. He approached Ethan, shaking his head.

Ethan shoved out his hands, which were almost numb now from lack of circulation.

Garvin produced a pair of snips with a snarl. "Stand back."

Ethan pulled back, holding out the heels of his hands to give Garvin the best access.

Garvin glanced at Ethan's wrists. He stabbed the tool under the zip tie and clamped down. The moment Ethan felt it release, he twisted his shoulders and swung his elbow up hard, breaking Garvin's nose. Ethan felt a rush of pleasure seeing the oaf stumble backwards, stunned. Karma patting Ethan on the back. Like a comic-book character, Garvin touched his nose and stared in disbelief at the blood on his fingers. Ethan moved away from the gantry and rubbed his wrists with satisfaction, watching Garvin's expression morph into outrage. Ethan's hands were at the pins and needles stage.

Ethan kept Joey in his sights as Garvin charged. He moved like a tank: brute force with little agility. Ethan sidestepped him and landed a hit to his neck as he sailed by. Garvin lurched off course with the momentum and lost his footing. He bowled into Joey, who caught him. As Joey righted him, the snips fell from Garvin's pocket. Ethan glanced away, not wanting to draw attention to the potential weapon. Garvin's eyes were wild with shocked disbelief.

Ethan's thoughts swirled around how to maneuver himself to get his hands on those snips. He repositioned, keeping his front to Joey, who was the real threat. Garvin was no more than an annoyance who was too stupid to quit. Garvin charged again, his face smeared with blood and fury. When his shoulder projected the coming punch, Ethan rushed backwards, matching his speed. Garvin swung into fresh air. Ethan nailed him in the groin.

Garvin dropped to his knees, temporarily out of play. "Had enough?" Ethan said. When he got no argument, he sought out Joey, who had stepped back and crossed his arms. Enjoying the show. Ethan's gaze darted to the floor. The snips were gone.

The boss and Dal each held a gun. Dal's was alongside his thigh, and the boss's was in one of his hands, which he'd clasped in front. Joey's gun was in Dal's pocket. The odds made Ethan want to hang his head, but he wouldn't give them the satisfaction.

His best—and maybe only—chance of escaping this death sentence was to take out Dal and the boss before they saw him coming. But first he had to survive Joey, who was across the room, loosening his hands at his sides. Ethan centred himself, gathering strength and mentally preparing for the most critical fight of his life.

Joey came in hot, forcing Ethan back with a flurry of fists. Ethan dodged and then retaliated. They exchanged blows, but neither gained the upper hand. Joey was quick, but Ethan landed a kick to Joey's knee, which left him limping. Ethan went in for another hit and connected with

Joey's eye, opening a cut. Joey replied with a blow to Ethan's ribs, adding more damage to the hit Garvin had landed earlier.

With each punch Ethan threw, his back shot out a painful reminder from where the broken-armed idiot had kicked him. His damaged quad felt weak, threatening to give out. The injuries slowed him down, as did his biker jacket, but it provided a layer of protection. Joey had likely left his jacket on for the same reason. Ethan struggled against the doubt that would be deadly if he let it get purchase and burrow in. They circled again, throwing punches that were getting harder to dodge.

And then Joey's attention broke. He looked up over Ethan's shoulder. The three men behind him also looked up. Ethan took the gift and landed another solid jab to Joey's cut eye. Dal left their little party at a trot. Joey sidestepped. Ethan caught a glance of Dal taking the stairs to the catwalk two at a time.

57 | Jane

Sadie and Jane both jumped back, Sadie rubbing her knuckles where the door had bashed them. The man who'd opened the door had been caught off guard. But his look of surprise quickly turned into an arrogant sneer.

He stepped out, and the door banged closed. He crossed his arms and tilted his head. "Can I help you ladies?" A broken-toothed smile and a lazy eyelid suggested nerve damage, probably one too many fights if the scars on his hands were anything to judge by.

Jane and Sadie had seen this overconfident reaction a dozen times, and it never got old.

"'Ladies' is so not PC," Sadie said, drawing his attention with a coquettish smile. He returned her smile, flattered, as most men were in the glow of Sadie's attention. "We prefer to be called women."

Jane swiftly positioned herself opposite Sadie, putting him in between so he could only see one of them at a time. The hoodie he wore under his leather jacket had bunched up at the back of his neck.

"You a fucking feminist?"

"Now that's just rude," Jane said, and as he turned to her, she pivoted, dipping her shoulder, and clipped him in the chin with her boot. Sadie caught him on the rebound, executing a roundhouse that effectively kicked him back to Jane. He staggered forward. Jane jumped out of the way as Sadie flew through the air, nailing him in the back with her shoulders. He landed on his face and stopped moving, but it wouldn't be for long. Jane ran for Ethan's bag. She threw Sadie the duct tape and yanked out a handful of zip ties. She secured his hands behind his back and looked over to see that Sadie had been overly generous with the duct tape, running it all the way around his head. Twice. He'd be plucked bald if he ever got it off. Jane reached for the tape and secured his feet. She then scooped up the scattered zip ties, stuffed them in her pocket, and jogged back to the rooftop door. Sadie joined her. "Ready?"

Sadie jerked her head toward the door. "I got your back."

Hand on the doorknob, Jane inhaled a calming breath and pulled. Halfway open, it let out a grinding squeal. She froze. When there was no reaction from within, she stepped inside and held the door open for Sadie.

They stepped into an equipment room. A few metres away, light leaked in under an interior door. Jane approached the door as if it were a bomb on a hair trigger. She wrapped her fingers around the knob and slowly turned. When she felt the latch release, she eased the door open a crack and looked through.

Beyond the door lay a steel, checker-plated landing and, beyond that, the grid of a catwalk. Sadie tapped Jane's hip. She shifted so Sadie could crouch and look out as well.

Noises drifted up. Not voices, but grunts, punches: the unmistakable sounds of a street fight.

Jane widened the opening. Below, toward the front of the building, two men circled one another. Joey and Ethan. Relief flooded her at the sight of him. But what the hell was Joey doing? Why were they fighting? Damn it, Joey!

Beyond them, three men stood in a row. Garvin had a hand to his face. Dalton Reddy and the man Jane recognized as the boss held guns, and Garvin was sure to have one in his pocket. The situation felt dire, and Joey's presence wasn't boosting her confidence.

Blood dripped down Ethan's face, and he favoured one leg. His shirt was torn. Joey kept a fist high, guarding one eye that looked swollen. He too favoured a leg. Given their conditions, they'd been at it for a while. Jane wanted to scream at Joey, *What the fuck!?*

Jane pulled the door closed, and she and Sadie stepped back. She pulled out her phone and texted Hunter. *Ethan and Joey are having a pissing match right now, inside the warehouse. Where's Porter?*

It felt like an eternity before he replied. *Get the fuck out of there.*

Jane squeezed her eyes closed. She texted him again. *Garvin, Dal, and his boss are here. They're armed. Guy on the roof is out of commission. Where's Porter?*

A long moment passed before Hunter replied. *Get. The fuck. Out. Of there.*

"Let's go," Sadie said.

Jane's thoughts scattered as she followed Sadie out past the lookout who was now conscious and worming his way across the roof. They jogged to the rooftop ladder, and Sadie swung her leg over.

Jane halted. "I can't." She reversed course and headed back to the rooftop door.

Sadie glanced up, confused. She scrambled back up and ran after Jane, grabbing her sleeve as she neared the door. "Where are you going?"

"Hunter didn't say Porter was on his way. For all we know, he won't get here until eight. I can't leave Ethan. It wouldn't be right."

"Then I'm going with you."

Jane threw her arms around her, hugging her fiercely. This is why she loved Sadie with all her heart and soul.

Sadie opened the rooftop door and eased it closed behind them. When they returned to the interior door, she asked, "What's your plan?"

Seconds later, the inside door burst opened, and light flooded the room. Dalton filled the door frame, pointing his gun at Jane's head.

58 | Ethan

Between hits, Ethan strategized. They would kill him the moment Joey put him on the floor, so he couldn't let Joey get the upper hand.

Dal had disappeared up the catwalk and his absence was another gift Ethan had to make the most of. If he could get Joey close enough to Garvin and the boss, he had a chance. He'd bowl Joey into them and make a run for the office door, lock it behind him, and then escape to the street.

Joey was efficient, wasting little energy, yet Ethan sensed he wasn't working very hard to end the fight. Ethan had left himself open twice now, and Joey hadn't taken advantage. A mistake? Ethan couldn't figure out Joey's game plan. He launched another kick to Joey's gut, but Joey arched away, and the kick had minimal impact. They circled again.

Joey moved into place. Ethan moved quickly, kicking Joey back, punching fast to keep Joey's hands up, moving him into position. Joey was close enough to his boss and Garvin that the two men felt the need to step back.

Ethan made his move. He flew at Joey, twisting his shoulders and hitting him with enough force that he stumbled backwards. He raced straight for the office door, not waiting to see if he'd scored a strike. He yanked the door open and skidded to a stop. He'd caught a reflection in the glass. Jane stood on the catwalk. Ethan spun around. No! His chest tightened. Dal had his gun pointed at her back. Sadie stumbled along beside her.

Jane had her gaze locked on Ethan's. She mouthed *Go!*, but how could he? Garvin's heavy footsteps rapidly approached. He jabbed the barrel of his gun into Ethan's skull. "Going somewhere?" Ethan closed his eyes. His mistake was going to get them all killed.

Garvin kept the gun's barrel to his head and prodded him back to Joey, who was tugging at the bottom of his jacket. Dal marched Jane and Sadie down the staircase and across the floor toward them. The boss held up his hand, and the advance stopped.

Dal pointed his gun at Jane. "This one matches the description, wouldn't you say?"

"That's her," Garvin replied. He shoved Ethan in their direction.

"Let her go! She has nothing to do with this," Ethan said.

"Shut the fuck up," Garvin said.

The boss brought his phone to his ear. "Bring my car inside." He slipped the phone back into his pocket and nodded to Garvin, who jogged back to the office and a door opener, just like the one at the rear of the building. The ramp's receiving door rattled upward.

The boss addressed Jane. "You and I are going to have a conversation." To Dal, he said, "Where's Raj?"

"Incapacitated," Dal said.

The boss frowned. "These two?"

"So it would appear."

The boss looked to Jane. "Resourceful. Who's your friend?"

Sadie crossed her arms, defiant.

Dal jabbed Jane in the shoulder with his gun. "Answer him."

Jane shifted to her left and swung her elbow into Dal's head. He lurched sideways, his gun clattering to the floor. Ethan spun on Garvin, but the oaf held his gun steady. Ethan turned back. The boss had his foot on Dal's gun and his own pointed at Sadie, who'd rushed him. Sadie raised her hands and stepped back. Dal rubbed his ear as he shuffled to his boss's side and bent to collect his gun.

Joey closed in on Dal as he was straightening, his hand outstretched. "My gun?"

Dal looked from Joey to Ethan. "You going to finish what you started?"

Their attention shifted to the vehicle entering the warehouse. A black BMW X model. It stopped just inside the door at the far end of the warehouse. "Garvin, escort the women to my car. Pat them down." The boss looked pointedly at Jane and Sadie in turn. "And secure their hands."

59 | Jane

"Hands out front," Dal said with his gun pointed at Jane. Though it grated her, she did as instructed, praying that Joey had a plan or was at least wearing a wire.

Jane glared at Joey. "What's he mean 'finish what you started'?" Garvin whipped out a zip tie and zippered it closed around her wrists.

Dal cut Joey off. "That would be none of your concern." He waved his gun impatiently in her direction.

Jane's focus swung to Ethan whose fists were clenched in tight balls. His nostrils flared. "Do what they say. Get out of here."

Jane shook her head. "Not without you."

Dal laughed. "Unless you can outrun a bullet, sweetheart, you got no choice in the matter."

She shot Joey a what-are-you-going-to-do-about-it look. He responded with a barely perceptible shake of his head and crossed his arms. Was he signalling her to go along with them? What was his fucking plan?

Garvin secured Sadie's wrists next, and then patted the women down, enjoying the procedure just a little too much. He took their phones and the zip ties Jane had stashed in her pocket, but he'd missed Jane's knife, so no gold star for him today.

Garvin retrieved the gun he'd stashed in the waistband behind his back. "Move it." The BMW idled at the other end of the cavernous space. Garvin herded them the length of a football field to the back of the warehouse, where he opened the rear door of the BMW with blacked-out windows. "In."

Sadie got in first. Jane spared a glance back toward Ethan, praying it wasn't the last time she'd see him. She forced a smile, hoping he could see it from this distance, and then slid in beside Sadie, feeling like she was abandoning Ethan. She pressed her lips closed, barely keeping a scream of frustration in check. An announcer was calling out a hockey game on the radio, turned down low.

"Keep an eye on them," Garvin said to the driver. He swung the door closed. The driver adjusted the rear-view mirror and engaged the door locks.

Through the windshield, they watched Garvin jog back to his boss as Dal took off up the stairs. He crossed the catwalk and disappeared into the equipment room. Moments later, he came out. Alone. Jane guessed he'd freed the lookout and left him in place. She wished she hadn't told Hunter the man on the roof was out of commission.

Sadie nudged Jane's leg, glanced at Jane's boot, and then at the mirror. "I'm Sadie," she said to the driver's reflection. "This is Jane. What's your name?"

The driver's gaze slid to Sadie, who offered up her best flirty smile. Jane took her cue and reached for her boot knife.

"You're kinda cute," Sadie said.

"Quiet." The driver glanced at Jane, but she'd already pulled her shoulders back.

She positioned the knife between her legs and inched the blade between her wrists. With her attention trained forward, Jane began to work the blade through the hard plastic. Even with a blade as sharp as hers, it was tough going, a challenge to hold the hilt securely enough to make headway.

And why the hell was Joey circling Ethan again? They both had blood running down their faces and both limped. Jane couldn't tell who was winning the fight. Was Joey buying time or delivering payback?

Jane shifted her wrists for a better angle. When the zip tie finally broke free, she darted a look at the mirror, but the driver's attention was trained on the men. Jane slipped the knife to Sadie and pushed the broken zip tie under her thigh. The ramp door behind the vehicle was still open. She and Sadie might be able to get out and run for it, but that wouldn't help Ethan.

She studied the vehicle's interior. Headrests topped the bucket seats in front, which were separated by a wide centre console. The driver didn't look particularly big. She could reach around the headrest and sever his carotid, but she couldn't guess if his hands would go to his throat first, or the horn.

Minutes later, Sadie's hands were free. She passed Jane her knife.

Jane tapped Sadie's thigh. She turned her face to the side window and casually raised her arms holding her wrists as if they were still tied. She kept the driver's side mirror in her peripheral vision and saw the driver's attention swing to the rear-view mirror. Jane brushed at the hair that had fallen in her face, a harmless gesture. The driver turned his gaze back to the fight in the distance. But Sadie paid attention and saw Jane rake her thumb across her throat as she lowered her hands.

Sadie nodded, and nudged Jane's thigh. Jane followed Sadie's line of sight to her lap where she held her hands upright, open in question. Though Jane couldn't be sure, it looked like Sadie had also identified the driver's hands as the weak spot in Jane's plan. Jane shrugged.

Sadie nudged her again and gestured toward her crotch, making a fist. Sadie would try to punch him in the jewels. It would be a trick shot—if she could even pull it off. But what choice did they have?

"Whatever you two are planning, give it up."

Jane and Sadie darted a look in the mirror. The driver had caught them communicating. He met their gaze in the reflection and then turned in his seat, draping his left hand over the centre console. He glanced at their hands, wrists clasped, fingers forward to hide the missing zip ties. Jane felt sure he could hear her heart pounding.

"Not much we can do trussed up like this," Sadie said, pouting. She could be the spokesmodel for Cool Under Pressure.

"That's the point," the driver said. He flipped them a mocking smile then turned back around.

Jane sucked in a ragged breath. That was too close. And then she realized what he'd done. She stared at where his hand had been on the console and looked over to Sadie, who was staring at the same spot. Their gaze met in a shared smile. This time when she sucked in a breath, it was to relax her jangled nerves.

Jane shifted the knife to her right hand. Sadie nodded.

"Where do you think they're going to take us?" Sadie said.

"Quiet." The driver didn't even bother to look in the rear-view.

"No place good," Jane replied.

"Driver," Sadie called. "You release the door locks and Jane and I will forget we saw you."

The driver's shoulders shifted. Jane waited until he'd fully committed. Words tumbled from his mouth as he turned, but Jane didn't hear him; she swung her knife and nailed his hand to the console. Before he had time to scream, Sadie followed up with a punch to his throat. His head snapped back. He stopped moving.

"Is he dead?" Jane asked, keeping a firm grip on the hilt of her knife.

Sadie was already crawling over the centre console, wriggling herself into the front passenger seat. The man hadn't moved. Sadie kept her head down and opened the glovebox. "Zip ties," she said, producing an elasticised bunch of them. "Come on. We've got to get him tied before he comes around."

If he comes around, Jane thought, pulling the knife from his hand. She helped Sadie pull the driver's upper body toward the passenger seat, keeping his arms behind his back. Sadie zip-tied his hands. His face was planted near the dashboard edge of the seat, his hips twisted, but his legs were still in the driver's footwell.

She and Jane checked the fight club crew. Their attention was elsewhere despite Jane feeling exposed, as if Sadie were flopping about on the floor of the warehouse and not just climbing her way over the driver's body. Sadie rearranged herself again, this time pressing her back to the driver's door. She shoved her feet against the man's hips and thighs, pushing him farther into the passenger seat, freeing up the gas pedal.

The man groaned. He was still alive.

Sadie slid into the driver's seat, her hand on the gear shift. "Ready?" she said to Jane.

"Keep low," Jane replied.

"You too." Sadie put the car in gear and hit the gas.

Jane pressed forward, her chin close to the driver's hip still occupying the console between the front seats. She stared out the windshield. Joey and Ethan halted. And then Dal looked in their direction, his face balled up in a frown.

60 | Ethan

"I thought you were a tough guy, Joey," Garvin said.

Joey laughed. "How's that nose of yours, Garv?"

Ethan had been in enough fights to know when one felt off. Either Joey was dragging this out, or he was hiding a more serious injury. Ethan sensed he could end the fight, put Joey on the floor, but that only brought him closer to being shot. He spun and landed another kick to Joey's knee. Joey hopped back with a grimace.

Joey and Ethan circled again.

"You're making me dizzy," the boss said. He looked at Dal and tapped his watch. "Finish this. We're out of here in five."

Dal raised his gun in Ethan's direction, but even as he leveled it, a look of alarm clouded his features. Dal swung his arm forty-five degrees and fired. Ethan spun sideways. Wheels squealed. The SUV was on the move, coming straight at them. Yes! Jane or Sadie must have been behind the wheel.

Ethan leapt out of the vehicle's path as a shot rang out behind him. The boss's gun. The shot missed Ethan but hit Joey. He fell into Ethan and took them both down, landing like a dead weight on top of him. The SUV accelerated.

Ethan shoved at Joey, not keen to be pinned down in the SUV's path. He wrenched his neck to locate the vehicle. His hand slipped off Joey's shoulder, covered in blood—not Ethan's. The boss's gun rang out again, and Ethan felt the impact of it through Joey's torso. The boss was shooting at Ethan through Joey? *What the fuck?*

More shots thudded into the moving vehicle from Dal's direction. The SUV swerved. Ethan shoved at Joey again, and this time he rolled off him with a groan. As Ethan clambered to his feet, he felt an unfamiliar weight in his pocket. Reaching inside, he pulled out the pair of snips that Garvin had dropped. How the fuck? He glanced down at Joey, who remained motionless. And then Ethan's attention shifted as he caught a glimpse of the boss and Garvin scrambling in different directions. The boss was headed for the office door.

Dal was down, writhing on the floor. Vehicle impact. The SUV squealed to a stop and reversed. It took another run in Garvin's direction, missed him, and smashed the front passenger side into the office wall. The engine emitted a high-pitch squeal as the vehicle reversed again. Sadie peeked above the driver's side door frame. Dal lurched toward the back of the car, firing his gun. Ethan glimpsed Jane's face rising from the back seat through the rear window seconds before Dal's bullets pierced holes in the glass.

"No!" Ethan ran toward Dal, ramming into him. Dal went down hard, his gun clattering to the floor. Ethan went down as well, but rolled and rose to his feet, his gaze seeking Jane. The car had rolled to a stop. By some miracle, Jane was unscathed, already getting out of the SUV, her knife in hand. She looked past Ethan with narrowed eyes and a furrowed brow. She threw her knife with a vengeance. A shot rang out. Garvin screamed. Ethan turned. Jane's knife protruding from Garvin's wrist. His gun had hit the floor. Ethan raced for it.

61 | Jane

Jane jumped out of her skin at a voice over a bullhorn. *Put your weapons down.*

She turned toward the big open door and saw a dozen people in black swarming the place, weapons raised, shouting instructions. Flashing light played across the interior walls. She was shoved to the ground, face down. Someone told her to put her hands behind her back. She was zip-tied. Again. Her ears rang, deafened by the gunshots.

Boots clanked on the metal stairs to the roof.

Sadie and Ethan were also face down with their arms behind their backs. Garvin was squealing, but he too was lying down. She couldn't find the boss, but Dal was down. Joey was the only one standing, if you could call it that. He leaned heavily on one of the black-clad men and hobbled toward the back of the building. Veering toward Dal, he stopped, delivered a kick to Dal's ribs along with some choice words, then resumed his trek.

Jane closed her eyes, relieved. She'd seen Joey go down and thought he'd been killed. And then she saw Garvin all over again, raising his gun, aiming at Ethan's head. She shivered at how close she'd come to losing him.

A pair of boots stopped at her shoulders. She looked up. Porter. "You're as big a pain in my ass as Hunter. Neither one of you does what you're told. But you'd best mind my words now. You're not to speak to anyone until I tell you to. You hear me?"

Jane nodded. He helped her to her feet and handed her off to a guard who marched her outside. She was pleased to see the boss hadn't gotten away after all. He stood in front of the *For Sale* sign, his wrists in handcuffs—the real deal, not the zip ties the rest of them wore. Another guard stood over him.

A crowd had gathered on the sidewalk at the front of the warehouse, a few of them holding up their cellphones. Jane turned from their scrutiny. Uniformed police kept the sidewalk paparazzi out of the driveway.

An ambulance came around from the back and blipped its siren as it eased onto the road. A second ambulance followed it.

Sadie was escorted out of the building next and deposited close to Jane. Sadie's face eased into a wide smile, relieved to see her. Sadie glanced across to where the boss stood and called out, "The name's Sadie, by the way." She winked at him. The guard reminded her not to speak. Soon after that, the boss was loaded into the back seat of a cruiser and driven away. The man who'd been guarding the roof came out, duct tape still fixed to the back of his head. He was put into the back of another cruiser.

When Ethan finally emerged, his escort was Porter, who guided him by the elbow. Hunter was with them. Ethan's gaze sought out Jane and when he found her, relief flooded his features. The carnal intensity of his stare as he swaggered toward her made her insides quiver. They came to stand in front of her. "We'll be taking your statement at the station," Porter said. He signalled to someone in the distance.

Ethan took a step toward Jane, leaned in, and kissed her soundly on the lips. If Jane's hands weren't locked behind her, she would have pulled him closer, wrapped a leg around his hip. Porter jerked him away. Ethan teetered like a love-struck puppy with a silly-assed grin. Jane returned a slow smile and mouthed *I love you.*

Sadie, Ethan, and Jane were brought to the station in separate cars. Jane was put in a room similar to the one she and Sadie had occupied when they were Porter's visitors.

Porter came in with a second officer and told her their conversation would be recorded. She sighed, all too familiar with the process. And this was just the beginning. She envisioned many more hours in her future sitting in the Crown counsel's office. Would Monica Fowler be assigned again?

"How's Joey?" she asked.

"Dylan? He'll live, but he's going to be sore for a while. Took a bullet to the shoulder. Another to his back. Without the body armour, he'd have been paralyzed, if not dead."

"He was wearing a vest?"

"A close-combat unit. Light weight but effective."

Jane found herself unexpectedly relieved about that. "I didn't see Dal come out of the warehouse."

"Dal?"

"Dalton Reddy."

Porter checked his notes. "They took him out in an ambulance."

Jane could still see the expression on Dal's face when Sadie drove the grille of the SUV into him. The jerk looked surprised, as if she'd stop and let him get a better shot. Or was it Joey's exiting kick that had done the damage? Dal had nearly killed them. She hoped he was in considerable pain.

The interview lasted hours. Now that she knew how much impact these statements had, she was meticulous with the details, not giving up anything connected to her dreams. She'd shared enough of her Crown counsel experiences with Ethan and Sadie to know that they, too, would be careful. This time.

Hunter was waiting for her when she was released. He drove her home. He tried to give her grief for going into the warehouse after Ethan, but she would have none of it. She'd saved Ethan from Garvin's bullet, and that's all that mattered. She dished out as good as she got, giving Hunter an earful about him telling Porter she'd witnessed a murder. It rolled off him in a fit of laughter. She was pretty sure he called her a ballbuster, but he wouldn't repeat it.

Sadie knocked on her door close to midnight. "We're not supposed to talk about it, but I'm not sure I can keep it inside," she said, pointing to her chest.

"You're my hero," Jane said. They hugged, and then Sadie carried on home.

Ethan came by an hour later. Jane threw her arms around him. They stood there, wrapped in each other's embrace for a long time.

Ethan pulled back first. "So Joey's a cop."

"Yeah, he is."

"He dropped a pair of snips in my pocket when we were fighting. Tried to give me an edge."

"He did?" Jane felt a new wave of respect for Joey.

"You saved my life," Ethan said. Steri-Strips closed the gash on his forehead.

Jane stroked his stubbled cheek, leaned up, and kissed him. She then took him to her bed and expressed with her body all that she felt in her heart. She didn't dress before she let herself drift off. She wasn't leaving him for a moment tonight.

62 | Ethan

"You awake?" Jane opened her eyes. "I am now."

Ethan grinned. "Just checking." He rolled on top of her and eased her legs open. They made morning love, languid, with long strokes and no end in sight. And when the end arrived, it was wondrous.

They showered, and Ethan left the bathroom to put the kettle on. A knock at the door startled him. He checked the peephole. It was Sadie. He opened the door.

Her gaze slid to the towel around his waist.

"We're not dressed yet."

Sadie inhaled. "You drink coffee, right?"

He frowned.

"She doesn't have a coffee maker. When you're dressed, come for coffee. Bring Jane. We need to talk."

When Sadie opened her door, a look of concern crossed Jane's face. "You sleep okay?" she asked.

Ethan had been inside Sadie's small apartment only once before, when he'd helped her move out of Jane's place. He'd been so happy she was moving out that he hadn't noticed how dingy it was. It was also smaller than he'd remembered.

"I'm fine." She handed Ethan and Jane mugs—his coffee, hers tea—and they went to sit side by side on the bed.

Sadie sat in her office chair and rolled up opposite them. She looked at Ethan. "You and I have to clear the air."

Ethan tried to interrupt, but she stopped him.

"I've made mistakes, I admit it. I fucked up with Rick and Andy big time. And maybe you can't forgive me. Maybe you'll always judge me by my mistakes, but I'm asking you to try to see past who I used to be. That photo you have of me and Cynthia? It was a fucking coincidence, that's all. I bumped into Cynthia on the street. Honestly. I'm making an effort here. I love Jane. And you and I at each other's throats is going to make all of us miserable."

Ethan held up his hand. "I know. And I owe you an apology."

Sadie sat upright, her expression one of surprise.

"I've been hard on you, and I'm sorry." Ethan couldn't meet Sadie's shocked gaze, and instead, studied his cuticles. "I don't forgive easily. When I saw you with Cynthia, I lost it. Thought you were bringing that shit home to Jane again." Ethan paused, swallowed, and took a breath. Finally, he looked at her. "I was wrong. You were fearless last night. I owe you more than a second chance. If you hadn't helped Jane find me, and gotten control of their car, we might all be dead right now." Ethan raised his mug in salute. "Thank you."

A tentative smile curled Sadie's lips. She clinked her coffee mug with his, and Jane added hers.

"Did you get a look at the expression on Garvin's face when you were gunning for him?" Ethan said. "Man, it was perfect."

A wide grin spread across Sadie's face. "I didn't think the fat fuck could move that fast."

Whatever tension had been in the air dissipated in their shared laughter.

"Seriously. I know now that you're out of the business," Ethan said. "I'll do better, too, and try not to jump to conclusions." He laughed again, looking around the tiny apartment. "Jane never doubted. Not for a second. And she was right—you couldn't work a john in here."

"No more talk of johns, okay? Another thing," Sadie said, this time looking at both of them. "You two need to spend some of that bedroom time talking."

Ethan and Jane glanced at each other, frowning. They looked back to Sadie.

Sadie turned to Ethan. "Jane got fired. She doesn't work at the nursery anymore."

She looked to Jane. "You *do* need Ethan's protection. You're vulnerable when you dream. Deal with it."

63 | Jane

Jane couldn't let go of her curiosity about Dylan, and Ethan wanted to see Connor. So when Hunter told Jane that Dylan was under police guard at the same downtown hospital as Connor, Sadie volunteered to drive them over. She admitted that Jane's obsession with Dylan had piqued her interest. She wanted to meet the man she'd only seen briefly in the grainy video feed in Porter's office before catching a glimpse of him in the warehouse.

Jane knew that the police had already questioned Connor following the beating. But after last night's events, they'd be back. The statement Ethan had given to the police last night put Connor in play. Ethan felt the need to prepare him. Whether Connor would be charged with anything, no one would say, but Ethan felt he should at least bring him up to speed on Joey being a cop and what had happened at the warehouse.

"You guys go ahead," Sadie said, leaving them at Connor's door. She'd never met Connor and didn't think he'd want strangers visiting when he was at his worst. "I'll see if I can find out which room Dylan's in."

Jane followed Ethan into Connor's room. Even though Ethan had warned her, she wasn't prepared. The parts of his face that weren't covered in gauze were bruised and scraped. After she'd said her hellos and expressed her sympathy, she left them to find Sadie.

Sadie had already asked at the information desk, using both the Joey and Dylan names, and was told no such person had been admitted. They dismissed the party line in favour of Hunter's intel, and walked the wards, playing at being lost when anyone questioned them. Eventually, they found a hallway with a uniformed cop milling around.

"That's got to be his room," Sadie said, as they approached.

The cop glared at them when they stopped in front of him. "I'm Jane Walker. This is Sadie Prescott. We'd like to see Dylan O'Brien." Jane thought the cop looked familiar, but she couldn't quite place him.

"Check at information on the ground floor. They can locate your friend for you."

"We talked to Dylan last night. From Porter Bick's office," Sadie said. "He'll want to see us. Just ask him."

The guard hesitated.

"I know you," Jane said, as the memory of his face clicked into place. "You're the rent-a-cop who works at the parkade on Davie Street."

He raised an eyebrow, put a hand on his gun. "Move along."

Okay. Not a rent-a-cop. Maybe the real deal, working undercover with Dylan. Just then, the door to the room opened, and Porter exited. He stopped mid-stride.

"What are you two doing here?"

"I need to talk to Buddy," Jane said.

"I thought we made it clear you weren't to discuss the investigation."

"Of course not," Jane said, wishing she had an ounce of Sadie's charm. "Is he in there?"

Sadie glanced beyond Porter. "Hey, Dylan. Want to tell your boss to let us in?"

Porter looked back into the room. Dylan nodded. Porter then opened the door wide. He let Sadie in, but barred Jane's entrance.

Porter leaned down close to Jane's ear. "That murder you didn't witness? The CCTV cameras on the port crane got a real good look. We have a clean reel of the murder. Traced the body dump through traffic cams. Tied it to a burned-out vehicle in Surrey. This time, we'll credit an anonymous tip." He stepped back and let her pass.

Porter called into the room. "Don't talk about the case, and don't tell anyone he's here."

As the door closed behind them, Porter told the guard to kick them out in five minutes.

Sadie stood on the far side of Dylan's bed, uncharacteristically tentative and awkward as she handed him a water glass with a bendy straw. His shoulder was wrapped in gauze. He was sitting up, the head of the bed having been raised.

"Jane Walker," he said, all business as she approached his bed.

Jane looked into one brown eye, one hazel. It felt strange to be here with this man, who wasn't Buddy but was. Other than the gauze, he was naked, at least from the waist up. He was built, tatted. Gorgeous. She had to drag her attention away from his twelve-pack.

His gaze slid to Sadie, and his face lit up. "Hello, Sadie." That eye-twinkling smile of his was pure Buddy. Jane felt tears well and beat them back. Buddy was right here, alive, and not the gang-banging monster she'd imagined him to be ever since she'd first seen him at Riptide.

His smile flipped from flirtatious to serious when he looked back to Jane. "You have my attention, Jane. How do you know me?"

"Do I look familiar to you at all?"

He tilted his head, left then right. "We met at Riptide."

"Not earlier?"

He paused. "You tell me."

Jane felt the dance move. He was leading, hoping she'd follow. Not confident enough to put himself out there—to admit that he saw an apparition that looked like her in a Davie Street parkade. She gave him a break. It would be a tough admission for anyone, inviting ridicule or worse. Jane knew the repercussions well.

Jane offered an alternative narrative. "I met your mother. It was when I worked for Anna and Lucas Bakker. They own Positively Plants. Anna's son, Pieter, was born the same day as you. Your mom knew Anna. When Mary stopped by the nursery with a tray of butter tarts, she mentioned they were your favourite."

"We haven't lived in the West End since I was five. Where did you meet me?"

"I don't remember exactly." Which was the truth. "Downtown somewhere. Maybe the Pacific Centre?" Also the truth. He'd been trading that beautiful smile for spare change.

"And how do you know my nickname?"

Jane shrugged. "Probably from your mom." He wouldn't believe the truth if she told him. Who would? Maybe one day she'd get the chance to explain it to him.

"At Riptide, the day we met, you nearly blew my cover. I'd been embedded for two years and you damn near got me killed."

"I'm sorry. I didn't know."

He shrugged, as if nearly getting killed was nothing. "It's one of the risks of undercover work."

Jane nodded to his bandages. "Are you going to be okay?"

"My skull tat took a bullet," he said, glancing disapprovingly at the white swaddling. But I'll have it fixed when it heals." He turned to Sadie. "Porter tells me you were behind the wheel at the warehouse last night."

"In fairness," Sadie said. "Their driver was a bit of a wuss. Didn't even break a nail getting him out of the driver's seat."

"Maybe you could teach me some of your moves."
Jane was beginning to feel like a third wheel. The guard saved her.
"Time to go, ladies."
Sadie shot a glance at Jane and laughed. "*So* not PC."

64 | Ethan

"Guys like him are connected," Connor said, speaking with a wired-jaw slur, in reference to the man they all called the boss. "He's probably already out on bail."

"Fanny says the cops are at Riptide doing an inventory," Ethan said. "Might take a day or two, but we'll be able to open when they finish up."

Connor and Ethan looked up as Hunter came in. Ethan introduced them.

Hunter handed Ethan a newspaper. The front-page headline read "Cops Pull Plug on Gang's Cash Laundry."

Ethan scanned the article, which included a marked-up map of the downtown core, identifying the businesses that were now under investigation. Including Riptide. "Looks thorough. Didn't expect Wilde would get the story out so fast." Ethan handed the newspaper to Connor.

"He didn't have a choice," Hunter said. "The law caps all media coverage the minute charges are laid. This is a big story. Wilde didn't want to miss his opportunity."

Connor opened the newspaper and continued to read. "Bastards had their filthy hands everywhere. I'll have to thank Wilde. A piece like this will be great for business. It'll bring in the rubberneckers. It's true what they say about there being no bad publicity."

"Any news on how Joey's doing?" Ethan asked.

"Dylan?" Hunter asked. "I heard he had a bullet removed from his shoulder, extensive bruising where his body armour stopped another."

"Pretty sure that bullet to his back was meant for me. I saw Joey—Dylan—take the hit to his shoulder. He fell on me. I think he did it intentionally. I owe him. Still can't believe he's a cop."

"I owe him too," Connor said. "A punch to the head. If you ask me, he took the gangbanger role a little too seriously."

"I heard a BOLO last night for Dalton on the scanner," Hunter said. "Seems he slipped his hospital escort after his x-rays."

65 | Jane

"We'd better go," Jane said, observing the guard's growing impatience. "But I'd like to keep in touch."

"I'll find you," Dylan said. He turned to Sadie. "And I'll find you, too."

Sadie's face reddened. She scooted out ahead of Jane without a goodbye.

"You like him!" Jane said, teasing her once they were inside Sadie's car. Jane had never seen Sadie lost for words in a man's company.

"Did you see the man in that bed?" Sadie said, starry-eyed. "The glorious washboard, the dragon, the dice."

He was definitely Sadie's type.

Back in her apartment, Jane organized a video chat with Ariane.

"What did Rosa have to say for herself?" Jane asked. Ariane sat alone at her family's kitchen table in Lima.

"She's sorry. She wanted to apologize, but my abuela's livid about what she did, sending you that bracelet as if it were a gift. Won't let her in the house. She's embarrassed by what Rosa did. Feels it reflects badly on the old families. I hope you can forgive them."

Jane wasn't at the forgiveness stage yet. Being trapped in a dream state had been terrifying.

"Tell Rosa that Hunter knows where her family's offering bowl is. Whether the museum will part with the artifact, I don't know, but that's her problem."

"I'll tell her. Eventually. The artifact isn't going anywhere, and I'm still angry with her. She can stew in her mess a while longer." Ariane gazed at her new diamond ring, twisting it so it twinkled. "The next time we speak with her, we'll be looking for answers. Like where she learned about the unbroken circle that trapped you. She's been holding out on us. We want to know what else she learned. I'm not telling her about her bowl until we have our answers."

Rosa had been holding out big time. And though Jane's curiosity about what else she knew caused her some restless nights, she agreed with Ariane. Rosa had betrayed all of them. She could soak in her guilt until she pruned up beyond recognition.

"The dreams?" Ariane asked. "Have they finished telling their story?"

"For now, I think. At least I didn't dream last night." Jane shuddered to think she very nearly repeated Pedro's mistake by acting too quickly. "I thought the dream about the murder was the final dream, the key, the wrong I was supposed to set right. But it wasn't. There was something much bigger going on."

Jane explained what had happened, her dream that revealed Joey was a cop, and the events that led up to the warehouse.

"The Joey dream came after the murder on the waterfront. If I'd acted sooner, I would have made the situation worse. Everything hinged on knowing Joey was inside the organization."

Jane thought back to her second dream of St. Paul's and the night Buddy and Pieter were born. Jane hadn't told anyone about it. She'd been embarrassed. She'd felt weak for not being able to fix her mistake.

But now she thought differently. It was strength, not weakness, that had held her in check. Watching history unfold, even knowing the damage it would cause Pieter and Anna, knowing she couldn't change it—that took fortitude. She wasn't weak. And because she'd shown strength, the able-bodied Buddy existed, and he'd become a cop. She never thought she'd be grateful for the mistake she'd made, but she felt grateful now.

She couldn't say the same about Rosa. "If I hadn't put on Rosa's bracelet, I might have been able to use the dreams as they were intended. But instead of warning Ethan, who could have helped Joey, I was stuck in that museum. We could have died in that warehouse, and the gang would still be in business."

"I'll make sure Rosa hears that. But I have other news," Ariane said. "We finished with Pedro's diaries." Her gaze shifted down. *To her notes?* "I'm sorry to say he lived much of his later life dodging authorities. Never stayed long in one place. Never married. Had no children."

Not notes. She looked everywhere but at Jane. Ariane continued. "He wrote of powerful people who began to fear they might not get away with their misdeeds. These people targeted Pedro, discredited him, tried to lock him away. It was the old families who harboured him. Kept him safe." Ariane finally met Jane's gaze, her expression filled with sorrow.

Jane sighed. "Something else to look forward to."

"I used to think if we could get proof of what you can do, what Witnesses have been able to do for hundreds of years, we'd be able to open minds. But I was wrong. I should have learned from your experience with Rick. I know better now. You must keep your dreams hidden."

A text came in. "Ethan's here with Hunter. I have to go let him in." Jane texted him back that she was on a call with Ariane. He replied, asking her to keep Ariane on the line. Hunter wanted to talk with her.

Jane let them in, and they huddled around her phone. Ariane and Hunter exchanged a few words of Spanish. "I didn't know you spoke the language," Jane said.

"Badly. I'm just learning. I have news. Dalton Reddy is dead. Shot in the abdomen."

"Who shot him?" Jane said.

"Good question," Hunter said. "The tech who logged in the bullet they removed noticed that it matched bullets he'd logged into evidence earlier from the warehouse. It had a distinctive thatch on it, a thatch attributed to Dalton's gun."

Jane frowned. "Dalton shot himself? In the abdomen?" An unlikely choice for a suicide bid. "Was it an accident, or did someone get hold of his gun?"

"No," Hunter said. "His gun's been in lockup."

Jane puzzled it out. "Then it was a ricochet shot from the warehouse."

"That's what we thought, too," Hunter said. "But we checked the film the hospital took before he escaped. He didn't have that bullet when he was x-rayed."

Ethan took Jane's hand. "Dal shot at the back window of the Escalade last night. I saw the holes in the glass. He was aiming at you, Jane. Your head was lined up in his sights. Did you duck down before he pulled the trigger?"

Jane shivered. "No." She felt like she'd ventured onto thin ice, her footing unsteady. "I remember him pointing his gun at me. I saw the holes too."

"Those bullets should have hit you," Ethan said, stroking his thumb over the back of her hand. It did little to sooth the uneasiness building in her chest.

"It's the promise of the blood marks," Ariane said. "Anyone who tries to take your life pays with their own. Your marks are still protecting you."

The ice cracked under Jane's feet. She plunged and the frigid water stole her breath away.

66 | Sadie

Sadie stared at the blinking cursor, unable to concentrate. She'd lost three days—and her mind, apparently—because she couldn't get Dylan out of her thoughts. He'd left her a voice message. She hadn't recognized the number, so she hadn't picked up. He wanted to see her. A cop should be the last person she was attracted to, but the sparks were undeniable.

It saddened her to know he would run faster than Mike the minute she told him about her past.

She sighed, picked up her coffee mug, and trotted down the hall to Jane's place.

Ethan answered the door. He had his jacket on, so he was either coming or going.

Jane sat on the sofa with her feet on the trunk. "Hey, Sade."

"Good to see you, Sadie," Ethan said. "I gotta go, get the bar open." He turned to leave and then turned back. "Sadie? Would you be interested in doing the bookkeeping at Riptide? Just until Connor's back on his feet?"

Sadie paused, momentarily stunned. "Uh, sure."

"That'd be great. See you later." He started down the hall.

Sadie snapped out of it. She called down the hall after him. "Good to see you, too."

Jane had a stupid grin on her face.

"What? He was nice to me."

"That makes me very happy."

"Me, too," Sadie said, making herself at home on the sofa. "I'm glad things are working out for you two. He's doing pretty good, considering."

"Considering what?" Jane said, sounding offended.

"Your dreams—what else? They're not just hard on you, you know. Take it from me. It's unsettling to know there's nothing we can keep secret from you. There's no privacy."

Jane paused. "I suppose. But you know I'd never share anything private."

"I know." Sadie stared into her coffee mug. "Dylan called."

"I knew it!" Jane said. "Did he ask you out?"

"I haven't called him back. Do you think someone like Dylan would stick around if he knew about my past?"

"Because he's a cop?"

Sadie shrugged. "I'm not keen on setting myself up for another round of Dump Sadie. And I'm not going to hide my past. Any guy in my life is going to have to accept all of me."

"I think that's what everyone wants: acceptance. You'd think it would be easier to come by."

It occurred to Sadie that this was what Jane had been forced to deal with all her life. And Jane had found Ethan, so maybe there was hope for her, too.

Jane's phone buzzed. "It's Hunter. He's at the door." She got up to go let him in.

"How's the NASCAR driver doing today?" Hunter said, breezing in behind Jane.

"I didn't know you had a sense of humour," Sadie said, laughing. She stood. "I'll give you two some privacy."

"No. Stay." Hunter waved at her to sit back down. "I'm going to need some support here."

"Oh?" Jane said.

Hunter took the chair opposite the sofa. Jane and Sadie exchanged a glance and settled back in their seats.

"What's on your mind, Hunter?" Jane said.

"Two things. First, my retainer."

Jane's features fell. "Oh no. I'm sorry. I thought you'd waived it."

"I did. This time. But I have a feeling you're going to need me again. Which got me thinking, how did that Huan kid make out?"

Jane blinked, confused. "What does your retainer have to do with Huan?"

"You were keeping an eye on him."

"Yeah," Jane said. "But not anymore. Nelson, our former social worker, called a few days ago. One of his colleagues got Huan's mom into rehab. He's staying with his grandparents out in Richmond. He's doing okay."

"That's good. Glad to hear it. How old's Huan? Twelve, fourteen?"

"Yeah. What are you getting at?"

"That charity you set up, the Morrow-Walker Foundation. It's to benefit vulnerable kids, right?"

Jane frowned, but Sadie had caught the scent of where this conversation was going.

"You're in a unique position, Jane. You can help people in a way no one else can. I'd like to continue working with you because I find what you do fascinating, and I'd like to contribute. But I can't keep working for free. I have bills to pay, a business to run. And you've got a charitable foundation whose aim is to help vulnerable kids. I think we can help each other; you just need to broaden your thinking about where those funds go. Because when those funds go to services like mine, the benefits trickle down to kids like Huan. It was a team effort, but we just took a major drug supplier off the street. That's one less gang for a vulnerable kid like Huan to join. It's a reduction in the number of times gang violence will erupt and send a stray bullet into an innocent bystander. You and I working together has already changed lives. Think about what else we could do."

"Good one," Sadie said, nodding. She turned to Jane. "He's got you there."

To her credit, Jane considered his words. "I hadn't thought of it like that. I'll have to talk to the investment firm, but yeah." Jane's smile widened, as if she'd surprised herself. "I'll make it happen."

"While we're on a roll here," Sadie said, turning to Jane, "Hunter's right about you being in a unique position to help people. But that's only going to happen if you're living someplace safe. Using your inheritance to keep a roof over your head when you're unemployed could benefit a lot of people—kids, too." Sadie had been harping on Jane about spending the funds on herself for months.

"I'll give it some thought. Promise," Jane said. She addressed Hunter. "You said there were two things. What's the other?"

"It has to do with Joey. You said you knew him as Buddy, that his given name was Dylan O'Brien. But he didn't know you. Was he in one of your dreams?"

"Yes. I told you that."

"You told me you dreamed of Joey. I checked my notes. You never mentioned the names Buddy or Dylan. Which makes me wonder who Buddy is. Or was?"

Sadie felt Jane's stillness like a chill. And then Jane told him the story.

67 | Ethan

Ethan met Fanny and the cook at Riptide, and together they put the bar, kitchen, and storage areas back together. The police had been thorough with the inventory, and hadn't left a mess, but they weren't cooks or bartenders. There was a flow to the jobs that required everything to be in its proper place.

After the temp bartender arrived, Ethan left to see Connor.

He found him sitting in a chair, a walker nearby. "You're up."

"Yeah. Got the neck brace off, too. Feels great." He must have been getting used to the wired jaw, because he sounded a little clearer.

"Riptide's open."

"Thanks. The police came by. They didn't arrest me, at least not yet. Took my statement."

There was a knock on the door, and Dylan stepped inside. "Hey, Connor. Ethan. May I come in?" His arm was in a sling.

"Depends on what you want," Connor said, none too happy.

"Thought I'd start with an apology."

"You going to tell me that decking me was part of the job?"

"Sorry, man. But yeah. Thought if we ever got out the other end of this case alive, you might forgive me when I told you that punch was meant to give you a defence for putting that restroom reno on the books."

"That right?"

"Sure is. If I'd known Garvin was ordered to do a number on you, I'd have gone along, tempered him. Any permanent damage?"

"Nah. You?"

"Nothing a change of scenery won't fix. The name's Dylan, by the way. Dylan O'Brien." He shook Connor's hand.

"I owe you my thanks," Ethan said. "The pair of snips you somehow got in my pocket? Thanks, man. Took me a while to figure out you were stalling for time with the fight, though. I thought you were trying to waltz with me."

Dylan laughed. "This operation was big, biggest one I've been involved in. We had teams set to raid a dozen places simultaneously that night, but not until eight o'clock. That's the time I'd set up for the big buy. So, when Dalton called me in early, Porter had to shave two hours off our go time. Wasn't sure he'd pull it off."

"Did you catch the dealers?"

"We did. Hunter stayed on them until we could send a unit in. Hunter said he owed Porter. Figures they're even now."

"I'd like to have a proper fight with you one of these days. We'd be a good match."

"Thanks, but I'll pass. I've seen you fight. Last year, Porter sent me down to the old boxing gym where you hang out. He wanted me to know what I was up against. Maybe you can train me, though."

68 | Jane

Jane got to her door and found an envelope had been slipped underneath it. She picked it up and hurried down the hall to let Ethan in. He walked her back to the apartment with an arm around her shoulder, and the moment they were behind closed doors, he pulled her into an embrace that curled her toes. The kiss was textbook Ethan, unrushed and thorough.

"I'll never get tired of that," Jane said, pulling away from him.

"You'd better not."

"You made Sadie's day earlier. Thank you."

"Ah, she'd earned it. Besides, we need someone. I can't do it all."

"And here I thought you were Superman."

"I am. Cape's in the laundry, though. What's that?" Ethan said, referring to the envelope she held in her hand.

"Found it slipped under the door just now," she said, sliding her thumb under the flap. She pulled out the sheet of paper, unfolded it, and froze. Fear gripped her. She glanced up at Ethan and passed him the note.

I'm not done with you.

He gripped her shoulder. "We shouldn't touch this." Ethan dropped the letter on the table.

Jane added the envelope, pulled out her phone, and dialled Porter. "It's Jane Walker. I just had a note pushed under my door. It's a threat."

"From whom?" Porter asked.

"I don't know." Jane's head swam with possibilities. How had she become the bait for so many predators? "Could be someone from the gang. Or it could be the man who kidnapped me. Maybe his accomplice." Jane gave him the details. He asked her to hold.

A moment later, he came back on the line to assure her that both Rick and Andrew were still in custody at Vancouver Pre-Trial. Garvin and the boss were as well. But there were no such tabs on the rest of the gang.

"We'll get a cruiser stationed outside your building. A uniform will be by to collect the note. We'll have it tested for fingerprints."

"Whoever delivered it got inside the building."

"I'll advise the landlord to have the lock changed."

After they hung up, she dialled Monica Fowler. Jane owed her a heads-up in the event the note was tied back to the kidnapping case.

Monica took the news in her stride. "If the note came from Rick or his accomplice, we'll be adding charges. Now that I've got you on the line, I've also got an update. I was going to call in the morning, but the news isn't going to get any better for waiting a night. Rick and Andrew have entered not-guilty pleas. We're going to trial."

After the police took the note away, Jane huddled on the sofa, still shaken.

Ethan rubbed her arm in soothing strokes. "They can't get in here. Not with a cruiser parked at the curb."

Jane wanted to remind him that two of the five in custody, Rick and Andy, had gotten in before, but she checked herself. She was overreacting. Though, with five killers out there who'd like to see her name on a tombstone, no one would blame her.

"And then there are your blood marks."

Jane pictured the photo Ethan had taken of her marks glowing. "Ghost marks now."

Despite the reassuring warmth of Ethan's presence, and her marks, a worrying threat loomed.

"Monica knows I'm not being honest with her," Jane said. "She's testing me. At our last interview, she asked questions to trip me up."

"Then we'll review everything. Together. Figure a way through it."

"If she doubts me, she'll negotiate a plea deal. Rick and Andy might get off. And if she's assigned this new case, Garvin and his boss might get off, too."

"They won't. We'll figure it out."

"I hope so. Because anyone who gets to me can do a lot of damage before these marks kick in."

Ethan managed to calm her with his reassuring words and gentle touch. Later, they crawled into bed, and he helped her forget, at least for a little while. Afterward, he wrapped her in his arms, and with his breath on her neck, he whispered, "I love you back."

Jane closed her eyes, his words swirling around her like a warm summer breeze. She luxuriated in the scent of him, the heat of him tucked against her back. She reached for her bedside drawer and pulled out the shiny new keys.

Turning in his embrace, she pressed the keys into his palm, and folded his fingers over them. "I'm all in, too."

The End

Thank You

Thank you for reading *Ghost Mark*. If you enjoyed it, please tell a friend or consider posting a short review where you purchased it. Reviews are the lifeblood of books and help other readers discover them. (They're also much appreciated.)

—JP McLean

Excerpt from Scorch Mark

Jane is in a race against time to recover a powerful artifact that's fallen into dangerous hands. But first she must convince a skeptical cop of the supernatural forces at play before a lethal chain of events engulfs them all.

Read on for an excerpt . . .

NOW THAT JANE WALKER knew where her mother had been laid to rest, she felt drawn there. It wasn't out of respect or duty—she'd never met her mother in the flesh—it was simply the only thing she could do as the daughter she was never allowed to be. The visceral loathing she felt for Rick Kristan, the man who'd taken her mother away from her, grew deeper as the day of his trial approached.

Heat rippled off the asphalt parking lot. It had already been a long, hot ride, and they had two hours yet to go. Jane dismounted her Honda Rebel, glad for the opportunity to stretch her legs. Ethan Bryce pulled in beside her and killed the ignition of his Fat Boy. Across a swath of summer-scorched lawn, Windermere Lake sparkled like a cool oasis. This was their last stop before the final leg to the cemetery on the outskirts of Canmore, Alberta.

She removed her helmet, shook out her dark, cropped hair, and brushed the road dust from her jeans. Ahead, just before the path to Kinsmen Beach, a tailgate party had taken root, spilling onto the lawn behind a row of pickup trucks. The tailgaters, mostly young men flaunting their abs and red Solo cups, had confiscated a collection of the park's picnic tables. Music pounded out of speakers, and the scent of barbecue made Jane's mouth water.

After the helmets were locked, Ethan pulled their towel rolls from one of the saddlebags. He stretched his neck and raked his fingers through his comically flattened hair. "Ready?"

Jane let a saucy smile cross her lips. She'd happily watch Ethan Bryce's backside all day long. "Lead the way."

Ethan came to stand toe-to-toe with her, his light brown eyes sparkling with mischief. He leaned down and kissed her. "I love it when your mind's in the bedroom." He started across the parking lot and Jane held back a moment, admiring his swagger and the broad shoulders under his leather jacket. She quickly caught up and matched his stride, looking ahead to the lake, anticipating the splash of relief from the cool water.

Her focus was on the lake, so she wasn't paying attention to the tailgaters as she and Ethan passed. But when Ethan took her hand—an unusual gesture for him—she glanced at him, and then at the men who had stopped their partying. One by one, they nudged each other and, in turn, stared at her. Startled, Jane looked away.

"You know them?" Ethan asked.

"No." Goosebumps skated across her arms. Jane surreptitiously checked her boots and jacket, smoothed her hair, searching for something—anything—to explain their attention. Anything other than the one thing the goosebumps foretold.

Ethan's carefree smile hid the tension she felt in the firm grip of his hand as he wove his way through the families who'd laid claim to patches of sand with beach blankets and umbrellas. They followed the shore to the thinning edge of the crowd, far from the tailgaters.

"That was weird, wasn't it?" Jane said.

"Depends." Ethan kicked off his boots. "Regular weird or your stratosphere weird?"

She'd already considered how a handful of men she'd never met looked at her like they knew her. Like they'd seen her before. Or met her ghost.

"They know our rides now," she said.

"We can't change that. Let's cool off and get out of here." Ethan kept an eye on the distant parking lot as he stripped down to his boxers, but he left his T-shirt on, unwilling to endure the stares his burn-scarred stomach would draw.

Jane removed everything but a tank top and bikini bottoms, an unthinkable disrobing had she still borne the blood-red birthmarks that had haunted her until the year before. The final birthmark had disappeared on her twenty-fifth birthday.

She glanced back, relieved the tailgaters hadn't followed. "Race you!" she said, and took off for the water at a run. Ethan laughed, a competitor through and through. She rushed into the lake, high-stepping until the water was above her knees, and then dove under. The water felt like an ice-cold beer on a sweltering day, a delicious quenching for her overheated skin.

They kept to the shallows, sparing an occasional glance at their belongings. Afterwards, they lay on their towels, drying off.

"Another dream's coming. I feel it." Jane hadn't had a visiting dream since the night she'd learned what had become of the man she'd once known as Buddy. A man whose life she'd accidentally and irrevocably altered. He was now Dylan O'Brien, an undercover cop. That was five months ago. But her reprieve was over.

"Because of the tailgaters?"

"Why else would those men behave like they'd seen me before?"

Ethan scrubbed his face with his hands. Accepting Jane's visiting dreams was easier for him when the dreams were dormant. Once they started up, they didn't stop until whatever events Jane was destined to witness had finished playing out. There was no avoiding it: Jane's dreams identified her as *una testigo*, a Witness in the Inca tradition.

They opted to take a longer route back to the bikes to avoid the pickup trucks, but the party had been packed up and the trucks were gone when they returned to the parking lot. With sighs of relief, they remounted and continued on their way.

The heat of the day was behind them when they rolled into the Canmore Cemetery. Jane had a map of the grounds and the location of her mother's grave. They parked the bikes nearby, left their helmets on the seats, and searched the headstones. It shouldn't be too hard to find, given the recent exhumation. The Crown prosecutor needed to establish that Jane was Rebecca Morrow's daughter. DNA testing was the only way.

Rebecca's grave marker was a flat black stone embedded in the ground above the still-mounded earth. Jane brushed the dust off the polished stone. Other than her name, Rebecca's birth and death dates were the only adornment. Not a beloved wife or a cherished mother. Not resting in peace. In the public's eye, Rebecca was a murderer who would have been convicted had she not taken her own life.

None of that was true. Rebecca was beloved by Jane's father, David Banner. She was cherished by Jane, who'd only seen her mother in dreams. She was at peace because everyone Rebecca had cared about knew she was innocent of David's homicide. And before she was murdered, she'd arranged for the blood marks that protected Jane from the man who'd killed Jane's parents: Rick Kristan, a deluded and corrupt psychiatrist who'd treated Rebecca against her will.

It pained Jane to know Rick would never be held accountable for her parents' murders. He'd taken her family from her. She'd never get to know them. She'd never feel their embrace or hear their words of praise or encouragement, things most families took for granted.

But killing her parents hadn't been a thorough enough erasure for Rick—he'd wanted Jane dead, too, severing all the connections to his crimes. So the only justice Jane could get was a guilty verdict at his upcoming trial for her aggravated kidnapping and attempted murder. Ten to twenty-five years behind bars wasn't nearly enough.

Jane and Ethan continued on to the Super 8 hotel they'd booked. The sun had slipped beneath the horizon, painting the sky in burnt orange. Ethan joined her on the balcony and handed her a Corona. He glimpsed the photo she'd been staring at on her phone. It was a snapshot of the cryptic note that had been slid under her apartment door in the days following the police takedown at the warehouse. *I'm not done with you yet.* The arrests at the warehouse had ended a drug gang's hold on Riptide, the bar Ethan managed, but they'd earned her a handful of new enemies. She still didn't know which one had sent her the note, but it achieved its intended effect.

She turned from the rail and took the beer. "Thanks." Their balcony faced the parking lot. "Do you think any of those pickup trucks are from the lake?"

Ethan glanced down at the bleached asphalt. "We're in Alberta. Everyone drives a pickup."

"They saw our rides, our licence plates. They could find us."

"Not at this hotel. Even if one of them was a cop, the best they could do is get our Vancouver addresses." He tipped back his beer. "You hungry?"

She faked a smile and went along with his change of subject. Who could blame him? The thoughts banging around in her head were probably the same as his and not fit for human consumption.

They finished their beers and headed out on foot to find Patrinos Steak House & Pub, which met their criteria: nearby and not fancy. They bypassed the pool table, several big screen TVs, and were seated on an outdoor patio, where they ordered the pizza special and two beers.

Ethan scrutinized the people at the other tables before his gaze strayed into the bar and the baseball game on the TV. His shoulders finally relaxed. Jane hated that her dreams caused him such stress. Whoever said sharing a burden lessened the load had lied.

Jane absorbed every detail of the restaurant and the other diners. Other than the colour of their licence plates, she couldn't make out a difference between Albertans and British Columbians. It was the first time she'd been outside British Columbia, at least that she could remember. She'd been born in Alberta, at the Wild Rose Psychiatric Hospital near Banff, but Rick had made sure there were no records of her birth. She had been less than a day old when she was found abandoned at the Joyce Skytrain station in Vancouver and taken to BC Children's Hospital, making Vancouver her official place of birth.

Back at the hotel, Jane climbed onto the bed and snuggled into Ethan, draping an arm across his chest. She'd been looking forward to this time away with him for weeks, but the tailgaters had ruined it.

Ethan didn't say anything, but Jane knew he was thinking about the last time she'd dreamed. She felt the weight of it, too. She'd been trapped in a dream and couldn't wake up. Ethan had to watch helplessly for days while she lay comatose. Not knowing if she would survive the dream had left its mark on both of them.

On any other night, they'd be getting busy, rolling in the sheets, but the tension of what was to come had flatlined their libidos. And if fear of the unknown hadn't done it, then Jane joining him in bed, fully dressed with her knife secured in her boot, would have. But it wasn't like she had a choice. Because if the dreams started up again, whatever she wore to bed was what she'd be wearing in the dream. She was done being caught underdressed and unarmed. If she was destined to meet the tailgaters tonight in a visiting dream, she'd be ready for a fight.

Chapter 2 | Sadie

Sadie Prescott stretched out on the king-size bed surrounded by a sea of pillows. She smoothed her hands over the cool, 600-thread-count sheets. Air-con droned in the background, releasing a steady supply of chilled air and enough white noise to drown out neighbouring hotel guests. She inhaled the rich scent of a properly brewed Americano that wafted over from the silver room-service tray.

And then she opened her eyes.

Daydreaming about her former life was how Sadie dealt with the relentless heat and the a-hole upstairs stomping around in construction boots. Hell, who was she fooling? Fantasizing was how she dealt with any stress these days. In her weaker moments, she longed for the old Sadie, the one who earned a grand for a few hours of making some sad sack feel like a million bucks. She sighed at the memory of the high-end hotels that Cynthia Lee, her former madam, insisted upon for the "students" in her Teacher's Pet escort business. It took effort to remind herself why she'd given it up.

Though it hadn't been even a year, the life she'd led felt like the distant past, like someone else's life. But one thing that hadn't changed was her distaste for mornings. If the goddess had intended for her to wake early, Sadie wouldn't need the alarm on her phone.

She dragged herself out of bed, and while the coffee brewed, she signed into the new bookkeeping module she'd started yesterday. A few hours in, Sadie lifted the hair from the back of her neck and turned her face to the small fan she'd set up on a stack of books. The breeze blew her blonde curls away from her forehead, providing a little relief from the suffocating heat, but it did nothing to lower the temperature in her pint-sized apartment.

She pushed away from the laptop and stretched her arms over her head. With the exception of the inconsiderate neighbour living above her, she felt sorry for the tenants on the upper floors of the Victorian mansion that had been butchered into apartments. At least she was in the basement, where it was coolest. *Coolest?* The word caught in her throat. *Coolest level of hell, maybe.*

It was still early afternoon, and she'd already finished the module. Tomorrow, after she took the end-of-section test, she could put another tick mark in the program calendar. If she didn't run into a roadblock, she was on track to finish her accounting certificate early next year. She'd then be a certified bookkeeper. She couldn't wait to get it behind her and start earning real money again. Living on a tight budget was an oxymoron: not her idea of living.

She figured she'd earned a break, and a few hours at Kitsilano Beach would lift her spirits. She changed into a bikini, pulled a short dress overtop, and dug out a sunhat from under a stack of laundry. After tossing her purse and phone into her tote, she slid into her sandals.

Too bad Jane's away, Sadie thought as she passed by her friend's apartment, which was right next door. Sadie would have dragged her along. Come to think of it, she should have heard from her by now. Sadie knew Jane had been anxious about her road trip. She hadn't had one of her paralytic dreams in a while, but the narcolepsy never left her in peace for long. It was why Jane lived in perpetual readiness, always sleeping behind solid doors with quality locks. That was something she couldn't be sure of on the road.

At least Ethan was with her. He'd learned first hand how vulnerable Jane was when she fell into one of her paralytic dreams. Though Jane had stubbornly resisted his help, he'd stepped up. And Jane had let him, which was a minor miracle.

Sadie walked the few blocks to the beach. At the water's edge, she removed her dress and stuffed it in her bag. Her Tommy Bahamas cut the glare from the water's surface as she strolled through the shallows up to her thighs, sandals in hand, cooling her legs.

Afterwards, she found a shade-dappled spot in the sand near the pathway, away from the marauding gangs of kids with their water cannons. She laid out her towel, set her hat and sunglasses aside, and lay on her back, using her bunched-up dress as a pillow. Music streamed through her earbuds, pushing the surrounding voices and laughter into the background.

A light breeze caressed her body. Her thoughts turned to Dylan O'Brien. After months of creative negotiating, he'd finally broken down her resistance and she'd agreed to a date. They'd seen each other a handful of times since then. There was no denying their chemistry, but she couldn't bring herself to sleep with him. So far, he'd been patient, a perfect gentleman, which only made it worse. She'd promised herself she wouldn't sleep with anyone again before telling them how she used to earn her living. Dylan would dump her ass the day she did, and she really liked the guy. It's why she'd been putting off the inevitable. He worked undercover, but he was still a cop. *Thou shalt not date a former hooker* was probably a commandment in their rookie handbook, printed in bold and underlined.

Soon, she told herself for what felt like the hundredth time. She'd tell Dylan soon.

She picked up her phone and skimmed through the latest videos on social media, but her scrolling jerked to a stop at a newsfeed headline: "Local Kidnapping Case Heads to Court." She clicked on the link. The story was a recap of the charges against Dr. Roderick Atkins and his accomplice, Andrew Ness—the men she and Jane knew as Rick Kristan and Andy Ness. They'd pleaded innocent, which was bullshit, and the reporter's liberal use of the word *alleged* pissed her off. Another link led to a related article: "The Tragic Life of Joyce Walker."

Sadie bolted upright. "Oh shit." Joyce was Jane's legal name, an unnecessary reminder of the place where she'd been abandoned. She skimmed the article. Jane's photo was a deer-in-the-headlights shot of her in the back seat of a cruiser on the night the warehouse was raided. The night Sadie had met Dylan. Jane looked like a criminal in the photo. The article included a grainy newspaper image of the Joyce Skytrain station and rehashed the story of the night she'd been found. It sensationalized the prominent birthmarks she'd been born with and hadn't stopped there. The reporter had uncovered the news stories of the fire that had killed her adoptive parents and the car accident that had taken the couple who had fostered her. Nice. He'd dug deep, and it was going to hurt.

"Chloe?" The man's voice, coupled with the name he'd called her, sent her heart racing. Chloe was her Teacher's Pet name when she'd been one of Cynthia's escorts. She shielded her eyes and squinted up. "I thought that was you. How are you, doll?" His unapologetic gaze crawled over her body.

She searched her memory for the name of the doughy, middle-aged man standing at the foot of her towel, not that he would likely have used his real name. "I'm good, thanks."

"Keeping up your grades?" A lecherous smile gave away his thoughts.

"I'm out of the business. Have been for months."

He bobbed his head. "That explains why I couldn't find your profile. You live around here?"

Sadie smiled, neither yes nor no. So much for a peaceful break on the beach. She remembered he liked to roleplay as a visiting professor who lectured on insurance fraud, an infraction he considered on par with taking a life.

His name came to her. "Brian, is it?"

"How about I come by your place? For old time's sake."

"How about you move along?" Sadie said.

His smile faded. "Seems only fair you adjust the fee, though, now that you don't have a pimp fronting the business. Less for me to pay, more for you to keep? A win-win."

Sadie took a beat. Doughboy's attitude needed an adjustment. She raised her phone and snapped a photo of him. "Brian Maddock. Have I got that right?"

He laughed, but the tone rang hollow. "You should treat your customers with more respect." He narrowed his eyes. "I'll see you around, Chloe."

Chapter 3 | Dylan

Dylan O'Brien felt like an automaton, skimming first the ballistics report, then Dalton Reddy's autopsy report, and finally the X-rays taken of Dalton before he'd escaped custody at the hospital on the night he died. The fruitless daily routine had become a compulsion. One of those reports had to be wrong, because it was physically impossible for Dalton to have been killed with a bullet fired from a gun that was in police lockup at the time of his death.

Dalton Reddy's demise wasn't what bothered Dylan, it was how it had happened. Dalton had climbed to the upper echelons of a gang that laundered its drug money through the coercion of local businesses. Dylan had been imbedded in the gang for months gathering evidence that culminated in a warehouse raid. Dalton hadn't been shot during the raid, he'd been injured by a motor vehicle and taken to hospital.

Dylan had checked and rechecked the security feed from the evidence cage; Dalton's gun had been logged in before Dalton died, and the gun hadn't moved. The chain of custody for the bullet that killed Dalton was flawless, and the ballistics report that matched the bullet to Dalton's gun was solid. The X-rays taken of Dalton's chest and abdomen before he'd escaped custody showed no bullets lodged anywhere. This left the autopsy report, which ruled Dalton's death as the result of a gunshot wound. The X-ray taken at autopsy showed the bullet in situ.

It was impossible, and it left Dylan right back where he'd landed every other time he'd gone through this routine. The frustration gnawed at him. Dalton's death was a puzzle he was determined to solve. There had to be a clue there somewhere. He just had to find it.

"O'Brien. My office."

Dylan looked over the lip of his cubicle and acknowledged Staff Sergeant Nowak with a tip of his chin. The sergeant had a bark like a rottie, but his thick neck wasn't red, which Dylan took to be a good sign. He logged off and followed him.

Nowak walked behind his desk and plunked himself in the chair. "Close the door. Have a seat." A single file folder rested on the desk. The sergeant slid on his reading glasses and flipped open the file.

Dylan sat with his elbows on the armrests and steepled his fingers.

"Your psych eval came in." Nowak ran his finger down the page, dotting his Is and crossing his Ts. "The doc says you're fit to resume duties." The sergeant flipped the page. Dylan tapped his forefingers together until the sergeant glanced pointedly at the offending digits. When Dylan stilled his hands, the sergeant repeated the finger slide. "You passed your physical." Another page flip. "Aced your firearms proficiency test." Another page. And another, and then he closed the folder. "Looks like you're green-lighted for active duty."

Dylan inhaled a deep breath and blew it out with relief. Finally. He'd worked hard to regain full use of his shoulder. The surgeon who'd removed the bullet had done a fine job, but it had taken months of physio and training to regain his full range of motion. The training was thanks to Ethan; the man was a machine. And when Dylan's scar settled down, he'd have his skull tat re-inked.

"Your transfer to Olsen's team has been approved. You still interested?"

"Definitely." Sergeant Dawn Olsen led a guns and gangs team. It was a sideways move from the drug squad, but it would give him a wider range of experience. A solid career move.

"All right, then. You're in. She's holding a briefing in one hour." He rested his arms on the folder. "Any questions?"

"No. Thank you, sir."

The staff sergeant extended his hand. "Welcome back."

An hour later, Dylan joined seven other officers around a table in the boardroom. He knew each of them by name and reputation. Doc was from the K9 unit. His German shepherd, Thor, sat alert beside him. Two of the men he called friends. Each of the officers in the room acknowledged him with a nod. All except Viktor Jenko, a goateed man Dylan considered dangerous. Viktor liked to test limits and play loose with rules. Regardless, this team was tight—Dylan was joining a family. The members would have had a say in the decision, though he doubted Viktor had gone along with the choice.

One of them quipped, "You get tired of flying a desk, O'Brien?"

Jeremy Nolan, one of his friends, swiped an image from his phone onto the smart board. The room erupted in laughter. Olsen glanced at the image and fought a smile. The drawing was a rudimentary rendition of a handgun with a stickman drawn facing the barrel end of it. The stickman's eyes were x's.

"This ain't the drug squad, O'Brien," Jeremy said. "This team works from the grip end of a gun."

"We've got work to do," Olsen said, putting an end to the friendly jibes. "You all know Dylan O'Brien. He'll be brought up to speed over the coming days." Olsen had ten years on Dylan and a reputation as a no-nonsense ball-buster. You'd never know that to look at her. She was quick to smile and didn't have a mean line on her face.

She pointed to an image of five evidence-tagged, putty-coloured M4 rifles on the screen. The weapons could be mistaken for kids' toys, but they were deadly. "A new player is making 3D ghost guns. We need to find them and put that printer out of commission." The guns had been seized from a cube van in Pitt Meadows. "These aren't the enthusiast's 3D guns we see at trade shows, the ones with dragon-head barrels and ball-sack grips. Those are made to test a printer's limits and impress your buddies. These M4s are straight up production units." 3D printers produced gun frames that bypassed the government-issued serial number. The metal parts that made up the remainder of the gun were not regulated.

After the briefing, the team cleared out, and each of the members welcomed Dylan with a nod or a pat on the shoulder. Viktor nodded as well, but from him it felt more like a challenge.

When Dylan got back to his cubicle, lying on top of it was a printed copy of Jeremy's drawing. Dylan smiled and tacked it on the partition, right beside the paper target with the centre blown out: three perfect shots right through the heart, and a fourth through the target figure's forehead.

Sergeant Olsen sent over a stack of background material with instructions for Dylan to familiarize himself. She'd also assigned him the task of sifting through social media feeds for chatter on 3D guns. Social media was where they often found leads.

At the end of the day, Jeremy wandered over and hung his elbows over the edge of Dylan's cubicle. His arms were ripped, an indication that fatherhood hadn't eaten into his gym time. "Want to get a beer?"

"Sure. Riptide?"

"What's up with you and Riptide? The Red Lion not good enough for you anymore?"

"Ethan's away. I told him I'd stop by, make sure the place is still standing." He didn't mention that his favour to Ethan brought with it the possibility that he might bump into Sadie. Dylan wasn't yet ready to let his friends in on that intel, and he wouldn't until he was more certain Sadie was on the same wavelength. She'd successfully kept him at arm's length since they'd met, which had suited him during rehab only because it let him focus—Sadie would challenge any man's focus. But now that he was back on active duty, rehab was officially over. Next time he saw her, he'd pour on the heat and melt that barrier she kept between them. If that was tonight, all the better.

"Okay, but next time, it's the Red Lion."

"Deal," Dylan said, and he logged off the computer. "Meet you there in fifteen."

He headed to his car, a 1969 Dodge Charger. It was a gift from the only dad he'd ever known. The two of them had spent Dylan's high-school years rebuilding it. Clever man, his dad. *The project*, as they'd called it, had kept Dylan out of trouble during those treacherous years when he might have fallen prey to a gang. He approached the car as he always did, with a smile on his face. He got behind the wheel and turned the key in the ignition. The throaty growl made him think of Sadie. She'd been impressed the first time she'd heard it. That Sadie appreciated his wheels kicked his smile up a notch. He eased out and drove to Riptide.

The bartender recognized Dylan and let him slip down the hall to the office. He knocked on the door.

"It's open." The voice belonged to Riptide's owner, and Ethan's boss, Connor Boyd.

Dylan poked his head inside. "Sadie around?"

"She was earlier."

"Okay. Thanks. I'll see you around." Disappointed, he ducked out of the office and joined Jeremy, who'd arrived and claimed a table against the back wall. A server dropped off the beers Jeremy had ordered. They clinked glasses, toasting Dylan joining the team.

"You think it's safe for you, coming in here?"

"Yeah, I'm good. The major players are sitting in Vancouver pretrial, and anyone else who could ID me as Joey Hampton is shit-scared to step foot in here." Joey was the street name he went by when he'd been embedded. The first time he'd gone out with Sadie, he'd had to warn her that if she heard someone call him Joey, she was to walk away and pretend she didn't know him.

"How are Tracy and the baby?"

Jeremy's face split into a wide grin. "Great. Can't believe I put off having a kid. Best decision I've ever made."

"*You* made?"

Jeremy laughed it off. He was a good-natured guy, and smart. They'd met in training at the Justice Institute and were roommates for a while. Even back then, Tracy had wanted to start a family. "Fatherhood looks good on you."

"Would look good on you, too. You need to get busy, my friend. Having a kid will put your life in perspective."

"You think I need perspective?"

"You work too much, and when you're not working, all you do is train."

"Doesn't mean I'm not looking. Just waiting for the right woman." Maybe even someone he'd already met. Sadie.

Acknowledgements

This book may have started off in my imagination, but the words didn't get into a fully formed book without the help of many talented people along the way.

Donna Tunney, you knocked my socks off with a structural edit that took *Ghost Mark* up to a level I didn't know was hiding inside the draft. Thank you so much! It was lovely to work with Amanda Bidnall, for the first time, and Ted Williams, again. Thank you both for the buff and polish that makes the words shine.

To JD&J Cover Designs, you've done it again! I love how you transform a short story summary into a stunning cover that hits all the right marks. Thank you.

My thanks and appreciation go to Mickey Mikkelson of Creative Edge Publicity for his encouragement and representation.

I'm so very grateful to have met Maura McGivern, who provided invaluable first-hand details about BC's Crown counsel. I took artistic license and veered off the official path a time or two, but the devil is in the details, which I sure hope I got right. (And I apologize for Jane's misbehaviour.)

Thanks to Will Wigle for the newspaper headline (so many choices!), and to Rob Christopher for the terminology in credentialed professional investor circles.

My admiration and gratitude go to Elinor Florence and Donna Tunney for their friendship, critiques, laughter, and wisdom. I love our Monday chats and wouldn't trade them for the moon.

This acknowledgement wouldn't be complete without a shout-out to the Creative Academy for their moral support, cheerleading, and technical expertise.

I am also indebted to a keen Beta team that never fails to improve the story at all its stages of development. Thank you to Sue Cox, Jean McLean, Kathy McLean, Annie Siegel, and Gee Wigle.

Despite all of this tremendously talented help, there will still be oversights. All errors that remain are entirely my own.

About the Author

JP (Jo-Anne) McLean is a bestselling author of urban fantasy and supernatural thrillers. She is an Eric Hoffer Award winner and was a finalist in the Wishing Shelf Book Awards, the Chanticleer International Book Awards, and the Independent Author Network Awards. She is a B.R.A.G. medallion honouree and a three-time Literary Titan award winner. Reviewers call her books *addictive, smart* and *fun*.

JP holds a Bachelor of Commerce degree from the University of British Columbia's Sauder School of Business, is a certified scuba diver, an exploratory chef, and an avid gardener.

Raised in Toronto, Ontario, JP now lives with her husband on Denman Island, which is nestled between the coast of British Columbia and Vancouver Island. When she's not writing, you'll find her cooking dishes that look nothing like the recipe photos or arguing with weeds in the garden. She enjoys hearing from readers. Contact her via her website, jpmcleanauthor.com, or through social media.

 Sign up for JP's monthly newsletter for FREE short stories and insider scoop at jpmcleanauthor.com.

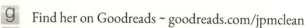 Find her on Goodreads ~ goodreads.com/jpmclean
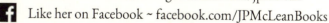 Like her on Facebook ~ facebook.com/JPMcLeanBooks
 Follow her on Instagram ~ @jpmcleanauthor

Manufactured by Amazon.ca
Bolton, ON

43930126R00169